D0480629

Deadly
Inheritance

Deadly Inheritance

An Ursula Grandison Mystery

Janet Laurence

*To Susan with thanks for all your
support, encouragement and help over the years
and for your wonderful friendship.*

First published 2012

The Mystery Press, an imprint of The History Press
The Mill, Brimscombe Port
Stroud, Gloucestershire, GL5 2QG
www.thehistorypress.co.uk

© Janet Laurence, 2012

The right of Janet Laurence to be identified as the Author
of this work has been asserted in accordance with the
Copyrights, Designs and Patents Act 1988.

British Library Cataloguing in Publication Data.
A catalogue record for this book is available from the British Library.

ISBN 978 0 7524 7001 6

Typesetting and origination by The History Press
Printed in Great Britain
Manufacturing managed by Jellyfish Print Solutions Ltd

Chapter One

April 1903

The boat train from Liverpool was crowded with passengers newly arrived from America.

The trip had been rough. Looking pale, a pretty girl of some seventeen years occupied a corner seat in a First Class carriage. She smoothed her smart, pink linen travelling suit with a careful hand. Her straw boater was set neatly on long, blonde hair. Her eyes were large and pale blue.

Opposite, sitting with her back to the engine, was a woman ten or so years older, who showed no sign of having suffered *mal de mer*. Where the girl was dressed in the height of fashion and displayed all the polish that money could achieve, her travelling companion's costume was restrained and serviceable. Chestnut hair was drawn back in a plain knot, under a hat that would never catch anyone's eye. Her gloves were cotton and her boots very ordinary. Her face, though, was rather fine, with classic features and a pair of exceptional grey eyes. She wore an expression of amused tolerance. After the porter had organised their heavy luggage and she had supervised the stowage of hand luggage onto the racks above the seats, she asked the girl, 'Belle, dear, will you need a magazine or a book to read on the train?'

'No, Ursula, how can you think such a thing? It would make me seasick all over again. Anyway, we are in England, on our way to London. How can I read when there will be so much to see?'

There came a whistle from the stationmaster followed by a louder, longer one from the train. The coal-fired steam engine began a slow and noisy progress, rather like a huge, lumbering elephant that required time to achieve momentum. Ursula Grandison, the girl's companion, found their gradual increase of speed thrilling.

'May I?' asked a middle-aged man, taking hold of the leather strap that operated the door window. 'It's the smuts.'

He pulled up the window, secured the strap, and sat down again next to a well-dressed woman who Ursula took to be his wife. On her lap sat a King Charles spaniel.

'Oh!' said Belle with a charming smile. 'What a cute little dog. May I stroke him?'

Ursula watched. Children and dogs, she thought, are a passport to instant friendship.

Soon Mrs Wright had exchanged names with Belle Seldon and they were in lively conversation.

'Are you planning a long stay in England, Miss Seldon?' asked Mrs Wright, sounding very English to Ursula's ears.

'I'm visiting my sister,' Belle said, caressing the little dog's long, silky ears. 'She's been married for over seven years but this is the first time I've come to England.'

'Over seven years, is that so? You will be longing to see her again.'

'Oh, yes! Though she and the Earl have visited us in New York.'

It was too late for Ursula to intervene and she watched the information Belle had so naively offered take root and blossom.

'Your brother-in-law is an Earl?' Mrs Wright strove to sound as though this was an everyday occurrence. 'Then ... then your sister must be a Countess?'

'She is,' beamed Belle. 'And I am to become one too.'

'You are? Which Earl are you to marry?'

'Oh, I don't know. Helen only knows titled people, or so it seems from her letters, and she is to find me a husband.'

Mrs Wright did not appear to find this at all incredible. 'And shall you like to be a Countess?'

'Oh, yes! To have a title and have everyone look up to you and live in a beautiful house must be great.'

'Belle,' said Ursula gently. 'Mrs Wright cannot be interested in your prattle.'

Belle smiled happily. 'I do go on,' she said to her neighbour. 'Papa is always saying I should talk less and listen more. But I like to talk.' She gave an extravagant caress to the dog. 'Why don't I take your little doggie for a walk down the corridor? I am sure he would like some exercise.'

'If you are careful with him,' said Mrs Wright.

'Oh, I'll be careful,' laughed Belle. She took the little dog's lead. One of the other passengers opened the door into the corridor.

'She is a delightful girl,' Mrs Wright said to Ursula. 'Would you be another sister?'

'I am her companion,' Ursula said briefly.

Mrs Wright could not contain herself. 'Is her sister really a Countess?'

'The Countess of Mountstanton,' Ursula said; her voice did not invite further comment.

'Good heavens,' breathed Mrs Wright. 'And you are going to stay with her and the Earl?'

Ursula nodded.

Mr Wright cleared his throat. 'I think, my love, we should consider whether we wish to take luncheon on the train.'

'Of course we will take luncheon,' his wife said in surprise, then coloured slightly. 'I'd be grateful if you could reach up for my bag, James; I want my book,' she added, a little belligerently.

Her wish was instantly gratified.

Allowed to retreat into her own company, Ursula studied the countryside as the train passed through. She failed to take in any of its features.

The mention of Mountstanton House had reminded her of the task she had been given. It was one she found daunting.

* * *

At London, a change of trains provided Ursula and Belle with a carriage to themselves.

As they racketed along towards Somerset, Belle exclaimed over the neatness of the countryside. 'Everything is . . . is, well, so nicely arranged. It's as though it's all waiting to be painted. There are so many hedges, so many tiny roads; the people should be small too but they seem a normal size.' She seemed totally recovered now from the effects of their voyage.

Ursula smiled at Belle's enthusiasm and hoped it would last until they arrived at their destination.

By the time they pulled into a small station decorated with tubs of wallflowers, the sun that had sparkled all the way from London had disappeared behind dark clouds. Ursula shivered slightly as she stepped down onto the platform, where a smartly uniformed stationmaster and a neatly dressed porter were the only signs of life. Where, she wondered, was Belle's sister?

No other passengers left the train so the porter had only their baggage to unload. Ursula pointed out their belongings and he started on the task with no sense of urgency.

'Where is Helen?' asked Belle. 'She promised to meet me.'

At that moment a large carriage drew up outside the station. A dashingly liveried footman jumped off and opened the door. Without waiting for the steps to be let down, a young man leapt to the ground and hurried onto the platform.

'My dear Miss Seldon, a thousand apologies. Your sister has been forced to remain at Mountstanton. Her mother-in-law, the Dowager Countess,' his face twisted in comic distress, 'has returned unexpectedly. So I have come to welcome you instead.' He swept off his hat, chucked it onto a bench, took Belle's hands in his and smiled down at her. 'Do say that you are not too desperately disappointed.'

Belle looked anything but disappointed.

Ursula studied the young man. He was extremely attractive. Looking to be in his mid-twenties, he was tall with hair carefully greased to repress a tendency to curl, eyes of a sparkling blue, a straight nose, and a mouth curved in a happy smile under a bold moustache.

'The Countess told me that you are the prettiest girl in the world. I did not believe her but it is true.' Another of those charming smiles.

Belle seemed unable either to remove her hands from the young man's grasp or to utter a word.

'It is very kind of you to meet us,' Ursula said serenely. 'Perhaps we could introduce ourselves? Miss Seldon's name you know and I am Ursula Grandison, her companion. Whom have we the pleasure of addressing?'

He released Belle's hands and with one of his fists hit his forehead. 'My wits have been sent scattering by Miss Seldon's beauty. William Warburton, at your service, ladies.' He gave them a graceful bow. Now, let us see about your bags.' He looked down the platform at the pile of luggage that was being assembled. 'Porter, don't hang about, bring that stuff over here.' His voice was curt and authoritative. He snapped his fingers at the two liveried servants who had appeared. 'Help him or we will be here all day.' He turned back to Belle and Ursula. 'Ladies, may I escort you to the carriage?'

Belle happily laid her hand on the arm that was offered to her.

Ursula said, 'Mr Warburton, I think I should check that all the luggage has been retrieved from the baggage compartment. If you will allow, I will join you in a moment.'

He gave her a brief nod, retrieved his hat, and escorted Belle in the direction of the carriage.

★ ★ ★

Ursula never forgot her first glimpse of Mountstanton.

The journey had been no more than some twenty minutes through neatly ordered farmland. Then the carriage swept through a matching pair of stone lodges set either side of massive wrought-iron gates that stood open in welcome, before following a long drive through parkland where deer cropped grass beneath mature specimen trees. Finally, in the distance appeared the house.

Ursula had expected grandeur but could not suppress a gasp of surprise at Mountstanton's size and majesty. As they drew closer, the house grew more and more imposing; the impressive façade with its rows and rows of windows, lightened a little by the way the frontage had been broken into three sections, with wings stretching back on either side in perfect symmetry. She found the total effect of the building and everything it represented overwhelming. Then, bending down sideways to see through the carriage window, she noticed a small domed and pillared pavilion sitting atop the central portion of the house with an almost frivolous grace. It was so delightful, her spirits rose. Maybe what awaited them would, after all, be a pleasant experience.

'Ladies, welcome to Mountstanton,' Mr Warburton said with a grand flourish as the carriage drew up on a gravelled area.

An elaborate and pillared stone portico shielded a heavy front door.

As the steps of the carriage were let down, the Countess of Mountstanton emerged.

'Belle, darling, I'm so sorry I could not meet you at the station.'

Belle tumbled into her sister's arms with incoherent cries.

The Countess searched her sister's face as though she was seeing it for the first time, then she kissed Belle again. 'I am so pleased you are here at last. You have grown even prettier. You will take Society by storm.'

As Ursula emerged from the carriage, the Countess held out her hand in a limp gesture.

'I regret that Papa failed to give me your name. His last message merely said that Belle would be travelling with a companion.'

Ursula supposed she should dip a curtsey. She remained standing.

Belle slipped an arm through hers. 'This is my dear friend, Ursula Grandison,' she said cheerfully to her sister.

The Countess's face froze. '*You!*' she said.

Chapter Two

For a moment there was an ugly silence.

Helen stared at Ursula with baffled rage while Belle looked from one to the other in bewilderment. Then William Warburton said jovially, 'I have never seen two more beautiful sisters, or two who looked more alike.'

Belle laughed and the moment was broken. 'That's not true. Helen is more beautiful; she is taller, her hair is more golden, and her eyes are green, not blue like mine – and her nose is straight.' They all looked at Belle's own nose; small, *retroussé* and quite charming.

The Countess smiled at her sister. 'My mother-in-law is waiting to meet you, she has returned from her visit to Yorkshire especially.' There seemed to be a note of warning in her voice.

A distinguished figure in a black tailcoat and striped trousers stepped forward. 'Miss Seldon, welcome to Mountstanton.'

'Thank you.' Belle gave a quick, uncertain look at Helen.

'This is Benson, our butler.'

'If there is anything you need at any time, Miss Seldon, please let me know.' The butler inclined his sculptured head with a practised movement that combined courtesy with a consciousness of his own standing.

A middle-aged woman with a stern face, dressed in unobtrusive black, a heavy ring of keys hanging from her waist, emerged from the shadows behind the butler. 'I am Mrs Parsons, the housekeeper. I, too, welcome you to Mountstanton, Miss Seldon,' she said.

As the sisters were about to enter the house, the Countess glanced back over her shoulder. 'Come along, William.'

Mr Warburton threw a quizzical glance at Ursula, then hurried to follow.

Ursula Grandison stood for a moment on the gravel. She had told Mr Seldon how it would be.

'You girls,' he'd said lightly. 'All that nonsense was years ago. I doubt if Helen remembers any of it.' He looked at Ursula. 'Belle needs someone to accompany her and business keeps me here. Anyway, I need both Helen and that husband of hers, that Earl, to be off their guard. They wouldn't be if I was there.'

Chauncey Seldon commanded attention wherever he went. Over six foot, with the broad neck and powerful back of a fighter, his small dark eyes were astute and his face, with its razor-shell cheekbones, full of an intelligence that warned no one should attempt to double-deal him.

'But no one is going to notice me, is that it?'

'Don't be bitter, Ursula, it doesn't suit you. It's not Helen's fault things turned out the way they did.'

Ursula had taken a deep breath. They were in Mr Seldon's panelled study, the engine room of the gothic house he had recently commissioned on Fifth Avenue. Everywhere in the mansion was evidence of the vast wealth he had accumulated. It was a world that once she had inhabited by right. Now she must remember that he was offering her a lifeline.

'It will not be easy,' she said slowly. 'But if what you suspect is true, Helen will need help. I am already very fond of Belle and I think I could be of use to her. And,' she gave him a brilliant smile, 'I would love to go to England.'

'Good! I know you will not disappoint me. Or Helen. Send regular reports. If they're urgent, do not hesitate to cable.' Mr Seldon rose, went over to a side table and picked up an ornate silver goblet. 'Have I shown you my latest purchase? It's Italian, sixteenth century, belonged to a Medici.' His large hands with their carefully manicured nails caressed the decoration lovingly, before passing it over to Ursula for her appreciation.

She admired the workmanship and asked pertinent questions on its history, but she did not envy its new owner. It was, after all, only a goblet. Chauncey Seldon valued the past for its treasures; she for its memories. He seemed to think it possible to dismiss them. She knew he was wrong.

Ursula sighed and entered Mountstanton. Heavy panelling and murky tapestries seemed hungry for daylight, despite the size of the windows. Huge pieces of well-polished furniture stood on a flagstoned floor inadequately covered with Turkish rugs.

The Countess was in whispered conference with the housekeeper.

Belle moved towards Ursula. 'What has happened to Mr Warburton?' she murmured.

The young man who had met them had vanished.

'No doubt he has matters to attend to.'

'Now, Belle, we will find your room.' Helen took her sister's hand.

'What about Ursula?'

'Mrs Parsons will look after her.'

With a lost little look, Belle allowed herself to be led out of the hall and down a long corridor.

'I am afraid I am unable to show you to your accommodation quite yet, Miss Grandison,' Mrs Parsons said smoothly. 'Allow me to take you somewhere you can refresh yourself after your journey.' She flicked a finger at a footman standing at the side of the hall with all the animation of a waxwork figure. He approached, received her low-voiced instructions, gave an expressionless nod and disappeared. The housekeeper turned an unsmiling face to Ursula and took her up an imposing flight of stairs.

The room Ursula was shown into was undistinguished. A brass bedstead was covered in a chintz spread; a tired brocade armchair stood in one corner, and a washstand in another. Only two good watercolours offered any sense of style.

'You will have had a long journey today. Is there anything from your luggage you require immediately, Miss Grandison?' The enquiry was courteous but without warmth.

'There are two dressing cases. The crocodile one belongs to Miss Seldon, the plain leather one is mine. We would both find them very helpful.'

'Of course; I will see that they are delivered immediately. Tea is shortly to be served in the Blue Drawing Room.'

The housekeeper hovered for an uncertain moment. 'We all hope Miss Seldon and yourself will be very happy with us,' she added, without conviction.

A few minutes later a maid knocked, entered and placed a jug of hot water on the washstand. 'Will there be anything else, miss?'

Ursula shook her head and asked the maid her name.

'Sarah, miss.' The girl was tall, with a plain face lit by lively eyes. Soft brown hair escaped from a mobcap.

There were a hundred things Ursula would have liked to ask but knew it was too soon. 'Thank you, Sarah. It is a great pleasure to be here.'

The girl grinned. 'Quite a place, isn't it?'

At last a servant who appeared normal.

Another knock at the door announced the arrival of Ursula's dressing case. Sarah took it from the footman and laid it carefully on a luggage stand. 'There's a bell if you need anything else, miss.' She indicated a silk rope hanging beside the bed.

Ursula thanked her again.

★ ★ ★

Hat discarded, travel grime removed, hair brushed into place, Ursula descended the stairs.

She should, she supposed, be feeling nervous. Helen had shown every sign of being as difficult as Ursula had anticipated. Was she planning to accommodate her in the stables? Or would she try to dismiss her? Perhaps she was sending a cable to her father at that very moment.

The stairs were shallow, offering easy passage. On the walls hung huge oil paintings, their subjects half hidden by over a century of candle smoke.

Ursula was not nervous. On the contrary, she found herself pleasantly excited by the prospect of battle – and of discovering what the exact situation was in this extraordinary house.

The waxwork footman came to a semblance of life when Ursula asked him for directions, and led her down a corridor lined with marble columns as discoloured as the oil paintings.

The Blue Drawing Room was as gloomy as the entrance hall. Curtains insufficiently drawn back prevented a clear view of its décor. Ursula longed to grab the lengths of velvet and yank them clear of the glass so that light could flood the room and illuminate the dark blue flock wallpaper. Almost immediately, though, she realised that that would only expose the shabbiness of the furniture.

Sitting rigidly upright in a large wing chair that would have dwarfed someone less powerfully aware of her own identity, was a figure dressed entirely in heavy black silk. A row of jet buttons enlivened the bodice; an elaborate silk fringe edged the skirt.

Behind Ursula, Helen entered with Belle. They could not have spent much time in the privacy of the bedroom catching up on their different lives. Belle looked bewildered. Her shoulders were rigidly held back, her chin lifted in a manner that betrayed nervousness.

'Mama, may I present my sister, Belle Seldon? Darling, this is the Dowager Countess of Mountstanton, my mother-in-law.'

Belle dipped the curtsey Ursula had made her practise.

The Dowager lifted a lorgnette and studied the newcomer, then snapped the hinged spectacles shut. 'Come closer, girl.'

Belle advanced a couple of steps, her chin rising even higher. 'Speak to me.'

Belle gazed at the Dowager Countess, her eyes wide with astonishment.

'And don't stare. Speak, I said. I am sure you can utter since I would have been told if you were a mute.'

'Mama, Belle is a little shy,' Helen said hurriedly.

Belle glanced at Ursula, who gave her the tiniest of nods and a smile of encouragement. She felt a moment of triumph that the girl had looked to her rather than Helen.

'Your . . . your ladyship, I am very happy to see my sister and to visit England.' Belle's voice, after the initial stumble over the correct form of address, was steady.

'No nasal twang; I am relieved. And you really are very pretty and quite suitably dressed. If you allow yourself to be instructed by your sister, you will do very well.'

The lorgnette was once again opened and raised. 'And who is this?'

Ursula took a step forward. 'I am Ursula Grandison, Miss Seldon's companion, your ladyship.'

'Indeed?' Cold eyes surveyed her. 'Necessary for the time being, I suppose. Your appearance is acceptable and you, too, lack that particularly ugly vocal characteristic so many of your fellow Americans display.' She gave a small shudder of distaste.

Ursula wished she had adopted a Brooklyn accent, then reflected that it would only have upset Belle and done nothing to repair relations with Helen.

'Here is tea, Mama,' Helen said with a note of relief as a procession of footmen arrived.

The bustle of service allowed seats to be found and something approaching a sense of ease to come over the little group.

'Where is Richard?' The Dowager Countess had refused the cucumber sandwiches and sat holding her porcelain cup with unstudied dignity. Her voice was sharp.

'Out riding somewhere, Mama,' Helen said negligently. 'None of us expected you to arrive back today.'

'I do not understand why not when it was common knowledge your sister was to arrive this afternoon.'

A small boy ran into the room, fair hair curling round his face, bright blue eyes alight with excitement. He was followed by a comfortable-looking woman wearing a grey work dress enveloped in a large white apron. She dipped a curtsey, saw her charge was safely inside the room and then withdrew.

'Mama! Mama!' the boy cried.

Helen opened her arms to him. 'Darling Harry.'

'You should not allow that child so much licence.' The Dowager's mouth set into a grim line.

Harry leaned against his mother's knee and looked resentfully at his grandmother. A little nudge at his back propelled him in her direction.

Reluctantly he approached. 'Good afternoon, Grandmama,' he said and, feet placed together, one hand held across his front and one behind, gave her a bow.

'Good afternoon, Harry. What have you learned since I last took tea with you?'

'I can recite the Kings and Queens of England, Grandmama.'

'Excellent. Tomorrow I will ask you to do so. Now, you must greet your Aunt Belle. Belle, this is the Viscount Hinton, your nephew.'

Belle gave him a brilliant smile and held out a hand. 'Come

and show me this book, Harry, it looks so interesting.' She indicated a large volume of architectural sketches lying on a table near the window. 'And I would love to talk and get to know you. Have you been to New York? It is such an exciting city. Do you know its buildings almost reach the sky?'

Ursula saw that Belle knew just how to interest children.

'It is most neglectful of Richard not to attend a family tea.'

Ursula had chosen a seat a little apart. She watched as Helen tried to parry her mother-in-law's increasingly acid comments on her son's general lack of respect, ending with, 'It's not what is expected of a Mountstanton.'

Over by the window, Belle teased and played with her nephew, encouraging him in a game of hide-and-seek with a floor-length chenille cloth covering a round table.

Little shrieks of delight drew a frown from the Dowager.

'Harry,' she said sharply as the boy climbed on the window seat. 'Stop that.'

Helen advanced, saying, 'Darling, come down ... '

But she was too late. He jumped off with a cry of 'Look at me,' stumbled on landing and caught at the tablecloth.

A large porcelain bowl fell off the table and broke, shards scattering over a wide area. As Helen rushed to pick up her son, he broke into shrieks of distress.

Belle stood aghast.

The Dowager Countess rose. 'Harry,' she said in an awful voice. Harry fell silent.

'You should know better at five than to behave like a hooligan. I have warned you before about the necessity to control your excessively high spirits. You will be beaten and sent to bed without supper.'

'Mama!' protested Helen, hugging her son.

Belle looked at the Dowager, her eyes wide with horror. 'He mustn't be beaten!' she said passionately. 'It wasn't his fault. He's only little.'

The gorgon stare switched from the small boy to young Belle. 'You dare to question my authority, girl?'

Holding her son in her arms, Helen joined battle with her mother-in-law. 'Mama, he realises how badly he has behaved.'

'It was an accident,' Belle said. 'If the bowl was valuable, my father will replace it.'

'The bowl is not the issue.'

Harry was now sobbing, quietly but relentlessly.

Ursula knew there was no point in saying anything, but she came and stood beside Belle in an effort to lend her support.

The Dowager narrowed her eyes and took a deep breath as the door opened to admit a tall man dressed for riding.

'Mama, I apologise for not being here earlier,' he said smoothly.

Ursula gazed in fascination at the Earl of Mountstanton. He had inherited the chill of his mother's eyes. Like those of a fish, there seemed nothing behind them. His features were unmemorable. His figure was too thin for true elegance but he moved with a certain ease.

A kiss was dropped on the Dowager Countess's cheek, then, ignoring his wife and crying son, the Earl turned to Belle. 'Why,' he drawled, 'it's my little sister-in-law. Welcome to Mountstanton, Liberty Belle.'

Chapter Three

Little dimples appeared on either side of Belle's mouth as she smiled shyly up at the Earl.

'I'm so happy to see you again, my lord,' she said.

'Come, come! Not "my lord" please. My name is Richard and I am delighted you have at long last paid us a visit.'

'Belle has only just left school, Richard; it would have been inappropriate before,' Helen said, her tone sharp.

'Of course.' The Earl gave Belle the sort of look that, in Ursula's experience, belonged to a man assessing the points of a horse.

'I think with a little tuition, Miss Seldon could possibly be an asset to the Mountstanton name, Richard,' said the Dowager.

Belle flushed and looked towards her sister. The Countess said with a hauteur of her own, 'Belle is already an asset to the Seldon name.'

There was a flash of something indecipherable in the Earl's eyes. 'Quite,' he said and looked around the room. 'Warburton not here?'

'Apparently you had letters requiring his attention.' Helen picked up her cup of tea and sipped at it.

The Earl looked at his son, now leaning against his mother, biting on his thumb. 'Harry, you stand to attention when I come into the room.' He looked at his wife. 'I hope the boy is not going to grow up a disgrace to his name.'

'Harry is not waiting to grow up.' The Dowager Countess waved an imperious hand towards the shards of porcelain littering the carpet.

'How now, what's this?'

Harry shrank against his mother's side and tears began to well up in his eyes.

'We were playing a game and . . . and there was an accident,' Belle's words tumbled out. 'I will replace the bowl. Please do not beat Harry – or send him to bed without any supper.' No angel could have pleaded more prettily.

'And has this punishment been suggested?' There was little more than polite enquiry in the Earl's voice.

'It is no more than the boy should expect.' The Dowager sounded implacable.

'Ah, but he is not *your* boy,' the Earl said softly.

'He is a Mountstanton.'

'Quite. So I am the one to dictate his punishment.'

Harry trembled and his tears spilled over. His mother put her arm around him. Neither said anything.

Belle grabbed the Earl's hand. 'Please, don't be so cruel as to beat him.'

He detached his hand from her grasp. 'Harry, stand up straight. Look at me.'

The boy reluctantly unglued himself from his mother's side and fixed a fearful gaze on the tall, unyielding figure before him.

'You will go upstairs now and remain in the nursery. You will have no supper and I will be up later to demonstrate exactly how displeased I am with you. Helen, send for Mrs Comfort.'

Ursula had remained standing after the accident with the bowl, her whole body rigid with distaste. She hoped that the woman's name reflected her nature.

The Countess rose without expression and went to pull on the long silk cord that hung beside the fireplace.

A footman appeared, received his instructions, and left.

The Earl flicked his gaze round the silent room. It rested for a moment on his mother, then passed on until it fell on Ursula.

The cold, fish-like eyes studied her for a moment. 'And you are?' he said in an indifferent voice.

'Ursula Grandison, companion to Miss Seldon, sir.' She deliberately did not give him his title nor dip a curtsey.

He raised an eyebrow.

She was silent and stood looking straight at him. Then he said, 'So,' and turned to his wife. 'Do I see tea?'

By now there were several servants in the room, brushing up the broken pieces of china and filling empty cups.

'Come and sit by me, Richard,' the Dowager Countess said to her son, indicating a chair set next to hers. 'I have been waiting to hear what you have been up to while I've been away.'

'Later, Mama. I wish to learn what Liberty Belle thinks of her first sight of England and Mountstanton.'

Ignoring the flashes of red that flamed in the Dowager's cheeks, the Earl settled himself next to Belle. 'No doubt now you are so grown up, I shall have to call you Miss Seldon,' he said pleasantly.

* * *

By the time it came for Ursula to be shown to her room by Mrs Parsons, she was exhausted. It was not the rigours of the travel; looking back on that morning's train journey, it seemed positively tranquil compared with what had awaited at Mountstanton.

The life of Ursula Grandison had been full of ups and downs. Using her wits, she had extricated herself from potentially disastrous situations. Tragedy had visited her and so had extreme happiness. She had learned to survive in situations that would have swamped girls less courageous than herself. Never, though, could she remember having to witness such powerful cross-currents of tension. With no part to play in the scene, Ursula had found the afternoon more challenging than the time she had found herself separating men seemingly determined on beating each other into extinction.

Relief came when Ursula was handed over to the housekeeper to be shown her accommodation. And Helen's announcement that dinner would be at seven o'clock, giving a clear indication that Ursula should not expect further contact with the family until then, was received thankfully.

There was careful politeness in every line of Mrs Parson's carriage as she led the way back along the corridor towards the great staircase. As she followed in her wake, Ursula realised that the housekeeper could well provide a key to much that happened at Mountstanton. Would she, though, be able to reach through the impregnable reserve displayed by so many of the servants? Maybe even achieve a cosy chat?

'This seems a very ancient house,' she said, a note of enquiry in her voice.

'Indeed it is, Miss Grandison.' Mrs Parsons sounded pleased at her interest. 'The original house was built in the reign of Elizabeth but the classical front was added some hundred and fifty years later.'

'There are so many interesting pictures and pieces of furniture.'

The woman dipped her head in acknowledgement of this truth. 'No doubt, America being such a new country, Miss Grandison, there will not be such houses there.'

Ursula thought of the treasures in the Seldon New York mansion and in some of the others built in that city over the last few decades. After visiting them, you would not be blamed for thinking that there could hardly be an antique piece of furniture, sculpture, painting, panelling or ancient hall left in Europe, so much had been transported to the New World.

'It is a great privilege to be allowed to stay in a house such as this,' she said. 'Would you, perhaps, be able to give me a tour one day?'

'Why, Miss Grandison, I would be privileged. But I am sure that her ladyship will wish to do that.'

'The Countess must have a great many calls on her time. As indeed, must you,' Ursula added hurriedly. 'But your knowledge of Mountstanton must be unrivalled. How many years have you been here?'

'Nearly thirty.' They had reached the stairs. 'I started as a maid, as my mother did before me. And my grandmother had charge of the laundry.'

Ursula looked at her in admiration as they moved upstairs. 'Why, that could be called a dynasty! I do not believe we have any such tradition of service in America.'

Mrs Parsons paused on the landing. She looked pleased. 'There is a tradition in England called *noblesse oblige*. It means that titled families, indeed, any with great estates whether titled or not, have a duty to those who serve them. We at Mountstanton believe that those who serve also have a duty of loyalty and dedication to the Stanhope family. That is the family name of the Earls of Mountstanton,' she added in a helpful manner.

Ursula was fascinated. 'I would very much like to hear more about Mountstanton, Mrs Parsons, when you have time.'

They started up a further flight of stairs.

'It would be an honour, Miss Grandison. And I shall hope to hear from you what America is like.'

The higher in the house they went, the more the grandeur dropped away. By the time Ursula was led along a corridor there were no ornate balustrades, no great oil paintings on the walls, few pieces of furniture, and the floor covering was no more than serviceable.

A door opened as they passed and Mrs Comfort stood there, looking apprehensive. Then her expression lightened. 'Oh, I'm sorry, miss, I'm sure. I thought . . . '

Ursula realised she must have thought it was the Earl come to discipline his son and heir. She smiled at the nanny. 'Has the young Viscount recovered from the unfortunate incident in the drawing room?'

'Unfortunate is the word, Miss Grandison. I never knew such goings on. I'll be pleased when a new nursemaid has been engaged. 'Tis too much on my own, Mrs Parsons, as you well knows. I can't manage the boy and his washing and ironing and everything else.'

'Quite, Mrs Comfort.'

The nanny gave the sort of nod that said she hoped due note had been taken of her words and closed the door.

Where, wondered Ursula, as Mrs Parsons continued along the corridor, did the nanny figure in the accommodation hier-archy? No doubt above the position of the ordinary servant but well below the status of family or honoured guest. Well, that surely summed herself up as well.

'Here we are,' said Mrs Parsons and threw open a door. 'I hope you will be comfortable.'

Remembering how lacking in charm the room she had been shown into on arrival was, Ursula did not expect much in the way of décor or furniture, and she was not disappointed. There was an iron bedstead covered with a cotton spread, a washstand, an upright chair, a simple chest of drawers, a small table and a deal wardrobe. A mirror hung on the wall above the table. There was also a text: 'Be thou thrifty and the Lord will provide', and a badly foxed print of a small child kneeling beside a bed to say her prayers, eyes closed and a deep frill round her otherwise plain nightgown. Ursula's trunk had been placed against one wall.

Mrs Parsons ran a hand over the surface of the chest of drawers, as though checking that dust had been satisfactorily removed. 'Do you require assistance to unpack?' Her voice was distant; it was as though she was removing herself from the decision to award this inadequate room to Ursula.

'Thank you, Mrs Parsons, but I am well able to undertake that task myself.' Ursula grinned inwardly as she thought how seldom she had had the luxury of a personal servant in recent years. 'May I enquire if the maid the Countess informed Mr Seldon would be provided for her sister is looking after the unpacking of her luggage?'

Mrs Parsons nodded. 'Didier, as she has informed us she is to be called, is in the process of doing that right now.' Her voice was noncommittal but Ursula received the distinct impression that the maid had not endeared herself to the housekeeper. 'You will no doubt require a gown to be pressed for dinner this evening. I will send Sarah up to collect it shortly.'

Left on her own at last, Ursula sank onto the bed. The mattress was thin and supported by a hard, unsprung base. It did not matter. At least she could close her eyes and try for five minutes or so to blank out everything that had taken place since her arrival at Mountstanton.

After a little while she remembered that Sarah was to collect a gown for pressing. As she unlocked the trunk and picked out a dark grey silk gown, the door was flung open and Belle entered.

'At last I have found you!'

Ursula rose and found herself wrapped in urgent arms.

'Oh, Ursula, this is a horrid place. I was so looking forward to being with Helen again. My big sister who always cared for me. And now all she can do is tell me I must do this and I must do that and I mustn't do the other.' Belle burst into tears.

Ursula sat her down on the bed and found a handkerchief.

'Hush, hush,' she said gently and stroked the distraught girl's hair. 'Helen has a great position to maintain. She has a child to raise and this enormous house to run; she is no longer a carefree girl with all her choices in front of her, she has chosen her role and now has to make it work. Think how complicated her life must be, particularly with the Dowager Countess for mother-in-law.'

'And that's another thing,' Belle screwed the sodden hand-kerchief into a tight ball and dabbed at her eyes. 'Why didn't you tell me you knew Helen?' She gazed at Ursula, all tears now gone. 'She says I am not to trust you. She is going to try and send you away, I know it!' Belle flung her arms around Ursula again. 'I don't want you to leave, I need you. I hate this house. If you leave, I'll leave too. I'll go home to Papa.'

Ursula held Belle tight. 'Shhh, shhh, I am staying here with you. And you know how much your father wanted you to come here and enjoy a London season.'

'But why didn't you tell me you knew Helen?'

'It's a long story,' Ursula said slowly. 'Helen and I were at school together, first in New York and then in Paris.'

Belle looked at her with wide eyes. 'In Paris?'

Ursula nodded. 'You were probably too small to remember but I often used to visit with you in New York during the holi-day. So did my father. You called him Uncle Ogden.'

'Uncle Ogden?' Belle stared at Ursula. 'I remember him. He was very tall and had a loud laugh.'

Ursula smiled. 'That was my father.'

'He used to give me liquorice ropes, and pinched my cheek. What happened to him?'

'I'm afraid he died.'

Belle placed a soft hand on Ursula's knee. 'I'm so sorry. You must miss him very much.'

Ursula blinked rapidly. 'Just as you miss your mother.'

'What about *your* mother?'

'She died when I was born. I never knew her.'

'How sad.'

Ursula took Belle's hand. They sat together in silence for a moment then Ursula faced the young girl. 'Darling, we are in a foreign country and things are very different here from at home.'

'I thought we were all the same. I mean, we talk the same language and we, well, we came from England originally, didn't we?'

Ursula grinned at her. 'You may have done. My father's grandfather was Norwegian. My mother came from Poland with her parents when she was a little girl. Americans are a stew-pot of different nationalities.'

'And are proud of it,' said Belle passionately.

'And are proud of it,' agreed Ursula. 'And you and your sister are showing this ancient nation that a new one can be just as good and behave just as well.'

'I don't think these English behave at all well.'

'We all behave badly at times,' Ursula said mildly. 'Don't be too hard on them. And you like little Harry.'

'I love Harry.'

'I think he loves you, too. And what about Mr Warburton, didn't you like him?'

Belle flushed. 'I asked Helen if he would be at dinner, and she almost flew at me. I wasn't to give him a second thought, she said, he was not for me. And then . . . and then, oh, Ursula, I couldn't believe it but she said something about my future husband having been chosen for me and it wasn't Mr Warburton.'

Chapter Four

Max Russell winced as he fastened the stud in his wing collar, then he released the tender piece of skin it had caught and took the bow tie from his valet.

Holding up his chin and working blind, he secured it, then checked his appearance in the mirror. 'Will it do, Jenkins?'

'Undoubtedly,' said the servant, tidying away riding clothes.

'You might at least make a pretence of looking at me.'

'If I thought anything I said would make a difference, I would.' Jenkins closed the wardrobe door, went over to the tallboy, picked up a watch and chain and handed them over. 'You'll do.'

'Jenkins, do I get the impression you have something on your mind? Something other than my appearance?'

The man shifted his feet uneasily then looked straight at Max. 'I've had an offer, sir.'

Max halted the act of anchoring his watch chain across his waistcoat. His expression went blank. '"Sir" is it, Jenkins? The offer must have been good.'

'It is, sir.'

'And you are minded to accept.' It was not a question.

'It's a matter of circumstances, sir.'

Max jammed the watch into his waistcoat pocket. He should have seen this coming. 'I know, I haven't paid you for several months. Is the offer from anyone I know?'

Jenkins' face was without expression. 'No, sir.'

Well, at least his servant had not been pinched by any of his acquaintances; he'd hardly call any of them 'friends'. The man must have approached an agency. He had known there was no point in asking for a rise. Well, the timing could be fortuitous.

'I will miss you, Jenkins. You have served me well.' Which he had, apart from a certain surliness every now and then which, given the fact that he was often forced to go without his wages, was forgivable.

'Thank you, sir.'

'When do you wish to leave?'

'I am asked for in one month's time, which is the length of notice I am bound to give.' The valet handed over Max's loose change.

Max gave him a nod, 'I have no objection.' He adjusted his cufflinks then slipped his arms into the sleeves of the jacket the valet held ready for him. He did not bother to check its set. 'I just ask that you do not let Lady Frances know you are leaving.'

'As you wish, sir.'

'Good night, Jenkins. Don't wait up.'

'Thank you, sir.'

Max left the valet picking up the shaving bowl and towel and strode along the corridor. He paused outside his mother's room, summoned up a warm smile, knocked and entered.

'Mama, how do you feel this evening?' he asked, his voice low and gentle.

Lady Frances Russell, daughter of an Earl, relict of the Very Reverend Russell, an austere but charitable dean who had died some eight years previously, smiled at her only child. 'I am well, thank you my darling.'

Max looked closely at her pale face and pain-laden eyes. The thin hand that lay on the coverlet looked almost transparent.

'I saw Doctor Mason after his visit to you this morning, Mama. He said he'd given you something to ease your suffering.'

The doctor had been blunt. 'There's nothing I can do for her, Mr Russell, the disease has advanced beyond medical aid. Even my strongest opiates cannot rid her of pain but I hope what I've left will help.' He'd looked compassionately at Max. 'She's a brave woman.'

'How much longer?'

The doctor shrugged. 'I would say no more than a few weeks. But I have found we doctors are not arbiters in these matters; they are decided by a higher authority.'

'Have you time to sit with me for a moment, Max?' Her breathing was harsh, her speech laboured.

He sat down beside the bed, brought her thin hand to his mouth and kissed the palm. He turned his head away from her and closed his eyes for a moment.

'You look so smart, my darling. Is it for Mountstanton?'

He nodded. 'I'd rather be with you. Shall I cancel and stay here? Would you like that?'

She shook her head and struggled to sit a little more upright.

He helped her, rearranging the pillows, smoothing them and then carefully settling the lacy wool comforter round her shoulders. Her bones felt so frail it was agonising.

His mother smiled at him. 'Leave an empty place at the table? The Countess would never forgive you.'

Max sat down again, taking her hand in his. 'That would be nothing compared to your comfort.'

She smiled. 'I like to think of you there.'

They sat for a moment in silence.

'Can you ever forgive me, darling?'

'What for, Mama?'

'Giving birth to you.'

He drew a quick breath. 'There is nothing to forgive. All my life you have given me such love. I am much, much luckier than – well, than many men I know.'

'Thank you for staying here. Without me, I know you would have left the country.'

Before he could protest, she started to cough and he had to pour some of the medicine Doctor Mason had left, then hold her close as the racking threatened to tear her chest apart.

Ann came in and took her mistress from him. 'Go, sir. It's for the best. She'll be all right later. Tomorrow she'll want to know how everything went.'

Safe, stolid Ann, who knew exactly how to care for his mother. She had always been part of his life. He placed a brief hand on her shoulder as she laid her mistress back on the pillows, the poor lungs gasping for air.

Outside, the horse and trap were waiting. He thanked Jethro, the groom, and told him not to wait up. 'I can stable Cobbley,' he said.

When the Very Reverend Russell died, Max and his mother had moved from the large rectory back to her father's estate, into a small but pretty house several miles from Mountstanton. Max's uncle had inherited the Viscountcy and Max had expressed his gratitude.

'Was always fond of my sister, Frances,' his uncle, the Viscount of Broome, had said. 'Thought my father behaved disgracefully towards her. It's a small thing; sorry there's no money to go with it; finances very dodgy, you know?'

Yes, Max did know. The family circumstances had always been straitened. Still, he and his mother managed, just. It looked as though her capital would last just as long as herself. As for him ...

Max clicked the horse into action and set off. With his mother gone, there would be nothing left for him here. It was as well Jenkins had found other employment. His uncle would find something for Ann and for Mrs Sutton, their housekeeper. That would leave him completely free to go where he would.

He pushed away the thought of what he would be leaving behind.

★ ★ ★

At Mountstanton, Max handed over the pony and trap to one of the waiting grooms and entered the house.

The butler took his hat, driving cape and gloves. 'Good to see you, sir,' he said, sounding pleased.

Max smiled. 'Everything going well here, Benson?'

'Indeed, sir. Miss Seldon, sister to the Countess, has arrived from America. The dinner tonight is in her honour. And, sir,' Benson continued, leaning towards him with as much excitement as a butler might ever be allowed to express, 'soon we expect Colonel Charles home.'

That was the Earl's brother, Colonel Stanhope. 'On leave, is he?'

'I believe he has resigned his commission.'

Now why should such a successful soldier leave the army?

More arrivals entered and Max moved on.

Helen greeted him with the usual, slightly distant courtesy she always showed towards him in company.

She seemed oddly tense and Max resisted the temptation to tease her. Instead he greeted the Earl, who clapped him on the shoulder. 'Good to see you, Max. Might like your advice on a filly I found the other day.'

'Any time, Richard.' Max hoped his equine expertise would earn him an income one of these days. In the meantime, he was happy to build his reputation for assessing a horse's potential and revealing any unsuspected shortcomings.

Helen took his arm. 'I want to introduce you to Miss Grandison, my little sister's companion. You will take her into dinner.'

He winced inwardly. The companion rather than the heiress was to be his lot. No doubt she would be at least forty years of age.

A servant approached. 'My lady, the Dowager Countess wishes a word with you.'

'Your mother-in-law has returned?' Over the other side of the drawing room Max saw the Dowager, her face thunderous. As she caught his eye, she deliberately turned away. 'I am amazed you did not send to cancel my invitation for tonight.'

'I shall be allowed to have whom I choose to my own dinners.' Helen's voice was tightly controlled. 'Ursula, may I present Mr Russell, one of our neighbours. Max, this is Miss Grandison.'

And then she was gone.

Max was pleasantly surprised to find that Ursula Grandison looked less than thirty and had a remarkably fine pair of grey eyes, now looking at him with startled interest, the reaction of so many around here.

'If you are companion to Miss Seldon, may I assume you, too, are American?'

'You may.' Her voice was cool.

'Our hostess has neglected to introduce me to her sister. May I ask which she is?'

Helen's deliberate discourtesy nagged at him. He regretted revealing his irritation to Miss Grandison but she appeared to have the good manners not to notice anything amiss.

'She is in the pink silk gown with roses in her hair, over by the fireplace talking to Mr Warburton.'

Max swallowed renewed irritation at finding William Warburton so firmly ensconced at Mountstanton and looked across the room.

The girl was talking vivaciously, her blonde hair, with the roses, beautifully dressed. Max was no expert on women's fashions but he could see she was perfectly turned out. Even at this distance, Max knew that there would be an aura of Parisian fragrance about her to match her gown. And yet her most noticeable feature was how naïve and innocent she looked.

Dinner was announced and he offered his arm to Miss Grandison.

As they waited for the more distinguished members of the party to pass onwards to the dining room, he mused over the news that Benson had given him. Why had Charles resigned his commission and when, exactly, would he be returning to Mountstanton?

'I think we should follow,' murmured Miss Grandison and Max saw that they were in danger of being left alone in the drawing room.

With a muttered apology, he led her smoothly towards the door.

They were a party of twenty-four. Max and Miss Grandison were, as he expected, seated in the middle of the table, as distant as it was possible to be from both their host and their hostess.

The Earl had his mother on his right and Miss Seldon on his left. Her cheeks were bright with excitement.

Max stopped himself from checking who was on either side of the hostess. Instead he turned to his partner. 'When did you arrive in England, Miss Grandison?'

'Three days ago, Mr Russell.'

'Then you will not have had much time to form an opinion of the natives?'

The cool grey eyes surveyed him with amusement. 'They afford me much interest.'

Wine was poured and Max sampled his. 'This is a splendid vintage,' he said. 'Richard has a wonderful cellar, much of it laid down by his father. I don't know if you have had much experience of French wines?'

She looked at him for a moment, raised her glass and sipped assessingly. Then she gave him an engaging smile and said, 'Montrachet, I think. I'm afraid I can't tell the year.'

'I'm stunned. Not only that you have recognised the wine but that you know how to pronounce the name. Not a "t" to be heard.'

She chuckled, a warm sound with a hint of irony. 'Not bad for a Yankee?'

By now he was enchanted. 'Are you making it a mission to transform the usual English opinion of our American cousins' sense of culture – or lack of it?'

'I think that would be doomed to failure. But it would be nice to think I have converted at least one Englishman?' Her head slightly on one side, she gazed at him with a hint of a challenge.

He put down his glass and held up his hands. 'I surrender. But, having known Helen ever since she arrived, I am well aware that American women can be educated, sophisticated and charming.'

'And there must be other American belles you have met; I understand English society is threaded through with our well-heeled sisters.'

Max laughed. 'You mean, our poverty-stricken landed gentry have been looking to fill their coffers with the riches garnered by enterprising Americans?'

Her expression lost its vivacity. Max followed her gaze and saw Helen's little sister ignoring Mountstanton, who was no doubt involved in dodging his mother's inquisition into his activities. Instead she was looking down the table and smiling beguilingly.

Max followed her gaze and saw William Warburton give her the tiniest of salutations with his glass. He was rewarded with a blush from Miss Seldon, who then looked down at her plate.

Miss Grandison's eyes narrowed and Max saw her glance at the Countess. As she turned her beautiful face to the aged Duke of Aberdare, seated on her right, her hand fiddled with the stem of her wine glass. A moment later, the glass had over-turned. Benson retrieved the situation in a moment and the Duke never hesitated in whatever the story was he was relating.

'What level of title is Miss Seldon expected to attract?' Max asked as his empty plate was removed.

Miss Grandison looked at him thoughtfully. 'Do you really expect me to answer that question?'

He shrugged. 'You Americans are so open and frank, it was worth asking.'

'Mr Russell, I am sure you realise my social training is sufficient to understand that, much as I have enjoyed our conversation, it is time for me to give my attention to the guest on my other side.' She gave a polite nod of her head and addressed a remark to her other partner, Aberdare's third son, a young man of little brain and less personality.

Reluctantly Max turned to do his duty to the female seated on his left. She was the eighteen-year-old, not-very-pretty, not-very-intelligent, but gentle and sweet second daughter of a local baronet. He knew her and prepared himself for a polite query on his mother's condition.

Instead she looked wistfully up the table at Miss Seldon and said, 'Mr Russell, that gown is the most beautiful I have ever seen. What must it be like to be very pretty and very rich?'

'I imagine that, like everything else in life, Miss Cary, it has its problems.'

'Problems?' Her pale eyes widened.

'For instance, it must be difficult to decide if someone, a young man for instance, likes you for yourself or because you are very rich.'

Her mouth formed an 'O' of comprehension. 'I never thought of that.'

'Then I also think it must be very, very difficult to decide which gown to choose if you have a vast number. And what about which shoes or hat?'

She stared for a long moment then laughed a little uncertainly. 'Oh, Mr Russell, you are teasing me.'

He was very glad when the moment came in the long, drawn-out meal when he could reclaim Miss Grandison's attention. She turned back to him with what, if he was not flattering himself, was similar relief.

'In England do none of society's young men occupy themselves with a profession, Mr Russell?' she asked abruptly.

'Work is beneath our station in life, Miss Grandison.'

Her eyes flashed, as though she suspected him of laughing at her. 'Do you do nothing, then, Mr Russell?'

For a moment he saw himself through her eyes and inwardly winced. 'I am something of an historian, Miss Grandison. I am currently studying the French Revolution and intend to write a book.'

She thought about this for a moment. 'Is that what the male members of English society do? Study?'

He laughed. 'Very few do. No, let me explain. Gentlemen in England only follow three ways of life. First they can be gentlemen of leisure. The eldest son will inherit the family estate. He will ride, travel, socialise, amuse himself in any number of ways. If he is a peer, he may take his seat in the House of Lords, attend and contribute to debates.'

She regarded him with fascination. 'And the other sons?'

'They may well also be gentlemen of leisure. They may indulge in politics as Members of Parliament. Or they have a choice of two professions. They can serve His Majesty.'

'Which means they become a soldier or a sailor?'

'Indeed. Or they are ordained into the Church.'

'And do these professions produce a reasonable income?'

He shook his head. 'The sort of regiment a gentleman desires to join requires a substantial income. The Church may well provide a stipend but it is unlikely to be generous.'

'So what does a gentleman do if he has no money?'

'Then he finds a wife who brings a large dowry, or he lives abroad.'

'He doesn't find an occupation that brings him in a suitable income?'

'Only if he no longer wishes to be regarded as a gentleman.'

She applied herself to eating for a moment, her brow creased in thought. He was amused at her difficulty in grappling with the concept he had outlined.

'In America,' she said, 'It does not matter how rich a man is, he works at a profession.'

'And is regarded as a gentleman?'

'Ah, that depends on his breeding and education.'

'I think I would like America. Perhaps I will try living there. I have a desire to try my hand at prospecting for gold.'

She laughed. 'The days of the gold rush are over. There are, however, silver mines,' she added provocatively. 'But there are many, many ways a man may make his fortune. Even in America, however, wealth does not guarantee a place in society. Mr Russell, what can you tell me about Mr Warburton?'

'Ah!' He remembered that look from the Seldon girl.

'William is the grandson of a Marquis; his father was the second son and accepted a commission into the Hussars, one of the most fashionable of cavalry regiments. He died a Colonel in the Sudan some years ago.'

'Mr Warburton has not become a soldier?'

'No. He is a gentleman of leisure.'

'With the money to follow the pursuits he enjoys?'

'Alas, no. He relies on his uncle, the present Marquis, to see that he is not quite destitute.'

'Whilst he searches for a rich wife?'

Max said nothing.

'You know him well?'

'Not well, no. I was at Eton with his cousin, who will eventually inherit the title, but, as you can probably tell, William is rather younger than I am.'

Again there was that steady gaze before she attended to her meal. Then she placed her cutlery neatly on her plate and said, 'Mr Russell, I did not answer your earlier question about Belle, Miss Seldon. Perhaps I should tell you that her father hopes she will not form any connection during her London season but return to New York before the end of the year. He would like his younger daughter by his side.'

There seemed to be an unspoken warning in her words.

'Miss Grandison, with you to keep an eye on her, I am sure her father will gain his wish.'

She made a curious sound that was almost a snort. 'Applesauce, Mr Russell. You know as well as I, when a young girl takes it into her head to fall for a man, there is little anyone can do about it. Now, tell me about the French Revolution. I have read Mr Carlyle's work on the subject and am interested to know whether you agree with his views on the causes of that uprising.'

There followed for Max the delight of a discussion on a matter close to his heart with a person of intelligence. The rising of the Countess to collect the women to withdraw came far too soon.

As the men regrouped around Mountstanton for their port and cigars, Max found himself studying William Warburton.

He was undoubtedly a handsome young man; little brain but a good deal of personal charm. Would he dare, Max wondered, to follow up that so-innocent invitation from rich little Miss Seldon? And just what would Helen do about it?

They did not remain long in the dining room. Instructions had undoubtedly been issued prior to the meal.

Filing into the drawing room, the men found that music was in progress. Max, bringing up the rear, looked around for Miss Grandison, but she was in conversation with Miss Cary.

Accepting a cup of coffee, Max moved out into the conservatory and settled himself on one of the wrought-iron seats beside a lush palm tree. Looking around, he saw he was not the only one who had sought a little peace and quiet – or was it privacy?

The weather had produced the first blush of summer and the doors onto the terrace had been opened, allowing a welcome breeze to freshen the air.

He half listened to the pianist, a local heiress whose looks if not her pearls left a great deal to be desired. He had decided to ditch his intention of securing a private conversation with Helen, however brief; now part of him wished to return home to his mother as soon as was polite, but another part of him wanted more conversation with Miss Grandison.

Polite applause signalled the end of the Chopin étude and he returned to the drawing room.

Almost immediately, he found Miss Grandison by his side. 'Mr Russell, have you seen Belle, Miss Seldon?' she said quietly.

She looked worried. He remembered the pink gown he had noticed at the far end of the conservatory.

'Could she have needed a little fresh air?'

'I do not see Mr Warburton either,' Miss Grandison's voice was low but tense.

He looked around the room. Helen seemed deep in conversation with a woman he knew was a good friend. She could not have noticed the absence from the room of her sister and William Warburton.

He smiled and offered his arm to Miss Grandison. 'Let me show you the conservatory,' he said pleasantly. 'The ferns are extraordinary.'

The conservatory was empty. Through the open doors, across the lawn, he caught the flash of a pink skirt. Max felt unexpected anger. This was a cad's trick.

Chapter Five

Helen Stanhope had arranged the dinner party to introduce her sister to friends with offspring who might provide Belle with companionship, and assist with her debut into Society, and to a few suitable young bachelors.

Now it seemed Belle was threatening social disaster by disappearing from sight. Helen could see her nowhere in the drawing room. Nor could she see William. All around Helen were the almost imperceptible signals that indicated people would shortly be leaving. Belle had to be at her side. It was so important that the Dowager Countess should not be able to make any complaint about her behaviour.

Where was Ursula? She should be looking out for her charge. Why else had she come to Mountstanton? Fury began to build in Helen. She stopped one of the footmen attending to the supply of coffee and drinks. 'John, have you seen Miss Seldon?'

His warm brown eyes that always seemed as though they saw a joke that had eluded everyone else, frowned slightly as he balanced a tray of empty cups. 'No, my lady. Not for a little while.'

'You haven't seen her go to her room?'

'No, my lady.'

'Thank you, John.'

The footman moved away. Helen gazed after him thoughtfully. There went one who managed to keep just the right side of what Mrs Parsons called 'getting above himself'. There was no doubt he was attractive. If Helen wanted to indulge in bed-room activities with a servant, a pastime followed by several upper-crust women she could name, he would undoubtedly be at the top her list. Her tastes, though, did not incline that way.

Could Belle have gone outside? Helen drifted gently towards the conservatory, exchanging remarks with friends as she went. If William had had the gall to take the girl out there on her own, she would have something to say to him; though she could hear the excuses he would give: 'Helen, sweetheart, the girl begged for some fresh air, how could I refuse?' Or, 'Helen, I just happened to mention your astonishing ferns and nothing would serve but that she had to be shown them. What was I to do?'

Into Helen's mind slipped the memory of a time when her father had, in his autocratic way, announced some project or other that ran counter to her mother's wishes. Giving in, as she always did, her mother had said to Helen, 'You Seldons won't let anything stand in your way. Relentlessly self-centred, end-lessly manipulative; I don't know why I put up with you.'

Until now, Helen had not thought of Belle in that way. She hardly knew her young sister. Separated from her, firstly by her own schooling in Paris (an arrangement her mother had vetoed for Belle, triumphing for once over her husband's wishes) and then by marriage to an Englishman, she and Belle had spent little time together. However, Helen had retained the impression, fortified on a visit home several years ago, of a deli-ciously malleable child growing into a docile young woman.

Now Helen was beginning to wonder if her sister was more like their father than she had realised.

She sighed. Were all her plans for Belle's debut into Society going to be upset? And would it be fair to blame William for this small act of rebellion? Better to chastise him for not taking the girl over to Ursula.

Just where was Ursula? Helen's slow burning anger focused on her sister's keeper. Such had been her rage at Ursula Grandison's appearance that Helen had not been able to bring herself to confront her ex-schoolfriend since her arrival. This, she now realised, had been a mistake.

A quick glance round the conservatory showed her it was empty. Then, through the open doors to the garden, Helen saw Belle and Ursula coming towards her, walking arm-in-arm. Strolling behind them, each smoking a small cigarillo, were William and Max.

For a moment all Helen could feel was relief. Then her anger ignited into rage. Rage against Belle, rage against William, even rage against Max, who could hardly be blamed for any part of the situation, but mostly rage against Ursula.

'Helen,' said Belle happily. 'You surely have a splendid garden – such fun to view it by moonlight. William, Mr Russell, thank you sirs for showing it to me.'

'Belle,' Helen controlled herself. 'Guests are about to leave. I need you beside me to bid them farewell.' She gave a cool nod to the men. 'Ursula, I would be grateful if, after everyone has left, you could attend me in my boudoir.'

'Of course, Helen.'

'I shall take my leave now,' said Max. 'Thank you, your ladyship, for a delightful evening. Miss Grandison, I hope we shall meet again during your time at Mountstanton.'

Ursula offered him her hand. 'I hope you will find your mother in better spirits, Mr Russell.'

Helen realised that, with everything else she had been thinking about this evening, she had neglected to ask Max how Lady Frances was. And there was that other matter. It was too late, though, to do anything now. She would go over in the morning and call at The Beeches. She could take Belle with her.

★ ★ ★

It was well over an hour before Helen said goodbye to the last of her guests. Richard had already taken William off to the billiard room, heedless of any offence he might give. The Dowager Countess had retired some time ago with only the briefest of good nights.

Helen turned to Belle. 'Go to bed. I'll talk to you in the morning.'

Belle looked at her with limpid eyes. She did not look at all tired, in fact she glowed. 'I hope I was a success for you, Helen.'

Helen, conscious of the two footmen straightening furniture and clearing the room of glasses and cups, restrained herself. 'I said, we'll talk in the morning.'

Belle walked away with a bounce in her step. It did not escape Helen how the footmen followed her with their eyes.

The girl was a minx.

'Thank you,' Helen said to them. 'Everything went very well.'

Suddenly conscious she was tired, Helen went to the foot of the staircase, then paused. She had intended to take a last look at Harry. The sight of her darling son peacefully sleeping could always soothe her spirits. On the staircase, the oil lamps flickered; they needed cleaning. In New York, the Seldon mansion was lit by electricity; it sprang into life at the touch of a switch.

Helen turned away, deciding not to visit the nursery suite now; Mrs Comfort should not be disturbed.

Helen wondered if she should talk to Mrs Parsons about the necessity to replace Polly, the nursemaid who had walked off in that infuriating way. The girl had been cheerful, hardworking and with a knack of knowing exactly how to handle Harry. He had been very upset when she left.

Mrs Parsons had been furious at her departure. 'Just upped, my lady. Took her box and left. Mrs Comfort thinks she had another offer. As though her chances anywhere else would be better than here, or there could be a more delightful child to look after than his little lordship.'

Delightful Harry certainly was, but he could also be very temperamental. One advantage with Belle's arrival was that she and Harry had formed an immediate bond. With an effort, Helen dismissed the problems with her sister; it was time now to deal with Ursula, no doubt already waiting for her in her boudoir. Helen for once was pleased that both her suite of rooms and her husband's were on the ground floor. Their facilities left a great deal to be desired, but at least she did not have to negotiate a long staircase.

Outside the door of her boudoir, Helen paused for a moment, drawing strength from her grievances.

★ ★ ★

Ursula sat with a straight back in a little buttoned chair. The room was the most charming she had met with so far at Mountstanton. It looked recently decorated. The soft, fresh blues and creams and pretty furniture gave quite a different impression from the rest of the house. There was a Watteau on one wall, and two interesting Impressionist paintings on another.

The room brought back the Helen Ursula had known throughout her youth: a volatile, pretty and gregarious girl, one who broke most school rules while managing to evade retribution. Many times Ursula had lied to save her friend from disaster.

What was going to be demanded of her now? And how was Belle to be handled? Walking towards that flash of pink in the shrubbery, Ursula had seen the girl standing far too close to Mr Warburton; they might almost have been in an embrace. She had exchanged a speaking glance with Mr Russell and they had quickened their pace. As they approached, Belle had looked at Ursula with the satisfaction of a cat that had stolen the cream. 'Do not be unkind, Ursula, I could not bear it,' she said, laughing.

Ursula could not catch what Mr Russell said to Mr Warburton but she heard a protest from the younger man.

'Come,' said Ursula calmly, 'Let us walk back to the house. Her ladyship will be looking for Belle, I am sure.' She had placed her hand through Belle's arm. After a moment's resistance, the girl had walked with Ursula, leaving the two men to follow.

That Helen was very angry when she met them was obvious but Ursula admired her control. Ten years ago she would have exploded into a tantrum. Now she managed to handle the situation to a nicety.

Ursula turned from the problem of Belle to the enjoyable time she had spent seated next to Mr Russell at the dinner table. He was a delightful conversationalist and if Englishmen in general were more like him rather than the Earl, whom in other respects he greatly resembled, then perhaps the next few months would not be as difficult as she feared. There might even be another meeting with Mr Russell.

The door opened and Helen entered.

Ursula remained sitting.

Helen stood as though expecting her to rise, then seemed to decide that, for once, she would not insist on the courtesy due to her position.

'You look very tired, Helen.'

The Countess went over to the fireplace and tugged on the bell pull. 'It was a long evening,' she said, sounding surprised. 'I think we could do with something to drink.'

This was not what Ursula had expected.

A footman arrived.

'Whisky and some soda, please, John.'

'Water for me, please,' said Ursula.

'Of course, my lady.' The footman bowed with a twinkle in his brown eyes that said he liked the idea of the two of them enjoying a nightcap.

Ursula waved at the two Impressionist paintings. 'You have good taste,' she said.

Helen looked at them as though for the first time. 'Part of my wedding present from Papa. Richard doesn't like them so they hang here.'

'Renoir, I think, and Monet?'

Helen waved a dismissive hand. 'If you say so.'

'This house seems to have many treasures. And its patina of age is attractive,' she added, wondering what this would bring forth.

Helen hardly seemed to hear. She sat down and removed her shoes.

It was almost as though they were schoolgirls again.

Helen looked ruefully at Ursula. 'I have hated you for ten years. When I saw you with Belle the day you arrived, I was almost consumed with hatred.'

'And now?' Ursula sat very still.

Helen dragged a hand across her forehead. 'I feel empty. Seeing you sitting there, remembering what we once were to each other, the hate suddenly seems pointless. It's as though rotting flesh has fallen away, leaving clean bones.'

'An interesting metaphor,' Ursula said dryly.

'I suppose you think that I have no reason to hate you. After all, I have my belted Earl, and an historic mansion, not to mention a house in London.'

'And a beautiful son.'

Helen's expression softened. 'Yes, I have Harry.' There was a moment's pause before she said, 'And you, Ursula, what do you have?' There was a note of satisfaction in her voice that suggested the answer had to be, 'nothing'.

'Memories, mostly damaged ones.'

The footman knocked and entered. He bore a silver tray holding a whisky decanter, glass tumblers, a soda siphon, a gracefully shaped jug of water and a bowl of ice.

There flashed across Ursula's memory a vision of an unlabelled, dumpy bottle of gut-blasting moonshine, tin mugs on a rough board table, raised voices, and a haze of tobacco smoke. She closed her eyes for a moment and blanked it out.

'Thank you, John,' said Helen. 'We will serve ourselves.'

Ursula opened her eyes to see Helen holding out a glass of whisky with ice.

She took it and added a splash of water.

'Papa wrote that Jack was killed in an accident in California. Were you there?' Helen sat down with her own, amber-filled glass.

Ursula nodded. 'It wasn't an accident. He had a devil of a temper when drunk.' She wasn't prepared to go into details. She enjoyed the smoky-peat flavour of smooth liquor. After a moment she added, 'If he hadn't died, I would have left him.'

Helen looked at the contents of her glass. 'He was a devil of a man every which way. I haven't forgiven you for taking him from me.' There was a streak of acid in her voice.

Ursula shook her head. 'He wasn't yours, any more than he was mine.' She looked full at Helen. 'He told me when we reached St Louis that you would have been too easy.'

Helen flushed. 'But I had money. Oh, don't look at me like that, Ursula. Men want money. They need money.'

'Jack said that real power didn't lie with money, it was to do with knowing how to handle people. Give him people he could set against each other and it was as though he'd been filled with alcohol. Look at how he set you against me. He'd have made one hell of a politician.'

Helen said nothing.

After a moment Ursula added, 'I didn't steal Jack, Helen. He had no "sold" notice on him.'

Helen tossed down the contents of her glass and refilled it, then leant against an antique secretaire, nursing her drink.

'What made Papa send you with Belle?' she asked abruptly. 'He must have known it would annoy the hell out of me.'

'He wanted someone with her he could trust.'

'He thought he could trust you?'

'He knew he could. He rescued me from the slums of San Francisco.' Ursula looked down into her glass. 'After Jack died, a friend of his employed me to run a boarding house. The clientele were the lowest of the low and I could see no way out. Then your father arrived.'

'He likes power, too,' Helen said bitterly.

'He said he needed someone to help with his younger daughter. I was starving and he offered me a feast.'

'What does he intend with this debut season for Belle?'

'Have you not discussed this with him?'

Helen sat down again. 'Belle was about to finish her education and I suggested she might enjoy a London Season. He agreed.'

'So why do you ask what his motives are?'

'Papa never does anything without motives.'

Ursula shrugged. 'If you mean do you think he's hoping for another marriage into the aristocracy of England, you can rest easy. He wants her to have a good time and then return to New York to brighten his days.' Ursula watched to see what the effect of this would be on Helen. Belle's tearful complaint that her sister had already chosen a husband for her was very much in her mind.

'But if Belle were to fall in love?'

'Ah!' Ursula studied the handsome tumbler she was holding. 'Belle's happiness is important to him,' she said slowly.

'Anything Belle wants, Belle gets, is that it?'

Ursula was silent.

'I'm surprised he didn't come with her.'

'He would have liked to but business keeps him in New York for the moment.'

'Business, always business!' Helen topped up her glass and waved the decanter at Ursula, who shook her head.

'It's business that gives you your money. Without it, do you think you would be here?'

Helen gave her a searing look and Ursula realised she had been clumsy. As she cast around for a way to defuse her remark, Helen said stiffly, 'Thank you for rescuing Belle this evening.'

Ursula shrugged again. 'She is very young and untrained in formal behaviour. I am sure you can make her aware of what is required. I will, of course, help in every way I can.'

Helen drained her glass for the third time. 'It's late. We must go to bed.'

Ursula rose. 'Helen, let me say that it's good to see you again.' She placed her half-finished glass on the silver tray. 'Thank you for this evening.'

Helen said nothing.

★ ★ ★

Going back through the main hall, Ursula saw a door open and the Earl and William Warburton stagger out. It was the Earl who seemed the worse for wear. His arm was around the younger man's shoulder; he was laughing inanely and slapping the other man on the chest. 'I sank them; I said I would sink them and I did, I did, I did.'

The light in the wide corridor was very dim, the lamps flickering. Ursula drew back into a doorway and hoped to remain unnoticed.

The footman who had brought the whisky to the Countess's boudoir appeared and draped the Earl's free arm around his shoulder. 'Come along, my lord,' he said. 'We'll see you to bed.'

As the little party drew level with Ursula, she distinctly saw the footman wink at her.

Chapter Six

The morning had promise. There was a mist but behind it the sun was shining and Ursula thought it would soon clear.

Helen had announced at breakfast that she and Belle would go for a drive and visit some neighbours, including Lady Frances Russell. The Dowager Countess was to be taken on a tour of the estate by the Earl.

Ursula decided she would explore the village of Hinton Parva, the nearest to Mountstanton, and applied to one of the footmen for directions.

She should go down the drive, then turn left at the end and follow the road. 'It's not above a couple of miles or so,' the footman added.

This was not a distance to trouble Ursula, especially on such a fine day. She put on stout footwear, changed her linen skirt for one of ankle-length in plain drill cotton, and donned a short jacket.

As she passed the nursery, drawing on her gloves, Mrs Comfort emerged with Harry.

'Morning, Miss Grandison. Going out for a walk? That's the ticket. Me and his lordship are off for a pony ride.'

'I'm to jump today,' Harry announced in a proud voice.

'I'm to jump today, what?' pressed Mrs Comfort.

Harry looked down at his boots. 'Miss Grandison,' he muttered.

'That sounds splendid. I'm sure you will jump beautifully. Will Mrs Comfort ride with you?' Ursula asked with a smile.

Harry laughed. 'Nanny don't ride! She will watch me. And clap when I jump. You will clap, won't you, Nanny?'

'Yes, my love, of course I will.'

'And then I can show Papa how I jump.' He gave a little skip as they all walked together towards the stairs.

'Where be you off to, Miss Grandison, if I may ask?'

'I thought I would see what an English village was like, Mrs Comfort.'

'Somewhat different from your American ones, no doubt.'

Ursula laughed.

'And will you walk through the wood?'

The idea of a wood sounded interesting.

'Which way is that?'

Mrs Comfort stopped beside a window. 'See, over there, Miss Grandison?' She pointed.

Beyond the formal garden, a path led up to a thickly wooded hill.

'Goes right over and down into the village. Bit rough in places but probably nothing to you.' Mrs Comfort glanced at Ursula's sensible footwear. 'Us staff always uses it if we're going to Hinton, shorter than by the road, see. Polly loved to take that way.'

'Polly?'

Mrs Comfort's face creased with some indefinable emotion. 'Polly was the nursemaid here.' Ursula remembered that the nanny was without an assistant. 'She seemed happy with us, and the little lord loved her.'

'So what happened?'

'Took and left, she did. Without a word of warning. Anyway, miss, she liked the wood. And the bluebells are out; they're early this year. It'll be quite a sight.'

'Can you ride, Miss Grandison?' asked Harry.

'Yes. Perhaps one of these days we could ride together. Do you think that might be possible?'

'I will speak to Papa,' he said seriously as they started down the stairs. 'Papa says it is important for ladies to ride well.'

'And your Mama, does she ride with you?'

'Mama rides exceedingly well but I do not think she really enjoys it.'

Ursula was amused at the pedantic way he said this. 'Has she told you so?'

'No, but she does not ride out with Papa. She says he rides like the devil.' He grinned at her.

'Lord Harry, I've told you before about your language!'

Harry slipped his hand out of Mrs Comfort's and ran down the rest of the stairs. 'I'll be first at the stables,' he shouted.

The nanny smiled at Ursula. 'I do like to see him enthusiastic, Miss Grandison. And he does love riding, as does her ladyship, whatever Lord Harry says. He spends too much time at the stables, though.'

'Harry!' came a stern cry.

The Dowager Countess was in the hall. 'You do not run like a common lad. You walk steadily, like a gentleman.'

Harry stood with downcast head. 'Yes, Grandmama.' Then he looked up at her. 'I am going riding. And we are to jump.'

For a fleeting moment Ursula thought she saw the ghost of a smile on the Dowager Countess's face. 'I look forward to hearing all about it later, Harry. But, remember, walk steadily.'

She saw Ursula. 'Ah, Miss Grandison, going for a walk, I see.'

'I thought I would explore the village, your ladyship.'

'In that case, my dog will accompany you. I was going to ask the under gardener but you taking her will allow him to continue with his work.'

'A dog, your ladyship?'

The Dowager Countess moved slightly and Ursula saw for the first time that she was holding a lead. On its end was a small spaniel with long ears, soulful eyes and an attractive red and white coat.

'This is Honey.'

Ursula crouched down. 'Hello, Honey.' She caressed the dog, gently rubbing between its ears and underneath its neck. Honey licked her face. 'I think we can be friends,' she said as she rose and held out her hand for Honey's lead.

This time the Dowager Countess did smile. 'I can see Honey will be in good hands. You will not let her chase rabbits or get over-excited. When you get back, apply at the stables and they will give you a brush. She always needs one after a run.'

'By all means,' Ursula said, amused.

* * *

As she left the house with the spaniel, Ursula saw Helen and Belle setting forth in an open landau. Helen looked strained and Belle sulky. Ursula waved at them.

'What a lovely day,' she called as the carriage moved forward. There was no response.

The hill was steep, the sun had burned through the mist, and Ursula soon removed her jacket and tied it round her waist. She laughed with enjoyment of the day and the spaniel trotted happily alongside her.

At the top, Ursula stopped to catch her breath and admire the countryside. She looked up at what was now a brilliant blue sky. Birds sang, liquid and sweet, in the soft spring air. She drew a deep breath. Compared with the vast open spaces of America, this countryside before her was a patchwork of handkerchief-sized pieces. But each piece was miniature perfection. For the first time since she had left on this trip with Belle, Ursula felt a sense of freedom. She bent down and released the dog.

Honey looked up at her uncertainly, her head on one side.

'Come on, let's go into the wood and see if there are any rabbits.'

After the brilliance of the sun, the darkness was almost sinister and the air was cold. Ursula shivered. She loosened the sleeves of the jacket from round her waist and put it on again, rubbing at her arms.

Gradually her eyes adjusted to the shaded light and she saw that the path continued straight ahead. Then she caught her breath. On either side of the path were the bluebells Mrs Comfort had spoken of. Slender, arching stems supported sprays of small, bell-shaped blossoms, carpeting the floor of the wood in an intense blue that yielded a sweetly fragrant and intense aroma. 'Oh!' cried Ursula. 'How beautiful!' The emotional force of this quietly enchanting sight was overwhelming.

She moved slowly through the wood. She forgot about the dog, forgot about Belle, Helen, and Mountstanton House; she forgot about Mr Seldon and her mission and just drank in the vision before her.

Honey ran through the bluebells, bounding in delight, her ears flying. Then she flushed a rabbit and streaked away after it. Ursula laughed and clapped her hands in encouragement.

Suddenly, Honey disappeared from view. One moment she'd been there, racing through the bluebells, the next she had vanished.

Ursula hurried after and found that the wood ended abruptly along the top of an escarpment. Both rabbit and spaniel appeared to have gone over the edge.

'Honey!' she called, 'Honey!'

There came an increasingly frantic series of yelps, then they stopped. The only sound was that of rushing water.

Ursula grabbed the support of a slender tree trunk and peered over the edge. An almost vertical slope studded with outcrops of rock and the occasional scrubby tree led down to a fast-moving river. Nowhere could she see the dog.

'Honey!' she shouted as loudly as she could.

Again no answer. Then, looking frantically around, her eyes caught sight of a wagging tail right down beside the water.

Ursula's first thought was relief that the headlong flight down the slope did not seem to have harmed the animal; then came the realisation that, in order to retrieve the dog, she was going to have to tackle the descent to the river.

Well, she had managed worse climbs, she told herself; it would merely take a certain amount of care. And at least the odd stunted tree could offer support. Tying the leash around her waist, Ursula started down the perilous slope.

At first all went well. The outcrops of rock from time to time could act almost like steps. Every now and then there was a tree to provide a handhold. Gradually she gained confidence; then a protruding root caught her foot and, just as the slope was at its steepest, Ursula lost her balance.

Frantically she reached out for the tree whose root had been her downfall. Her hand grazed the bark but couldn't grab a hold. She found herself tumbling over and over, spears of sunlight flashing across her eyes, jolting agonies of pain racking her body as she bounced from rock to rock. Terrified of breaking a limb, Ursula tried to roll herself into a ball, protecting her head with her arms.

Her flight ended in an almighty splash as she fell into the river.

For a moment she was aware of nothing. Then, gradually, her senses returned. She was lying in shallow water that flowed swiftly but gently over soft sand.

A tongue licked her face.

'Honey,' she groaned. 'What have you done?'

Soaking wet ears brushed her cheeks as she received another lick.

With an effort, Ursula managed to raise herself into a sitting position. Nervously, she moved her aching arms and legs, testing for broken bones. It seemed at first as though she had survived the fall with no more than severe bruising. But when she attempted to rise, pain shot through her right ankle and she collapsed back into the water with a cry. At the very least it was badly sprained.

Ursula sat and assessed her situation.

Just before it reached the river, the steepness of the slope gave way to a narrow bank. On it was the odd, bleached branch, no doubt brought down by winter winds.

Weighed down by her wet skirt and petticoats, Ursula struggled to crawl onto the bank and then to reach a stout-looking stick. With its support she managed to get upright. Then realised that once again the dog was gone.

This time Honey was easy to see, engrossed in examining something in the river a little way away.

Ursula wrinkled her nose as a stray breeze carried a most unpleasant, rank aroma towards her. Oh dear, trust a dog to find something unspeakable. The last time she'd smelled anything so odious, it had been the carcass of a cow in a Californian gulch. Calling Honey had no effect. Finally, using her branch, Ursula hobbled towards her. Here, half a rotten tree had got caught by an outcrop of rock and provided a quiet pool. In the pool, humped up, was what appeared to be a washerwoman's bundle.

Reassured by the fact it obviously wasn't a dead cow, Ursula clipped the leash onto Honey's collar then attempted to pull the dog away. Honey dug her feet into the shallow water, growled at Ursula, and returned to the bundle.

Impeded by her damaged ankle, Ursula staggered a little closer, took a grip on the animal's collar and once again tried to pull the animal away.

Suddenly she let go of the dog. There was something unsettling about the sodden, bleached hump of chequered cloth. Despite the sun, Ursula felt arctic cold suffuse her. Balancing on one foot and trying to control her rising gorge, she poked at the bundle with her branch. Then she once again fell back into the water as a nauseous belch of gas was released.

Her hand clamped to her mouth, Ursula watched the bundle roll on its side. A head was revealed. Once there had been a face, now the features had been eaten away. Half an arm briefly rose in the air then flopped down.

Chapter Seven

Ursula vomited, retching until her stomach was empty. She had thought the last few years had made her impervious to the most horrific of sights. This, though, was too much.

Finally she dragged herself up, sat on the sandy bank, and shouted to the dog. Rather to her surprise, Honey left the corpse and came, nestling into her side as though realising comfort was needed.

'Oh, Honey,' Ursula groaned.

Her eyes closed, she took deep breaths. Gradually her heartbeat slowed. On the inside of her eyelids, though, was the picture of what she had seen revealed in the water.

Eventually she brought herself to look at it again.

The skin was covered with an excrescence like a velvety veil, yet underneath it looked as dark as a negro's. Judging by what clothed it, the corpse was that of a woman.

Ursula looked at the steep slope she had fallen down. Whoever she had been, the dead woman must also have slipped and fallen. Perhaps she had knocked herself out, landed in the water and drowned. If it had not been for that dead tree caught in the river bank, her body would have been carried downstream.

So much for what had probably happened. More important was how Ursula could alert the authorities. Another glance up the slope told Ursula that, with her wounded ankle, it was an impossible climb. Did the river run all the way to the village?

And how far was that? Could she hobble along the bank with the aid of her branch, contact the authorities and then get some-one to drive her back to the house?

Grimly, Ursula attached Honey's lead, struggled upright and started to limp painfully along beside the river. She had not gone far before she saw that an outcrop made further progress impossible.

She looked again up the slope to the bluebell wood. Mrs Comfort had said that staff used the path as a shortcut when going to the village. What were the chances someone would be coming along and could hear her cries?

Very unlikely; all the servants would be going about their tasks at Mountstanton. However, when it was realised that Ursula had failed to return to the house, Mrs Comfort would direct the search into the bluebell wood.

How long would that take?

Ursula started to shiver. The sun was still shining but this early in the year it did not have enough heat to dry her wet clothes. Ursula rubbed her cold arms and tried to get her blood moving. Then she looked along the river in the other direction. That way must surely lead towards Mountstanton.

She started to hobble along the bank. The dog trotted hap-pily beside her.

As she drew level with the remains of the poor, dead wom-an's battered corpse, Ursula looked straight ahead, grasped Honey's leash tightly, and tried to think of something else.

Then, above the sound of the river, she thought she could hear someone whistling.

She stopped hobbling and listened hard.

Yes, it was definitely whistling. Someone must be walking through the wood.

With all her force, Ursula yelled, 'Help, help!' trying to bring the breath up from her diaphragm the way an actor had once taught her.

The whistling stopped.

She yelled again, and after a moment a figure appeared on the edge of the escarpment. 'What the hell are you doing down there, woman?' he shouted.

'I fell. My ankle is sprained,' she yelled back. 'There's a dead woman in the river.' She waved in the direction of the sad bundle.

The man immediately discarded his cap and shouted, 'I'm coming down. Stay there.'

Ursula wanted to say that she had no intention of moving but saved her breath.

He negotiated the steep slope facing inwards. As she saw him sure-footedly using the rocks and trees to help his descent, she understood what a mistake she had made in trying to go down face-forward.

She admired the lithe way he moved. A little above middle height, he was dressed in grey-green tweeds, his jacket's waist marked with a band of matching material, his trousers neatly nipped in below the knees. Muscular calves were covered in long socks of a colour that matched his suit. His footwear was as sensible as hers.

After a remarkably short time, he jumped the last little way down onto the bank and turned to face her. He looked to be in his early to mid-thirties, his features open and not unattractive. But Ursula saw what she had come to recognise as an upper-class Englishman's belief in his God-given right to rule the earth.

'Now, tell me what happened,' he said; then his authoritative air softened slightly. 'We'd better get you sitting down first.'

He helped Ursula towards a large boulder, then removed his jacket and placed it round her shoulders.

The feel of dry material on her freezing body was incredibly comforting and Ursula held the jacket tightly around her as she told her story as succinctly as she could, Honey sitting beside her wet-booted feet. Only now did she realise how lucky she was not to have been drowned in the river like that poor woman.

The man stood in front of her, listening, hand on hip, his weight negligently poised on one leg, sharp grey eyes studying her face as though probing the verity of her words. When she described how she had found the body, he wheeled and looked at where she pointed. Then he held up a hand to arrest her tale and strode over to the corpse.

She heard an intake of breath but he gave no other indication that the sight moved him. Then he was back in front of her again.

'Do you recognise her?' Ursula asked.

'How do you imagine I could identify that poor remnant of humanity?'

'But negroes can't be common in this area.'

'Negroes?' He sounded perplexed. Then he said, 'Ah! No, I'm afraid the body is almost certainly that colour because of prolonged immersion in the water.'

'Oh.' Ursula wondered at his knowledge of what drowning could do to a body.

'I don't understand why you were walking through the wood, you don't sound from these parts.'

Ursula resented his tone. 'I was walking from Mountstanton House to the village. I was told it was a shortcut.'

His eyes narrowed. 'From the house? Who are you? Despite your current appearance, your air is not that of a servant.'

And, obviously, not that of a guest either. Ursula became exasperated. 'I'm freezing. I have a damaged ankle and there is a dead body in the water. I don't want to visit with you, I want action. Can't the inquisition over my exact status wait for now?'

'American, that's what you are.' His expression cleared. 'Of course, you are some connection of Helen's.' He looked suddenly suspicious. 'Not her sister, are you?'

'No, I'm not.'

Suddenly he became all sympathy. 'I am a pig. We need to get you back to the house and into a hot bath. And I need to inform the police about . . .'

Ursula averted her eyes as he waved towards the corpse.

'Now, I can't see getting you back up to the wood is a starter. Are you able to ride?'

Ursula nodded.

'Can you bear it if I leave you here whilst I fetch some mounts? It'll take some time but I think it's the only way.' He indicated the direction Ursula had decided led towards Mountstanton.

'Honey can keep me company.' Ursula may have disliked his attitude but she found she had complete faith in his ability to do what he said. 'Can you, though, help me to sit over there?' She indicated a rock some way away from the dead woman's remains.

'Of course.' In a most ordinary manner, he placed her arm around his neck and helped her hobble further along the bank. Honey followed.

Determined not to show how much her ankle was paining her, Ursula was able to ignore the intimate contact she was forced into with her rescuer. She was merely thankful that he was only a little taller than herself.

Neither of them said anything until he had sat her down on the boulder.

Then he stood back and looked at her and the dog, once again nestled against her legs. 'Would you like me to put that animal onto your lap? It could act as a hot water bottle. I'm sorry I do not have another coat.'

'I shall be fine,' Ursula said, summoning the last of her energy. 'At least the sun is shining. By the time you return I shall be dry.'

'I won't take that long.' He raised his hand in a sort of salute, then set off to climb the escarpment back to the wood.

Ursula held her face up to the sun and clutched the warm tweed jacket around her shoulders. It had a masculine smell of tobacco and carbolic soap and a faint, elusive male fragrance that recalled Jack. For a brief moment, she wondered who her rescuer was. Neither of them had introduced themselves but it was hardly the most social of occasions. Even so, Ursula thought grimly, the Dowager Countess would doubtless disapprove.

Etiquette was the least of her concerns. More important was to consider the identity of the corpse she had discovered. That might keep her mind off the pain in her ankle and the cold gathering in her bones.

★ ★ ★

Sooner than she had dared to hope, two horses thundered round the river bank.

Her rescuer, still wearing his tweed breeches, handled both mounts with consummate ease. Even before the horses drew to a halt, he was dismounting beside her. 'Are you all right?' he asked.

'I'm fine,' she said, trying to control her shivering.

'Miss Grandison, you are a doughty lady.'

So, as well as organising mounts, he had ascertained her name. But if he thought flattery was going to get him anywhere, he could think again. Then Ursula remembered just what a wet and bedraggled picture she must present and that this did not seem a man who practised empty compliments.

'I'm afraid I have been very remiss,' he continued. 'I should have introduced myself. I'm Richard's brother, Charles. He's out riding, and Helen is off somewhere with Miss Seldon. But I've alerted the household as to your state. Also I've sent a lad from the stables to inform our local constable of the situation.

This, Ursula realised, must be the Colonel Stanhope who had been expected, so she had been told a number of times, to arrive home within the next few days. She wondered that he should have been returning in such an informal fashion.

The Colonel helped her onto her mount. She was amused to see it was equipped with a side-saddle. It was many years since she had used one; riding astride had been her practice in California, and was so much easier.

Colonel Stanhope adjusted her stirrups, careful not to jolt her injury.

Before he could remount, Ursula forced herself to say, 'If you could manage to get a piece of the dress, Colonel, an identification might be possible.'

'You mean, the dead woman's dress?'

She closed her eyes briefly. What else could she have meant?

'Of course,' he said swiftly and handed her the reins of his horse. She didn't watch to see how he carried out her request.

When he returned, he was stuffing a scrap of fabric into a pocket. 'Right, Miss Grandison, let's get you back to Mountstanton. I'd better take the dog, otherwise she might not be able to keep up. Can you hold her whilst I mount? Then you can explain exactly why you think that piece of material is important.'

* * *

Back at the house, Albert and James, two of the Mountstanton footmen, were waiting in the stable yard. They would, Ursula was informed, carry her upstairs to her room with their hands locked together in what she was informed was a 'bosun's chair'.

'You should be safe enough like that,' the Colonel said, helping her to dismount.

Then Harry clattered up on his pony, with Mrs Comfort puffing hard as she followed behind. She greeted Colonel Stanhope with an unaffected warmth.

'Uncle Charles, how splendid,' Harry said eagerly.

He nodded, 'Good to see you, young Harry. How you've grown! Been riding, have you?'

'I jumped lots of fences and I only fell off once.'

'Excellent! You are obviously going to be as great a rider as your papa. Now, I think you should see that your pony is properly rubbed down.'

The boy dismounted and took the animal into the stables.

The Colonel turned his attention to the nanny. 'Mrs Comfort, I'm delighted to see you again. I'm afraid, though, that something tragic has happened. I wonder if you recognise this piece of material?' He handed her the scrap of cloth he had pocketed beside the river.

'I don't know why you should think I might know anything about this.' Mrs Comfort held the drenched rag distastefully. The Colonel was silent. Ursula watched her carefully.

'Oh, my lord, it looks like . . . ' She screwed up her eyes then gave a cry. 'Yes, Polly has a dress made of just this stuff.' She looked up at the Colonel. 'You said something tragic has happened. Do you mean that Polly . . . ' her voice wobbled and failed.

'A moment, please, whilst I see Miss Grandison taken to her room.' The Colonel swiftly checked the footmen's grip then helped Ursula to sit on the linked hands and place her arms round their shoulders. 'Right, take her upstairs, and see that the crutches I asked for are there.'

'But, Polly?' wailed Mrs Comfort.

The two footmen looked at each other across Ursula. Their usually poker faces expressed profound shock.

'Take her inside now.' Authority quenched any possibility of enquiry.

Without a word, Ursula was carried into the house and up the stairs.

Chapter Eight

With extraordinary deftness, Ursula was lowered onto her bed.

'Here are the crutches the Colonel asked for.'

They were lying against the only seating in the room, a little upright chair. Albert placed one on the bed beside Ursula. 'Is there anything else you require, Miss Grandison?'

His manner was unusually subdued. Ursula thought how devastating the news of the girl's death must have been; she was someone they had lived with, seen every day. 'No, thank you,' she said. All she wanted now was to be left alone. Her ankle was aching, so was her badly-bruised body, and her mind reeled from the impact of her discovery.

She remained sitting upright on the bed until the door closed behind the servants, then she lay down, pulled up her knees into a foetal position and closed her eyes. She shivered with cold, but dragging the bedcover over herself was more than she could manage.

Some time later Mrs Parsons knocked and entered. 'Doctor Mason has arrived. Colonel Charles sent for him. May he come in, Miss Grandison?'

Ursula pulled herself into a sitting position again. Was there anything the Colonel had not thought of?

Doctor Mason was a tall, thin man with grey hair and cadaverous cheeks. His manner was nicely deferential without being obsequious. As he investigated her damaged ankle, causing her considerable pain, Ursula wondered if he modified his approach according to the rank of his patient.

'It does not seem to be broken, rather badly sprained.' He bound the foot and advised her to rest it as much as possible. 'If an ice pack was available,' he said to Mrs Parsons, 'it might help reduce the swelling.'

'Of course, Doctor. I will see to it.'

'And keep the rest of yourself warm, Miss Grandison. You have had a bad shock.' He took a small bottle out of his bag and placed it on the night table beside the bed. 'If you have trouble sleeping, or your ankle pains too much, take a dessertspoon of this.'

Ursula nodded and thanked him; she had, though, no intention of resorting to the laudanum she was sure the bottle contained. She needed to keep a clear head.

As soon as the doctor and the housekeeper had left, she removed her still damp dress and underclothes, sucking in her breath as she saw the livid bruises beginning to emerge, and dragged on her nightdress. Then, with the help of a crutch, she limped over to the chest of drawers and found a wrap for her shoulders.

Underneath the bedclothes, warmth gradually began to penetrate her bones.

Soon there was another knock on the door and Mrs Parsons reappeared, followed by a footman carrying a tray. On it was an icepack, a stone hot water bottle and a bowl of hot soup.

Mrs Parsons took the tray. 'Thank you, Albert, that will be all.'

The icepack was applied to the ankle, the hot water bottle, wrapped in a piece of flannel, was slipped into the bed, and the bowl of soup was given to Ursula. 'It's chicken. I am sure it will do you good.'

As Ursula started on the soup, the housekeeper placed a dessertspoon beside the bottle the doctor had left.

'Thank you, Mrs Parsons, you are very kind.'

The housekeeper remained standing beside Ursula's bed. She seemed suddenly to have aged.

'Miss Grandison,' she said finally. 'Is it certain that the poor body you found is that of Polly Brown?'

For a moment, Ursula laid aside the soup, which was delicious, and said gently, 'I cannot say, Mrs Parsons. Even if I had known Polly Brown, I would not have been able to recognise her, too much damage had been done by her immersion in the water.' A brief shudder went through her.

'Then how . . . ?'

'While the Colonel was fetching the horses, I had time to think. I had heard that a nursemaid had left here quite suddenly. Mrs Comfort told me this morning that the path through the wood was regularly taken by staff to the village. I thought it seemed just possible the nursemaid may have had an accident there – that she'd fallen down into the river and drowned. I asked the Colonel to obtain a piece of fabric from her dress. When he showed it to Mrs Comfort, she said that Polly had a garment of just that pattern.'

Mrs Parsons's mouth pursed. 'That girl's off-duty dress was most unsuitable. She could be a disruptive influence in the house.' She seemed to sense that a different attitude was expected of her. 'Mind you, she was a splendid help in the nursery. His little lordship loved her.' Again there came a suggestion that a slice of lemon had been placed between her lips. 'If it is Polly who ended up where you found her – and I have to say, Miss Grandison, we all regret that you should have been put through such an unpleasant experience – well, if it is Polly, that is a tragedy, one we will all find difficult to come to terms with. Bad enough that she should up and leave like that but to have such an unfortunate accident and meet her end in that way, well, it is a sad day.'

Ursula wanted to question Mrs Parsons about Polly's 'disruptive influence'. But Belle rushed in.

'Dearest Ursula, what happened? Are you very injured? Was it so awful? We have only just returned from our visiting – and to hear such a terrible tale. Oh, please tell me you are all right.' She sat herself down on the bed and passionately embraced Ursula, who had difficulty in preventing her soup bowl from ending on the floor.

Mrs Parsons took it from her and picked up her tray. 'I'll leave you now, Miss Grandison. If there is anything else you require, please ask Miss Seldon to send me a message. And, Miss Seldon, luncheon will be served very shortly.'

'Thank you,' Ursula said, stroking Belle's shoulders; the girl seemed really distressed. 'You have been very kind and I am sure I have everything I need.'

The housekeeper sailed out of the room.

Belle buried her head in Ursula's shoulder and burst into tears.

'Come, come, dear. I am fine, merely a sprained ankle that will soon heal. Finding the remains of that poor girl was very unsettling but I have experienced worse things.' Ursula was not sure she had but her task at the moment was to calm Belle. 'Now, tell me about your visits.'

Belle released herself. 'I must be careful not to hurt your poor ankle. Is it aching very much?' She looked at the bandaged foot, which had the bedclothes neatly folded back from it so that the ice pack, a collection of ice chunks in a calico bag, did not make them wet.

'Not nearly as much as it did.' This was true. Having it raised up, together with the anaesthetising effect of the ice had reduced the angry throbbing to a dull ache. She sat back and attempted to coax Belle into better spirits. 'Who did you meet?'

'Oh, they were all boring, boring, boring.'

Ursula waited.

'Helen got me in that room she calls her boudoir,' Belle sounded so scornful, Ursula could not help smiling. 'She lectured me for at least half an hour on how disgracefully I had behaved last night. I nearly told her she did not own William, that is, Mr Warburton.'

'It was foolish of you to disappear into the garden like that with him,' Ursula said gently. 'You must have known it was wrong.'

'Oh, don't you start! I am so tired of being told what I should not do and what I should do. Ursula, if I had had any idea of what it would be like, I should not have pestered Papa to send me over.'

'You will soon find your way around. Did you not like anyone you met? How many houses did you visit?'

'Only two – and no young men at either of them. First we went to Lord and Lady Anstruther. They live in a darling old house with low ceilings and lots of porcelain everywhere and two sweet little Pekingese dogs. I was allowed to have one on my lap. Lord Anstruther was awful. He was like a dried bean pod, tall and thin and wrinkled. All he said was "hello" and would we mind awfully but he had some business to see to on the estate.' Belle aped an English accent and giggled. 'After he left, Lady Anstruther said what a pretty girl I was and how Anthony, her son, would have liked to meet me but he was on the Continent somewhere, and how she wished her daughter was with her but she had gone to stay with a friend in Scotland. So Helen had dragged me over there for nothing.'

'Not for nothing, Belle. Now Lady Anstruther has met you, she will send an invitation as soon as her son and daughter return. Where did you go next?'

'That was even worse! We went to see the mother of the man who was with you when you dragged William and me out of the shrubbery.'

'That must have been Mrs Russell.' Ursula felt a rush of warmth as she recalled how friendly and amusing Max Russell had been at dinner.

'Lady Frances Russell,' Belle said with a note of triumph. 'Helen explained that daughters of an Earl are always called Lady, even when they are married to men with no title. But the sons, apart from the eldest, are only "The Honourable", not lords. I don't think that's fair, do you? Helen said Lady Frances was married to a vicar, the Very Reverend George Russell.' Belle giggled again. 'How would you address them if they were both together?'

'The Very Revered George and Lady Frances Russell,' Ursula said, remembering the lessons in etiquette she and Helen had suffered at their Paris finishing school.

'Oh, my, such a mouthful! Anyway, I did not really want to see Mr Russell again, he looked at me in such a way last night and was very unpleasant to William, but when we arrived, he wasn't there. And Helen was told Lady Frances was too ill to come downstairs but would she please go and visit with her in her bedroom.'

Belle pouted. 'So I was left in the drawing room to look at some boring old books. There wasn't even a dog to play with. There was a piano but I didn't like to try it in case it disturbed Lady Frances.'

'That was thoughtful of you.'

'And, anyway, it was locked.'

'Was Helen upstairs very long?'

Belle sighed heavily. 'It seemed forever. The house is very small with a very small garden. I should be quite ashamed to live in a place like that, but there were some pretty pictures and I found a box that had lots of little boxes inside it. Just as I

was trying to open the smallest – I knew it must open because
something inside it rattled – Mr Russell came in.'

'And how was he?'

'Much friendlier than I expected,' Belle confessed. 'And he
showed me how to slide open one side of the box in a most
ingenious way. And what do you think was inside?'

'I cannot imagine,' Ursula laughed, but she found herself
curious.

'A ring! I don't think it was valuable but it was very pretty;
little pearls set in enamel so it looked like a flower. I asked
whose it was and Mr Russell said it was his mama's. I wanted
to ask why she did not wear it but Helen came downstairs then
and spoke to me quite sharply. She said I should not have been
messing about with things that did not belong to me. And Mr
Russell said he had been showing me the secret box and it was
not my fault. Even though, I suppose, it was,' Belle added. 'But
it was not fair to leave me alone for so long.' She thought for a
moment then added, 'Helen and Mr Russell did not seem at all
easy with each other. But I think it was because of Lady Frances
being ill. Helen said she was shocked at her condition and Mr
Russell said he did not think it would be very long now. I asked
Helen when we drove away what he meant and she said Lady
Frances was nearing the end of her life. That is sad isn't it?'

Ursula agreed.

'And she asked Mr Russell if he still meant to do what he'd
said, and he said "yes". What do you think that meant? And
why do you think Lady Frances would keep a ring in a secret
box? I asked Helen but she said she didn't know, in quite a
nasty way. All she wanted to talk about on the way home was
Richard's brother, Charles, who is a Colonel in the army and
has been fighting in the South African war. She said that the
war finished last year and he was to arrive today or tomorrow
and that I would like him very much. He was very brave, she
said, very handsome and very interesting. It was just as though
she was a salesman trying to get me to buy a horse!

'And then we get back here and this Charles has arrived and
I don't find him at all attractive.' Belle gave a disappointed pout
and smoothed down her tussore silk jacket over its matching
skirt. 'He's not nearly as tall as William – or Richard – and all
he said to me was that he hoped I was enjoying my stay.'

Oh, dear Belle, thought Ursula. 'I expect he had to tell Helen about the tragedy that I discovered.'

'He did. And it sounded something awful. So I had to come and see how you were. Are you really all right? I would hate for you to be badly injured.'

'I had a shock and sprained my ankle, that is all. I will be downstairs again this evening. Look, they have found me some crutches.' Ursula pointed to them. 'You had better go and wash your hands before luncheon. Will Mr Warburton be there?' The ploy worked.

'Yes! He was in the drawing room with Richard and the Colonel when we got back. They all seemed to think finding that dead girl was very serious.'

'I think it is, Belle. There will be a lot of formalities, including with the police.'

'Do you think it will be in the newspapers?'

'I certainly hope not.'

After Belle had left, Ursula pondered that question. She was sure Richard and his mother would be very keen not to have any publicity over the death of their nursery maid. If, indeed, the corpse was that of their maid.

* * *

Ursula awoke a couple of hours later feeling greatly refreshed. So much so that she rose and dressed. She longed to have a bath but to ask a servant to bring one upstairs and then to carry up the hot water seemed too much of an imposition, so she made do with a thorough wash, balancing herself on one leg. The bruising on her body was now so shocking, Ursula found it almost comical. At least it could be decently concealed.

Dressed, she consulted her watch: four o'clock. Mrs Comfort would take young Harry down to tea and then return to the nursery.

Ursula gave her ten minutes then walked along the corridor, learning to manage the wooden crutches.

Mrs Comfort arrived at the door of the nursery at the same time as she did.

'Why, Miss Grandison, you are up – how do you feel?'

Ursula decided she would have to get used to that question.

'The ankle is a bother but apart from that I am fine, thank you, Mrs Comfort.' She hesitated for a moment then said, 'This morning was a terrible shock and the idea that the dead woman could have been your nursemaid I find very troubling. I wonder – would you be willing to talk to me about her?'

'Oh, my dearie, there is so much I would like to say about poor Polly. Come in and share my tea.'

The nursery was a large room with a shabby charm. It was evident it had done duty for several generations of children. A large table in the centre of the room had sturdy chairs around it. Painting utensils and sketching paper were in use and Ursula glimpsed colourful attempts at wild beasts in a jungle. Two comfortable chairs stood either side of an iron fireplace. A fire ready for lighting was in the grate. On the floor in one corner stood a large castle complete with brightly painted lead knights in arms. Beside it was a dappled-grey rocking horse with red, snorting nostrils, a long white mane and tail, and a tattered saddle. On a side table stood what looked like several regiments of lead soldiers, some dressed in khaki, others in more colourful uniforms. Mrs Comfort saw Ursula looking at the display.

'Them brown ones were sent to Harry by his uncle, Colonel Charles. Most of the others belonged to his lordship and his brother when they were young.'

'Were you the nanny then, Mrs Comfort? Not that you look old enough,' Ursula added hastily.

'Bless you, I was here. Nursery maid first and then when Nanny Porter retired I took over. After the young sons went away to school, I was put in charge of the linen; watched both of them grow into such handsome men. When his lordship chose a wife, we were all so thrilled. And when the waiting was over and we knew her ladyship was in an interesting condition, well, what a thing it was to be sure; bringing this nursery back into service! Maybe soon there'll be another little treasure. But, there, Lord Harry is everything we could desire, even if he does get a bit too lively at times. He's hoping Mr Charles, I mean the Colonel, will demonstrate his battles with the Boer for him.'

'Harry's not too young for games of war, then?'

'Bless you, it's born in them, that's what I think.' Mrs Comfort took a box of matches from the top of the mantelshelf and lit the fire. It blazed up instantly.

A knock on the door preceded James, one of the footmen who had carried Ursula upstairs. All of the Mountstanton footmen seemed to be tall and handsome. He brought in a tray of tea complete with sandwiches and cake.

'Thank you, James. I'm glad to see Chef hasn't given me short commons. I've got a guest today, Miss Grandison is joining me.'

'Glad to see it, Mrs Comfort.' The young man put the tray on the table and left.

The nanny went over to a cupboard and retrieved a second cup, saucer and plate.

'Now, you sit there and I'll be mother.'

Ursula limped over to one of the chairs by the fire. She was soon supplied with tea and fish paste sandwiches.

Mrs Comfort brought her own cup and sat opposite, settling down into the chair with a sigh. 'It was a real shock, being shown that piece of dress this morning.'

'I'm sorry but it seemed as if the chances were that you would know what your nursemaid wore. Didn't you say that she left without notice?'

Mrs Comfort picked up a sandwich and ate thoughtfully. 'I held it was a joke, the way she left I mean. "Don't expect me back," she said, and laughed. She was to go over to the village, see. I thought it was to meet a young man. She was always joking; always laughing with Lord Harry and me.' Mrs Comfort flicked tears away. 'I expected her back in time for supper, no matter what she said.'

'If she meant to leave, wouldn't she have taken her things?' asked Ursula.

'She had a box with her, a round cardboard thing, once held a hat I reckoned. When she didn't come back and no one had seen her, I looked in the bedroom she shared with Lord Harry. Nothing of hers in there at all – apart from her uniform. But, then, poor thing, she didn't have much. She'd have been wearing most of what she owned.'

Ursula had a sudden vision of Belle's trunks crammed with delightful outfits. Even the contents of her own would have seemed a wardrobe fit for a princess to one such as Polly. She smoothed the linen skirt she was wearing and tried to forget the times when, like Polly, most of what she owned was on her back.

'Came to us from an orphanage, she did; no family,' Mrs Comfort continued.

'If she really was leaving, where would she be going?'

'Well, now, that's what got me, Miss Grandison. Wasn't as if she received any mail, Mr Benson would have known. Wasn't as if she had any callers, Mrs Parsons would know.'

Ursula had a sudden sense of a household where, despite its huge size, there must be something approaching thirty indoor staff; nothing went unnoticed. Her ankle started to ache and she moved it uneasily.

'You need something to put that up on.' Mrs Comfort leaped up, brought over a cushioned stool and gently arranged Ursula's foot on it.

'You must have known her best, Mrs Comfort. What was she like?' Ursula wanted to be able to convert the horrible bundle she had found in the river into a living, breathing girl. Only then could she exorcise the awfulness of her discovery.

'She was a delight.' Mrs Comfort sounded in no doubt about this. 'She loved Harry, was kind to me, and never skimped on her duties. If anything went wrong, she turned it into a joke. I remember when Harry trod on his favourite toy and broke it. In an instant she had the place turned into Florence Nightingale's hospital, with Lord Harry as the doctor. She left him arranging his toys as if they were in bed, went and found John – he's so good with his hands – and brought him up with a hammer and nails. Then there had to be an operation and Polly made John be the surgeon. Lord Harry had such a time of it!' Again the nanny had to wipe tears from her eyes.

Ursula said nothing.

After a moment Mrs Comfort added, 'There was some as thought she was too forward, but she was only young. Trouble was, the maids was jealous of her looks and the footmen were after her.'

'Did any of them catch her?'

Mrs Comfort gave an uneasy laugh. 'She kept things close to her chest. I'd ask her sometimes, in a joking way, you understand, which of the footmen she fancied and she'd look up, bright as a sparrow, and say, "Oh, Nanny, none of them is worthy of me." But I'd see the way she'd look at one or another of them sometimes and wonder.' There was silence for a moment then she said in a sad, small voice, 'Such life she had;

I can't believe it's been snuffed out just like that. What happened? Did she slip and fall? If you move off the path near that slope, it can be right dangerous, especially if it's wet.'

'Had it been raining the day she set off?'

The woman took several minutes to think. 'Can't say, but probably. Awful lot of rain we've had this spring. But it's brought on the flowers a treat. Did you like the bluebells this morning, Miss Grandison?'

'They were wonderful. Mrs Comfort, would Polly have taken her box for any other reason than to carry her possessions?'

'Now there you have a point, Miss. Polly did use to take it if she was to get something in the village that needed carrying. She'd bring me back toilet waters sometimes, or stockings if I needed them. And then there was books from the circulating library. I offered her a proper basket but if the weather was fine she liked her box. It had pretty paper round it, see? And she did look a picture carrying it. It had a wide ribbon for a handle that went over her arm.'

Suddenly Mrs Comfort rose. 'Oh, my goodness, I'm letting my tongue run away with me; her ladyship asked would I collect Lord Harry early today.'

Ursula immediately stood up and apologised for taking up so much of the nanny's time.

'Now don't you move, Miss Grandison. You finish your tea in comfort. I'll be back with Lord Harry in a moment; he'll like to see you.'

Sure enough, it could not have been above ten minutes before the nanny and her charge returned to the nursery. The boy did not seem at all downhearted at having his tea time cut short.

'And Uncle Charles says he will come and make battle with me tomorrow,' he was saying excitedly as they entered. Then he saw Ursula. 'Perhaps, Miss Grandison, you will come and watch,' he said, very politely. Then he saw her bandaged ankle and the crutches. 'We can pretend that you have been wounded in action.'

A very pertinent description of her plight! Ursula thanked him and watched the woman and the boy for a moment; Harry almost dancing with energy and chattering away to the person he saw most of in his life.

★ ★ ★

Much later, Ursula wrote a letter to Mr Seldon detailing what had happened that day, starting with the discovery she had made in the morning. Then she continued:

At present there is nothing to suggest that the girl's death was anything but an accident. However, I think you will agree that there are several oddities surrounding it that may well turn out to be more sinister.

The discovery seems to have changed the atmosphere here. The servants appear on edge. Twice this evening at dinner a plate was dropped. Benson, the butler, reproved the offender, most unobtrusively, as was to be expected, but his attitude to my mind lacked fire. To be sure, to lose a member of what is more or less a family must be most upsetting. At first it was thought the girl had left, though no one has produced a reason why; now it turns out that she is almost certainly dead.

As far as identification of the corpse is concerned, a post-mortem has apparently been arranged and the fact that the girl broke an arm shortly after her arrival at Mountstanton should provide certainty whether or not it is poor Polly. I hope it is not, but fear that it will prove so.

The Earl, the Countess and the Dowager Countess are all very anxious to avoid any sort of publicity. The Earl has asked the coroner to call tomorrow morning and apparently will ask him if the inquest can be held, I believe the phrase he used was, 'in camera'. If it is open to the public there will certainly be members of the press there. Colonel Charles Stanhope has suggested that that might be an advantage since publicity would almost certainly produce any contacts the girl had, but he was over-ruled. He also suggested that the Earl should ride over to see the coroner, rather than ask him to come here, but the Earl insisted that the full weight and power of the Mountstanton name and position could only be brought to bear in the house itself. I think, sir, that you would consider the property's state would mitigate against this but it seems in England things work differently.

As for Colonel Stanhope, it appears that Belle has been chosen by his family to be his partner in life. I have to say

that neither he nor Belle seem to feel this is something
either of them desires.

Ursula put down her pen for a moment and remembered the
scene she had found in the drawing room before dinner. After
changing, she had negotiated the broad stairs, using the crutches
with extreme caution, then moved more easily along to the
drawing room where the family were gathered for dinner.

It appeared that the Earl's appearance there was his first of
the day amongst his family and he had only just heard of the
morning's news. He and his mother were anxious to pick over
every aspect of the incident; Helen, however, was more interested in pairing off Belle with the Colonel, it seemed without
success. Belle insisted on flirting with Mr Warburton and the
Colonel was far too involved with his brother and mother to
pay Belle any attention.

He had, however, almost immediately noticed Ursula's
entrance and came straight over to her. 'The wounded soldier,'
he said quietly. 'I trust the ankle is not too painful?'

She shook her head. 'I have to thank you, sir, for all your
thoughtfulness. Including arranging for these,' she managed a
slight wave of a crutch as he escorted her to a comfortable
chair. 'Who needed them originally?'

'Why, I did. When I was sixteen I fell off my horse jumping a
high fence. So I know how damnably, forgive me, how uncomfortable it is to lose power in one of one's legs.'

He saw her settled, surveyed her with interest, then grinned,
'Miss Grandison, I have to say you have transformed yourself.'

'Colonel,' protested Mr Warburton, 'is that any way to speak
to a lady? Though I have to say that Miss Grandison does
indeed present a picture of feminine beauty.'

'Ursula always looks pretty,' said Belle, insinuating herself
into the circle.

'Please, Charles,' said the Earl. 'Can we continue with how
we are to handle this sorry event?'

Much to Ursula's relief, attention switched from her and she
was free to play the part of onlooker. If it hadn't been for the seri-
ousness of the subject under discussion, she would have enjoyed
a high comedy of manners. She did, though, allow herself to be
pleased that the maid, Sarah, had appeared before dinner, insist-

ing on dressing her hair more elaborately than Ursula usually managed, and helping her into her grey silk gown.

'I will not,' announced the Dowager Countess with emphasis, 'allow the pig-swill of the gutter press to pollute Mountstanton.'

'Pigs do not live in the gutter, Mama,' said the Colonel, straight faced.

'Charles, I thought army life would have removed that vein of levity. I am disappointed.' The Dowager stared glacially at her younger son.

'Once the press get a hint of the story, they will dig and dig,' said the Earl, looking furious. 'What they don't find they will make up.'

'Such as, for instance,' said the Colonel, 'why a Mountstanton servant can go missing and no one wonders why?'

'She left,' said Helen coldly. 'She said she was leaving and she left. There is no mystery about it, merely sheer inconsideration.'

'At Mountstanton,' said the Dowager, 'we have a reputation for looking after our servants.'

'Mama!' the Earl sounded exasperated. 'Let us keep to the point. You will be the first to agree that the Mountstanton name matters. We cannot allow those press rats to throw it to the wolves.'

'As a mixed metaphor, that is a triumph,' said the Colonel. 'No,' he held up his hands in surrender, 'I will be serious. Look,' his tone became cool and reasonable. 'I know how intrusive the press can be but if, once they are alerted to the story, we try to cover up matters, they will write a far worse account than if we issue a plain statement of the facts.'

'What are the facts?' asked Helen.

Silence fell.

'We shall have to wait for the result of the post-mortem examination for positive identification,' said the Earl, uncertainly.

Ursula stared at him. Did he have a faint hope that the body was not that of Polly Brown? If it was not hers, whose could it be?

'Why, we have driven Belle and William into the conservatory,' said Helen in a tone that signalled this conversation was at an end. 'Charles, do go and bring them back amongst us.'

* * *

In her bedroom, Ursula continued her letter:

> I am not sure why the Earl and Countess appear to favour
> a match between Belle and the Colonel, who to my eye
> seem wildly unsuited.

Ursula paused and looked at her last sentence. After a moment,
she gave a little nod and continued:

> As I have mentioned before, William Warburton's charms
> seem to have made a deep impression on Belle. The
> Colonel paid her no attention before dinner but during
> the meal studied her with close, though unobtrusive,
> attention. It could be that he is making up his mind as to
> her suitability for the position of his bride. Whether Belle
> would succumb to a determined wooing, remains to be
> seen. I will keep you informed.

Ursula signed her letter, folded it and addressed the envelope.
Benson would organise its despatch.

Then she wondered if allowing the butler to know how
frequently she was sending letters to his mistress's father was
a good idea. At the moment, however, with the immobility
brought by her sprained ankle, what alternative did she have?

She suddenly felt very tired. Balancing her travelling writing
desk on her knee while working in the poor candlelight of her
room had been exhausting and her ankle was now throbbing
badly.

She tried to keep movement to a minimum as she put away
her writing impedimenta and got ready for bed. Today had
been a marathon. What would tomorrow be like?

Ursula blew out her candle and, not for the first time,
longed for the electric light of the Seldon mansion. Were all
English aristocratic houses living in the past? She wondered if
she could request an oil lamp. Over everything, though, there
loomed the big question she needed to find an answer to: what
was Helen doing with her dowry?

Chapter Nine

The following morning Ursula, using her crutches with increasing skill, managed to negotiate the stairs and the corridor along to the breakfast room; a much smaller and even shabbier version of the stately dining room.

Belle came in some twenty minutes later. She was dressed in a dark green riding habit, her blonde hair pulled back into a tight knot at the nape of her neck. She stopped in the doorway and surveyed the room.

'Ursula, I didn't expect to see you. Aren't you tired after yesterday? Shouldn't you be staying in bed?' She sounded almost resentful that this was not the case.

Ursula helped herself to another piece of toast and more of the dark, thick marmalade. The Mountstanton preserves were outstanding.

'I slept well last night,' she lied. 'The idea of staying in bed and wondering exactly what had happened to that poor girl was not attractive. Much better to be up and about.'

'Oh, you are always so positive!' Belle sat herself at the table. There were just three places laid. The arrangement suggested that earlier there had been more. Belle eyed the still unoccupied place.

'Is that Helen's?'

Ursula shrugged. 'I have no idea.'

As was customary, staff were not in attendance in the breakfast room. Silver dishes, equipped with domed lids and laden with cooked items were kept warm by little paraffin heaters gently flaming beneath them. Breakfasters helped themselves to their contents. There were rolls in a covered basket and fresh coffee had been produced soon after Ursula came into the room, with an inquiry as to whether there was anything else she wanted.

She had thanked the girl and said everything was perfect.

Belle fidgeted on her seat for a few minutes, then got up and inspected the contents of the silver dishes.

The serving girl entered with another pot of coffee and placed it on the table.

'Will there be anything else, Miss Seldon?'

Belle replaced the last silver lid. 'What I should really like would be dollar pancakes.'

'Dollar pancakes, miss?'

'You know, those little pancakes, with maple syrup, oh, and streaky bacon, thin and crisp, not like those soggy slices in there.' She gestured to one of the serving dishes.

Ursula held back the comment that rose to her lips.

'And the Countess, my sister, has she had her breakfast?'

'Her ladyship is having it in bed this morning, miss. I'll tell Chef about the pancakes. Is there anything else you would like?'

'Just them.' Belle sat down in a manner that said she was not prepared to wait long for her breakfast.

The maid gave a little bob and disappeared.

'I never knew dollar pancakes could hold such attraction,' said Ursula mildly. 'I found the devilled kidneys and scrambled eggs extremely tasty.

'I don't see why I shouldn't have what I want.'

Ursula decided that it was Mr Warburton's absence that was upsetting Belle, rapidly reviewed possible comments, rejected them all and said, 'You obviously intend horseback riding this morning. I wish I could join you, the weather looks wonderful, another sunny day.'

Belle said nothing, her eyes still on the empty place at the breakfast table.

The door opened and in came Mr Warburton.

'William!' Belle exclaimed, clapping her hands together. 'I am so glad to have you join us; I was afraid you had breakfasted.'

'Little Liberty Belle,' he said, seating himself in the third place. 'What a delight to find both you ladies here.' He gave a gracious tilt of his head to Ursula then immediately returned his attention to Belle, smiling at her with warmth.

In response, she glowed. There was no other word for it, thought Ursula. It was as though a candle had been lit inside her.

'Where are we to ride, William? Do let's have a real good gallop somewhere.'

He held her gaze with his for an intimate moment; it was as though they were alone in the room, and a dreadful thought occurred to Ursula. She tried to dismiss it as absurd; they would surely not have had the opportunity. Yet Belle was an enterprising and determined girl. Anything she set her mind on, she usually achieved.

Mr Warburton rose and started lifting lids.

Ursula saw that he was dressed in a country suit.

'I'm afraid, Belle, that our ride will have to be postponed. Your sister has other plans for this morning.' He piled kedgeree on his plate, and came back to his place.

Mutiny crossed Belle's face.

'Another boring visit to another of her boring friends? Well, I won't go. I am having no fun at all.'

The Countess entered the breakfast room in time to hear Belle's remarks, and took in the situation with one comprehensive glance.

'Belle, darling, I am sorry about your ride but there will soon be another opportunity. Please change into that elegant yellow muslin dress of yours and be ready to leave with me in half an hour. Lady Paxton has all three of her extremely handsome sons eager to make your acquaintance. One has recently visited New York and wants to know more about life there.'

'I am waiting for my breakfast.'

'Ah, yes, breakfast. I am afraid, my dear, that dollar pancakes are not part of Chef's current repertoire. He will research and produce some for breakfast tomorrow. You should know, Belle, that if we ride in the mornings, we do so much earlier than this. Richard and Charles have already returned from their exercise. I will arrange for coffee and rolls to be brought to your room so you can eat while you change. Julian Paxton really is extraordinarily attractive,' she added in a throw-away voice.

Belle looked at Mr Warburton. He had risen on the entrance of the Countess and stood, holding his napkin, his face expressing no more than mild interest in what was being said.

Ursula saw the rapid flicking of Belle's gaze from him to her sister and back again.

With a sulky flounce of her head, Belle rose. 'I will be ready in thirty minutes, your ladyship,' she said, giving a bitter emphasis to the last two words.

'I think I need a cup of coffee,' said Helen as the door banged shut.

The secretary helped her into a seat then poured her a cup. He was all attentiveness.

Helen glanced at Ursula.

'My dear, I should have enquired how you are feeling this morning. How is your poor ankle?'

'I am fine, thank you, Helen.' Ursula went back to her toast and allowed Mr Warburton to refill her coffee cup.

Helen tapped her fingers irritably on the tablecloth. 'Did you encourage Belle to think you were to take her riding this morning, William?'

He shrugged. 'Something may have been mentioned last night when it seemed as if you were to be involved in this ghastly business over Polly. However, when you told me of your intention to visit the Paxtons with your sister . . . ' A graceful wave of his hand indicated that the riding suggestion had instantly been dropped.

Helen's eyes narrowed.

'*I* am not "involved in this ghastly business", as you put it, and I would prefer that Belle was not encouraged to believe you will dance attendance on her every whim.'

William Warburton sat down with a little assenting dip of his head.

Helen drank more of her coffee. 'Perhaps tomorrow morning we can all ride together, William?'

He looked up eagerly.

'I have missed our early morning rides; there seems to have been so little time since Belle's arrival,' Helen continued.

A slight flush coloured his face. 'I would like that,' he said quietly.

'A pity you cannot join us, Ursula. I hope in a few days your ankle will be recovered sufficiently to make riding possible.'

Ursula refrained from pointing out that she had managed to ride back to Mountstanton after she had damaged her ankle.

'I hope so too.'

Helen managed a slight smile. 'I did not realise just what a task you must have had in chaperoning my sister from New York to here.'

'She was little trouble, Helen. The fact that I was not family must have helped.'

Another slight smile in acknowledgement. 'I know what you mean. Ursula, if you were able to advise my chef this morning on how dollar pancakes are cooked, I would be greatly in your debt.'

'I shall be delighted,' Ursula said cheerfully. 'I wonder if after that, Helen, I might be permitted to practise on your drawing room piano? My playing skills, such as they are, are so rusty.'

'Of course.' Helen rose. 'Until luncheon, William?'

He nodded, half rising in his seat. 'I shall be there, Helen.'

After the Countess had left the room, Ursula said, 'Did you know the nursemaid well, Mr Warburton?'

'What, Polly? No, of course not, Miss Grandison. What on earth makes you think I might have done?'

'I apologise. It was just the way you referred to her, that is all.'

'Oh, I see. Well, I knew her, of course.' He helped himself to a piece of toast, placed butter and marmalade on his plate and thought for a moment. 'I would have seen her with Harry, taking him for a walk, or bringing him down to tea.'

'Was she pretty?'

William Warburton broke a piece off his slice of toast, smeared it with butter, added some marmalade and ate it while considering his answer. 'I can't say I thought much about the matter. Comely, I suppose. Certainly she was not ugly.'

'No, I suppose you would have noticed that.'

The young man looked at her suspiciously and Ursula chided herself for her tone. 'I've noticed that men are always aware of ugliness in a female. It's as though they distrust the owner of such an appearance, though why it should be, I cannot understand. No one chooses to be ugly. On the contrary, everyone, I think, would prefer to be pleasant to look at.'

Immediately he brightened. 'I agree! A pleasing appearance in a woman, or a man – or indeed a piece of furniture – is to be valued.'

'And yet,' Ursula said reflectively, 'there are other qualities that could be equally valued, if not more. Kindness, for example, or honesty.'

'Oh, quite,' said William Warburton quickly, buttering another piece of his toast. 'I do see what you mean, Miss Grandison, and, if you will allow me to say so, it does you a great deal of credit. However, may I be allowed to hold that all those virtues of character are more appreciated in someone who is agreeable to look upon?'

He smiled ingratiatingly at her.

Oh, poor Belle, thought Ursula. She smiled back at the young man. 'You are not from these parts, I understand, Mr Warburton?'

'No. My family is from the Midlands; Derbyshire to be precise.'

'Ah, was that not where Mr Darcy was from?'

'Darcy? I don't recognise the name. My uncle is the Marquis of Buxton.'

Ursula laughed. 'Easy to see that you are not a fan of Miss Austen, Mr Warburton. Mr Darcy is the hero of *Pride and Prejudice*, one of her novels.'

'Oh, a novel. I am afraid I am not a great reader. *Sporting Life* is what I study. Amazing range of information.'

'How interesting,' Ursula murmured.

Mr Warburton swallowed the last of his coffee, muttered something about 'getting on with things' and hoped Miss Grandison would excuse him.

Ursula sat for a moment alone at the table and wondered precisely what the young man's function in the Mountstanton household was.

★ ★ ★

Ursula had listened to the superb sound of the Mountstanton piano on the night of the dinner party and envied Helen its possession. Once they had vied with each other to receive applause for their performances. Over the last few years, though, her playing had been confined to popular songs on ramshackle instruments.

Propelling herself along on crutches was tiring and Ursula found it a relief to hop onto the piano stool.

She started with scales and arpeggios and was soon lost in the rigour of the exercises. Stiff and clumsy to begin with, her fingers gradually began to loosen and acquire something of their old mastery. As her hands dedicated themselves to the mechanical movements, Ursula's mind drifted to contemplation of what the coroner was reporting to the Earl and his brother. Would Richard be able to ensure that there would be no publicity surrounding this death? Would the Mountstanton influence stretch to a neat tidying away of the facts? Would the circumstance that Polly appeared to have no relatives be of assistance there?

The scales grew faster and faster; the arpeggios acquired more of a flourish.

Finally Ursula rose from the stool and, balancing herself on her good leg, raised the lid to find what was available inside.

A few moments later, a thick copy of Beethoven's Diabelli Variations was on the piano's music stand.

It had been a delight to find something she knew so well. Ursula had studied the variations with her Paris tutor, immediately attracted by their complexity, power and beauty. It had been so long, though, since she had played the pieces. She struggled with the first variations, working on difficult passages over and over again.

She had lost track of time when the drawing room door burst open.

'There you are!' said the Colonel. 'Come on, I'm taking you for a drive.'

Startled, deep in Beethoven's subtleties, for a moment Ursula could only stare at him.

Dressed in a light brown tweed suit with a similar belted jacket to the one he had worn the day before, the Colonel hit his leg with a pair of gloves.

'I've got to get away from this place,' he said irritably. 'I've ordered the trap to be harnessed.'

As Ursula continued to stare at him, his expression changed.

'Can you manage?' He came forward and picked up the crutches.

She looked at him with a raised eyebrow.

'Sorry, for a moment I forgot you're not one of my men,' he said with an apologetic grin. 'Would you, please, come with me? Can I fetch you a wrap?' he added.

Resentment at being ordered about dissolved into amusement. Ursula abandoned Beethoven. 'It's a lovely day but maybe one would be sensible for driving in a trap.'

The Colonel strode over to the fireplace and rang the bell. Then he held the crutches out to Ursula.

'Good girl.' He watched as she rose, positioned them beneath her arms and started to walk slowly but confidently towards the door.

As she reached it, the butler entered.

'You rang, sir?'

'Yes, Benson. Be so good as to send someone to collect a wrap for Miss Grandison from her bedroom. Do you know where it would be?' he asked Ursula.

'In the middle drawer of the chest, knitted, with a fringe. And perhaps whoever fetches it could also bring the hat and bag that are sitting on top of the chest?'

'Of course, madam. It shall be done.'

'It's very good of you, Benson.'

'Not at all, madam.'

'And, Benson,' the Colonel continued, 'get Chef to put up some cold meat with rolls and butter and a bottle of wine. Nothing fancy, I need it in double-quick time. Miss Grandison and I are going for a drive. We shall not be back before this afternoon.'

'Of course, sir.'

'Get it sent out to the stables, we'll pick up the trap there.'

'Indeed, sir. Will that be all, sir?'

'Yes, thank you, Benson.'

The butler gave the smallest of bows and melted through the door.

'That man is a marvel,' said Ursula. 'Your family is very lucky to have him.'

'Benson has been a Mountstanton fixture ever since I can remember.'

The Colonel held open the door for Ursula.

As they proceeded along the corridor, there was a flurry of red and white fur and Honey flung herself at Ursula with small squeals of excitement.

'I'm sorry,' she said to the dog. 'I can't get down to stroke you but I'm very pleased to see you again.' She looked around, expecting to see the Dowager Countess.

Instead a footman hurried towards them. 'Sorry, Miss Grandison. She got out before I knew what was happening.'

'Got out from where, John?' asked the Colonel.

'She was shut in the pantry, till someone had time to take her for a walk, sir. The Dowager is out visiting.'

'Poor thing! Colonel, can we take her with us?'

'If you're content to sit whilst I walk her, I don't see why not. As long as nothing else delays us.' The Colonel snapped his fingers at Honey, and Ursula hid a smile as she instantly came to heel. John produced a lead; Ursula's wrap, hat and bag were brought to her by one of the maids, and they were ready to set off.

Soon Ursula was seated in the trap, a wicker basket of comestibles in the back, Honey, all panting eagerness, placed between her and the Colonel.

Having taken one look at her companion's grim face, Ursula said nothing for some time. Instead, she enjoyed their progress through rolling farmland, the Beethoven phrases still resonating in her head, one hand on Honey's warm back, occasionally caressing her silky ears.

After a little Ursula said, 'Are we going to Hinton Parva?'

The Colonel glanced at her and seemed almost surprised to realise that he had a passenger.

'She was with child.'

For a moment Ursula was taken aback. 'Polly?'

He nodded.

'What is the coroner going to do?'

'Hold the inquest *in camera*. No press, no public.'

'Can he do that?'

'He says, yes. He said he sees no point in exposing the poor girl to more public scrutiny than absolutely necessary.' He took a deep breath. 'My brother has more or less demanded that the matter be kept as quiet as possible. He may talk about protecting the girl's reputation; what he means is the reputation of the Stanhopes.'

The Colonel's voice was cold.

'You do not agree with him?'

He turned and Ursula was shocked at the raw anger in his face.

'They are saying Polly committed suicide because she knew she was expecting.'

'And you do not believe that was the case?'

He turned his attention back to his driving.

Ursula waited.

'Polly was a children's nurse, she adored Harry.'

'You knew her?'

'She was here when I returned two years ago from South Africa, injured. I was unable to do much. So I spent time with little Harry, he's a delightful child – and that meant with Polly as well. Polly was a welcome contrast to all that had gone on out in Africa.'

Ursula thought of the faded magnificence of Mountstanton House; of the social life that Helen pursued there. Had life in the nursery been a refuge for the Colonel? And exactly what role had Polly played in that refuge?

'Don't imagine, though, that I conceived a *tendresse* for her,' he continued, as if reading her thoughts. 'We were just friends. But I got to know her and her commitment to children. Believe me, she would never have killed her child as well as herself.'

'Not even if that child meant a ruined reputation?'

'She was tough; she would have been sure something would turn up to save her.'

Ursula thought of the poor bundle of broken body she had found in the river.

'Mrs Comfort told me yesterday that Polly had set off for the village that last day in high spirits, saying, "Don't expect me back". Mrs Comfort thought that meant she was going to meet a young man and that she would be out some time.'

Nothing was said for several minutes as the horse trotted along the dirt road, her head held high.

'What do *you* want to happen?' asked Ursula.

'I want a proper inquest. I want to know who fathered that child. I want to know if it was a pure accident Polly fell and finished her life in the river.'

'Would an inquest reveal who was responsible for her condition? Surely the man, whoever it is, is not going to own up?'

'Somebody must know something,' he said obstinately, his face set and hard. 'Trying to cover up what has happened will not help anyone.'

Ursula thought of the proud nature of the Earl; the supreme self-confidence of the Dowager Countess; the determination of Helen.

'Why are we going to Hinton Parva?'

The Colonel allowed the reins to slacken and the horse to slow its gait.

'I had not intended to when we started out,' he said, sounding surprised. 'I just wanted to get away and I thought . . . ' His voice tailed away.

'You thought that nice Miss Grandison, who found dead bodies, would make an entertaining companion, was that it?'

He looked at her again, this time with the glimmer of a smile. 'How well you know me!'

'I know nothing about you. Except that you appear to have a highly developed sense of justice – and that your sense of loyalty to your family is rather less than that of your brother's.'

'Damn Mountstanton and all it stands for!' The anger was back. 'I thought I had got away from all that. Instead, what do I find? That the death of one of its faithful servants matters less than its standing in the world. Why am I not surprised?'

'Why did you return, if that is what you feel?'

'Why, indeed?'

After a moment, Ursula said, 'I have to confess that I have not visited the village and have no idea how large it is.'

He gave a curt laugh. 'Quite small. But it has a police station and a constable who is ostensibly in charge of the investigation into Polly's death. I want to find out if he means to do exactly what my brother and the coroner tell him, or if he is going to hold out for a wider justice.'

'Does he have the power to do so?'

Her companion shrugged his shoulders. 'That's another thing I need to find out. There is also a village shop, hotbed of all village gossip. I thought I might hear something about Polly there. The tittle will certainly be tattling.'

'And what would you like me to do in the meantime? I am afraid I am unable to walk the dog.'

He hit his forehead in a gesture of frustration. 'My dear Miss Grandison, I am a complete and utter fool.'

'By which I assume you had forgotten about me,' Ursula said cheerfully.

He gave her a rueful look. 'I think I have remarked before on your intelligence, Miss Grandison. I now turn to you for the solution to the problem. Shall we return to Mountstanton and allow you to have lunch there? Or shall we abandon the village. I can, after all, come back on my own later this afternoon.'

'Nonsense, Colonel. Not when you are as fired up as Don Quixote. I think the answer is that you assist me to descend at the village store and allow me to venture in and see if I can gather anything from the gossip. As I am not a Mountstanton, and a foreigner not bound by English conventions of loyalty, they may hope I can provide some meat for their gossip.'

'And in the process may provide you with some meat of their own?' He looked admiringly at her. 'Miss Grandison, you understand the way small societies work much better than I.'

Ursula gave a peal of laughter. 'Colonel, you beat everything! I dare you to tell me this is not what you intended from the start.'

'Miss Grandison, you disappoint me. How could you impugn such Machiavellian motives to me? I'm just a bluff, honest soldier.'

Ursula gave him a straight look. He grinned at her but said nothing.

How very different this man was from the Earl, Ursula thought. Helen's husband had no wit, and little sense of anything beyond his own importance. She wondered what made Helen think she could persuade Charles Stanhope to make a match with Belle. Why, in fact, did she want to achieve such an unsuitable union? And what sort of relationship did she have with her brother-in-law?

The trap reached the first cottages on the outskirts of Hinton Parva. Neat, thatched, with gardens planted with colourful flowers, they led up to a large green. This had a pond with ducks and a couple of white swans. On one side stood an inn with a sign illustrating its name: The Lion and Lamb. There was a rough table outside with a bench. On it, enjoying the sun with a tankard of what Ursula thought had to be some local beer, sat an elderly countryman wearing a large-brimmed hat. Not far from the inn was a church and beyond that a street, which seemed to offer several shops.

As the Colonel brought the trap to a halt, the countryman lifted his wrinkled face and gave him a warm smile. 'Master Charles,' he called. 'You'm be back then?'

'As you see, Joshua. How's yourself?'

'Fair to middling. Mustn't complain.'

'I'll come and drink an ale with you in a little while. But first I have business to attend to.'

'Aye. Soon as I saw you, I knew what you'd come for. Constable's at home, wrestling with what he calls them awk'ard pieces of paper.'

The Colonel laughed. 'You haven't changed, Joshua. You always did know everything. This is Miss Grandison, who accompanied her ladyship's sister, Miss Seldon, over from America. This is Joshua Barnes, Miss Grandison, one of the oldest and most valued members of the community.'

Ursula raised a hand in greeting. 'I am pleased to make your acquaintance, Mr Barnes.'

Joshua pulled at a forelock. 'Glad to make yours, miss.'

The Colonel put the horse into motion again and drove down the little street. Ursula noted a butcher's, a cobbler's, an ironmongers and, halfway down, a general store. The trap was brought to a stop outside this emporium.

The Colonel got down, retrieved Ursula's crutches from the back of the trap, then helped her descend. As Ursula gingerly stepped onto the ground, gripping her escort's arm tightly while he handed her first one and then the other crutch, two respectably dressed women came towards the shop entrance, nodded at them both, then opened the door. A gust of busy chatter came forth.

The Colonel looked at Ursula. 'It's a serious matter, Miss Grandison, and I'm relying on you,' he said in a low tone. Then, loudly, 'Well, I've brought you here. I will be no more than half an hour, do not keep me waiting.'

With a tilt of his hat, he hoisted himself into the trap, picked up the reins, and drove off down the street.

Ursula took a deep breath and worked her way towards the shop door. How on earth, she wondered, could she achieve what he wanted?

Chapter Ten

'She was a hussy,' a voice said as Ursula entered the shop. Then silence fell while she negotiated a couple of steps down into the interior.

The space was larger than she had imagined but so full of goods that the four or five customers it contained took up most of the room.

All there looked round as Ursula wielded her crutches. 'Why,' she drawled, hamming it up, 'I surely do need to sit awhile. That trap throws a body around like I don't know what. I declare it was almost as bad as the racketing I received the time I travelled by covered wagon over the Sierra Nevada.'

She moved forward towards the counter. As one, the others drew back – and revealed a bentwood chair standing beside the counter.

'My, that gives a body ease,' Ursula said in heartfelt tones, lowering herself onto it. 'If you all will forgive me, I'll just sit a few moments.' She closed her eyes and leaned against the back of the chair. A soft motion of customers said they were settling back into the pattern she had disturbed.

'And how be Lady Frances, Mrs Sutton?' The voice was soft but composed and Ursula, running through the brief look she had gained of the shoppers as she moved towards the chair, decided it had to belong to a small, neat-looking woman dressed in clothes of a faded gentility.

'Not so good, Miss Ranner, I'm afraid.' A voice with a

stronger local accent. Its owner sounded genuinely regretful. 'Don't reckon she can last much longer.'

There was a general muttering of concerned regrets from the other shoppers.

'And what about young Mr Russell?' asked the same soft voice that had spoken before.

'Poor lad is like a ghost,' said Mrs Sutton. 'Don't know what to do with himself, he don't. Talks of America. Wants to go there, after . . . ' she faded to a stop. For a moment nobody said anything, then: 'Not much of a life they've had, either of them,' a third shopper entered the conversation.

Ursula realised with a slight shock that they were talking of the delightful partner she had had at Helen's dinner party. It had only been the other night but now it seemed weeks ago.

'Your sins will always find you out,' said another, and it was the same voice that had been stridently proclaiming someone a hussy.

Ursula opened her eyes in time to see the shopkeeper, a man with a gentle face and skin the texture of fine suede, lean forward and say in a peaceable tone, 'Now Mrs Clarke, if that be true, we'll all be for the hangman's rope.'

'She's right about that little strumpet from the big house, though.'

The women tutted. The speaker was a slight man, his shoulders bent, his thinning hair long and straggly. He looked, decided Ursula, like some minor clerk fallen on hard times, his clothes shiny with wear, the waistcoat plentifully stained with food. 'I saw her, in the woods, flaunting herself.'

Ursula shivered at how he managed to sound both vitriolic and lecherous at the same time.

'Who with, Mr Snell?' breathed out a wispy woman of uncertain years, dressed in what looked like an assembly of scarves that floated around a dowdy-looking skirt and jacket. A romantic who had never had her day, Ursula wondered? Both this woman and Miss Ranner seemed to be in the store on their own account; the others shopping for their employers. She was amused for a moment at how confident she was of this analysis of status.

'Were you looking for something in particular, Miss Grandison? It *is* Miss Grandison, isn't it?' said the shopkeeper, bending towards Ursula. There seemed to be a note of warning in his voice, but the warning was not for her.

'Why, I thank you, sir. I was wondering, could you supply knitting needles and wool? See, I have time on my hands,' Ursula said cheerfully.

'Miss Grandison,' said Miss Ranner with a quick gasp. 'You came with Miss Seldon from America, did you not? She who's come to see her sister, the Countess? Of course, you hurt your ankle, didn't you? When you found poor Polly Brown.'

A murmur ran through the little group; it was obvious not everyone had realised until now who they had in their midst.

The shopkeeper started to hunt through a series of drawers that ran along the wall at his back.

In front of the counter were sacks and barrels of flour, beans, potatoes, carrots. Cabbages were in a crate and gave off a freshness that was welcome. The store was redolent with a combination of lamp oil, kerosene, candles, well-matured cheese, brown sugar, soap, loose tea, coffee, and other comestibles. It caught at Ursula's throat. All at once she was back with the horror of the worst time of her life.

'Are you all right, Miss Grandison?' asked Miss Ranner. 'You look terribly pale. Mr Partridge, a glass of water for Miss Grandison.'

With an effort Ursula wrenched her mind away from the Sierra Nevada and back to the safety of a small village in the English countryside.

A glass of water appeared and she sipped at it gratefully.

'Who did you see Polly Brown with, Mr Snell?' The romantic spinster was not going to leave the matter alone.

'There'd be the devil to pay if I were to say,' said Mr Snell. 'But I'm not. There's some matters as should be left alone.' He sounded horribly sanctimonious.

'Which means you have no idea who she met,' said Mrs Sutton decisively. 'You shouldn't go round spreading rumours, Mr Snell. Rumours are the work of the devil. Now, Mr Partridge, if you please, and if you have finished serving Miss Grandison here, Lady Frances is needing eggs. Our lot's gone broody on us.' She sounded confident of a certain status as housekeeper to a titled lady.

'Of course, Mrs Sutton, in just a moment. Here are knitting needles, Miss Grandison.' The shopkeeper placed a selection on the counter. 'What colour wool was you interested in?'

Ursula had no idea what she wanted; knitting had only occurred to her as she entered the shop. 'Please, serve Mrs Sutton while I think.'

'Kind of you, I'm sure,' said the woman graciously. 'Two dozen eggs, if you please, Mr Partridge.'

She handed over her basket and the shopkeeper started to place creamy-white eggs carefully in paper bags before arranging them in the carrier.

Glancing around at the other women, Ursula became aware that she was the only one wearing a knitted wrap. She had not expected Helen to possess such a mundane article, but did not countrywomen knit themselves warmth and comfort?

Suddenly Ursula wanted to make herself something fragile and feminine instead of her fiercely practical dark brown shawl. However, its very plebeian status may have given her a certain anonymity amongst them. And tied about her in the mountain cold, it had provided welcome warmth.

Mrs Sutton left. No one else seemed in a hurry to place an order. They stood fingering items on shelves: tins of preserved vegetables and fruits, bars of soap, mops and brushes, dusters, books from the circulating library shelves. Conversation had ceased. Ursula felt everyone's attention fixed on herself.

When the shopkeeper turned back and asked if she had come to a decision on the shade of wool she required, she said, 'Cream,' as though she had been nourishing the idea for some time. She picked up a pair of thick needles. 'A fine wool, if you have one, Mr Partridge, it's to be a lacy wrap.'

Skeins of a fine cream wool were placed beside the needles.

'I don't suppose you would have a pattern, Mr Partridge?'

He shook his head. 'Patterns here be copied down from knitter to knitter. Baby shawls be most popular and everyone has a pattern for them.'

'I'm right sorry, Mr Partridge, to have troubled you over such a thing. I'll take this wool and these needles. Could you please wrap them for me?'

Miss Ranner said, 'I have a pattern for a lacy wrap as might suit, Miss Grandison, if you would be interested. I would be most willing to lend it to you.'

Ursula looked at the steady hazel eyes in the soft face. 'Why, Miss Ranner, you are most kind. I would surely be grateful for the loan. How many of these skeins do you think I'll need? And would these be the right size needles?'

Soon the needles and the wool were parcelled up and Mr Partridge offered to send them up to Mountstanton House.

'Too much trouble,' Ursula said briskly. 'I'll take them with me. They can sit in the Colonel's trap. Mr Partridge, what do I owe you?'

She paid the shopkeeper and took the parcel.

'Shall you come with me to see the shawl and its pattern?' Miss Ranner looked up at Ursula hopefully.

'I'd be delighted. I'll wait for you to finish your shopping.'

'Oh no, I can do that any time.'

'Then lead the way. Perhaps, Mr Partridge, if Colonel Stanhope arrives to collect me before I return, you can tell him where to find me?'

As Ursula left the shop with Miss Ranner, she could feel the gaze of everyone else following her. She wondered if she imagined the long drawn out sigh that came as the doorbell rang on her departure.

Her companion lived a few doors down from the store, in a little cottage no more than one room wide. A narrow staircase led upstairs and there appeared to be another room at the back. One glance, though, was enough to tell Ursula that, for Miss Ranner, life was lived in the room that gave straight onto the street. A fire was laid in a gleaming black grate. On the mantelshelf above stood a pair of small china houses, roses climbing round the doors; windows and chimney picked out with colour. A round table in the centre of the room held an assortment of needlework, books and letters. Beside the unlit fire was a comfortable chair. A wooden armchair with a round back and spindle supports was drawn up to the table.

'Perhaps you'd like a cup of tea?' Miss Ranner took off her bonnet and adjusted the set of her hair. 'There may be some coffee,' she added doubtfully.

'Tea would be very pleasant, ma'am.'

Her hostess gave a small, embarrassed laugh. 'I like the way you talk, Miss Grandison. It's more interesting than the Countess, if you don't mind my saying so. Though you can, of course, tell that she is not English.'

Ursula laughed. 'Her ladyship hasn't spent time in the far West of America. We were at school together but my life has been more rough and ready than hers.'

'Goodness, you don't say!' Miss Ranner gave another, smothered laugh. 'Do, please, sit down and rest that ankle. I'll ask Ellie to bring us tea.' She disappeared into the room at the back.

Ursula loosened the ends of the unfashionable wrap she had tied around her waist, then inspected a couple of framed samplers displayed on one of the walls. Judging from the dates, and the fact that the name on each was the same, it would seem that her hostess was called Amelia.

'Are these your work?' she asked when Miss Ranner reappeared.

'Oh, dear, they are.' Miss Ranner peered closely at one of the samplers and her index finger traced the line of patterned cross-stitch that framed the sampler's rows of different stitches. 'Now, I'll just pop upstairs and find that shawl.'

She was soon back with a cobweb-fine wrap.

Ursula expressed her delight with the intricate garment then watched as Miss Ranner dug out a large box from the bottom drawer of a dresser and found a couple of much-fingered pages covered with neat knitting notations.

Rather as she had with the sampler, Miss Ranner ran a hand over the first page. 'My dear Mama copied this from one in the possession of her mama. She was a vicar's daughter in the North of England, you know?'

Ursula expressed interest.

'She met my Papa when he was on a walking holiday. He was a curate; so suitable.'

'So, she became a vicar's wife as well as daughter?'

'Why, yes, and brought up a large family as well as giving succour to the parish. She used to say that, poor as we were, we had much, much more than others.'

'It must have been a tough life for your mama; forgive me,' Ursula gave a little laugh. 'That's my far Western vocabulary speaking. I mean it must have been difficult for her.'

'She managed. Ah, here is Ellie with our tea.'

A small and very nervous maid brought in a tray with a brown teapot and two porcelain cups and saucers and placed it on the table, Miss Ranner clearing a space.

Ursula was pressed to take the upholstered seat.

'Are you comfortable at Mountstanton House?' Miss Ranner asked as she supplied her guest with a cup of the tea. 'I am afraid, though, that the unfortunate discovery yesterday must have upset you.'

Ursula admired the skilful innocence with which Miss Ranner had introduced the subject.

'Did you know the girl, Polly Brown?' Ursula allowed herself to be as direct as her hostess.

'Why, yes. All the Mountstanton servants visit Hinton Parva when they have free time. Or are on an errand for someone.' Miss Ranner sat down, her pleasant countenance very sad. 'Polly was full of life. Always ready to chat.'

'About Mountstanton?' Ursula drank a little of her tea. It was hot and strong. She was coming to like this English obsession.

'Not about the Earl and Countess, dear me, no. But she would always tell us tales of young Lord Harry. Adored that boy, she did. And then there would be comments about some of the other servants. Because she was in the nursery, Polly gave herself a few airs; she thought herself better than most of the other young ones.'

'How about Mrs Parsons and Benson?'

'Full of respect for them she was. She had to be.'

'Was she pretty?'

'Very pretty! She had blue eyes that were so large. Such a pleasure to look at, she was. And her nose was small and straight. She held her head up as though she knew she looked as good as anyone and better than most. Bit of a saucy air about her.' Miss Ranner stopped for a moment and gave an apologetic smile, 'How I do go on.'

'Please, Miss Ranner, I'd so like to put a face to that poor body.'

'Oh, Miss Grandison. How terrible it must have been.' Miss Ranner looked as though she might burst into tears.

'Tell me more so I can picture her alive.'

Miss Ranner thought for a moment. 'Full mouth she had. "Made for kissing" is what someone told me once.' She gave a deprecating little laugh.

'Would that have been Mr Snell?'

'Goodness, no. That man never says a kind word about anyone.'

'He seems to have noticed Polly in a very particular sort of way.'

Miss Ranner looked her straight in the eyes. 'I do not like to speak ill of others, but Mr Snell is not a nice man.' She took a quick breath. 'I was the local schoolteacher, Miss Grandison. I taught Polly and others from the orphanage. Polly was a bright girl who liked to be helpful. I had hopes for her. When she came down to the village, she sometimes used to spend a little time with me.'

'Mr Snell seemed to suggest she was involved with a man, indeed, perhaps with more than one. Did she confide in you?' Ursula asked gently. She had been sure that Miss Ranner had wanted to talk to her about Polly rather than show her a shawl.

Miss Ranner gazed into her teacup as though it would yield up what she should say. Finally, as though she had made some decision, she looked up and said, 'I saw her once walking with one of the Mountstanton footmen. Laughing they were, and very close with one another.'

'Do you know which footman?'

'He's called John. I teased her, said she looked as though she was in love. But she laughed it off, said it was nothing. It did not, though, look like nothing to me.'

Ursula thought of the footman: his handsome features, his elegant figure, the knowing way he could look.

'Did she say she was interested in anyone else? Forgive me for being so curious but discovering her body makes me want to know everything about her.'

'I think I understand, Miss Grandison. But there's nothing much else I can tell you. Except when I heard she'd left, I thought how strange she had not come to say goodbye to me. Then, yesterday, when the news came that she was dead, I cried. She was such a little piece of sunshine. And when I hear her called a hussy,' her voice suddenly strengthened, 'I cannot bear it. Jealous, that's what they were.'

They were interrupted by a knock on the door.

Miss Ranner looked round. 'Now, who can that be? Ellie, someone's called!'

The little maid appeared and opened the front door.

There stood Colonel Stanhope.

He removed his cap. 'Good morning. Is Miss Ranner at home? I believe she has Miss Grandison with her.'

His formality surprised Ursula; he could not help but see both of them sitting there. But it was pleasant how he respected the conventions in this little village he knew so well; that here, at least, he forgot his abrupt army ways.

Miss Ranner rose. 'Colonel Charles, please, do come in. Can I offer you a cup of tea?'

Chapter Eleven

Belle walked with quick, angry steps towards her bedroom. On her way she encountered one of the footmen.

'John, tell my maid to come immediately.'

He looked at her with that familiar twinkle. 'Of course, Miss Seldon. At once.'

There was just a trace of something in his voice. It could not be called cheek but Belle was conscious she had not been as courteous as she had been taught. Ursula would have said, 'Please and thank you cost nothing, Belle, and they ease our transactions with those less privileged than ourselves.'

'Thank you, John,' Belle said, trying to sound gracious.

The twinkle became a little more pronounced. 'Think nothing of it, Miss Seldon.'

The fellow was flirting with her! Belle gave him a sidelong glance and her mouth curved in a small smile before she continued on her way, her steps not quite so angry.

She felt guilty. It was not Ursula's fault the morning had gone so badly wrong. Belle gave a bad-tempered shove to her bedroom door.

On rising, when she had told her maid that she would be riding and to bring her habit, Didier had pursed her lips and asked in that high and mighty French way of hers if her ladyship knew she was to ride. As if the woman had the right to question her!

Casting herself onto the room's small sofa, Belle gnawed on a finger. Helen seemed determined to prevent William spending any time with her. Didn't she want Belle to enjoy herself? Helen was unkind, overbearing, never considered her needs, did not respect her wishes, treated her like a doll to be ordered about. It was too bad!

A breakfast tray arrived. Belle listlessly poured herself a cup of coffee and buttered a roll.

Then her maid entered. 'Mam'selle requires me?'

Didier was another source of Belle's bitterness with her sister. Middle-aged and severe, Didier was no fun. Look at her now! No smile, she seemed almost grumpy. After all, the whole point of her being at Mountstanton was to serve Belle, so why couldn't she be pleasant to her?

'I am not going riding; the Countess and I are to pay a call and I need my yellow muslin.'

'*Bien sur, mam'selle.*' At least there was no hint of triumph.

Didier went and found the gown. '*C'est ravissante, mam'selle.*'

'Speak English.'

The maid reverently laid the garment on the bed. 'I said, it is pretty.'

Didier started to undo the fastenings of her habit.

'Madame, La Comtesse, 'er French is so good. But you, mam'selle, you do not seem to speak French at all. 'Ow is this? You are sisters, no?' She laid the riding jacket neatly on the sofa.

Belle felt the ancient jealousy rise in her chest. 'My sister went to school in Paris. That's how she knows French. My school was in New York.'

Didier unfastened the habit's skirt and removed it along with Belle's undergarments. '*Maintenant*, we 'ave the *jupon de soie, n'est ce pas?*'

A moment later silk slipped down Belle's body, its cool touch on her skin infinitely comforting.

Whalebone stays were tightly laced around her upper body, pushing up her small breasts into soft, seductive shapes.

With Belle seated at the dressing table, Didier unfastened the knot of blonde hair, brushing it until it was a shining swathe, then clipped it back with ivory clasps.

When she was finally ready, Belle looked at herself in the long, cheval mirror. 'My pearls,' she said, darting to the dressing table, opening her little jewel case and taking out the string.

'Ah, no, mam'selle, not for the morning.' Didier inspected the contents of the case then picked out a cameo brooch. 'This, I think.' She fastened it at the neck of the yellow dress, just below the narrow ruffle that showed off Belle's slender neck, then stood back.

'*Ravissante*,' she declared. 'You are very, very pretty, mam'selle. And I am proud to 'elp you look so, so chic.'

Belle impulsively hugged her maid. 'Thank you. No one has ever dressed my hair so beautifully as you.'

Didier blinked. '*Mais, votre chapeau!*' She found a pretty Leghorn straw with a tie of the same muslin as the dress. She fastened it with a bow under the girl's chin, then stood back and gave a final nod of satisfaction. '*Mais oui, parfait!*' She handed over a pair of white lace gloves and a parasol that matched her dress.

Belle found Helen giving instructions to Mrs Parsons, the housekeeper who was even more severe than Didier.

Helen gave her sister a quick, assessing look, seemed to approve, turned back to Mrs Parsons and said, 'Miss Seldon and I will be here for luncheon, as will Mr Warburton and Miss Grandison. The Dowager Countess is visiting friends. You must enquire of the Earl and Colonel what their plans are.'

'Yes, my lady.' Mrs Parsons took herself off.

'The carriage is already outside, Belle, we must not keep the horses waiting.'

It was the closed carriage today. As they drove at a steady pace through the park and onto the road, Belle asked, 'Helen, why do you and Richard not have a motor vehicle? Papa uses one now all the time. So do many others in New York.'

Helen was frowning over a small notebook. 'Too expensive, the vehicle needs a mechanic for its maintenance and propulsion and is too liable to break down.'

The horses' hooves clipped a steady beat on the dusty road. The carriage was so old fashioned! However, they were private inside.

'Tell me, Helen, why have you not redecorated and modernised Mountstanton?'

Helen gazed out of the window for a long moment. 'Plans are being made.'

'But you have been married more than seven years!'

'Richard has not been Earl that long.'

'Didn't your papa-in-law pass away just after Harry was born? That must have been some five years ago.'

'Belle, it is no concern of yours how Richard and I manage our affairs.' Helen's tone made it clear that the matter was closed.

Belle watched her sister attempting to write in the note-book, her pencil jerking with the jolting of the carriage. 'Helen, why was I not sent to school in Paris as you were?'

Once again the notebook was put down. 'Belle, dear, why on earth do you ask this now?'

'Didier wanted to know why I did not speak French. And I thought how I would have liked to go. My friend, Sarah-Anne, she went and she wrote me that it was wonderful,' Belle said wistfully. 'I don't think it fair that I wasn't sent,' she added more forcefully.

'Papa wanted you at home.' Helen said in a warning voice. After a moment she added, 'You must know that Papa writes me everything. There is nothing I am not aware of.'

She should have known, Belle reflected a little bitterly. Papa was always telling her how she should look up to her sister, how important it was to obey her in every respect.

'And, of course,' Helen continued smoothly, 'Without Mama, he would have felt too lonely with you abroad.'

Belle sighed deeply. She was seven when her mother had disappeared from her life. Mama had been so much fun. She was always laughing, always had wonderful ideas for expedi-tions, always bought Belle lovely little presents. 'I do miss her,' she said with a little gulp. 'I wish . . . '

'I know, dear.' Helen laid a sympathetic hand on Belle's arm. 'It would have been so wonderful to have had her here with you. She would have been so proud of you and I think of me, too.'

For an instant Belle felt completely in tune with her sister. 'I am so sorry she died. Home seems empty. And Papa will never speak of her.'

The pressure on her arm increased for a second. 'She would want us to enjoy ourselves,' Helen said in a rallying tone. 'And I hope that that is what you will do this morning. The three Paxton sons are extremely handsome. Meeting them now means that they will all ask you to dance at the London balls.' Helen hesitated for a second, then added, 'Darling Belle, you do realise what a chance you are being given, don't you? Much more valuable than a year or two at finishing school in Paris.'

Belle twirled the point of her parasol on the carpeted floor. 'By chance, you mean, for marriage?'

'Of course I mean for marriage, you little goose.'

'But I could always marry one of the boys back home. I'm not sure I want a lord of some sort if it means I'm stuck with a draughty, run-down old rabbit warren of a house, a mother-in-law who thinks she has the right to lay down the law, and a husband who never seems to want to be with his wife.'

Helen closed her notebook and turned to her sister. 'Darling, don't you understand we have no entrée into the top rank of New York or Washington society? Papa's millions can buy us *haute couture* gowns from Paris, hunters from Ireland, and travel to anywhere we want to go, but it can't propel us into the Vanderbilt and Astor circles.'

'But why should we care?' Belle asked passionately. 'Did you marry Richard so that you should have the entrée, as you call it, into London society? Did Papa's millions buy him for you?' she ended on an acid note.

'He fell in love with me,' Helen said decisively.

'Well, I want someone to love me. I want to have fun and enjoy myself. Isn't it possible to get married and have fun? And does a husband have to have a title? After all, didn't you want me to marry Richard's brother, the Colonel? He only has an army title, or does that count as much as being a Lord?'

'He is Colonel the Honourable Charles Stanhope. Please, Belle,' Helen said persuasively, 'be sensible. I admit, I was wrong over Charles. I hadn't realised how much he had changed. When I first came to England he was a dashing young captain and every girl who met him fell head over heels.' She fiddled with her pencil. 'I thought what fun it would be if you and he made a match of it. You see, Belle, you do rather let your emotions run away with you. I think you need to find a man who can perhaps, well, take charge.'

For a moment Belle could hardly breathe. How dare her sister make her sound like a schoolgirl who had to be managed? But Helen's jibe about her not being able to control her feelings resonated uncomfortably. She gripped the handle of her parasol and took several deep breaths the way her father had advised when something boiled up inside her.

'Belle, my sweet,' he'd said after she had thrown a temper fit over not being allowed to have something she'd really, really wanted. 'You are full of passion. All the Seldon females are. Helen has learned control and you must too. Whenever you feel you must lash out, or fall into howls of rage, or fling yourself into some unsuitable chap's arms, take three deep breaths and tell yourself, it will all go away; that nothing is that important. Or, if it is, then the only way you will achieve your desire is to use your head and not your heart. Do you understand?'

He had looked so concerned and so loving, Belle had sat on his lap, wound her arms around his neck, and buried her face against his chest. 'Darling Papa, you are so, so wise.'

There were so many things Belle wanted to ask Helen about her marriage and her life but she felt she had been warned off. Her questions would have to wait.

'I want a son just like Harry,' she said instead.

Helen smiled. 'Well, first you have to find a husband.'

Belle adjusted the muslin folds of her skirt, not looking at her sister. 'Helen, why don't you wish me to spend time with Mr Warburton? He is so very nice,' she added in a rush. 'He makes me laugh.'

'Belle, I have told you,' said Helen wearily. 'William is with us to learn how to be a secretary. He handles Richard's affairs. He has no money and will have to earn his living. So you will do him no service by distracting him from his duties.'

'It seems to me he spends more time with you than with Richard,' said Belle slyly, back to twirling her parasol.

Helen gave an exasperated sigh as the carriage turned in through high, wrought-iron gates.

'We're here. Please, Belle, for all our sakes, be the well-behaved young lady I know you are.'

There was a note of entreaty in Helen's voice that Belle had not heard before. A little kernel of satisfaction sat in the pit of her stomach as the carriage drew up in front of a solidly respectable-looking house.

★ ★ ★

As they returned home, Helen said briskly, 'That went very well. They were all charmed by you, Belle, as I knew they would be.'

Belle gave a little smile of triumph. She had made sure she simpered in regular young-miss style as the three Paxton youths had attempted to secure her attention.

'And weren't those young men attractive, and so very personable?'

'Oh, very personable.' They had indeed been handsome, very much in what Belle was beginning to realise was the English style: tallish, good bone structure, upright posture, wearing their unremarkable clothes well. 'They did not, though, seem very amusing.'

'I heard you laugh a lot,' Helen said curiously.

'Young men like a girl who laughs a lot. Surely you remember that, Helen?' Belle said with a superior air. 'All I had to do was think how very funny they looked with their high collars and faces that might just have been freshly scrubbed.'

'I am sure they all dance well.'

Belle was certain they were the sort of young men who would step on your best shoes the moment they took you onto the floor. 'Can we have some dancing at Mountstanton, Helen? I am sure Miss Grandison can play for us.'

'Why, that is a splendid idea, Belle. I will organise a small party for a few days' time. Tell me,' she added after a small pause, 'You get on with Ursula, Miss Grandison, that is? She is helpful?'

'I like her; she is very kind to me. I am so sorry she has hurt her ankle, it must be awkward for her.'

'Indeed,' said Helen dryly.

'Tell me about that poor nursemaid that Ursula found in the river.'

'Nothing to tell,' Helen said briefly. 'Harry was very fond of her, and it was upsetting when she left so suddenly. It's very tragic she should have suffered such a dreadful accident.'

Belle felt most sorry for poor Harry. She decided to take him for a walk or a ride that afternoon. Perhaps it might be possible to have William Warburton along as well.

★ ★ ★

While they were all assembled waiting for luncheon to be announced, the Earl said, 'Helen, we need a meeting with Mrs Parsons this afternoon.'

'Why, Richard?'

The Earl looked towards Belle in a pointed way. 'It follows on from the meeting with the coroner. I'll tell you everything after lunch.'

'Ah,' said Helen.

Belle contained her curiosity. She was, though, very conscious of William Warburton's gaze flicking between his employer and his wife.

They went into luncheon. No explanation had been given for the absence of both the Colonel and Ursula. Belle was not concerned about the Colonel, he was old and no fun, but she did wonder about Ursula.

'Will this meeting take long?' Helen asked her husband once they were seated.

'For heaven's sake, I have no idea! But we may have to talk to some of the other servants as well.'

Helen moved smoothly into a description of their morning's visit.

As soon as the Earl had finished his meal, he rose. 'Summon Mrs Parsons,' he said to his wife. 'We'd better get this over with.'

Helen looked at Belle. 'I expect you can find something to do, can't you?' She gave her a smile. 'William, show my sister the picture gallery.'

'Of course, my lady,' he said with a covert glance of conspiracy at Belle that gave her a flutter of excitement.

'Will there be anything else, Miss Seldon?' asked the butler. 'Coffee, perhaps?'

'I don't think so, thank you, Benson.'

'I can suggest something better than the picture gallery,' William whispered as they left the dining room. 'What would you say to a place no one would think of looking for us? A place where we can be alone?'

Belle's heart began to beat more rapidly and her breath came more quickly. 'Where?'

'Follow me.'

William went up the main staircase, past the first floor, up to the second floor, then he turned the opposite way from the nursery and led her down a long corridor to another, much smaller staircase that wound upwards.

Curiosity as well as excitement consuming her, Belle followed the young man up and up till they came to a door.

William opened it, Belle followed him through – and gasped in amazement.

They were on the roof of the house. The door had accessed a wide, paved area bounded by a parapet that ran all the way around the house and was decorated with urns. There were areas of pitched roof covered with slate tiles. Chimneystacks of brick built in twisted patterns rose everywhere.

'Look at the view,' said William, moving towards the parapet.

Belle reached nervously for his hand. 'Is it safe?'

He smiled. 'As long as I am with you, you are in no danger,' he said, holding her small, hot hand in his large, cool one, mesmerising her with his eyes.

She dragged her gaze away and peered over the parapet, looking down from the dizzying height to the formal gardens, the parkland and beyond to fields and woods.

'Are you pleased I brought you up here?'

'Oh, yes! It's magical.' Belle shaded her eyes from the sun, straining to make out more of the landscape. 'It's all so small. That's what I think of England, you know? It's like a land for children.'

'This is more than a toy house. Come, I want to show you something else.'

Set exactly over the front entrance was a darling little pavilion with a domed roof. It almost floated above the line of the parapet. William led Belle up its steps. 'It looks as though it's made of stone but actually it's wood, so much lighter, you see. Step inside, my lady.'

Belle looked at William's sparkling eyes and her blood began to speed through her veins.

The pavilion was unexpectedly large. Round the inside were a series of couches with neatly rolled ends.

'Two hundred years ago or so, parties would come up here for delicacies after a banquet. They ate early in those days. It would be cool in summer and perhaps they sat until the sun went down; maybe walked around the roof, perhaps had candles lit.' His breath was ragged, the pupils of his eyes huge, dark pools. 'I believe some of the servants use it now for assignations,' he added casually.

Belle saw a layer of cushions on one of the couches. She sat down, her heart beating faster and faster, her mouth a little open, her eyes half closed.

He sat beside her, so close she could feel the heat of his body. 'Oh, sweetheart, you are like the source of all water to a man dying of thirst,' he said and placed a hand underneath one of her breasts, as if it were a precious fruit.

'William.' It came out almost as a groan. She put up an arm and pulled his head down to hers. The softness of his hair at the nape of his neck sent a shiver through her. His moustache tickled her lip and Belle knew that she could no more stop what was about to happen than the sun could stop rising every morning. And she did not want it to stop; she wanted this with a passion she had never experienced before.

Chapter Twelve

The Colonel exchanged courteous greetings with Miss Ranner and extracted Ursula with smooth efficiency.

'Do come again, Miss Grandison; I'm always here.' Miss Ranner pressed both Ursula's hands with hers.

'As soon as I am mobile again,' Ursula promised her.

Once helped onto the front seat of the trap, she was welcomed by Honey, who squirmed her way onto Ursula's lap then produced enthusiastic licks.

'Did you have a useful meeting with the constable?' Ursula asked.

'Depends which way you look at it,' the Colonel said curtly. They trotted down the dusty street.

'We'll find somewhere to picnic then we can exchange what we have each learned from this morning's encounters.'

Ursula held the little spaniel safely on her lap as the trap began to jolt along an uneven road. She was not sorry to have time to put together the bits and pieces she had learned that morning with items from her chat with Mrs Comfort and comments from Mrs Parsons. The picture that was emerging was an uncomfortable one and she wondered how the Colonel would react to her conclusions.

They began to climb a hill and Ursula hoped she would not be required to propel herself up the last of it on her crutches. But the horse sturdily gained the top with the passengers aboard. The Colonel reined her in for a pause and Ursula gave a little gasp of delight at the vista of rolling meadows that was revealed, the land falling down in a steep slope to their left towards a strip of flashing silver reflecting back the sun. It had to be the river she had met so disastrously the day before. Far away could be glimpsed a thick wood, the green of the trees rendered almost blue by the distance. Up in the clear air a bird was singing, the same liquid notes she'd heard the previous day falling like a benediction.

'A skylark,' said the Colonel with an air of quiet satisfaction. 'Now I know that I'm back in England.'

'The deep blue thou wingest, And singing still dost soar, and soaring ever singest.' Ursula quoted.

'Keats,' said the Colonel, clicking the horse into resuming their trip. 'Hail to thee blithe spirit, yes?'

'Shelley.'

'Ah, I bow to your superior knowledge.'

'Though you're surprised to find that an ill-educated American knows English poets?'

He laughed. 'Miss Grandison, you seem to have a poor opinion of us English.'

'Not at all; I think that you are all charming.'

'But hold that you Americans are more straightforward and to the point? Do not suffer fools? In fact, regard bluntness as a virtue?'

'Is that your opinion of Helen?'

The Colonel concentrated for a moment on taking the trap round a tricky bend in the road.

'My sister-in-law is as charming as any English girl,' he said briskly, bringing the horse to a stop. 'Here I think is an excellent place for our picnic. If I help you and the basket of food down, would you be able to see what Chef has provided while I deal with Beauty?'

They had reached an open area beside a sheltering cluster of trees. Ursula was settled on a grassy promontory with a rug and a cushion on which to sit. Then the wicker picnic basket was unloaded.

Ursula's first thought was to see if there was some water in the basket that could be given to the dog. Her respect for the Mountstanton organisation grew as she removed a white cloth and found beneath it a container of water and a metal bowl that was obviously intended for the animal.

The Colonel unharnessed the horse and tied her on a long rein to one of the trees.

'Glad to see you follow campaign rules of attending to animals before men,' he said as he joined her.

'Pioneering rules as well,' Ursula said briskly, spreading the cloth on the ground and investigating what else was in the basket.

'Indeed? Have you done much pioneering?' He looked at her quizzically.

'I spent some time in the silver fields of the Sierra Nevada.' It was not a subject Ursula wished to pursue and she regretted the light-hearted way she had tried to match his comment. 'The chef has done us proud,' she said quickly. 'Look, roasted chicken, slices of game pie, hard boiled eggs, and potato salad!'

He sat on the ground and helped arrange the food on the cloth. 'Ah, I see a bottle of claret.'

'And a corkscrew!'

Glasses, cutlery and plates were also in the basket. The Colonel opened the wine and poured them both glasses. Ursula took a sip. It was excellent.

'Those back at Mountstanton can't be eating any better,' she said, 'and they certainly won't have this amazing view. Oh, isn't the sun wonderful?' She held her face up to the warmth. 'Look at those fluffy white clouds, don't they make the blue of the sky so much bluer?'

Holding a chicken leg, the Colonel looked, not at the sky, but at Ursula. 'Such enthusiasm for the simple things of life.'

'Aren't they the best?'

'So you would abandon the glories of Mountstanton, the pomp of position, the comfort of riches?'

'Isn't that what you have been trying to do?'

He said nothing but tore a piece of chicken off the bone and offered it to Honey, who eagerly gulped it down.

He attacked the rest of the leg with relish. Ursula gnawed at hers rather more delicately. She supplied them both with napkins.

He grinned as he wiped his fingers. 'We must not abandon civilisation entirely, I suppose.'

Ursula arranged a slice of game pie and a mound of potato salad on a plate and handed it to him with a fork.

'Tell me,' said Ursula after a moment, 'what did you learn from the constable?'

The Colonel rose with the plate in his hand and roamed the little area of grass as though the activity allowed him to think better. 'The constable has seen the report of the post-mortem examination,' he said, gazing into the distance. 'It would be unfair of me, I suppose, to suggest that the examination was carried out in some haste. Considering the amount of time poor Polly's body was in the water, it obviously had to be done as swiftly as possible.'

Ursula set down her plate, her appetite gone.

'Nevertheless, the constable gave me the distinct impression that the intention had been to establish an accident had taken place.'

'Was there any evidence to show it might have been anything else?'

The Colonel finished his piece of pie and placed the plate on the ground for Honey to lick. Then he poured more wine for them both. Ursula took her recharged glass gratefully.

'It seems the state of her lungs suggests she did not drown,' he said slowly.

Ursula looked up at him, shocked. 'That surely means she was attacked.'

He shook his head. 'Not necessarily. Richard and I went through this with the coroner this morning. He pointed out that Polly might easily have received a fatal blow from a stone when she fell down that slope. Her skull had certainly sustained serious injury. She might have lain unconscious in the river with her head above water and died of her injuries.'

Ursula shuddered. In her mind's eye she saw the helpless figure of a young girl hurtling down that deadly escarpment into the rushing waters.

She took a deep breath. 'It's difficult for me to remember exactly how the body lay; I was too shocked. Did you see whether the head was below the water?'

He looked at her with considerable sympathy. 'I'm sorry to bring back memories of such an unhappy event. But, yes, I did see that her head was beneath the water.'

Ursula suddenly recalled the position of the body – the head face down in the river. She gulped and looked around, trying to find some distraction.

The Colonel sat down and reached for her hand. 'However,' he continued. 'That means nothing. The force of the water or a wild animal could have moved the body.'

Ursula found unexpected comfort in the warmth of his grasp. She looked straight at him. 'Do you believe Polly was attacked?'

He frowned. 'I don't know. I just want to be certain that every possibility has been explored; that her death has not been tidied away under a convenient label of either accident or suicide if there could be another possibility. Suicide would be the worst conclusion.' He drank more of his wine. 'The constable says that the area superintendent could be looking into the case.'

Ursula gently retrieved her hand. Perhaps because of the way he'd held it, perhaps because of the wine, she had recovered much of her composure. 'Then surely you can be certain that every contingency will be considered?'

He rose to his feet again; it seemed impossible for him to keep still. 'I cannot, I am afraid, ignore the fact that my brother will make every attempt to ensure that a verdict of accidental death is brought in. He is no doubt at this very moment writing letters to such people as have influence over superintendents of police to ensure that this will be the verdict.'

'Is power in England concentrated in such a way that he can do this?'

'My dear Miss Grandison, are you trying to make me believe political corruption does not exist in the United States of America?'

Ursula could not help laughing. 'By no means. But it is politicians and powerful financiers who pull the strings to get the results they desire. Forgive me, but I did not understand that an earl could hold a similar position.'

The Colonel gave a bleak smile. 'The Earl of Mountstanton is part of a network of the top social order. He can eat financiers for breakfast and that goes for most politicians as well. The House of Lords can frustrate the aims of any government, voting down Bills that do not suit them. One of these days I hope this will change.'

She looked at him curiously. Was this a bitter younger son talking, one who would like to see his brother brought down in some way? 'You sound dangerously subversive, Colonel.'

'Richard would agree with you on that,' he said lightly. 'But now, tell me what you have learned about Polly from the gossipmongers.'

Ursula gathered her thoughts. 'Well, I think I told you earlier that I had a chat with Mrs Comfort yesterday?'

He settled again on the ground and looked interested. 'You mentioned that Polly had said not to expect her back when she set off that last day and that Nanny Comfort thought that meant she was going to meet a young man and would not be back until much later.'

Ursula nodded. 'I think she was really shocked when Polly appeared to have run off. According to her, Polly had no followers; she said she didn't receive mail or callers.'

The Colonel gave a snort of laughter. 'I'd like to see Mrs Parson's face if a young man called to pass the time with any of the Mountstanton female servants.'

'Are they not expected to have friendships, then?'

'Only if they are kept well outside Mountstanton. Of course what you might call "associations" are formed between various servants, despite it being forbidden. Sometimes they even get married. In my father's time, I remember a cottage being made available when two members of staff applied to him for permission to remain in our employ as husband and wife.' He looked at her. 'You seem shocked. Is servant life in America more free and easy?'

Ursula thought about Mr Seldon's smoothly run New York household and had to admit that she had no idea what the rules were there. 'But so much of American life is less formal than it seems here.'

'I can certainly accept that it would be very different in the Sierra Nevada mining fields,' he said with a laugh.

Ursula almost choked on her wine. 'You have no idea,' she said, laughing with him. 'But, rough and ready as life there was, a certain hierarchy existed. There's always someone top of the pile; what varies is what puts them there. However, back to Polly. Mrs Parsons did not seem to have such a high opinion of her as Mrs Comfort. She said she could be a disruptive influence and that the dress she wore out of uniform was, according to her, most unsuitable.'

'That's interesting.'

'Could what remains of her dress still exist, or has it been thrown away?'

He shrugged. 'It never occurred to me to ask. Do you think it important?'

'It might give some evidence as to Polly's view of herself.' Ursula looked down at her plain shirt and skirt and wondered for a moment what they were evidence of. 'As I went into the shop I heard a reference to "a hussy" but I did not catch the context.'

'You think it referred to Polly?'

She nodded. 'I'm sure of it; the conversation dried right up as soon as they saw me. But later, a rather unpleasant-looking man, Mr Snell, I think his name was, referred to the hussy remark. He claimed the speaker had been right. He talked of "that strumpet from the big house". There's something else. Mr Snell said he'd seen Polly in the woods. "Flaunting herself", he said. When asked who with, he wouldn't say, but hinted that it could cause trouble. I got the impression he loved making a mystery out of nothing very much. Miss Ranner, during our little chat in her house, said she knew Polly well; she'd taught her at the orphanage and thought she was very bright. She also said Polly was friendly with one of the footmen, John. Maybe that was who Mr Snell had seen her with.'

The Colonel was listening intently.

'Miss Ranner liked Polly very much,' Ursula added. 'The girl apparently visited her when she came down to the village. Miss Ranner called her a little piece of sunshine. And she thought it strange that Polly hadn't called to say goodbye before leaving. She did add, though, that Polly thought herself rather better than the other Mountstanton servants and Miss Ranner said there could have been some jealousy amongst them.'

There was silence.

'Do you really think,' Ursula said, 'that Polly's death was other than some sort of dreadful accident?' A cold shiver ran down her spine.

He looked up, his expression serious. 'What do *you* think?'

'I? I know nothing about the matter.'

'At this stage, I think you probably know rather more than anyone else.'

'But that does not mean that I know enough to give an opinion. This is not something that should be judged lightly or without knowing a great deal more about who Polly was walking out with.'

'You mean, who was the father of her child?'

Ursula nodded. 'There is one other thing,' she said reluctantly. 'What happened to the hatbox Polly was said to have with her?'

'Picked up by some passer-by?' suggested the Colonel. 'The very fact that she took it, though, suggests that she was not thinking of suicide.'

Ursula tried to shift her injured ankle into a more comfortable position and saw a horseman approaching them on a handsome pale gold palomino. 'Isn't that your brother?' she said in surprise, wondering why the Earl was not eating luncheon at Mountstanton.

The Colonel rose. 'Richard? I don't think so,' he said, his tone cold.

The horse came nearer and its rider raised a hand in greeting. 'Charles, I heard that you had returned, good to see you again. And, Miss Grandison, is it not?'

Of course, the newcomer was Mr Russell.

'You've met?' The Colonel sounded surprised.

'Helen was good enough to invite me to a dinner she gave for her sister and I had the pleasure of sitting next to Miss Grandison.'

Ursula smiled up at him. 'You'll forgive me for not rising, Mr Russell, I have hurt my ankle.'

'I am very sorry to hear that.' He swung himself down from his horse and held out his hand, first to her and then the Colonel, who seemed to hesitate a moment before taking it.

'I regret very much hearing the poor news of your mother's health, Max,' he said rather stiffly. 'How is she today?'

'No better, but little worse either, which is a cause for relief. You have been picnicking, I see.'

'Have you had lunch? There is plenty left over and we should be delighted to have you join us,' said Ursula in a spirit of mischief. It was patently obvious that the Colonel was not happy with the encounter but she was delighted to meet Mr Russell again. She could not forget either what a stimulating conversationalist he had been or how he had managed to smooth over the unfortunate disappearance of Belle into the shrubbery with William Warburton.

'I should warn you we have finished the wine,' the Colonel said, his voice slightly less hostile.

'Many thanks, but I need to return home. However, I hope I may have the pleasure of more conversation in the near future with you, Miss Grandison. I am seriously thinking of travelling to America after, well, when I no longer have ties here. I think it is somewhere I can make something of myself.'

'I should be delighted, Mr Russell. I believe it has much to offer.'

He mounted his horse again and sat looking down at the two of them. 'Miss Grandison, I am your servant. Charles, I understand you have resigned your commission. I wish you luck with whatever lies before you.' He raised his whip in farewell then trotted away.

Ursula looked at the Colonel in an enquiring manner.

His face worked in an odd way then he shrugged his shoulders. 'Is there anything else in the basket? I'd hate to offend Chef.'

Ursula inspected the basket. 'Fruitcake,' she said, unwrapping a greaseproof paper packet. 'What a pity there isn't coffee to go with it.'

He suddenly grinned. 'There speaks the American. An English girl would have expressed a desire for tea.'

'After luncheon, surely not?'

'Maybe you are right. But in South Africa I found I longed more often for a billy can of tea than coffee.'

'In the Sierra Nevada there was always a pot of coffee on the stove. Tea was unknown.' Ursula handed him a slice of cake.

'No doubt you Americans gave it up after the Boston Tea Party.'

Ursula laughed as she watched the retreating figure of Max Russell. She wondered why the Colonel should show such tightly controlled animosity towards someone his brother and sister-in-law appeared to treat as a friend.

Chapter Thirteen

The picnic was packed up in near silence. Max Russell seemed to have left a strained atmosphere.

The Colonel called Honey to heel and announced he would give her a quick walk, 'So long as you feel happy to be left on your own for a little, Miss Grandison?'

Ursula assured him she would very much like to sit quietly and contemplate the scenery. 'It is very beautiful here, Colonel,' she said, leaning against a wheel of the trap. 'I think I could look at this scene forever. Does any of this land belong to your brother?'

'All of it,' he said curtly.

'All of it?'

'As far as you can see – on every side.'

'How much land does he own?'

'Ten thousand acres here, another five thousand in the north of England, one thousand in Scotland.' He sounded stilted, as though these figures were embarrassing, then clicked his fingers at Honey and disappeared across the top of the meadows.

Ursula sat in awed contemplation of the fields and hills that rolled away from her and tried to imagine a total of sixteen thousand acres of Britain. This was such a small country compared with the seemingly unending expanses of America; to think of one family, one man, owning such a large portion of it was extraordinary. Then she wondered how much income the land represented.

'Rents are down, I know that,' Mr Seldon had said before she left with Belle. 'Large estates require large sums to be spent in maintenance. Helen complains of the burden death duties have imposed on them. However, I don't think that's the answer. Helen would not allow her dowry to be spent propping up failing farms.'

Ursula thought over what she had seen of the relationship between Helen and her husband, the Earl of Mountstanton. It hardly seemed a marriage made in heaven. An image flashed into her mind of the drunken Earl being supported by Mr Warburton and the handsome young footman along the corridor from the billiard room. To Ursula's eyes, Richard Stanhope seemed a cold and unsympathetic man. She remembered the passionate girl she had shared her schooling with. Had one unfortunate liaison made her settle for status rather than romance?

She could not help remembering Jack Dyke, the man both she and Helen had fallen in love with. She had been work-ing in Chauncey Seldon's office, earning her keep. Helen was preparing her society debut and moaning that she was not on either Mrs Astor's or Mrs Vanderbilt's list. 'I won't meet the right people if I'm not invited to their parties!' But Helen was welcomed everywhere else. Where she met Jack Dyke, Ursula had no idea. She herself had met him when he came into the office selling typewriters. He was funny, charming, tall and handsome. And an excellent salesman. He'd won a contract from the Seldon company for ten typewriters and taken her out to lunch to celebrate. Later, he'd told Ursula the idea to approach the company had come from Helen.

Jack invited Ursula not only to lunch but to the theatre, dinner, Coney Island. He seemed to be flush with cash and swore he was going places. Then the typewriter company went bust, the Seldon company lost money and Jack didn't dare show his face there again. 'California,' he said. 'That's the place for a man like me. I'll be running my own show in no time. Come with me, darling girl. We'll get married and have a won-derful life.'

So she'd run away with him. How was she to know Jack had been dating Helen as well? And when she did find out, she was ashamed to admit that she felt a sense of triumph that it was she who had captured his heart.

Down the meadow Ursula saw the Colonel throwing a stick for Honey to retrieve. Charles Stanhope was direct in his manner and stood no nonsense. Certainly not a romantic figure. He had, though, a warmth about him; look at the way he had taken care of her. No, he was not cold like his brother. To Ursula's American eyes, the difference in status between the two brothers was extraordinary. Did the younger man envy the Earl his position? Marriage to Belle would bring him money but that did not seem important to him, any more than did the pomp and position that his brother and mother took for granted. Nor did he appear close to his sister-in-law. Ursula had not seen them exchange more than the odd word.

In the Sierra Nevada she had suffered serious bruising and several cracked ribs, but nothing that had hampered her movements the way this sprained ankle did.

Soon after they'd arrived in San Francisco, Jack declared all his savings had been exhausted. It had taken less time for Ursula to lose her illusions about the man she had so hastily married in front of a drunken Bronx cleric. They'd travelled to St Louis by rail, then joined a covered wagon train. During the long, difficult journey over the Rockies and the Sierra Nevada, Ursula came to realise she had married a drinker and a gambler, and a man who found his greatest enjoyment in arguing, both with words and his fists. They'd been expelled from one wagon train and had to wait at a trading post for another, when Jack's charm had rescued them. For the remainder of the journey he had tried, with some success, to curb his worst instincts. In San Francisco he seemed to make no attempt to find employment, spending most of his time in various bars. Then he declared a drinking buddy had made him a partner in a silver mine claim that would make their fortune. Ursula hoped that, away from the temptations of a large city, he would once again be the charming man she had fallen in love with. It was not to be.

Ursula brought her mind back to Helen. How would she have dealt with Jack? Would her father have cut her off if she had married him? Maybe Jack realised that was how it would have been. But he knew that Ursula had no money; he must have loved her.

Was it after losing Jack that Helen had learned to control her passions? She seemed to show very little emotion these days. She was as cool with her husband as with her brother-in-law. The only people Ursula had seen her show genuine warmth towards had been Max Russell and William Warburton. Ursula realised Mr Russell had much of Jack's charm: less mercurial, perhaps. He was certainly more sophisticated and he had not shown any particular love for alcohol at the dinner table.

Ursula shivered. Dark clouds now obscured the sun and a chill wind was blowing up across the meadow.

The Colonel strode up the hill with the dog. 'It's going to rain, we should be going,' he said and started to harness the horse to the trap.

Ursula hauled herself to her feet. Putting any weight on her foot was still extremely painful; she wondered how long it was going to take to heal; she hated not being able to move easily.

Buckling the last of the straps, the Colonel checked that all was secure. He stowed away the basket Ursula had repacked, then helped her up on to the front seat.

'With luck we'll get back before the worst of the weather.'

'It was such a lovely day and the sun seemed so set this morning.'

'That's the English climate for you; we can get four seasons in a day.' The Colonel handed up Honey and Ursula settled her on the seat between them.

On the way back the Colonel concentrated on his driving. The easy relationship that had developed between them seemed to have vanished.

A fine drizzle started as they reached Hinton Parva. The Colonel slowed their speed. Then he gave an exclamation and brought the horse to a halt.

Outside the village store a girl was trying to pull away from a man who held her by the wrist. Ursula recognised Mr Snell, the unpleasant fellow she had seen earlier inside the shop. The girl looked to be in her middle twenties, with a plain face and brown hair dragged back beneath a simple bonnet. Her neat figure was dressed in an ill-fitting grey skirt and coat. She looked very distressed. No one else was in the street; any villagers had disappeared inside to escape the rain.

The Colonel thrust the reins into Ursula's hands and jumped down.

'Maggie, good to see you again. Do you need a lift up to the house?' He looked at the man. 'Mr Snell, do you have some business with Miss Hodgkiss?'

The man dropped the girl's hand. 'So the Honourable Charles Stanhope is returned from the wars. A fine mess you've found at home.'

'Maggie, where is your luggage?'

She dipped a little curtsey. 'I've left it with Mr Partridge, sir. I was going to walk back through the wood.'

'Run and ask him to bring it here.'

She disappeared into the shop.

The Colonel turned back to Mr Snell. 'I would ask you not to accost Mountstanton staff, sir. Please ensure there is no repetition of what I have seen this afternoon.'

The man flushed a deep crimson. 'Your family lords it over everyone but you have no right to speak to me like that. I will consort with whom I choose.'

'It is unbecoming of someone with pretensions to being a gentleman to press his attentions on unwilling females.'

'Ho! What makes you think all the so-called gentlemen at Mountstanton behave themselves?' Mr Snell's tone was full of innuendo and an abhorrent slyness.

The Colonel looked steadily at him for a long minute, then turned away as the storekeeper came out carrying a small, battered travelling case and tucked it in beside the picnic basket on the trap.

The Colonel thanked the man, helped Maggie up onto the seat beside Ursula, then climbed up and took back the reins. He gave a small salute to the storekeeper and drove off down the street.

'Miss Grandison, may I introduce Maggie Hodgkiss, a member of the Mountstanton staff. Maggie, Miss Grandison has arrived from America with the Countess's sister, Miss Seldon.'

Ursula smiled at the girl, but she seemed too distressed to take in the introduction.

'How is your mother, Maggie?' continued the Colonel. 'I hope, since you have returned to us, that she is better.'

The girl held herself very straight. 'Thank you, sir, she is much recovered.' Then she gave a small gulp and said in a completely different tone, 'Oh, sir, is it true what Mr Snell told me about Polly? Is she truly dead?'

'I am afraid that, yes, it is true.'

She gave a cry. 'How did it happen, sir?'

'What exactly did Mr Snell say to you, Maggie?'

The girl clutched her hands together. 'He . . .' she gave another gulp. 'He said I was not to expect to find my friend, Polly, at Mountstanton because she had suffered a . . . a grievous outrage . . . and was dead.' She ended on a sharp cry and brought her hands up to her mouth. 'What did he mean, sir? How did Polly die?'

The Colonel glanced at Ursula.

She took one of the girl's hands in hers. 'I'm so sorry, Maggie. She seems to have fallen down that steep hill from the wood into the river. I . . . well, I found her.'

Two astonished brown eyes looked into Ursula's. '*You*, miss?'

Ursula nodded. 'It is very sad. I think, though, to call it "a grievous outrage" is a little strange.'

'Do you know Mr Snell well, Maggie?' asked the Colonel.

She shook her head violently. 'Polly and I were with Miss Ranner one afternoon and he called, so she introduced us.' She gave a slight shudder. 'As Polly and I walked back to the house, we both said that he was a queer fellow all right.' Her hand clutched at Ursula's and she swallowed hard. 'Mr Snell was there when I arrived on the Salisbury coach. He grabbed me after I'd asked Mr Partridge if he'd look after my case and said what I told you. He came straight out with it. I was that shocked I didn't realise at first he had hold of my wrist. I mean, Polly dead! I can't hardly believe it.'

The rain was now falling in earnest.

'Get the rug out of the picnic case, Miss Grandison; it can shelter you and Maggie,' the Colonel ordered.

Ursula reached for the basket. She pulled the rug over both her and Maggie's heads. 'I'm sorry, Colonel, it's not large enough to include you.'

He gave her a quick grin. 'My men would have thought me unworthy of respect if I succumbed to being wrapped up against a light shower of rain.' He flicked the reins to encourage greater speed from the horse. 'I'm not going to suggest we shelter under the trees, this is going to get much worse and we're not far from home now.'

Despite the rug, Ursula began to feel the rain seeping through her clothes. She smiled at the servant girl. 'I hope you're not feeling too cold, Maggie?'

The maid gave her a nervous smile. 'It's much better than walking through the woods, miss, and it's very kind of you and Colonel Charles to give me a lift.'

'Tell me, Maggie,' said the Colonel, 'Who was Polly's young man?'

The brown eyes opened wide. 'What do you mean, sir?'

'Come on, Maggie,' he said gently. 'You're not going to tell me a girl as attractive as Polly didn't have a young man to tell her how beautiful she was? Or that she didn't confide in you her feelings for him.'

Another nervous smile from Maggie. 'Well, Colonel Charles, you never knew with Polly. One moment she'd be saying John had sworn he loved her and the next that there was someone else but she couldn't tell me his name. Loves a bit of a mystery, does Polly. I mean . . . she did. Oh, sir, I can't believe she'll not be there when we get back.'

'Did she not give you any idea who the mystery man might be? Drop you a hint, get you guessing at all?'

'Is it important, sir?'

He glanced at her. 'It could be, Maggie. It could be very important.'

She closed her eyes for a moment, as though that would help her to remember. 'Before I left she was very mysterious, more than ever I knew her.' There was a brief hesitation. 'Polly did say, though, that I'd be fair amazed when I heard what she had to tell – and that I could find myself curtseying to her. Only, she said it in such a way, I knew it was a joke. I mean, we used to say every now and then that a prince might appear and carry us off and that we'd live in splendour, like what you do at Mountstanton, sir, if you don't mind my saying it. We didn't mean anything by it, not really.'

He gave her a reassuring smile. 'Why shouldn't you dream, Maggie? Life's hard enough; without our dreams we'd find it insupportable.'

Did the Colonel have them? Ursula wondered. He'd left the army, what was he intending to do now? Was it anything connected with Mountstanton? Is that why he was so concerned about its staff? Or was it that he considered them part of his family and felt a duty towards them?

The horse increased its speed as the shelter of the stables drew near.

On arrival in the yard, a groom dashed out to hold the horse. The Colonel jumped down and helped Maggie descend.

'Thank you, sir,' she said and reached for her case. But he'd already got hold of it. 'I can take it now, sir, thank you,' she gasped as he swung it down.

The Colonel, though, instructed a stable lad to take the case up to the women's corridor. Then he retrieved the crutches and helped Ursula and the dog down. Maggie ran into the house as a footman came out with an umbrella. The Colonel took it and held it over Ursula's head. 'I hope you aren't too wet, he said as she limped towards the house.

Ursula laughed. 'I should tell you about the number of times I was soaked to the skin in the Sierra Nevada. No one held an umbrella for me then.'

'I look forward to hearing your Californian exploits.'

It seemed that the rapport established between them had returned. Then Ursula realised how much it had come to mean and told herself to be careful.

The Colonel left her at the back door and returned to the stables, no doubt to see that the horse was properly looked after.

Passing the kitchen area, Ursula looked in and complimented the Chef on the excellent picnic. When she reached her room, she found Sarah had brought up a big jug of hot water and had lit her fire.

'Colonel Stanhope requested it, miss,' she said, dipping a little curtsey. 'He said you and Maggie were wet through.

Removing the damp clothes and washing herself down with the hot water was instantly reviving. Ursula wrapped herself in the big towel Sarah had draped by the fire, now crackling nicely and bringing welcome warmth, then sat to dry her hair. Finally dressed in a muslin gown and with her hair arranged into what she hoped was an elegant chignon, Ursula realised it was time for tea. The family would be gathering in the drawing room. In the nursery, Mrs Comfort would be having her afternoon refreshments. Perhaps Mrs

Parsons, the housekeeper, would also take the opportunity of a break from her duties and this might be the time to engage her in conversation.

Ursula made her slow, careful way downstairs.

In the hall the duty footman assured her the housekeeper was likely to welcome a visit at this time and gave directions for her office. Ursula passed through the green baize door into the servants' area and eventually found a door with 'Housekeeper' painted on it. The upper half was glass but Mrs Parson's privacy was guarded by a curtain hanging on the inside.

Just as Ursula was about to knock, she heard someone sobbing and turned to leave. A small gap in the curtain showed Mrs Parsons with an arm round a bitterly crying Maggie Hodgkiss.

Ursula made her way to the drawing room. Inside were the Earl and the Countess, the Dowager Countess and the Colonel. No Harry, no Belle, and no Mr Warburton. Tea had been served.

The Colonel was relating how he had found Maggie Hodgkiss in the uncomfortable company of Mr Snell.

'Quite apart from upsetting Maggie, the man seems to be making vague accusations about Polly's liaisons,' he was saying as Ursula entered.

'Liaisons?' repeated the Dowager Countess. 'Really, Charles, I wish you would leave your coarse army language behind when you are at home.'

There was a sudden rush of red and white fur as Honey ran towards Ursula and sat hopefully before her.

'Ah, Miss Grandison,' said the Dowager graciously. 'I see you have formed a warm friendship with my dear Honey. It is most kind of you to exercise her.'

Unseen by his mother, the Colonel gave Ursula a wink and said smoothly, 'Since Miss Grandison's unfortunate accident, I, too, have been responsible for exercising your animal, Mama.' He came forward and helped Ursula to sit in a comfortable chair, placing the crutches beside her.

This attention was met with tightened mouth and a look of disapproval from the Dowager.

Helen sat by the fireplace. She was looking particularly lovely in a rose chiffon dress trimmed with heavy lace. Her blonde hair was piled elaborately on her head, an ivory comb inserted on one side. She had some delicate embroidery in her hand and stitched with the air of someone who had mentally retired to some other place.

As soon as Ursula was settled, the little spaniel looked ready to jump up on her lap, but the Dowager said, 'Honey,' in a sharp voice and the dog retreated to the shadow of her mistress's black silk skirt.

'China or Indian tea, Miss Grandison?' asked the Colonel.

'No need to do that, Charles, the footman will be back soon,' instructed the Dowager.

'I am well able to pour a cup of tea, Mama,' said the Colonel in a pleasant tone and raised a questioning eyebrow at Ursula.

'China, please, Colonel Stanhope.'

A moment later she was supplied with the fragrant tea and a cucumber sandwich. 'I see ready money was available,' she murmured to the Colonel.

He grinned delightedly. 'A devotee of Mr Wilde!' he said, returning to his chair, situated some distance from both his mother and his sister-in-law.

The Dowager turned impatiently to her elder son. 'So, Richard, who is this Snell fellow? Do I know him?'

The Earl was standing by the window, surveying the garden. To Ursula he looked even more bored than usual.

'Snell, Mama? He's been here a few years. Moved into that little cottage at the end of Hinton Parva, the one that stands on its own.'

'It matters not to me which cottage he inhabits, I want to know what sort of man dares make such personal remarks about us.'

'Hugh Snell moved to Mountstanton when he retired from his position as secretary to the Dean of Wells, Mama,' said the Colonel as his brother failed to provide any further information. 'I believe he was persuaded to retire early.' His tone was matter-of-fact.

The Dowager pounced. 'You mean there is something unsatisfactory about the man? He committed some malfeasance?'

'I mean the Dean finally found his presence insupportable.'

'Do you think Snell will insist on giving evidence at the inquest?' the Earl suddenly asked.

A footman entered bearing a tray of fresh tea.

'Evidence?' Helen looked up, her delicate eyebrows curved in surprise. 'At the inquest? Surely Snell is just a gossipmonger, he can't have seen anything, no matter what he says. Richard,' she added, as though some memory had just come back to her, 'Isn't he the man who made such a fuss about some repairwork he felt necessary on his cottage? I remember him accosting you in Hinton Parva in a most unpleasant way. Wouldn't accept that the work could only be done at his expense.'

There was an awkward silence for a moment as the tray was placed on a table, then the Dowager said, 'Thank you, James, we can serve ourselves.'

'Yes, my lady.' The footman exited smoothly from the room.

'Really, Helen,' said the Dowager, 'How could you be so indiscreet?'

Helen gave a little shrug. 'Don't you claim that the servants always know everything? Why do you try to hide things from them?'

Ursula wondered how difficult Helen found it to have her mother-in-law behaving as though she still ruled Mountstanton. 'Has an inquest been arranged?' She asked.

The Earl seemed to come to life. 'That ba—,' he broke off. 'Sorry, Mama. That bumped-up strutting turkey cock, Squire – as he insists on being addressed – Adenbrook, how Papa allowed him to be appointed Chairman of the Magistrates I will never know; anyway, he has arm-locked the coroner into announcing that a public inquest will be held the day after tomorrow.' Veins stood out on his forehead and a tic flickered in his left eyelid. 'Just when I thought that we'd sorted the whole matter out.'

'Perhaps, Richard,' said the Colonel quietly, 'if you hadn't insisted on taking the hunt over Adenbrook's land after his protest, the man would be more amenable.'

A silence fell in the room, broken only by the crackle of the fire. Helen added a new thread to her needle; the Colonel poured himself another cup of tea. The Dowager took a deep breath and said, 'Richard, I approve of your sentiments but there is no point in getting agitated about the matter. The law has to take its course.'

'Law be . . .' He walked across the room, then returned and took control of himself. For the first time he acknowledged

Ursula's presence. 'I am afraid, Miss Grandison, that not only will you be required to give evidence regarding the finding of the body, but a policeman will call tomorrow to take a statement. I told that damn coroner it was inappropriate that you, Mrs Comfort and Mrs Parsons should be expected to attend Hinton Parva police station, which is what Adenbrook insisted would be correct. How the man survives as a magistrate I cannot conceive.'

Ursula noted that he had neglected to mention Polly by name. To refer to your dead nursemaid merely as 'the body' seemed to her callous in the extreme.

'Thank you,' she said, feeling he expected her to be grateful. On behalf of the two older women, she was grateful. For herself, she would have found it interesting to visit the local constable to have her statement taken.

She looked across at the Colonel, half expecting him to grin at her in a way that signalled he understood her reaction. Instead, she found his gaze fastened on his sister-in-law as she drew her needle through the fine linen, anchoring drawn thread-work into place with something of the aura of a fairy princess.

Ursula felt shock as she recognised a yearning in his expression. After an unexpectedly difficult struggle, she managed to put her emotions aside. Then found that a piece of the puzzle slid into place with the smoothness of expertly fashioned machinery.

Chapter Fourteen

In the gloomy dining room that evening Belle shone.

Ursula watched as her charge chattered gaily, entertaining the entire table. Was she, against all protocol, allowed to do so because only Belle was uninvolved with the nursemaid's death and the imminent inquest? Or because there were no outside guests that night?

'You were able to entertain yourself this afternoon?' asked Helen as Belle finished describing an amusing incident involving a ride in New York's Central Park, a runaway bicycle and a dashing young man.

'William took me round the family portraits. It was so interesting.'

Ursula noticed for the first time that she was wearing one of her best dresses, a pale blue silk from Paris that was supposed to have been reserved for her London debut.

'There are some very fine portraits there, Miss Seldon,' said the Dowager. 'Was there one that particularly caught your attention?'

'Oh,' said Belle roguishly, 'I liked best the ones of the various Earls.' She turned to Richard. 'Isn't it amazing how you all look the same?'

'Do we?' he drawled. 'I have never noticed it.'

'Oh, yes, it is very marked. And I went and had a good look at Harry after my tour and it is quite clear that he is a Mountstanton.'

It was as though the oxygen had suddenly been sucked from the room.

'It's the nose,' said the Dowager after a moment. 'How very perceptive of you, Miss Seldon. There is a very definite Mountstanton nose.'

Belle looked across the table at the Colonel. 'You don't have the nose though, Charles, do you?'

He smiled gently at her. 'I take after my Mama,' he said, raising his glass to the Dowager.

'But you have the chin,' his mother said with what, for her, was warmth.

'Show me your profile, Charles,' Belle demanded. 'And you, Richard.'

'Belle, this is not good manners,' said Helen.

But the brothers complied. Ursula followed Belle in comparing their silhouettes.

It was true, the Earl's nose was slightly hooked where the Colonel's was straight. But they both had the same square, slightly pugnacious jaw.

The Colonel held up his left hand. 'Here's another Mountstanton feature,' he said and wiggled his little finger. Ursula could see that it was slightly crooked. 'Did you notice that Harry has inherited this as well?'

'I suppose your features are all part of belonging to an ancient dynasty,' Belle said. 'We don't have that in America, do we, Ursula?'

'The Indians do. They belong to tribes who guard their inheritance jealously.'

'Oh, Indians,' Belle said carelessly. 'I cannot count them.'

'All your nation needs is time, Miss Seldon,' said the Colonel. 'You must remember we have had hundreds of years of careful breeding.' He shot a look at his brother that was unreadable.

'I trust you appreciated the beauty of the Countesses,' the Earl said to Belle. He raised his glass to his wife at the bottom of the table. 'There is a particularly lovely one of Helen by Sargent, done just after we were married.'

It was almost the longest speech Ursula had heard him make, and certainly the first compliment to Helen.

Ursula turned to Mr Warburton. 'Is there a particular feature that runs in your family?' she asked.

He gave her a wide smile. 'Big ears.' He demonstrated that his were indeed large and slightly stuck out. Somehow they did not detract from his looks. 'My eldest brother, the heir, managed to avoid them though.'

'All this talk of personal appearance is exceedingly bad form, particularly at the dinner table,' said the Dowager repressively. She turned to the Earl. 'Have I told you that the son of one of our oldest friends has been appointed Ambassador to Peru?'

The conversation was successfully turned.

At the other end of the table, Helen asked the Colonel for details of the political situation in South Africa and Ursula pressed Mr Warburton for details of his home.

She received the impression of an open and fun-loving family. How different from this cold and unemotional house. 'Do you miss your brothers and sisters very much?' she asked impulsively.

He flashed a glance up at Belle, left marooned by talk of people she knew nothing about, then dropped his gaze as she beamed a warm smile at him. 'They are very kind to me, here,' he muttered.

Ursula had caught the exchange of glances. She felt deep unease.

Helen now brought the secretary into her conversation with the Colonel.

While duck plates were cleared and roast beef was brought in, Ursula studied Belle across the table.

Quite apart from the Paris gown, the girl had something about her that evening. It was almost as though she had drunk too much wine. Though she sat quietly while the Earl listened to his mother's talk of neighbours, longing looks from beneath demurely lowered eyelashes were sent down the table towards William. How long before Helen noticed?

The meal seemed interminable. Charlotte Russe followed the beef. Ursula forced herself to make conversation with the Dowager and achieved a minor triumph by discovering that they shared a love of music.

'It has been a great sorrow to me that I can no longer play the piano,' the Dowager told her, displaying hands twisted by arthritis. 'Do you play, Miss Grandison?'

Ursula confessed that she had been delighted to be able to practise that morning on Helen's superb piano.

The Dowager's eyes lightened. 'Ah, yes, the Steinbeck. It arrived with Helen and I envied her that instrument.' The admission following on the revelation of her physical disability somehow made the Dowager more human.

After anchovy fritters, Helen took the ladies to the drawing room but the men did not linger long over their port. Soon after they rejoined the party, the Dowager asked her daughter-in-law if she would play to them. 'It is a very long time since I have heard you, my dear.'

'Please do,' Ursula pressed. 'I remember so well your recitals in Paris.'

Helen did not look pleased. 'I am out of practise.'

'In South Africa, out on the veldt under the stars, I remembered your playing Chopin and hoped the fighting would soon be over so I could hear it again,' said the Colonel quietly.

'You have to excuse me,' said the Earl. 'I need to check on details for the inquest.'

Helen opened up the piano, sat down, gazed at the keys for a few moments then began playing Chopin études.

Ursula had a clear view of Belle sitting in a chair not too far from Mr Warburton. Her hand hung down over the arm, as though she wished him to take it. The secretary's gaze was firmly fixed on the pianist and he held his coffee cup in both hands.

Ursula had heard Helen play better and quite soon the piano was closed again.

Ursula picked up her crutches and excused herself. The Colonel held open the door for her. 'Thank you for your company today,' he said. For an instant a rapport flashed between them.

Upstairs Ursula wondered whether she should write another letter to Mr Seldon. Not only, though, did she lack the energy, there was too much that confused her. Something had been going on over the dinner table beyond the obvious; what, exactly, had it been?

Ursula blew out her candle and tried to sleep, aware that part of her difficulties lay with emotions within herself that she did not wish to acknowledge.

★ ★ ★

The breakfast room next morning was empty. 'They're all riding,' the maid told her. 'His lordship and the Colonel went out early and her ladyship, Miss Seldon and Mr Warburton left half an hour ago.'

Ursula looked out of the window. It was a fine morning at the moment but clouds were gathering. Servants were everywhere performing cleaning duties, but there was no sign of the housekeeper.

Exploring the back regions, Ursula came across a big, buxom maid carrying a large container of cleaning items and with a smear of soot along her forehead. She gave Ursula a happy grin.

'Was there something, miss? I'm Susan,' she added.

Ursula did not hesitate. 'Perhaps you can help, Susan. I'm just wondering what the system is with dirty washing. My underclothes have disappeared and ...'

'And you was wondering when they'd be back, I expects.'

Ursula nodded apologetically. Someone, probably Sarah, cleared the linen basket in her room daily but so far nothing had been returned. Did she need to explain that her supply of underwear was more limited than Helen or Belle's?

'Thing is, with Maggie away, laundry has had a bit of a pile up. Now she's back, though, should soon be sorted. If you want to ask if your stuff's ready, laundry's across the yard.'

At the rear of Mountstanton was a collection of outbuildings designed in keeping with the main house. The one that housed the laundry was indicated by the sheets, which could be seen through the windows, hanging in serried rows.

Ursula limped over and managed, with difficulty, to open the heavy door.

Immediately inside she was faced with rows of washing lines, hung almost to the floor with wet sheets and tablecloths. The air was heavy with the smell of boiling coppers and its humidity would challenge a Turkish bath. For a moment Ursula stood, fascinated by the number and variety of the hanging items. Many of the sheets were heavily trimmed with lace, unlike those on her bed.

Then she heard voices.

'Why didn't you keep her safe? She trusted you. What happened to her?'

'Now, Maggie, you know nothing about Polly.'

'I do! I do! We was best friends. She told me everything.'

There was a sudden silence.

"What did she tell you?'The voice was wary, suspicious.

'She told me that you was sweet on her. Then that something had happened. You're a bastard, John, a bastard.'

There was a sound that might have been Maggie hammering at the man's chest.

'Hey, easy, Maggie.'

Sounds of a brief struggle. Then sobs.

'Listen, Maggie. Polly wasn't the little angel you think her. She, well, she could be a right little tease.'

'I don't believe you!' More hammerings.

Ursula opened and closed the outside door with a bang and called out: 'Anyone here?'

Stock silence for a moment. Then the footman's voice. 'You'll get that tablecloth ready for Mr Benson, then, Maggie?'

'Right, John, it'll be done, be sure of that.' Maggie's voice started quavery but gained strength.

The footman, face blank, marched round the lines of hanging linen, gave Ursula a nod, and left.

'Miss Grandison! Can I help?' Maggie appeared, carefully skirting the clean washing lines, reddened hands smoothing down the huge apron that swamped her slight figure. Her eyes were red.

'I see you're back into your job,' Ursula said easily. 'I understand you have been much missed.'

Maggie waved hopelessly at the wet washing. 'Never seen a pile like it, miss,' she blurted out, her voice wobbling. 'Don't know what they've been doing last two weeks but it 'ain't been much washing.'

* * *

The interview with the police went smoothly but Ursula was driven almost mad by the slowness of the process. The constable took her statement with stolid competence, sorting through her account and repeating everything back to her as he slowly wrote it down.

After she had read the statement through and signed her name, inwardly sighing at the plodding quality of the language, the constable thanked her with solemn sincerity for her patience and help. Finally, gathering up all the paperwork, the policeman asked, 'Is there anything you wish to add, Miss Grandison?'

Ursula thought back to the snatched piece of conversation she had overheard in the laundry. Could it be classed as evidence?

'No, Constable, I think the statement covers my discovery of the body fully. Thank you for your assistance.'

As Ursula emerged from the library a peremptory voice said, 'Miss Grandison, it is time we got to know each other. Come and take coffee with me in my drawing room.'

'It would be a pleasure, your ladyship,' said Ursula, reaching down to pat Honey, frisking around her legs.

The Dowager Countess lived in a separate apartment in the west wing of the house. She was independent and yet able to join the family whenever she wished, which appeared to be most of the time. It seemed to Ursula a splendid arrangement for the Dowager and one that could be very difficult for Helen.

They travelled the long corridor that ran past Belle's room and the apartments belonging to the Earl and Countess. Finally the Dowager turned a corner and opened a door into her private quarters, which were as grand and spacious as the main house.

The drawing room was furnished in an elegant style. Grey brocade covered the Louis Seize chairs and settee. A set of porcelain birds lining the shelves of a display cabinet added colourful notes, as did crimson damask curtains that looked considerably newer than any Ursula had so far seen.

'This is my sanctuary,' the Dowager said. 'When the fifth Earl, Richard's father, died, these rooms were turned over for my exclusive use.'

'How very attractive you've made it,' said Ursula. There was a French window that led out to the garden. A large lawn was edged with herbaceous borders and, in the distance, was a stone pavilion.

The Dowager laid a hand on the sumptuous curtains and gave a satisfied smile. 'I wanted a break with the past.'

Had she indeed!

A bell pull was tugged and Ursula waved towards a chair that proved more comfortable than it looked.

'I was very sorry to hear of your injury,' the Dowager said, seating herself. 'Most unfortunate. Is it very painful still?'

Ursula stretched out the damaged ankle and tried not to grimace at the pain. 'It is making progress,' she said lightly.

'Exercise can expedite the healing, as I found when I suffered a similar injury.'

'Indeed, what sort of exercise, my lady?'

The Dowager rose, placed her weight on one foot and rocked it back and forth. She indicated that Ursula should imitate her.

Ursula swallowed hard as pain shot through her ankle. 'It does seem to help,' she said in some surprise after a few minutes. 'Thank you, my lady. I will persevere.'

A footman entered with a tray of coffee, served both ladies, then disappeared. Ursula sipped her coffee and wondered exactly what was coming.

'Now, Miss Grandison, I hope you have managed to settle into Mountstanton and that the tragedy you uncovered has not completely ruined your visit.'

Ursula put down her cup. 'The discovery of the body was a great shock. Since, though, I had never met the poor girl, I was spared the pain of loss.'

'I hope you will not find testifying at the inquest too stressful. Nothing like this has happened in Mountstanton before; you are probably aware that we are all finding it very upsetting.'

'Our English history lessons suggested the aristocracy frequently suffered scandals of various sorts,' Ursula could not resist saying.

'But not Mountstanton.'

'Ah, of course not.'

The Dowager smiled. 'I can understand that you find us unusual, Miss Grandison. America is such a new, raw and thrusting country, we must seem indolent beside many of your fellow countrymen. But we do not like bustle or money-grabbing ways. Of course, the upkeep of houses such as this one can be a heavy burden. The fifth Earl, my husband, fought a constant battle against dry rot, rising damp, roofs that leaked, tenants who couldn't pay their rent, and tax inspectors who insisted on far more than a pound of flesh.'

'Tax men are a universal enemy.'

'My husband's death was a great shock. To contract such a wasting disease at sixty is a tragedy, especially when the victim had always been so full of life. Anyone around here will tell you what a charismatic person he was.'

'I wish I could have known him.'

'His death has thrust great responsibilities onto Richard and Helen at a time when they should be enjoying their young family and a carefree social life.'

Was the Dowager hinting that the nursery should contain more than one child?

'And the death duties are a great burden.' Silence fell while Ursula tried to think of something to say that would lead the conversation into safer areas.

'I understand you were at school with my daughter-in-law in Paris, Miss Grandison?'

Ursula inclined her head. 'She was a very good friend to me.'

'Until I met Helen I had no notion that American girls could be educated at continental establishments.'

'Most of Europe seems to expect us to have no manners, live in log cabins and be hardly able to read,' Ursula commented mildly.

'That's a little harsh on us. We merely compare the centuries-old civilisation here with the pioneering spirit on your side of the Atlantic. We are not censorious; indeed we admire what I think is called your "get-up-and-go" spirit. And I find it most interesting that Americans can esteem our educational values. Tell me, was it mainly American girls who were enrolled at your Parisian establishment?'

'No, we were a mixture.'

'Indeed? And I suppose learning French and various social requirements were your main activities?'

Ursula smiled as she remembered the long school days that had started in the early morning and ended in the late afternoon, with more hours spent in the evening on preparation for the next day. 'It was not a finishing school, as I think you would understand the term, Countess. We underwent a rigorous academic programme. But we were also schooled in every aspect of the social scene. Plus the requirements of running a large establishment, handling staff, fulfilling social obligations, and so on. Everything an embryonic Duchess or Marchese might require.'

'So Helen fulfilled her destiny when she married my son?' The Dowager's tone was ironic.

Ursula decided she was enjoying this conversation. 'Helen has always been a romantic. Marriage for her meant union with a man she loved rather than social status.' That had to be true where Jack Dyke, the man she had accused Ursula of stealing, was concerned. Yet had not Helen longed to be on the prestigious Vanderbilt and Astor invitation lists?

'So it was merely chance that brought an English aristocrat within her orbit?'

Ursula put her coffee cup down again. 'I am afraid when Helen met your son, I was already on the other side of America. I do not know who or what brought them together.'

'It was unfortunate that Helen and Belle lost their mother. I should like to have met her. You must have known her?' The question was put with a certain negligence that set Ursula on her guard.

'Mrs Seldon was delightful.'

'I have not liked to ask Helen about her; it seems a subject she finds painful.'

'Losing a parent *is* painful.'

'Does Belle resemble her father or her mother?'

Ursula smiled. 'Both Belle and Helen look like their mother. Mrs Seldon was very attractive but not a classical beauty; so much of her charm was in her expression, the way she used her eyes, the musicality of her voice.' Ursula stopped abruptly as a vision of Clara Seldon rose before her.

'She sounds charming indeed. She died in a train crash, I understand?'

'Helen and I were completing our last term in Paris; it was a very sad homecoming.'

'It must have quite spoiled Helen's plans for her New York debut.'

Ursula strove to keep her hands steady in her lap.

'If you spent so much time with Helen and her family, Miss Grandison, you must have lost your own parents?'

Ursula wondered how much Helen had revealed of her old school friend's background.

'My mother died at my birth. My father was in business with Helen's father until he, too, died.' The firm had originally been known as Grandison and Seldon. 'The Seldons have all been very kind to me.'

The Dowager refilled their cups. 'So you had no hesitation in agreeing when it was suggested you accompanied Belle over here?' she said, handing Ursula hers.

'The opportunity to catch up with my old school friend, not to mention visiting one of the grandest houses in England, was irresistible.'

'I can imagine it must have been.' The Dowager was at her driest. She ran a finger round the edge of her saucer. 'I hope you feel able to report favourably to Mr Seldon?'

Ursula felt a sudden chill. Had Benson been reporting on her letters?

'He was very disappointed not to have been able to accept the Countess's invitation to visit alongside Belle, but the pressures of business were inescapable. I promised to let him know how Belle was settling down; he thought she was unlikely to prove an informative correspondent,' Ursula said smoothly and gave the Dowager a frank smile. 'I have told him how excited Belle has been at meeting her sister again and how much she is enjoying the social scene Helen has arranged for her.' She paused before adding, 'I felt I also had to inform him of my discovery, though I am sure Helen has done so also.'

'Of course.'

The Dowager put down her coffee cup. 'I shall watch Belle's London debut with great interest. No doubt she is hoping to capture an English husband and so be able to stay close to her sister?'

No mention of the plan to marry Belle off to her second son, Ursula noted. Nor the fact that, like Helen, she would be quite a catch, both in looks and dowry, .

Ursula shrugged. 'As to that, I think Belle is merely excited about attending dances and such events as the Ascot races and Henley.'

'You know about such matters, Miss Grandison?'

Ursula stared gravely at the Dowager. 'I may have spent some years roughing it, as you might call it, in California, but I have not forgotten my education, your ladyship.'

The Dowager returned her look with a steady one of her own. 'I do not think there is much you would forget, Miss Grandison. Some time I am sure we would all be most interested to hear of your Californian adventures.' After the smallest of pauses, the Dowager continued, 'I imagine Mr Seldon has plans for a generous settlement should Belle find someone over here she wishes to marry?'

Ursula drew in a sharp breath, shocked at this open curiosity. Then, quite suddenly, she understood the reason for this conversation. The Dowager Countess was as curious as Mr Seldon about what had happened to Helen's dowry.

The Earl entered. He seemed not to notice Ursula.

'Mama, it's as we feared. That damned rogue, Snell, has asked to give evidence at the inquest.'

Chapter Fifteen

After a night of troubled sleep, Matilda Parsons finally threw back her bedclothes and struggled up.

For a minute or two she sat on the edge of her mattress, looking at the legs that poked out of her white cotton nightgown. Every day the pain from the gnarled blue veins seemed to grow worse. She tried to remember when they were shapely and Walter had loved to slip his hand round one of her ankles.

'My, Tilly, they beat the fetlocks off all the horses in the stables.'

He'd not give them a second look now. So much of the position of head housekeeper depended on your legs. Inspecting the work of the maids; inspecting the condition of furniture, linen, carpets. So many windows to be washed, so many floors to be polished, so many surfaces to be dusted, pails to be placed under leaks in the roof whenever it rained.

If only there were money to be spent on replacement of worn-out upholstery, curtains, sheets and tablecloths – and so much else.

What had happened to the dowry the Countess was supposed to have brought with her from America?

Matilda hauled herself to her feet and drew back the thin curtains, handling the fraying material with care. The light outside was grey, a veil between the window and the outlines of trees. She could just make out the wood that covered the hill; the wood through which the path ran to Hinton Parva.

Matilda retreated to her bed, drew the covers up over her cold feet and lay fighting a desire to bury her head beneath the blankets and pretend she did not have to face the day. Yesterday she had had to make her statement to that policeman. The day before, the Earl and Countess had interviewed her. The same questions, the same answers. And last night she had tossed and turned knowing that she had not told them everything.

She felt so guilty. She should have said something at the time; done something. But instead she had hugged the knowledge to herself, feeling triumphant that she had been right about Polly Brown all along. It was only later that she began to feel that just knowing was not enough.

Where was Alice with her morning cup of tea?

Yesterday afternoon, after her statement had been taken, she had been summoned by the Dowager Countess. It was as though the last few years had rolled back and the Dowager was once again Mountstanton's chatelaine. Touching the small cameo brooch she always wore at the collar of her black bombazine dress, Matilda had fought frustration. Why could the Dowager not have retired to a house on the estate?

'Parsons.' The tone was sharp; the formidable figure sat sternly upright.

Matilda's eyes automatically checked that no speck of dust was evident on any surface, and that the fire was correctly laid in the grate.

'Parsons, I want to hear what you will say to the coroner tomorrow.'

Matilda drew a deep breath.

The Earl and Countess had asked if she knew of any liaison between Polly and another member of staff. The Countess had done the talking, her eyes intently focused on Matilda, her body tense. The Earl had stood by the window, his hands thrust into the pockets of his trousers, his manner wary. It had been he who had brought up the matter of *exactly* what she was to say at the inquest. Now it seemed she had to go through it all again.

'I am to tell the coroner that Polly was a girl of good character; that she was satisfactory in her conduct, and that I was not aware she was with child. Also, if asked, that when her condition became apparent, it would have been necessary to dismiss her, your ladyship, being as how we cannot tolerate such things here.'

The Dowager looked at her steadily. 'That and no more?'

'No, your ladyship.'

Fingers beat a restless rhythm on the chair's arms. 'How many years have you been at Mountstanton, Parsons?'

'Thirty-eight, your ladyship.'

Matilda had started as an under-maid at the age of fourteen. Her mother had been a maid here before her marriage to the local butcher.

'Work hard,' she'd said. 'And work at your letters and figures. You're a bright girl, you could become assistant housekeeper. Just mind your manners, do everything that's expected, and watch what goes on.'

And Matilda had. It had been the fourth Earl in those days: George, the present Earl's grandfather. What a tartar! They had all feared his temper. His Countess, though, had been the love-liest woman. Their son, Simon, had inherited all her charm – together with his father's autocratic ways. He too, though, had feared his father.

'Ah, yes, I remember,' said the Dowager. 'You were here when I arrived.'

All the staff, lined up in order of seniority, their uniforms clean, their expressions respectful, had gathered to welcome the new bride, all eager to know who it was their greatly loved Viscount Hinton – always known to them as Lord Simon – had been forced by his father to marry.

For Matilda had been told by Walter, the under-groom with the blond corkscrew curls and gentle hands who looked for every opportunity to spend time with her, that this was no love match.

'His lordship told 'im 'e'd gone too far this time,' Walter had said with awe. 'Servants was one thing, married women were acceptable, respectable misses was something else. 'E must get married, then per'aps 'e'd keep . . . well, be'ave 'imself,' Walter had finished hurriedly.

Tilly didn't ask how Walter knew this; he had an uncanny ability to overhear things that should have been private. The Earl failed perhaps to realise how sharp were his under-groom's ears when they rode out. And they all knew how Lord

Simon could be with the girls. There were a number on the Mountstanton staff who had fallen for his charms and found themselves packed off with a small pension. Now, apparently, he'd got involved with the daughter of the local auction house proprietor. She had, so word got out, been sent off to visit an aunt somewhere in the north, no doubt with a suitable sum of money in recompense.

As soon as the engagement was announced, the underground network of servant gossip had provided details of the girl who was to be their mistress. Lord Simon's mother had died two years earlier, so there would be no mother-in-law holding the household reins.

Bertie Fry, Lord Simon's valet, had filled them all in: 'Rich, her father is. A Viscount now, but made a fortune in India. Not trade, mind you. Respectable family but come into the title all unexpected. Regular train of deaths there was.' Bertie accompanied his master to various house parties so had had plenty of opportunity to observe the future Countess of Mountstanton.

Normally Mr Peabody, the butler then, would have told him to mind his language and his business but he was as keen as they all were to know every detail.

'Is she the only child?' he asked. Everyone wanted to know if the fortune had to be carved up between various offspring.

'There's a son and a beautiful sister. She's already been snapped up ...'

'Fry!' Mr Peabody said warningly.

'Been chosen in marriage she has, as has the son,' the valet had said with a mischievous look at the avidly listening maids.

'Is the Honourable Beatrice a beauty as well?' asked one.

He shook his head. 'Not a corker – but not bad looking. Pleasant and got a sort of, well, a sort of style, you know?'

On a fine day – and they all took that as a good omen – Lord Simon had helped out of the open landau a slim girl with an erect carriage and undistinguished looks. She had worn a green silk travelling costume in the latest fashion and on her brown hair a bonnet trimmed with roses. The only sign of nerves had been her tight grip on her new husband's arm.

Accompanied by Mrs Hastings, the housekeeper, and Mr Peabody, the bride had moved with her new husband down the long line of servants, greeting each one pleasantly.

Matilda had marvelled at her new mistress's ability to maintain her appearance of interest. But as she had bobbed and given her name, she noticed a glazed look in the pale blue eyes and it seemed to be with a feeling of relief that, after the last servant had been acknowledged, Beatrice Stanhope turned to her husband.

'I am very happy to meet you all,' she said, standing on the top step. 'Together we will ensure Mountstanton is as glorious now as in the past.'

Her father-in-law frowned at this suggestion the house might have deteriorated recently and Lord Simon quickly took his bride inside.

It had not taken long for the staff to realise the will of steel that existed beneath Lady Mountstanton's pleasant manner. And only her father-in-law managed to escape her organising ways.

'Mrs Hastings says she won't stand for it any longer,' Agatha, the assistant housekeeper, told Matilda a year later.

The cook had already walked. Two promising footmen had left for neighbouring estates and not been replaced.

'Her ladyship told Mr Peabody that they were not needed,' Agatha sighed. 'She said we was all lazy and it would do us good to work a little harder. A little! My heavens, Tilly, as if we didn't do enough polishing and sweeping and dusting as it is without having to run errands, and serve the tea and even dinner, which isn't right! Should be footmen. As for keeping all those danged chandeliers clean and deal with the candles, well, I don't know how we'll manage!'

Tilly said nothing but privately she reckoned that Mountstanton had never been so clean as under her ladyship; or so well organised.

If only they didn't have to put up with Enid Barnes, her ladyship's maid! The woman thought she was so superior, being as how she had been trained in a Duke's household. She was always running to her mistress with some tale of backsliding amongst the staff.

The last straw for Mrs Hastings had been the sheets.

'She told her ladyship it was time they was replaced,' said Agatha. 'One was that thin it tore as it was put on. Instead, her ladyship said they must all be turned side to middle. Mrs Hastings happened to say in the servants' hall that she thought this was a bit much just as Enid entered. So an hour later she's hauled over the coals by her ladyship for querying one of her orders.'

'Every sheet to be turned?' Matilda found it difficult to envisage sheets with a seam down the middle gracing the grand bedrooms.

'Course not, silly. Not the guests' All the servants' though *and* her ladyship says the family can very well suffer a slight discomfort.'

Matilda stood awestruck at this.

'And poor Mrs Carter has a pile of sheets as high as a house to deal with.'

Matilda had watched the battles that the new mistress fought and won. Her dowry was used for patching up some of the roof and then investing in the Home Farm rather than for redecorating Mountstanton's salons. The only time lavish food appeared was for entertaining and the Earl's temper deteriorated as he battled with his daughter-in-law over how many could be invited for his famed shooting weekends.

''E's the one insisted Lord Simon got married, and 'e chose 'is bride, so 'e can't complain, now can 'e?' Walter said to Matilda three years into the marriage. 'But 'e's on at Lord Simon to fill the nursery.' For there were no offspring yet.

The more the indoor staff grumbled though, the more Matilda decided she had to treat the constant surveillance and nit-picking as a challenge. The Viscountess began to notice her with the occasional approving nod.

The Viscount had a much easier relationship with his stable staff. 'Treats me like someone he can talk to,' Walter said to Matilda when she managed to snatch some minutes with him behind the carriage house one evening. 'Today he came as near 'e ever 'as to complaining about her ladyship.' Walter spread a horse blanket over the rough grass and drew Matilda down to sit beside him with her head on his shoulder. It had been a hard day, with the Viscountess even more demanding than usual, and she found the feel of his solid flesh beneath her cheek very comforting.

'Told me she'd said he wasn't to buy the 'orse he's set his heart on. 'E took me to see 'im last week. Bit flash it was; too long in the back and I didn't like the look of the 'ocks. Of course, 'e didn't take any notice, just thanked me and said 'e'd drop 'is price. Then today told me 'e wasn't buying it after all.'

'Because her ladyship had said "no"?'

'It was plain as any pikestaff. There's going to be trouble there, you mark my words.'

And sure enough, there was. Rumour was soon rife that the Viscount was being seen too often in the company of a highly connected and single young lady.

For a time it seemed that her ladyship was unaware of what was going on. The staff, though, knew that her husband's mood had changed. It was almost, Matilda thought, as though life had become beautifully simple for him.

Walter saw more of the situation than most since he often accompanied the Viscount out riding. 'I'm to say we've been somewhere quite different than what we 'as,' he told Matilda.

'Different? Why, where is it you go?'

'There's an old cottage in the east part of the estate. 'Is lordship has 'ad it cleaned and 'es put in a bit of furniture. They plays at 'ousekeeping there. Never seen 'is lordship so 'appy as after one o' those sessions.'

Matilda was horrified. 'What if her ladyship finds out?'

Walter's broad forehead creased and his brown eyes were very anxious. 'It's what I bin afraid of. That's why I go along with 'is stories of 'ow 'e's been checking estate matters or visiting town.'

Then, suddenly, it was all over. The young lady had married and gone away and the Mountstanton nursery was being brought back into service.

''E's different, Lord Simon is,' Walter told Matilda. ''E's like a man lost. Doesn't know what to do with 'imself.' He gathered her into his arms. 'If I lost you, I don't what I'd do. Tilly, we've got to get married, that's what. I reckon I can get 'is lordship to give us a cottage. Then you can make us an 'ome instead of working all the hours up at the 'ouse.'

They came together in a long kiss that was deeper and more passionate than any Matilda could remember.

There was no trouble about the cottage and Matilda gave up her ambitions to be head housekeeper without a pang. Indeed, such was the tension in the house, she could not wait to start organising her own home.

Marriage was everything Matilda had hoped for and the birth of little Alfred made her world complete. She rejoiced at the news of the birth of a Mountstanton heir, rejoiced again when the little one gained a brother, then mourned at the death of the fourth earl. But none of it really touched her.

Agatha would often come over for a cup of tea and envy Matilda her situation. 'We never see his lordship, he's always off somewhere. Her ladyship gets more sour and high handed by the day. I tell you, Tilly, she's that pernickety! I don't know how long I can stick it.'

When Alfred was four, tragedy struck. Within a week Matilda's darling boy was dead of diphtheria and her husband had been killed by a kick from a temperamental horse the fifth Earl had insisted on buying.

Two days after the second funeral, the Countess arrived at the cottage.

She sat in the small living room drinking tea. Her gaze swept the pristine room: the few items of furniture beautifully polished, a small cut-glass vase on the mantelpiece holding a tiny bunch of snowdrops. 'You will need to return to work,' she said after a brief expression of sympathy. 'The cottage will be required for the new under-groom.'

Matilda had sat, frozen.

'I can offer you the position of assistant housekeeper; Agatha wants to get married.' The Countess made it sound an extraordinary desire.

There seemed no other alternative. So Matilda returned to service at Mountstanton.

Something, though, had changed for her. She now understood about loss. She watched the battles between the Earl and the Countess and began to sympathise with her mistress's determination to keep what was hers. It enabled her to stomach the high handed ways and the zealous watching of expenditure.

Matilda's delight was to watch the Countess's two sons grow into young men. She welcomed the American bride, rejoiced at the long-awaited birth of Lord Harry, followed so soon after by the death of the fifth Earl from a debilitating illness. She knew what Walter would have said: 'Well, at least it means you'll be rid of 'er ladyship.' Except that she wasn't. Settled in the west wing, the Dowager came and went in the main house as she pleased. How the American Countess put up with it, Matilda could not imagine.

The discovery of Polly's body had been a terrible shock. When they thought she'd run off, Matilda's conscience over keeping what she'd seen secret had been stilled. Now, it seemed she couldn't stop thinking about it and wondering was it right to keep silent? But if she spoke out, there would be trouble, no doubt about that. Why could Polly not be allowed to rest in peace? The interview with the Earl and the Countess had been difficult. This one threatened to be worse. The Dowager had always seemed able to see into the darkest corner.

'Parsons, is there anything else you could feel tempted to tell the coroner?'

'No, my lady,' said Matilda quietly.

'I understand the Earl and the Countess asked if you knew of any liaison Polly was conducting.'

'Yes, my lady.'

'And you told them that as far as you knew, she was not involved with anyone at Mountstanton.'

'Yes, my lady.'

'And, of course, as head housekeeper you know of all involvements between staff, forbidden though they are?'

Not only of the staff, Matilda wanted to say.

'I keep myself informed, my lady.'

Rules could never be kept when blood spoke to blood.

There was a long silence. The Dowager's gaze remained focused on the housekeeper.

'I always thought, Parsons, that behind her demure exterior Polly Brown was an out-and-out minx.'

It was unusual language from the Dowager.

'Apparently, according to my daughter-in-law, she could do no wrong in the nursery.'

'Mrs Comfort was very satisfied with her conduct, my lady.'

'And I understand that is what she will tell the coroner.'

So the nanny had had a similar interview to herself.

'Now, Parsons, tell me what you know of this man Snell.'

'Mr Snell, my lady?'

The gimlet gaze hardened. 'Don't be stupid, Parsons. I understand that someone called Snell is claiming he saw something in the woods involving Polly.'

Matilda's heart lurched. 'Mr Snell is a gossip, my lady; nothing he likes better than making up tales. He can't be believed, whatever he says.'

'Not even when he announces he will act as a witness at Polly's inquest?'

Matilda's mouth almost dropped open in shock.

There was a glint of satisfaction in the Dowager's eyes. 'So, perhaps you have something more to say now, Parsons?'

Matilda gathered her wits together. 'There is nothing I can add, my lady, to what I have already told you, and his lordship and my lady.'

Another long pause. More rhythmic tapping on the arm of the chair. Finally the Dowager waved a hand at the housekeeper. 'Go, Parsons. You always were a fool.'

Matilda dipped her head and retired.

No sooner had she got back to her office than the butler appeared. It was twenty years now since Mr Benson had replaced Mr Peabody on his retirement.

'Will you allow me to ask, Tilly, how your interview with the Dowager went?'

Matilda sighed. 'When she finally dismissed me I almost scuttled out, Arthur.'

He gave her an understanding smile. 'May I suggest that we take a small glass of port to settle your nerves? Everyone will be changing for dinner and I have done everything necessary in the dining room.'

'Thank you, Arthur, that would be very pleasant.'

Clutching her glass, Matilda said, 'Do you believe that Snell fellow will really say something at the inquest, Arthur?'

The butler put his port down. 'I cannot think speaking up will be of any benefit to Mr Snell – and he has never been known to do anything that was *not* to his benefit.' His words were reassuring but to Matilda his eyes seemed worried.

'Does his lordship consider the verdict will be suicide?' she asked.

'Can it be anything else?'

Matilda drank down the rich, sweet liquid and felt a slow warmth begin to spread through her veins. Her glass was quickly refilled.

'An accident, surely.'

'Tilly, we have been through this. You know how sure-footed that girl was. And what reason would she have had to approach anywhere near that edge?'

Matilda sipped her port slowly and tried not to think of Polly's body spinning down to the river. 'But suicide! Oh, Arthur, I cannot say I liked Polly, she always had an air that said she thought she was better than you, but I did admire her spirit. I cannot believe she deliberately threw herself down into that river. Nothing's more terrible than suicide.'

She looked at her old friend, a colleague for so many years. His mouth was tight and an obstinate gleam lit his deep-set eyes.

'Now, Tilly, don't start looking for mysteries where there are none. That girl either fell or threw herself down into that river and nothing Mr Snell can say will make any difference.'

'But . . .'

'No, Tilly. Forget what you saw.'

'Suppose Mr Snell saw them too?'

'That is nothing to do with you.' Her hand lay on the table. He held it for a moment. 'Forget it, Tilly. Remember the family.'

She took her hand away and turned her head.

'Remember when her ladyship wanted to dismiss you and the Earl refused to let you go?'

How could she forget that battle? She had misunderstood an order and Mr Gladstone, the Prime Minister no less, had been given the wrong room. Mind you, he had had the best sheets, the ones with the Alençon lace edging.

'You will leave at the end of the month, Parsons,' the Countess had said.

The fifth Earl, though, had laughed when he heard what had happened. 'Mr Gladstone would not have minded wherever we put him. I am sure there was some very simple error and I will not see faithful Matilda Parsons turned off for it.'

Was it because he felt guilty over buying the horse that had killed Walter? Or was it because every now and then he had to assert himself with his wife? Or had he remembered a kiss he'd stolen one day in an empty corridor from a very young maid who had thrilled to him but fought to be set free?

Released, she had looked at him with frantic eyes. 'Oh, my lord,' she had said, stuffing her hands behind her. 'Please, don't.'

He'd laughed and gently pinched her cheek. 'You are very sweet but worry not, I don't seduce unwilling maids.'

A moment later he was gone and he'd never approached her again.

Whatever reason the Earl had had for persuading the Countess to retain her services, Matilda knew that from then on her mistress resented her presence. When the Earl died, it had been Lord Richard's American wife who had insisted on Matilda remaining in her position.

'You're right of course,' Matilda finally said to the butler. 'I can't bring trouble on the family. I am sure, though, that Polly met with an accident.'

Now, sitting in bed and waiting for her morning cup of tea, Matilda was not at all sure Polly's death *had* been accidental. She was certain, though, that it could not have been suicide. She might not have liked or trusted the girl, but to deny her a grave in consecrated ground would be a crime; as much of a crime as suicide itself. If it looked as though that was the verdict the coroner was going to bring, then she, Matilda Parsons, would have to speak.

Chapter Sixteen

Ursula feared she might break down when she had to recount her finding of Polly's body to the coroner.

At breakfast on the morning of the inquest, Belle sat next to her. 'Dear Ursula, are you feeling very nervous?'

Ursula produced a resolute smile. 'It will soon be over.'

'Shall I come too? So I can hold your hand?'

'Darling Belle, that is very sweet of you, but I shall be all right.'

'Promise?'

'Promise.'

Belle's concern filled Ursula with unexpected warmth. For a moment she felt some of the closeness that had existed between them on the voyage from New York.

Ursula smiled again, trying to hold on to this sense of rapport. 'Tell me, what are you going to do today?'

Belle's sulky look appeared. 'Nothing. Helen says she's busy, you'll be at the inquest, and William has disappeared.'

'Disappeared?'

'He's gone to see his parents, Helen says. He won't be back until next week. And he didn't even say goodbye to me!'

For a moment Ursula thought the girl would burst into tears. Then a maid entered and placed a fresh pot of coffee on the table.

'Her ladyship asks if you will spare her a few moments in her boudoir, Miss Grandison.'

'Of course, as soon as I have finished breakfast.'

Ursula took Belle's hand, only to have it snatched away. 'Belle, darling, I can see you are unhappy. Can't you tell me about it?'

Belle rose and walked rapidly around the room, pushing her hands through her hair.

'Ohhh,' she moaned. 'You don't know, you can't know.'

Ursula stumbled out of her chair, ignoring the pain in her ankle as she drew the girl into her arms. 'Belle, darling, don't. Nothing can be that bad. Talk to me, please.'

Belle pulled herself away. 'You can't help me, no one can.' She ran from the room, slamming the door.

Ursula remembered Helen at the same age and how impossible it was to talk any sense into her when she was emotional – and how trivial the reasons usually were for her temper. Once the inquest was over, she would find Belle and see what could be done to make her life at Mountstanton a little happier.

As she limped along the wide corridor to Helen's boudoir, the obvious decay in the fabric of the old house seemed more pronounced than ever. Entering the room, its charm and decorative order struck Ursula even more forcibly than it had the first time. She remembered the Dowager Countess's drawing room. How similar in some ways the two women were. Both strong minded, both determined to have things ordered the way they wanted. But the Dowager seemed dedicated to the Mountstanton name and standing in a way that her daughter-in-law was not.

Helen was sitting at her desk attending to piles of invitation cards and their envelopes.

'Ah, Ursula. I wanted to tell you that the under-groom will take you, Mrs Parsons and Mrs Comfort to the inquest in the trap. It will leave in half an hour.'

'You could have sent a message to tell me that,' Ursula said, anger suddenly rising as she thought of the long walk with her crutches from the breakfast room. Also, it looked as though rain threatened and surely Mountstanton's senior staff deserved the comfort of a closed carriage on the way to do their duty?

Helen put down her pen. She was dressed simply in cream *crêpe de Chine*, the high-collared, prettily tucked blouse and graceful skirt displaying her slim figure to perfection, a pearl-embroidered belt providing a touch of richness.

She looked coolly at Ursula. 'I thought you might need a word of advice about this morning. Do take a seat.'

Ursula remained leaning on her crutches. 'Now why should you think that?'

A slight flush stained Helen's smooth cheek. 'You are in a foreign country and it will surely be an upsetting occasion.'

'Oh, yes; it will be upsetting all right. Do I gather that it will be too upsetting for you to attend?'

'There is no need for you to take that tone with me. You cannot imagine that, in my position, I can be seen at such an event in our local public house.'

'But it's to consider the cause of death of your son's nurse-maid.'

The flush deepened and Helen dropped her gaze. 'No one is more upset at Polly's death than I am,' she said quietly. 'But nothing I can do now will bring her back.' She looked up again. 'No one will expect either myself or the Earl to be there. It's bad enough that Charles has to give evidence.'

'And, of course, myself.'

'The household cannot be kept altogether out of the pro-ceedings.'

Well, that made her status clear.

'Which is why I thought it best to speak to you beforehand. Richard and I have already talked with Mrs Parsons and Mrs Comfort.'

'So you can be sure they are not going to say anything det-rimental to Mountstanton? What do you think *I* can say? I'd only just arrived here when I found that poor girl's body. What, exactly, is it that you are afraid of, Helen?' Ursula was now so angry she was shaking.

'How dare you!' Helen flared back at her. 'As though there is any way *you* could demean *us*.'

'Then why are you so anxious to discuss my evidence?'

Helen took a deep breath. 'You have completely misunder-stood my intentions. I do not want to discuss your evidence; I only want to ensure that you will feel as comfortable as pos-sible with what is going to happen.'

'How many inquests have you attended, Helen?'

She flung up her hands. 'Oh, you never were willing to listen to other people. You'd better go and get ready to leave.'

'Willingly. But, before I do, what have you got planned for Belle today?'

'What has that to do with you?'

'Mr Seldon put me in charge of her. So far I have seen nothing to suggest that you have her best interests at heart. It is your fault she has formed that unsuitable attachment to Mr Warburton.'

'William has gone to visit his parents; he will not be here,' Helen said in a tight voice.

'So Belle understands. Was it you who told him to go? Did you forbid him to say goodbye to her?'

White patches appeared either side of Helen's mouth. 'How dare you speak to me like that. I care very much about Belle. There is plenty to amuse her at Mountstanton. There is her music to practise, she can go horseback riding, there are books in the library, countryside to walk in. Boredom displays a lack of character. These invitations,' she indicated the pile on her desk, 'are for her coming-out ball. William was to have addressed them but, because his mother is not well, I told him to go to her. Now I have to send them out.'

'If you really care about Belle, suggest she helps you so you can talk, discuss why she really wanted to visit you and make her debut here.' Ursula limped towards the door.

'Ursula,' Helen said in quite a different voice. 'Have *you* attended an inquest before?'

'Yes,' Ursula replied and closed the door behind her.

Moving jerkily down the corridor, Ursula used her anger at Helen to overcome her memories of the Californian inquest into Jack's death.

Reaching the hall, she asked the footman if he could be so kind as to collect her wrap from her bedroom. Then she went and joined the housekeeper and the nanny as they waited in the stable yard for the trap to be harnessed. She was surprised to find that the butler was to accompany them.

'I cannot allow you ladies to go through this ordeal on your own,' Mr Benson was saying as Ursula joined the little party.

She was touched to see how relieved Mrs Parsons seemed to be. She clutched at the butler's arm as though it was all that lay between her and disaster. Mrs Comfort seemed less overwhelmed by the occasion.

Halfway to Hinton Parva, rain arrived. Out came umbrellas but the protection they offered was minimal. As they drew to a halt in front of the Lion and Lamb, Ursula accepted the aid of someone's hand to descend from the trap, her attention concentrated on getting safely down and retrieving her crutches. It was only when they were handed to her that she found herself thanking the Colonel.

'I apologise on behalf of my family,' he said in an undertone. 'I rode here and it never occurred to me you were not all being brought by carriage.' He turned to help the butler aid the other women to alight.

The yard of the Lion and Lamb was seething with horses, carriages of all types, and a variety of people. The noise was overwhelming as people issued instructions, greeted friends and shouted comments. Ursula felt very vulnerable as she manoeuvred her crutches and was grateful for the Colonel forcing a way through for them.

Inside the inn, space had been cleared for a table and an arrangement of chairs. Sawdust covered the floor and already the seats for spectators were filled with a collection of locals who looked to be eager for sensation rather than attending a sad inquiry into the death of a young girl.

The Mountstanton party was seated to one side. Nearby was Miss Ranner, the teacher who had expressed such interest in Polly, together with the doctor who had attended to Ursula's sprained ankle. She exchanged greetings with them both. She looked for Mr Snell but could not see him.

'Morning, Dr Mason,' the Colonel said.

'Morning, Colonel. A sad business, this.'

The Colonel nodded, refused the offer of a chair next to the doctor and stood behind Ursula. She heard someone shout, 'Where's his lordship, then? What's he scared of?'

It wasn't possible to see who had spoken and he was immediately hushed down, but, clearly audible to Ursula, was the Colonel's sharp intake of breath.

Ten men filed in and sat themselves on the chairs set at right angles to the top table. Amongst them was a man in a sober suit with a dog collar.

'The jury,' the Colonel whispered, bending down to Ursula. 'The vicar is the foreman.'

A preacher had been the foreman at that other inquest. For a moment the room wobbled before Ursula's eyes.

'You look very pale, Miss Grandison,' said the Colonel. 'Can I fetch you a glass of soda water?'

She nodded gratefully. Somehow he found a barman and obtained the water.

The Colonel's unobtrusive care of her provided Ursula with a lifeline. He did not have to take her hand or express support in words. It was enough that he was there. Later she could worry about her dependence on his presence.

'Here's the coroner,' he murmured as a small, stocky man in a well-cut tweed suit threaded his way through the spectators and up to the top table.

He placed a thin file of papers before him and sat down. His air of competence calmed the atmosphere and almost silenced the spectators. A sharp look at the last of the gossipers over his pince-nez brought them into line.

'Good morning everyone. I am Geoffrey Matthews, general practitioner and the coroner. On my left are the jurors. It will be their task to decide how the deceased met her death: was it an accident, was there another person or persons involved, or did she take her own life? On my right are the witnesses who will be asked to give evidence to this enquiry. I ask that you allow them to speak without interruption. The only person allowed to question them is myself. If members of the jury have a query, please address it to the clerk.' Dr Matthews indicated a thin, insignificant-looking man wearing steel-framed spectacles, seated at the side of the table.

Then the coroner invited the jury to accompany him over to the ice house behind the Lion and Lamb to view the body and then to go to the location where Polly's body had been found. 'There is a cart ready to take us,' he said.

Ursula had not expected this; nor, it seemed, had many of the spectators.

'I do not envy them,' said Dr Mason as the jury filed out. 'After the autopsy I did what I could with poor Polly's body but it is not a pretty sight. How about a pint, Colonel? They'll take at least an hour.'

But the Colonel was already attracting the attention of a barman. 'I'd be grateful for a tray of coffee,' he said. 'Will you join us, Miss Ranner?'

Spectators were crowding the bar and tankards of beer appeared. The noise level rose. When the coffee arrived, Mr Benson poured the cups and Ursula took hers gratefully. She realised that the interruption in the proceedings was giving her time to come to terms with her ordeal. Despite the similarities – the sawdust, the informality of the spectators, the availability of alcohol – she could see that this inquest was to be nothing like that other one when interruptions and shouting had threatened the proceedings. Part of her, though, was back in California, unable to take in the fact that Jack's life, so full of energy and his own extraordinary mixture of aggression and charm, had come to an end.

Suddenly a tall, burly man dressed in riding clothes and holding a whip in a threatening manner appeared. 'Where is he?' he shouted. 'Let me through. I have to get through.' He looked distraught. His riding bowler sat askew on his head and he kept beating one thigh with his whip.

'Where is he?' he snarled, approaching the Mountstanton party. 'Where's his lordship?'

'He's not here, Gray,' said the Colonel. 'What do you want with him?'

The man stared through red-rimmed eyes. 'So, you're back, are you?'

A strong smell of whisky reached Ursula.

'I expect you've only just heard what happened, Mr Gray,' Mr Benson said, placing a hand on the man's arm. 'Must have been a shock. You being away, you wouldn't have known.'

With a mighty howl of rage the big man brought down his whip on the table. 'Dead and I knew nothing! Nothing!'

'We can't talk in here. Come outside and I'll tell you everything we know,' Benson said, exchanging glances with the Colonel, who gave him a nod of approval.

'Who is that?' Ursula asked as the butler led the man outside.

'Our agent, Adam Gray.'

'Agent?'

'He looks after the Mountstanton estate.'

'Mr Gray was in the north on estate matters,' said Mrs Parsons, her voice unsteady. 'He returned last night,' interrupted Miss Ranner. 'I met him this morning in the village shop. Mr Partridge said how sad Polly's death was and told him

what had happened. You never saw anyone so struck. Then he
erupted. No other way to describe it. Roared, just like he did
here. Ran out of the shop and headed for the police house.'

'He must have known Polly well,' said Ursula. The man had
seemed in agony. To learn such a terrible thing in such a casual
way must have been unbearable. She wondered why no one
had mentioned the possibility of a liaison before.

She saw Mrs Comfort look at Mrs Parsons and shake her
head. 'Never knew nothing about it,' she said. 'He wouldn't have
had nothing to do with Polly. He's married! And he's too old.'

Neither seemed good enough reasons to Ursula why the
agent should not have been besotted over the nursery maid.
Then she wondered if life had made her too cynical about
male intentions towards women.

'Would there have been opportunities for meeting?' she
asked, still struck with the agent's display of naked emotion.

'Polly and Harry went out every day,' the Colonel said, following the discussion with keen interest. 'Sometimes they'd
ride, Harry on his pony and Polly on a bicycle. Gray is always
moving around the estate, dealing with tenants, the home farm
and other matters. At the very least they would have been on
nodding terms.'

Mrs Comfort shook her head. 'Can't have been more than
that, that's what I say.'

Mrs Parsons said nothing.

'What about Mrs Gray in all this?' Ursula asked. She had
imagined that life in England would be straightforward and
ordered. Instead, it seemed there was a cesspit at Mountstanton
that was giving off a most unpleasant smell.

'Oh, my dear,' said Miss Ranner, 'Deirdre Gray has been
in an invalid carriage for ten years. How well named she is;
"Deirdre of the Sorrows" could not be more apposite. Adam
Gray has been something of a saint. He has nurtured and cared
for her ever since the accident.'

'With the help of his sister,' broke in Mrs Parsons. 'If anyone
deserves the name of saint it is Adele Gray. The devotion she
shows Deirdre is an example to us all.'

Ursula felt the Colonel's hand on her shoulder.

'Miss Grandison, I need to consult you; would you accompany me outside?'

Filled with curiosity, Ursula nodded and reached for her crutches.

The rain had stopped and outside crowds of spectators had spread themselves in happily gossiping groups.

'Wait!' called Ursula as the Colonel strode ahead faster than she could follow.

He came back. 'Miss Grandison, I am so sorry. I did not realise.'

She smiled. 'You imagine everyone is as athletic as one of your soldiers.'

He grinned as he guided her carefully outside and round a corner into a quiet space. He leant against the inn's wall. 'How does this latest development strike you?'

Ursula leant on her crutches. 'How on earth can I judge? I'd never heard of Mr Gray until he arrived here like some avenging angel. No one in your brother's household has mentioned the possibility of Polly having had a liaison with him. So what am I to think?'

He looked pleased. 'Exactly! Adam Gray has been a part of Mountstanton for a long time, as was his father before him. If he and Polly had been involved in a passionate affair, everyone would have known.'

'Yet the man is distraught. Her death has come as a very great shock.'

'That is why I wanted to talk to you. I am a plain and simple soldier, unused to emotional involvements. I need a woman's advice.'

'Colonel, you have tried that simple soldier tack with me before and it will not wash.'

He touched her shoulder. 'Now you are angry with me. I apologise. Perhaps I should just have said that I wanted your view as to whether a man such as Adam Gray could be attractive to a young, pretty and vivacious girl such as Polly.'

The brief contact was healing in a way Ursula did not want to analyse. Instead she said tartly, 'No one can say what attracts one person to another. I have seen pretty women bowled over by men that many would not have thought worth looking at. It is as though nature has implanted certain magnets in us which respond without any logic to similar magnets within others.' She smiled, pleased with her analogy. 'Contrariwise, there are members of the opposite sex who seem highly desirable in every way but who lack that inbuilt magnet that matches ours. We may tell ourselves the person is right for us in every way but know in our heart of hearts that the relationship will always lack real passion.'

He looked at her with a peculiar intensity, started to say something, then looked down at his boots. Then he began again and Ursula knew he had decided against revealing something of himself.

'Miss Grandison, what a wise woman you are.' He gave her a brilliant but impersonal smile. 'I wonder if Benson has managed to find out what lies behind the man's outburst; and if Gray intends giving evidence to the inquest. But what evidence could he give?'

'He might know of someone Polly had been involved with. Someone he was jealous of. Perhaps someone who had supplanted him in her affections.'

'Supplanted in her affections? My dear Miss Grandison, have you been reading penny dreadfuls?'

It seemed that moment of connection between them when he had been tempted to say something beyond the humdrum had been despatched beyond recall.

'If he does know anything that could throw some light on Polly's death, I'd back your Mr Benson to sober him up so he can tell the coroner.'

The Colonel gave a sudden snort of laughter. 'I agree. Come, let me find you somewhere to sit while we wait for the return of the coroner and jury; your poor ankle must be hurting.'

He was right about that. Ursula was happy for him to find and wipe dry a space for her on one of the outside benches. She let the swirl of activity all around occupy her mind in a senseless kind of way. She was conscious, though, of the Colonel's sharp eyes taking in every aspect of the scene. He must know most if not all of those present. Some greeted him, respectfully, but keeping their distance and throwing curious glances at Ursula when he introduced her as companion to the Countess's sister from New York. It seemed they all knew it was she who had found Polly's body and there was suspicion in the way they eyed her. Unexpectedly, she found herself missing the warmth and familiarity of that makeshift life in California.

Suddenly there was a shout. 'They're back!'

The long cart bearing the jury and coroner swept down the road from the river.

As they once again settled themselves inside the inn, Ursula looked around the little group of witnesses. 'Do you see Mr Snell?' she asked.

He surveyed the room and shook his head. 'Maybe he had second thoughts about giving evidence.'

'I am sure your brother will be relieved,' said Ursula, watching for his reaction.

The Colonel said nothing but she detected a sense of unease. What was it Mr Snell knew?

At the back of the room, Ursula saw Mr Benson enter with a subdued and now sober Martin Gray.

The jury filed in; they looked shaken by their experiences.

The coroner called the room to order and soon Ursula found herself asked to describe finding the body. She spoke slowly and clearly; concentrating on the facts but blanking out an actual picture of what she had seen.

'Thank you, Miss Grandison,' the coroner said as she finished. 'I am sorry we had to ask you to relive what must have been a most distressing experience.'

The Colonel was the next witness. He gave his evidence succinctly and unemotionally. Then he added a few words on Polly's suitability for her position. 'She never gave cause for any disquiet in the way she fulfilled her duties,' he finished.

'Thank you, Colonel Stanhope,' said the coroner, making a note on the pad in front of him.

After the Colonel came the constable, who took the inquest laboriously through the removal of the body and his investigation of the scene, which had failed to discover anything that could throw light on how the deceased had met her end.

Then Dr Mason gave the results of his autopsy.

There were gasps and an outburst of whispered comments as he revealed that when Polly had died, she had been three months gone with child. The coroner had to ask for silence before matters could proceed.

Not for the first time, Ursula wondered how the girl had reacted to her situation. Had she been fearful, worried? Or had she had reason to think that the father of her child would take care of them both; that they were on the verge of a joyous life together? But in that case, surely she would have told some-one? Bearing a child was one of the most important, yet often traumatic, events of a woman's life. She needed the support and commitment of the man responsible for her condition.

Mrs Comfort, clearly nervous, was next to give evidence. Many times she lost the thread of what she was saying and had to be prompted back on course by the coroner. Ursula admired his patience as he coaxed her into a declaration that Polly gave every satisfaction and she knew of no liaison between her and any man.

When she came to Polly's last words to her, she broke down. '"Don't expect me back," she said. I thought she was joking; wanted me to think she was running off with a young man. Well, I knew she wouldn't be doing anything like that. She was always having a laugh with everyone, me included.'

The coroner regarded her for a long minute. '"Don't expect me back," was what she said?'

Mrs Comfort nodded.

'And when she didn't return, then you decided she had meant it?'

'We all did!'

'Mrs Comfort, once you knew she was expecting, could you imagine that she had decided to take her own life rather than bear an illegitimate child?'

Mrs Comfort's hands worked her damp handkerchief. 'Sometimes I didn't know what she was about. She could go down into the depths; not often, mind, but every now and then. Not that she ever took it out on Harry. Well, we all find life a bit much at times, don't we, sir?'

Beside Ursula, Mrs Parsons shifted uneasily. She would be next to give evidence.

'Would you have said she was depressed that morning?' asked the coroner.

'Like I said, she'd been laughing. But, I don't know. I'd've said she would have told me if she was expecting. I couldn't have known her at all, could I?' Tears began to flow again.

'Thank you, Mrs Comfort, we appreciate your frankness. Now, if we can have Mrs Parsons, please?'

As the nanny took her seat, still upset, Ursula wondered if she realised how her evidence could have suggested to the jury that Polly had deliberately flung herself down that fatal slope.

The housekeeper seemed as nervous as the nanny but more in control. Yes, she said, she was in charge of all the female staff in the Mountstanton household. Yes, the nursemaid had had to conform to the rules of the establishment. These meant she was not allowed to fraternise with male members of staff.

'So,' said the coroner, a trifle wearily as though he knew the answer to the question he was about to ask. 'You were not aware of any liaison the deceased was conducting?'

There was a pause and suddenly the atmosphere in the room sharpened.

Mrs Parsons clasped her hands tightly together. 'There was, sir, one occasion when I saw Polly together with a member of the opposite sex in a compromising situation,' she said slowly, reluctantly.

The coroner's expression sharpened. 'When was this and who was the man?'

'I saw them in the wood, not far from where she fell down into the river. It was several weeks ago – I could not tell you exactly. I went to gather some primroses. I had some matters I wished to consider and was not studying where I was going. The trees suddenly opened and I saw two figures in a small clearing. They were . . . ,' she swallowed hard then gave a small cough. 'They were in an embrace. It was a private moment and I began to retreat. And then I recognised them.'

'And they were?' prompted the coroner.

Silence fell upon the room.

'Mrs Parsons?' the coroner said gently.

'I saw . . . ,' the housekeeper whispered.

'Please speak up, Mrs Parsons.'

'I saw that the girl was Polly, and the man . . . ' again she faltered.

'And the man?' prompted the coroner.

Ursula sensed an almost tangible anticipation in the room.

Mrs Parsons straightened her shoulders. 'The man was Mr Gray. He was kissing her passionately.'

'No!' shouted the agent from the back of the room. 'It was not like that!'

'So how was it, Mr Gray?' asked the coroner. 'I must ask you to come forward and give evidence. There is no one else I think due to speak?'

The clerk murmured some words in the coroner's ear.

'Snell? Snell? Well, is he here?' He looked around the room. No one moved. 'Send to find out where he is,' said the coroner tetchily. 'Meanwhile, Mr Gray, please come forward.'

Mr Benson guided the man, who was still a little unsteady.

'Mr Gray, do you or do you not admit that you were in the woods with the deceased?' asked the coroner.

The big man seemed to sag inwards, as though air had been drawn out of his body. All at once he appeared to age before their eyes. Where before Ursula would have gauged him to be in his early forties, now she would have said he was considerably older.

'Well, Mr Gray?'

'I was in the woods with Polly,' the man murmured.

'Speak up, man.'

With an effort the agent squared his shoulders. 'I met Polly in the woods, sir. That is true. She was upset. I comforted her. That is all. We had no sort of liaison, if that is what is being suggested.'

'Why did she need comforting?'

The agent bowed his head as though unable to meet the coroner's eye. 'She had been let down,' he mumbled.

'I shall not tell you to speak up again. Did I hear you to say she had been let down?'

Mr Gray nodded.

'Who had let her down?'

'I do not know,' the agent said helplessly.

The coroner sighed. 'Let me see if I have understood this right. You met the deceased in the wood. Was this by arrangement?'

Gray nodded. 'She left me a note in a place we both knew of.'

'So you were in the habit of exchanging notes and, one has to suppose, of meeting?'

Once again the shoulders sagged.

'You must answer the questions Mr Gray. Were you or were you not in the habit of meeting?'

'A few times.'

'For what purpose?'

'Polly had troubles, she needed advice.'

'What sort of troubles? What sort of advice?'

The agent clenched and unclenched his hands. 'There was a man she said she was involved with. It was he who let her down.'

'Who was this man?'

A hopeless pause, then, 'She wouldn't tell me.'

The coroner looked at his scribbled notes then sent a keen glance at the agent. 'What else?'

'There is nothing else I can tell you, sir.'

'Nothing,' the coroner repeated without inflexion. 'And you say there was no relationship between you and the deceased?'

'No, sir. I swear it.'

There was a long pause before the coroner sighed deeply and said, 'You may step down, Mr Gray.' He consulted one of his papers. 'I see I have forgotten not only Mr Snell but also Miss Ranner. My apologies, ma'am, may I ask you to come forward?'

Miss Ranner had little extra to add to what had already been said, merely that she had taught Polly and had always found her to be of sober character.

After she had finished her evidence, the coroner looked around the room. 'Is there any person who wishes to tell us anything further?'

There was a general craning of necks and some whispering but no one came forward.

'As Mr Snell has not had the courtesy to attend this inquest, I am removing his name from my list of witnesses.' The coroner studied his notes for a moment then summed up the evidence for the jury. Finally, he reminded them that they could find that the deceased had met her death by accident; or that a person or persons unknown had been responsible; or that the deceased had taken her own life whilst the balance of her mind was disturbed, owing to the unfortunate nature of her condition.'

He had, thought Ursula, managed to convey to the jury that the last possibility was the most likely verdict and the one that they should return.

As the jurors huddled together to discuss the matter, the outer door banged open and the clerk ran in, his face a picture of consternation.

'Sir! Sir! Mr Snell, he is dead, sir.'

Chapter Seventeen

After Ursula left the breakfast table, Belle sat there, emotions churning inside her.

She was not a girl who normally examined her feelings. Like a bird, she soared along the currents of her life. Her father had been heard to say, 'Don't ask Belle to think, just enjoy her.' And she had reached the age of seventeen confident in her ability to please, sure there was nothing that could be denied to her. For her desires, she told herself, were not many. Lovely clothes, people to tell her how pretty she was, lots of parties, and a beautiful home to live in. And, of course, a handsome man who would love her to the end of his days. He didn't have to be rich, because, thanks to Papa, she had masses of money. He didn't have to have a grand title – though to be called 'my lady' would be nice – he just had to be hers and she had to be the centre of his life. And together they would have lots of babies.

Helen's invitation to make her debut in London had been so exciting. All those wonderful clothes she was provided with. And a French maid, who might be as sour as a lemon without an ounce of human feeling but she sure could do hair.

Belle poured herself another cup of coffee, sat holding it in both hands and looked at the faded Chinese wallpaper. Everything in this place was so old and so shabby. Why did Helen stand it?

She remembered her father returning from his one visit here soon after Helen's marriage. Belle had been too young to go as well. 'Got some treasures there, she has. They ain't looked after, though. And the state of the place, you wouldn't credit. Still, Helen will see to all that. I've made sure she's enough funds to do the place up a treat. The Vanderbilt girl has done up Blenheim for the Marlboroughs and my girl will do the same for Mountstanton.'

Only she hadn't. Belle wondered what her father would say when he heard about the state of the house.

She finished the coffee and, finally, nothing could stop her thinking about William Warburton. She had fed on the memories of that afternoon with him on the roof, before the rain had driven them indoors to the picture gallery. She'd relived every moment of the passion they had shared. Even now, her body sang to echoes of what she had felt then.

Abruptly, she rose and went over to the window. Instead of the parterre garden with its regimented box hedges, she saw William Warburton standing on the station platform to greet them as they arrived.

The attraction had been instant. She had no sooner looked into those astonishing blue eyes with their long, dark lashes and seen the energy that lurked there, heard the hint of laughter in his voice as he apologised for the absence of her sister, than she knew that this was the man she wanted. He was so tall, so handsome, had such charm. And he had seemed as captivated by her as she by him. Those stolen moments in the shrubbery on the night of Helen's party had been worth the sermon she had endured afterwards. Then there had been the rapture of their union on the roof.

But she had seen so little of him since that afternoon. That night at dinner, she had caught his eye and been confident he felt exactly as she did, which was that she wanted to be alone with him, in his arms, enjoying their passion, not sitting at a stupid dinner table.

The following day, though, when she had hoped for at least a quick kiss in one of the many, many rooms this house contained, together with some words that would feed her soul, William was nowhere to be seen.

When the men had rejoined the women in the drawing room after dinner last night, there had only been Richard and his brother, that Colonel who made Belle feel that in his eyes she hardly existed. Nobody had explained why William was not with them and she had not dared to ask.

Belle had soon excused herself for bed, then wandered around the corridors trying to find the office where, she supposed, William was attending to some urgent correspondence. Not looking where she was going, Belle bumped into John, the footman with the twinkly brown eyes. He asked if he could help.

'I have a message for Mr Warburton,' Belle said casually. 'I thought he was in the Earl's office.'

'Mr Warburton has left, Miss Seldon.'

She stared at him. 'Left? What do you mean?'

'As I understand it, miss, he had a message from his family.'

Belle went straight to Helen's boudoir and waited for her sister.

'Where has William gone and why?' she demanded the moment Helen entered.

Her sister looked tired and strained. 'It is none of your business, Belle.'

'You don't want me to be involved with him, do you, Helen?'

'Involved? What do you mean?'

'You know, dummy.'

Helen's gaze grew glacial. 'Belle, your language is a disgrace.'

'Don't you come all high and mighty, all *English* with me. I am your sister; I know all about you. So don't try and pretend you don't understand exactly what I mean.'

Helen sighed deeply, sat down and put her hand over her eyes for a moment. Then she looked up at Belle.

'William's mother is not well; he has gone to see her.'

'Without saying goodbye to me? How long before he's back?'

'I have no idea. Belle, you must abandon any idea of forming a relationship with Mr Warburton, he's not for you.'

'So you've already said. But why? Do you think I should be looking for an Earl or a Duke? Well, let me tell you, sister, that titles mean nothing to me.'

'Belle, you need to control yourself,' Helen said coldly. 'These displays of emotion do you no good.'

Belle had cried out in frustration and left, slamming the door behind her. In her own room, she cast herself down on the bed and let out a scream of rage.

When Didier entered, asking what was the matter, Belle drummed her feet on the bed, then picked up a pretty clock from the bedside table and threw it at her. It crashed against the wall.

The maid looked at the ruined remains, muttered '*Salle putte,*' and retreated from the room. Belle didn't know what she meant and didn't care. Soon tears were streaming down her face. Eventually, still dressed, she drifted into sleep.

* * *

The view from the breakfast room window offered no comfort. Belle drummed her fingers on the glass and tried to think of something to do. Should she go up to the nursery and see if she could take Harry off somewhere? They could let off steam together. But then she remembered that Mrs Comfort would be at the inquest. Some maid would be looking after Harry and would insist on asking Helen for permission. The last thing Belle wanted at the moment was any involvement with her sister.

On impulse she ran to her room and rang for her maid.

'I am going riding,' she announced.

'But, Miss Seldon, it is raining.'

Belle glanced out of the window. 'It will clear.'

Belle presented her back for the line of buttons running down her muslin bodice to be unfastened.

The maid pressed her lips together and assisted her mistress into her London-tailored habit.

In the stables Belle got hold of the Head Groom and announced that the Countess wished her sister to ride her mare, Pocahontas.

The man looked worried. 'I understood Dancer was to be your mount, Miss Seldon.'

She gave him a dazzling smile. 'Today I am to ride Pocahontas. Her ladyship said she wanted to know how I found her. The rain has stopped and the morning will be perfect.'

The groom looked as though he did not agree but said, 'If that's the case, Miss, I'll saddle her up and tell young Dan he's to accompany you.'

'No!' said Belle sharply. The thought of any company but William's that morning was more than she could bear. She took a calming breath and gave the groom another smile. 'I will not need to be accompanied today. I am not going to be out long. I just need to see how Pocahontas goes. I just love the way you English are so formal,' she added with a laugh. 'We Americans do things differently. It's such a change for me.'

The Head Groom's face cracked in a smile. 'It took her lady-ship a while to get used to our ways,' he said, moving over to lift a side-saddle down from the wall.

Belle knew she had won.

Soon she was being given a hand up onto Pocahontas' back. A few adjustments needed to be made to the stirrup, and the horse moved uneasily as Belle locked her right knee over the top pommel and fixed her left thigh under the lower.

'That comfortable?'

'Just fine,' she assured the groom and with a smile of triumph took her high-spirited mount out of the yard.

With a fizz of satisfaction, Belle thought how angry Helen would be when she learned that her sister was riding her precious horse. She remembered the chestnut mare Helen had kept in New York. When it was announced that she was to go to school in Europe, Belle had clapped her hands and said, 'Then I can have Princess!'

'No!' Helen had declared. 'Princess is my horse. I'll get my friend Joyce to ride her while I'm away. Your hands are so heavy, you'll ruin her mouth.'

Belle had sulked.

Not long after Helen and Ursula had gone to their school in Paris, Princess had been hers. Helen had been so mad when she returned the first time, but Papa had said that Belle had out-grown her pony and the only horse she'd wanted was Princess. As soon as Helen was settled in New York again, he'd buy her an even better mount.

Helen had taken Belle to the stables soon after she had arrived in England. She'd patted the neck of a beautiful dap-pled grey and said, 'This is Pocahontas. I named her after that Red Indian princess. Do you still have my first Princess, Belle?'

'Yes, and I haven't ruined her mouth.'

'I'm glad to hear it. While you are here, you may ride Dancer.' This was a small, pretty bay with big, liquid eyes. Mounted on Dancer, Belle had felt the little sister and knew that nothing would satisfy her but a ride on Pocahontas.

Now here she was and Belle felt joyous for the first time since she had learned that William Warburton had gone away. She brought the horse to a halt and looked around.

Ahead of them was the wooded hill that led to Hinton Parva. That must be where Ursula had had her accident and found the nursery maid's body. Over to the left was the open country where Belle had already ridden with Helen and William. Over to the right were fields filled with some crop or other. A broad track led through them and up onto more hills.

'Shall we explore, Pocahontas?' Belle whispered into the horse's ears; they twitched forward endearingly.

Belle laughed and set off in a trot along the track.

The clouds were building into a heavy grey eiderdown above her head. She urged the horse up the hill and found the countryside opening before her with meadows and, in the distance, a thick wood.

'Let's go!' she shouted and kicked her left heel into Pocahontas's side.

The horse took off at a gallop; its exhilarating speed took Belle's breath away. She hardly needed to guide Pocahontas, the horse seemed to know exactly which way to go. When the rain started, the girl ignored it. She was flying above the ground. It was brilliant; magnificent; she wanted to ride like this forever.

Soon, though, the rain grew heavier. Just as Belle was wondering whether they should turn for home, they reached the shelter of the wood she had seen. There was a path through the trees, one the horse seemed happy to follow. Now the rain hardly penetrated the canopy of leaves.

After a little, a clearing with a building appeared.

'Oh my,' Belle said to herself. 'Hansel and Gretel!'

It had to be a woodman's cottage: stone built, a thatched roof, two windows and a door. There was a chimney but no smoke; the place looked deserted.

Belle slid down from the saddle. Without the shelter of the leaves, the rain was heavy. She saw a sort of shed with a stable door and led Pocahontas in, tied the reins to a convenient hook, then shut the lower part of the door and left the horse looking out as she went and knocked on the cottage door.

There was no reply, but she had not expected one.

She peered in through the dirty windows. The interior seemed to be roughly furnished but it had an abandoned air.

Belle shivered and rubbed at her arms. The rain was heavier now and the wood had acquired a sinister look. She tried the door latch. To her surprise, it opened.

Inside, all was dark and smelled of dust and absence. But at least it was dry. There appeared to be just a single room. In one corner stood a pump, its spout hanging over a cracked porcelain sink. In the centre of the room was a small, round, three-legged table and on it a brass candlestick and a box of matches.

Belle struck one and lit the candle, which produced flickering shadows. Shaking the rain out of her hat, she slowly turned, inspecting her surroundings. The place was cleaner than her initial impression had suggested. On a shelf by the sink was a small collection of unmatched crockery. Two thick wine glasses stood at one end. Beneath a draining board, its ridges dark from decades of dishwater, was a drawer that Belle opened almost automatically. It held cutlery: knives with cracked bone handles, forks of worn silver-plate with bent tines. Along one wall was a low, truckle-type bed covered with a rough but clean-looking blanket.

Belle sat down on one of the two sturdy yet comfortable wooden chairs that stood either side of the table and shivered. She did not feel comfortable in this place. But she did not feel comfortable at Mountstanton either.

Helen had grown into someone she hardly recognised. What had happened to the sister who used to laugh with her? What had gone wrong? Was it all connected with the death of that nursery maid which had upset everyone so much?

Belle shivered. Outside it was still raining. Suddenly, she screamed and leaped to her feet as a mouse ran across the dirt floor and into the sticks piled roughly in the fireplace.

For a long time Belle stood with her hands clamped to her mouth, her terrified eyes scanning the floor. But the mouse seemed to have disappeared. Gradually she relaxed. Should she, she wondered, light the fire? It seemed laid ready for a match.

She looked around again. There was a line of pegs by the door but they held no clothes. Hanging down from the chimney was a large, serrated jack that ended in a hook. And beside the fire was a pot with a handle that could be hung on the jack. And a kettle stood on a trivet at the other side.

Who used this place? Was it, in fact, on Mountstanton land or did it belong to a neighbour? Her curiosity thoroughly aroused, and on the alert for any hint of a mouse, she scanned every inch of the room. And was rewarded by the glint of something lying underneath the trivet.

It was a small button of dark blue enamel, ornamented with a tiny white flower. Belle stared at it and knew she had seen it before. After a moment she remembered where: Helen had a silk shirt with these buttons.

For a long moment Belle stood looking at it. Then everything came together. Helen and William were having an affair! This was their private place. No wonder the horse knew the way so well. Anger seared through her. How dare Helen lecture her on proper behaviour.

Rain or no rain, Belle didn't want to spend another moment in the cottage. She grabbed her gloves from the table, blew out the candle, checked there was no trace of her presence, and left.

Pocahontas snickered and nibbled at her shoulder. Belle stroked her neck. 'Good girl; you won't tell we've been here, will you?'

She led the horse out of the shed then looked around and found there was a moss-covered mounting block by the front door. 'How useful,' she murmured. Pocahontas stood perfectly still in exactly the right position while she mounted, then retraced her passage through the wood back to the open country beyond.

Belle was surprised what a long way her reckless gallop had brought her. She set Pocahontas into a canter towards Mountstanton. Drawing near the range of hills they had come down, she found a single horseman coming up behind her.

'Well, well, Belle, my dear sister-in-law,' said the Earl, drawing level. 'What have you been up to? And where,' he said, turning around in his saddle, 'is your groom?'

Belle gave him a lovely smile. 'Was it very naughty of me to say I wanted to ride alone? Is it not "the done thing" in England? Helen is trying hard to educate me.' She pouted. 'There seem to be so many "done things". How long did it take Helen to learn them all?'

Richard's face broke into one of its rare smiles. 'Long enough! My mother was a great help.'

I bet she was, Belle thought. Poor Helen!

'How far have you ridden? You seem very wet, you must have been caught in that downpour.'

He was wearing a wide-brimmed hat and a rubberised coat.

'It was fine when we set out. I didn't intend going far but Pocahontas is such a lovely ride and the countryside is so beautiful. It's been a wonderful change from hacking around Central Park back home.' She gave him another wide smile and gestured to the rolling hills and woods all around them. 'Is this all your land or have I trespassed onto someone else's?'

'No, it's all part of the Mountstanton estate, which stretches several miles behind us.' He turned and pointed towards the wood which held the stone cottage. 'Over to your left, the boundary is just beyond that wood. You look really cold, my dear. Not surprising, considering this rain. Come, let's gallop back before you catch pneumonia.'

It was the first time Belle had been alone in the company of her brother-in-law. Also for the first time, she did not feel intimidated in his presence and could almost believe that Helen had actually fallen in love with the man rather than his position.

They slowed as they tackled the hill that lay between them and the house.

'Feeling warmer?' Richard asked.

Belle nodded. She felt more comfortable altogether. She was dying to mention the cottage to see if Richard knew anything about it, then decided it was wiser not to.

'What do you think of Pocahontas?'

'She's wonderful.' Belle patted the horse's neck.

'I'm glad Helen allowed you to ride her. She was a marriage gift from me, I chose her with great care.'

'You are a good judge of horse flesh, Richard.'

He nodded. 'My father taught Charles and me what to look for.' He shot a sideways look at Belle. 'My brother is very taken with you.'

She laughed. 'It's sweet of you to say so, Richard, but he disguises it very well.'

'It would please Helen and me very much to have you properly in the family, you know?'

They had reached the top of the hill and paused to allow the horses a brief respite. Belle looked at her brother-in-law and realised he was serious.

'I'm much too young to think of getting married,' she said with a laugh. 'And I am having such a good time with you all. I do appreciate the compliment, however.' She gave him another sweet smile and hoped he would now drop the matter. 'There's the river,' she said, pointing. 'Does it ever flood?' she asked, looking at the fields it flowed through before it reached the wooded hill that hid Hinton Parva.

'Only very occasionally. Mountstanton stands well above it, if that is what you fear.'

Belle found she could not forget the poor nursery maid who met her end in its waters. 'You are not attending the inquest?'

'No, I am not needed,' he said tersely and set his horse down the hill. They returned to the stables without further conversation.

Richard walked beside Belle back to the house. As they approached the side door, Helen emerged looking very angry.

Belle flinched involuntarily. Trust Helen to have found out exactly what her baby sister had been doing.

Richard put an arm around Belle's shoulders. 'My dear, we have had a marvellous ride together; your sister is almost as good a horsewoman as you are. It was very generous of you to allow her to ride Pocahontas.'

'Richard has been telling me how she was a present from him on your marriage,' Belle said as lightly as she could manage. 'I thought you could not object to my riding her when you were otherwise engaged. We have had such a wonderful time.'

'I have been otherwise engaged writing the invitations for your ball,' Helen said in a icy voice.

'Why did you not ask me to help? I would have liked to.'

'You look drenched. Go and change. Richard, the inquest has returned a verdict.'

The hand on Belle's shoulder tightened for a moment.

'And?'

'Suicide whilst the balance of her mind was disturbed.'

'Ah! Pity. I do not suppose the shame of such a criminal act will escape us entirely.'

Belle was astonished at his reaction. It seemed all he worried about was the Mountstanton reputation. What about that poor girl?

'But it seems there will have to be another inquest,' Helen continued. 'Snell is dead and the doctor is refusing to sign the death certificate.'

Chapter Eighteen

There was uproar at Polly's inquest.

Dr Mason disappeared to attend to Mr Snell and the coroner called for quiet. 'I had already removed Mr Snell's name from my list of witnesses and his demise, if indeed he is dead, is regrettable but of no account to these proceedings. I now ask the jury to return to the task of deciding on their verdict.'

In California, the jury had taken some two hours of furious debate to reach their verdict; two hours that had seemed a lifetime to Ursula. At this inquest it took no more than twenty minutes or so before the vicar, as foreman, was able to announce the jury's verdict that the deceased had taken her life whilst the balance of her mind was disturbed.

There were gasps of shock from the audience.

'Owing to her delicate condition,' one of the jurors added from behind the vicar.

'Quite,' said the coroner. 'Note down the verdict,' he directed the clerk.

The inquest was over.

Ursula looked round at the Colonel. He was banging his hand against his leg as though he held his army baton. 'Wait for me outside,' he said to Ursula. Then he strode over to the coroner.

Ursula thought that Colonel Charles would never learn that 'please' and a few soft words would get him further than his customary curtness, and smiled to herself as she followed the Mountstanton contingent out into the courtyard of the pub.

The remains of another downpour was draining off the cobblestones and the benches were once again wet, but the sky was now clear. It seemed that in England the weather could change from fair to foul and foul to fair in less time than it took to boil a pot of water.

There was nowhere to sit that wasn't soaked, so Ursula stood against the wall, leaning on her crutches, and watched as Mr Benson found the groom and set him to harnessing up the trap. She felt very uneasy.

After the coroner's summing up, the verdict had been exactly as she had expected. And the evidence as it had been extracted from each of the witnesses would seem to back up that conclusion. The wound to the back of the girl's head had only been mentioned in order to be dismissed as a result of the fall down the rock-strewn slope.

When the Colonel had given his evidence, he had made a point of saying that he did not see the fall as a suitable means of suicide. Had Polly meant to kill herself, he'd said, she would have found a rope and hanged herself, or thrown herself off the railway bridge in front of a train.

The coroner had listened with barely concealed distaste. 'In many cases of suicide,' he'd said, 'the victim had not meant to complete the act; they had merely wished to draw attention to themselves. Or perhaps the nursemaid had hoped the fall would bring on a miscarriage.'

Ursula thought of the glimpses she had been given of Polly. A wayward, rebellious spirit who found discipline difficult but who loved children. A girl who believed she was on her way to a better life. No, the Colonel was right, this had not been suicide.

Did the verdict matter so very much? Nothing could bring her back. But the consternation that had run through those present underlined how very shocking such an act was. It was a criminal offence and meant that Polly could not be laid in hallowed ground. There would be no religious ceremony, and her body would be buried outside church boundaries.

Mrs Parsons and Mrs Comfort were talking quietly together. Everything about their postures suggested that they were now going to put what had happened behind them.

Mr Gray, the agent, had disappeared. Ursula wondered how he felt about the verdict. His was a troubled soul.

'Is your foot still very painful, Miss Grandison?' Miss Ranner's face was concerned. 'I heard the Colonel ask you to wait for him; would you like to do so in my little house? It must be most uncomfortable for you to have to stand with your crutches.'

'That is very kind but I think I must remain here. As soon as the trap is harnessed, we shall be expected to return to the house.'

'Of course; quite proper. But perhaps we could find somewhere to sit inside? There are a number of traps and carriages being harnessed and yours could take a little time. I am sure Mr Benson would not, as I expect Colonel Stanhope would say, "pull rank".' She flushed slightly. 'I would never normally sit in the Lion and Lamb but I am sure no one could raise an eyebrow if we were to be there under the present circumstances.'

She bustled back into the public house. Ursula gave a nod to Mrs Parsons and followed. She was sure it was not merely her comfort that Miss Ranner was concerned about.

Inside the hostelry, the rows of chairs were being put away and fresh sawdust spread. In a far corner, the Colonel was addressing the coroner in a low voice that didn't carry but had sufficient force to have the other man purpling up with affronted dignity.

The same friendly barman who had earlier produced the coffee, arranged a couple of chairs at a small table for them and, having refused the offer of further refreshment, Ursula and Miss Ranner sat.

'Thank you,' Ursula said with relief. 'You were quite right; it is difficult to remain standing with this wretched ankle of mine.' She stretched it out before her. 'However, I truly think there is an improvement. All the swelling is down and I can at least do up my boot again. Perhaps I may soon graduate to a stick instead of these clumsy crutches.'

Miss Ranner sat smoothing her gloves over her dark brown skirt, her forehead creased in deep wrinkles.

Ursula tried again. 'Are you dissatisfied with how the inquest has gone, Miss Ranner?'

She looked up. 'As to that, it is what I expected. Poor Polly,' she said with unexpected vigour. 'She has not been given justice but there is nothing I can do about it.'

'Then is there something else bothering you?'

'It is poor Mr Snell.'

Ursula was taken aback. 'Death is always distressing. But, forgive me, Miss Ranner, I have gathered the impression that very few in the village will mourn his passing.'

'Oh, Miss Grandison, I am afraid you are right. I hate to speak ill of those who have passed on but Mr Snell was not a nice man. However, I hope I can always regret a demise, particularly one that was so sudden.'

There was a just perceptible stress on the last phrase. 'He was not at all indisposed?'

Miss Ranner went back to smoothing her gloves. She gave a quick look around them, then said in a low voice, 'I am wondering if the Earl noticed anything amiss last night.'

This was totally unexpected. 'Last night?'

'It was so late, you see.' Miss Ranner leaned forward, eager to continue now that she had started. 'I usually walk Jessie, my little dog, just before I retire. Last night I was involved with a book from the circulating library. Such an exciting tale of the French Revolution and the rescue of those poor aristocrats from the guillotine, I could not bear to leave it until I knew exactly what happened. Do you ever find that with a book, Miss Grandison?'

Ursula smiled. 'I know exactly what you mean. So, last night you read late. Do you not find text by lamplight taxes your eyes?'

Miss Ranner dismissed this with a wave of her hand. 'Not when I can arrange my chair right beside it.' She gave her gloves another stroke. 'I did not realise quite how late it was until Jessie whined quite piteously and drew my attention with her little paw on my shoe. And I saw it was past eleven o'clock! I was so upset at being neglectful of her needs that I went for my shawl and took her outside. Mr Snell's cottage is a little beyond mine; it is the last in the village. I usually walk Jessie in that direction, as there is so much vegetation beside the road, you see?'

Ursula nodded.

'We had not gone as far as Laurel Cottage, Mr Snell's, when a rider came out and rode off in the direction of Mountstanton. It was a clear night with a full moon and I could see that it was the Earl.'

She stopped and looked at Ursula.

'You were certain it was him?'

'Oh, yes, his figure is quite unmistakeable, as is his white horse, though, of course, it should be called a grey.'

'No doubt he had some very good reason for calling on Mr Snell,' Ursula suggested in a colourless voice.

'Oh, I am sure,' Miss Ranner said in heartfelt tones. 'And no doubt when he hears the news he will tell Dr Mason that Mr Snell was alive and well when he left. The poor man must have had some sort of attack later in the night, or even this morning, for I am sure his lordship would not have left him if he had been in any distress.'

Ursula gave this rapid consideration. 'I suppose the moon being so bright, you did not need the aid of a lantern to walk your little dog?'

Miss Ranner agreed.

'And the night being so bright, the Earl would undoubtedly have noticed you?'

Miss Ranner dropped her gaze. 'Very possibly. Though, with that monster of a yew tree ... it leans right over the road and we have been saying to Mr Snell for an age that it needs to be cut back. No one knows how old it is and if a storm should bring down a branch, someone might be badly injured. Well, I was in its shadow and it could be that he did not see me. He rode away in the opposite direction, and so quickly.'

'I am sure if it was him, as soon as he knows about Mr Snell's demise, his lordship will come forward and let the doctor know what sort of state he left him in,' Ursula said soothingly.

Miss Ranner gave her an apologetic smile as the Colonel appeared.

'Miss Grandison, here you are, waiting for me?'

'I have been waiting for the trap to be harnessed,' said Ursula. Her eyes challenged him. 'Miss Ranner has been keeping me company.'

He immediately smiled and raised his hand in the manner of a fencer acknowledging a hit.

Miss Ranner rose. 'Colonel Charles, now that you are here I can return to my house and poor Jessie. Do reassure me; you have been instructing the coroner that the verdict was wrong?'

His expression darkened. 'We need more evidence, Miss Ranner, and I am making it my business to see that it is discovered.'

She took his hand in both of hers. 'Colonel Charles, I knew we could rely on you.' She turned to Ursula, 'Miss Grandison, thank you for listening. I hope you will visit me again soon?'

'I shall be sure to, Miss Ranner.'

The woman gave her a questioning look. Ursula glanced briefly towards the Colonel. Miss Ranner's face cleared as though she had received the message she needed. A moment later she was gone.

'What has Miss Ranner been saying that she was grateful you listened to, Miss Grandison?' The Colonel sat on the chair opposite her.

What a pleasure it was to deal with someone so quick on the uptake. Yet Ursula was reluctant to come straight out with what the woman had told her. The information could be entirely innocent, or it could be flawed, or . . .

'She is not happy with the way the inquest went.'

'I understood that. Neither am I, as you heard me say. And I do not understand Gray's part.'

'Perhaps you or your brother need to speak to him.' There, she had at least referred to the Earl.

The Colonel gave her a searching look. 'That should be Richard's task. I shall be speaking to him as soon as I return. But how did the man's evidence strike you?'

Ursula dragged her mind back to what the agent had said. 'He was emotional but very definite that he had not been involved with Polly.'

The Colonel whistled tunelessly for a moment. 'I can make no sense of things. I'd hoped this morning would throw some light onto Polly's death. Instead it has merely deepened the mystery.'

'Your brother will no doubt be relieved Mr Snell did not appear,' Ursula said and waited for a response.

'Snell would have produced some farrago. I suppose I should express regret at his death but I cannot.'

Ursula looked into his face. His eyes were a clear grey; she realised she had not before noticed how clear. He was frowning. 'You have something you wish to say, Miss Grandison?'

She took a quick breath. 'Miss Ranner has just told me she saw your brother ride away from Mr Snell's cottage late last night. A little after eleven o'clock she said.'

His face froze. 'What on earth was she about, walking in the lane at that hour of the night?'

Ursula repeated Miss Ranner's tale.

'Village busybodies,' came the bitter response.

She said nothing.

The Colonel put both hands on the table, laced his fingers together and studied the result.

'Your brother must have had a good reason for his visit,' Ursula said in her calmest voice.

'If it was him.'

'Miss Ranner said she recognised not only his figure but his horse. Are there many greys in the neighbourbood?'

'Not that I know of.'

'All that is needed is a word to your brother that his evidence as to Mr Snell's condition at the time he left him last night could possibly be required.'

The Colonel's expression grew thunderous. 'All that is needed! Miss Grandison you have no idea what you are suggesting. My brother is a law unto himself.'

The door to the pub opened and Dr Mason bustled in and went straight up to the coroner, who was now exchanging words and papers with his clerk.

'He's dead all right,' the doctor said, his words carrying clearly to where Ursula and the Colonel sat. 'But don't ask me to sign his certificate.'

Ursula and the Colonel looked at each other.

★ ★ ★

No more rain came on the journey back to Mountstanton.

There was little talk in the trap about the inquest. Instead there was a discussion on the qualities needed in Polly's replacement.

'And a very plain looking girl!' was Mrs Comfort's last, decisive word on the matter.

Back in the house, Ursula ascertained that the Countess was in the library.

There was a fire in the great stone hearth. A pleasant smell of wood smoke, beeswax and neat's-foot oil made the book-lined room welcoming.

Helen sat in a deep leather chair. Standing in front of the fire, gazing down into its flames, was the Colonel, still in his riding clothes.

'I'm sorry,' Ursula said, 'I didn't mean to disturb you, Helen. I came to give an account of the inquest but I see that you will already have received one.'

The Colonel turned. 'My horse was faster than your trap.' He smiled briefly at her and waved a hand towards a chair on the opposite side of the fire to Helen's. 'Please, join us.'

Ursula looked questioningly at the Countess.

'Oh, come in,' Helen said impatiently. 'You will know everything shortly anyway.'

'After you left,' the Colonel said once Ursula was seated, 'I asked Dr Mason exactly what his diagnosis of Snell's death was.' He had changed his riding boots for brogues and she was caught by the incongruity of the shoes with riding breeches. 'He was not at first inclined to offer any opinion. I pointed out that he had refused to sign the death certificate; he hemmed and hawed a little, then Geoffrey Matthews said he must have had some reason for this and he'd better tell us.'

How useful to have a name of such power as Mountstanton, Ursula thought.

'Mason said he'd found Snell in bed, lying on his back. His first thought was that the man had died of a heart attack. Snell was a patient of his but had no history of heart tremors. However, something had undoubtedly stopped his breathing. Then Mason said he'd looked at his eyes and noticed the unmistakeable signs of asphyxia. He could only conclude then that Snell had been smothered to death.'

Helen placed a negligent hand on the book she'd been holding. 'Did he explain what those unmistakeable signs were?'

The Colonel nodded. 'Apparently smothering causes tiny red dots to appear in the eyes – blood no doubt.'

Ursula gave a small gasp and gooseflesh rose on her arms.

'There's more,' the Colonel continued grimly. 'Mason then went downstairs and tested the doors. Both were locked but a back window in the little scullery-cum-kitchen was open and might have been forced.'

'Can he be sure?' Helen asked casually, as though the matter was of no great moment.

He shrugged. 'Matthews is getting the constable to investigate and has ordered Mason to perform an autopsy. There will undoubtedly have to be an inquest.'

'Another one,' Helen sighed, rising from her chair. 'Luncheon will be late, I've asked for it in half an hour's time. I hope by then both Richard and Belle will have returned; they are out horseback riding.'

The Colonel smiled. 'You have never lost your American habit of tautology. What else could they be riding but horses?'

'Donkeys, maybe, or pigs,' she said caustically. 'In America we prize accuracy.' She shut the door behind her with a decided click.

'You haven't told her Miss Ranner's story?' Ursula asked the Colonel.

'I need to speak to Richard first.'

★ ★ ★

Luncheon was a sombre meal. The Dowager banned any discussion of the inquest.

'That girl brought nothing but trouble to this house. I am not going to have her shade disturb us now,' she said.

'Mama, I have to agree with you,' said the Earl.

Ursula asked Belle about her ride.

Belle praised Pocahontas's spirit and speed, then turned towards Helen and added, 'I suppose you called her that because you think of yourself as some native American princess making peace with the English, then marrying one, coming over here and meeting the Queen.'

Helen narrowed her eyes.

The Colonel swiftly said, 'Is that what Pocahontas did? I don't know much more than her name and that she was a Red Indian.'

Belle looked pleadingly at Ursula.

'Belle has neatly summed up the story,' she said. 'She came from Virginia and helped maintain peace between the early colonists and the natives, and saved the life of an adventurer who was at the mercy of her tribe.' Ursula looked around the table. 'Had it been a properly romantic story, they would have fallen in love but she actually married another Englishman, one John Rolfe, and became a Christian.'

'I thought she married John Smith, the man she rescued,' pouted Belle.

Ursula smiled at her. 'No, it was John Rolfe. He brought her to England and she did meet the Queen.'

'That's romantic, I suppose.' Belle looked as though she was not quite sure.

'All you Americans want to meet our monarch,' said the Earl. 'For a republic you have an unhealthy love of titles and royal blood.' He rose from the table. 'I have matters to attend to.'

The Colonel also rose. 'I need to speak to you, Richard.'

'Now?'

'Now.'

'Then you'd better come to the library.'

The two brothers left the room.

The Dowager sighed. 'I don't know what has happened to manners these days. Helen, you should insist on proper behaviour at the table. Sometimes it's like bedlam here.'

Helen merely reached for an apple from the dessert arrangement.

'Belle, shall you and I go for a walk this afternoon?' suggested Ursula.

'I have arranged that we are to take tea with some neighbours,' said Helen swiftly.

'Oh, *more* boring people?'

'Belle!' said the Dowager sharply. 'No one likes girls who whine.'

'And what about Harry? Isn't tea time when we see him?'

'Harry will come down after we return. It will not take us long. Lady Moore is to give a ball for her daughter this season. I shall invite her and Lavinia to your ball and you will receive an invitation to the Moore's. It is right and proper that you meet her before then. You will like Lavinia; she is very pretty and well-mannered.'

A footman entered the dining room and spoke to the butler.

'Miss Grandison, his lordship asks if you could attend him in the library.'

Ursula stood up with a feeling of relief. 'Of course, Benson.'

She followed the footman down the corridor.

In the library the two brothers stood either side of the fireplace. Anger crackled between them.

The Colonel was very controlled; his well-shaped mouth firm, his eyes steady. But the hand that held the edge of the mantelshelf was white with the intensity of his grip, and the fingers of his other hand tapped a silent rhythm on his leg.

The Earl had his hands buried deep in the pockets of his beautifully tailored trousers. His face was red and his pale blue eyes, always slightly protuberant, looked as though they might pop out of their sockets.

As Ursula was shown into the room, he thrust one of his hands through his hair, smoothing it back in a gesture of frustration.

'Miss Grandison, my brother has told me some cock-and-bull story that he said he heard from you, who was told it by that village busybody Miss Ranner. I want you to repeat it to my face.' His voice was dark and disturbed.

The Colonel indicated a chair. 'Please sit, Miss Grandison.' He did not look at his brother.

'Yes, do,' said the Earl irritably. 'Accept my apologies for not offering one to you immediately.'

Ursula sat down and allowed the Colonel to place her crutches suitably to hand.

Speaking in an expressionless voice, she repeated Miss Ranner's story, editing her words into a concise account of how the woman came to be in the lane and what she had seen. 'I suggested she might have been mistaken in her identification of the rider but she said she recognised both his outline and his horse.'

The Earl brought a clenched fist down on one of the library tables with such force that a book fell to the floor. 'Damn it, woman, she could not have seen me. I was not there, I was here.'

'There are not many grey horses in the district, Richard.'

The Earl swung round on his brother. 'Do you dare to disbelieve me? God's sake, man, it was night! All cats are black and don't tell me it was bright moonlight. Yes, the moon was full but clouds scudded across.'

'How could you tell, if you were inside Mountstanton?' The Colonel sounded like a reasonable man with a reasonable question but his gaze bored into his brother's face.

'I said I was here, not that I was fast asleep behind curtains!'

The Earl raked his hair with his hand again, strode to the end of the library, turned and strode back. He had all the tension of a coiled spring. 'I smoked a cigar on the terrace, if you must know. In fact, I looked for you to join me but apparently you had gone to bed. Everyone had gone to bed, it seemed, but me.' He thrust his hands back into his trouser pockets. 'Even Benson was locking up. I had to promise to attend to the terrace door when I had finished. At least *he* trusted me,' he finished bitterly. 'I then had a nightcap and went to bed. I did not,' he added through gritted teeth, 'go to the stables, saddle Snowy and ride off to Hinton Parva.' He glared at his brother.

He sounded positive but did he protest too much? 'Is there anything further you wish to know, my lord?'

'What? Oh, no, Miss Grandison, you may go. Wait – I would rather you did not spread this story around. There is no need to distress my mother. I find it difficult to understand why Miss Ranner spoke to you in the first place. Had she even met you?'

'Yes, my lord. On a previous occasion, she and I had talked at some length in her cottage. The Colonel was busy talking to the coroner and I think she felt I might be someone who could, well, make you aware of what she believes she saw.'

The Earl said nothing.

Ursula took her crutches from the Colonel. He laid a hand briefly on the top of her arm as she prepared to leave the room. 'Thank you,' he said.

She felt very sorry for both men. Whatever the truth of the matter, trust between the brothers seemed to have broken down.

'Whatever the truth of the matter'; the words repeated themselves inside Ursula's head. However convincing the Earl might have sounded to her, she knew that his brother did not believe him.

Did the Colonel really believe that Richard, Earl of Mountstanton, had secretly visited a man whose stated intention was to give evidence at the dead nursemaid's inquest? A man who this very morning had been found murdered?

Chapter Nineteen

Later that afternoon, Ursula was quietly knitting in the small sitting room used for casual activities, and trying without success to engage Belle in conversation. The young girl sat playing a game of cat's cradle, silently refusing to respond to any of Ursula's light comments.

The door opened and Belle looked up, her eager expression changing to one of disappointment as the Colonel entered.

'I must change for this visit Helen wants to make,' she said, and left the room.

The Colonel courteously held the door open for her.

Ursula smiled and indicated a convenient chair.

'I thought you would like to know what has been decided regarding Polly's burial, Miss Grandison.'

Ursula put down her needles. 'I have been wondering what should happen. I suppose, the verdict being what it was, she cannot be buried in a church graveyard.'

He sat down. 'No, I fear not. However, I understand there is a space just outside the Mountstanton church environs where a grave could be dug, and Richard has agreed that this would be most suitable. The plot is now being prepared and Polly will be buried tomorrow morning. The Reverend Taylor has been consulted and he has agreed to say a few simple prayers at the graveside.'

'May I attend?'

He looked pleased. 'I hoped you might want to be there. The poor girl will not have many to say goodbye to her; there is the stigma of suicide and the lack of any family.'

'Perhaps she thought of her fellow staff as family?'

He coloured slightly. 'I hope so. What are you knitting?'

She held up the cobwebby confection. 'It's a wrap. I bought the wool at your village store and Miss Ranner lent me the pattern.'

He leaned forward to examine it. 'It is beautiful. If it didn't sound too fanciful, I would say it was fairy work! Who will be lucky enough to wear it? Perhaps Miss Seldon – over a ball dress?'

Ursula laughed. 'Knitted wraps are not fashionable.'

I have seen women knitting in South Africa,' he said. 'It seems a very peaceful and productive activity.'

Ursula smiled but said nothing.

'I thought coming home was going to offer me a period of quiet contemplation, a time to consider the future,' he said slowly, his gaze on the leaping flames of the fire. 'Instead . . . '

'Instead you've been plunged into a tragedy with unpleasant ramifications.'

'Quite so. In many ways it reminds me of war.'

'You mean, unexpected attacks, that sort of thing?'

He smiled. 'You understand, I think. Guerrilla warfare is always the most difficult for an army to counter and overcome.'

★ ★ ★

The next morning was sunny and warm. A small party set off from the Mountstanton side door towards the grey-stone church that stood in the grounds surrounded by a haphazard arrangement of headstones and tombs set in well-tended grass.

On the far side of a low stone wall, a grave had been dug. Waiting there was the local vicar, a light breeze teasing his surplice. Resting on webbing was a coffin of quality wood with brass handles, on its top a simple wreath of white roses. Four undertaker's assistants were in attendance.

Polly might not be allowed to lie in hallowed ground but Ursula was glad that an effort had been made to see that her burial was as dignified as possible. She suspected that it was the Colonel who had made the arrangements.

Both brothers were there, as was Helen. The Dowager had announced that it was unsuitable for either herself or Belle to attend and she was surprised at any of the family ignoring the criminal taint of suicide. Mrs Comfort walked beside the Mountstanton housekeeper and butler. Behind them came Maggie Hodgkiss, the laundry maid, and she was followed by several of the other servants. Ursula noted that the footman, John, was amongst them.

The vicar opened his prayer book.

Across the fields came a furiously ridden horse. All turned as Adam Gray, the agent, pulled up and dismounted, handing the reins to one of the assistants.

'Your note has only just reached me,' he said angrily to the Colonel, taking his stand beside the brothers.

There was a short committal service, then the coffin was lowered into the grave. Helen cast the first handful of soil, followed by her husband and brother-in-law. The Colonel handed Ursula a small quantity of the earth to save her the necessity of bending. She threw it in. The Mountstanton servants added their handfuls.

Last of all was Mr Gray.

Resting on her crutches, Ursula watched the way his square, rugged face worked and his light blue eyes blinked hard to clear them of tears. His generous mouth, though, was firmly controlled.

Then it was all over. The vicar exchanged a few words with the Earl and Countess, and the Colonel turned to the agent.

'Will you join me in a sherry, Gray?'

The agent shook his head. 'Thank you, Colonel Stanhope, but I have matters to attend to.'

'I'm sorry my note reached you so late.'

'Not really your fault; I was late getting home last night and didn't check my correspondence until this morning.'

The servants headed for the house and Ursula limped behind them.

* * *

The following day, Ursula spent the morning practising on the piano. Everyone else was out; the Earl and his brother off on some business in Salisbury, and Helen had taken Belle for a luncheon some distance away. Emerging from the drawing room, Ursula encountered Mrs Comfort and Harry.

'Miss Grandison!' exclaimed Harry. 'I have been wondering who can play cards with me.'

Mrs Comfort shushed him.

Ursula laughed. A simple game with a five-year-old boy sounded a perfect way of passing the time.

Negotiating the stairs, Ursula realised that her ankle, at long last, really did seem much stronger.

Harry ran to a cupboard and found a pack of cards. 'I like snap,' he said happily. 'I always win.'

'Who do you play with?' Ursula shuffled the cards. The pack seemed well worn.

For an instant his expression trembled. 'Polly liked to play snap.' He sat at the table and set his mouth in a straight line.

'And remember how Colonel Charles played with you and Polly when he was recovering from his wound?' Mrs Comfort said in an encouraging tone.

'Mama does not like me to play cards; she says they are a path to per . . . per . . . perdition,' he finally brought out on a note of triumph.

Ursula smiled. 'I think we can play a game of snap without dangerous consequences, Harry.' For an instant she remembered games of poker played in the mining camp; the high stakes, the tensions, the accusations of cheating, the spilling over of passions when fortunes changed hands, the shots that could be fired – but it was only for an instant, then she firmly closed a door on her memories.

For Ursula, card entertainment lay in speed and hilarity, and she forced the pace until Mrs Comfort almost collapsed in tears of laughter. She was first to lose her cards. Harry, though, even while laughing with them, demonstrated surprising powers of concentration and single-mindedness. Time and again his 'snap' came a split second before Ursula's, and not because she had deliberately hung back.

'I won! I won!' he crowed, gathering up the last pile of cards.

'You are a real champion,' Ursula acknowledged. 'I can see that your mama may well fear you turning into a gambler.'

'Are you a gambler, Miss Grandison?'

She looked at the eager face. 'No, Harry, I am not. I don't mind losing a game but I hate losing large sums of money. I have known many gamblers, though,' she added.

'Do lots of them win?'

She shook her head. 'Sometimes they have lucky streaks, then they play some more and lose it all. Sometimes they lose very, very large sums. I knew a man who shot himself because he had lost everything he owned – and more.'

'How could he lose more than he owned?'

She sighed. 'Because he lied and offered to bet something that wasn't his.'

Harry looked up at her, his eyes huge. 'And that's why he shot himself?'

'Yes. He had lost his honour as well as his possessions.'

'Well, let that be a lesson to you, my lad,' said Mrs Comfort. 'No wonder her ladyship doesn't want you playing cards.'

Harry's soft little mouth pouted. 'But I'm not going to lose anything.'

'Not if you don't play for money,' Ursula said with a smile. 'Play because you enjoy the game, not to win stakes.'

She stayed to have luncheon with him and Mrs Comfort in the nursery, enjoying much simpler fare than was served in the dining room, and entertaining both boy and nurse with tales of mining in the Sierra Nevada. Harry listened, open-mouthed, and had to be gently encouraged to eat his meal as Ursula told him of fights and the privations of living in a mining camp.

On her return downstairs, Ursula requested the loan of a walking stick. Abandoning her crutches, she tried to walk with only the aid of the stick. Her ankle was more painful than with the support of the crutches, but the feeling of freedom was worth the extra discomfort.

Ursula turned around at the end of the corridor, and saw the Colonel watching her.

'Congratulations, Miss Grandison. I commend your courage.'

'A short walk on friendly terrain hardly calls for bravery.'

'I am sure you need to rest that ankle now,' he waved a hand towards the library and Ursula was happy to enter.

'Did your business go well?'

He shrugged. 'It was nothing very important.'

'I have spent a very pleasant time with Harry this morning,' Ursula said brightly. 'We played snap. He won,' she added with a smile.

'Harry's a demon with the cards. I think he has an uncommonly bright intelligence.'

'You're very fond of him, aren't you?'

'He's my nephew, the Mountstanton heir. But he's a capital fellow; one can't help liking him.' His smile was endearingly natural.

'I agree,' she said softly. 'I enjoyed his company so much I ate luncheon in the nursery.'

He sat down opposite her. 'I'm afraid that your stay at Mountstanton is not offering you many opportunities for fun. I had hoped that perhaps, with the wretched inquest out of the way, I could suggest a diversion of some sort.' He grinned at her. 'You have, after all, promised to tell me about your Californian adventures.' The smile vanished as quickly as it had appeared. 'But now I find I have to go up to town.'

'Oh?' Ursula tried to sound disinterested.

'Business.'

'Of course.'

Silence grew and deepened. Ursula wanted very badly to know how long he was going to be away and just what he was going to be doing in London, but could not bring herself to display such bad manners as to ask.

The Colonel drew a quick breath. 'I'm hoping to stand for parliament in the next election. At the moment an election doesn't look likely. I should have abandoned the war in 1900, as my comrade Winston Churchill did. There was an election the following year but I wasn't a famous war correspondent and I doubt I would have won a seat.'

'You want to be a politician? Is that why you have resigned your commission?'

He looked down at his hands. 'I've experienced the splendid way the ordinary soldier can conduct himself. His class gets a raw deal out of life and I'd like to help change that.'

Ursula wished she knew how the English political system operated.

The Colonel gave her a contrite smile. 'This isn't the time to talk about such matters. I should not, perhaps, have mentioned it. Only Richard thinks I'm a fool and Mama refuses to discuss the matter with me.'

'And Helen?'

'Oh, Helen says she'll never understand politics and not to bore her with such matters.'

'I would be interested to hear about your aims and the party you hope to join.'

'It'd take too long now. I have a train to catch.'

Was he really to disappear up to London? 'What about your investigations into Polly's death?'

'I haven't forgotten her, Miss Grandison.'

'And Mr Snell?'

His gaze shifted to his beautifully polished shoes. 'Apparently the post-mortem examination has enabled the death certificate to be signed. Heart attack, plain and simple.'

Ursula felt deeply uneasy. Could it be that simple?

'I have to consider Richard,' he said awkwardly, fiddling with his gold watch chain. 'He's terrified of Mama and she's determined that the whole matter should be quietly wrapped up. No scandal must attach itself to the Mountstanton name.' He sounded bitter.

'You are surely not terrified of your mother?'

'I'd rather face a brigade of Boers than Mama in full cry, but there are times when I can summon sufficient courage to do my duty rather than hers.'

Was this the man Ursula had been certain would fight to a standstill to redress the wrong he saw being inflicted on Polly's memory?

He rose and held out his hand. 'I must say farewell for the moment, Miss Grandison. But I shall return shortly and then I hope we may be able to spend some time together.'

She inclined her head. 'I shall look forward to that, Colonel Stanhope.'

It was, she thought, a polite exchange of social niceties that meant nothing very much.

What had happened to the rapport she thought had been established between them?

* * *

Ursula was surprised at how empty the enormous house seemed without the Colonel. She told herself to banish such nonsense from her head. When she and Belle had arrived at

Mountstanton, the place had seemed overflowing with people and the absence of someone who had not even been present then could not, *would* not, make a difference.

She made determined efforts to practise walking with the stick rather than the crutches, played more cards with Harry and accompanied him to the stables to watch him ride his pony. She watched his face flush with triumph as he jumped the two low arrangements of rails cleanly. 'Won't Papa be pleased?' he cried to Ursula as he dismounted.

Days passed and then two weeks with no sign of the Colonel. When Helen had asked in a desultory way over dinner if they could expect to see him in the near future, the Earl had said, 'You know Charles, he does what he wants when he wants.'

Deprived of the Colonel's stimulating presence, Ursula tried to apply herself to the task Mr Seldon had entrusted to her: the discovery of why Helen was not spending her dowry on restoring Mountstanton. Ursula made friends with Mrs Parsons. She learned a great deal about running a mansion such as Mountstanton and soon realised that the housekeeper was as puzzled as she was about the lack of funds being spent on the house. Gradually the housekeeper become more and more forthcoming until finally one day she said, 'Forgive me for saying so, Miss Grandison, but we does wonder about her ladyship's dowry. It's not as if we've heard of sums being laid out on other areas of the estate.'

Ursula murmured something soothing about there possibly being some difficulty with stocks and shares, at which Mrs Parsons had looked so horror-stricken that Ursula gave up any further discussion of the subject.

She tried subtle approaches to Helen, though the Countess either failed to respond in any meaningful way, or she became waspish: 'If it's that my father has failed to supply you with sufficient funds, please ask straight out, Ursula. I hate the mention of money but I suppose occasionally one has to deal with the filthy stuff.'

Unusually flustered, Ursula told her she had no need of financial assistance. 'I suppose it's that I wonder why you have not put in hand any restoration of the house,' she said, coming right out with it.

To her surprise, Helen did not at once fly at her. She sat in her boudoir with red patches flaring in her cheeks for several minutes. Then she said, 'I wonder at you, Ursula. I would have thought you had been here a sufficient time to understand that Mountstanton follows tradition. If I transformed the whole place the way I have done this room, there would be outrage. We Americans cherish the new, the English the old. Now, I would be grateful if you could leave me to finish my correspondence.'

Ursula retreated. The story of Mountstanton and tradition was patent nonsense. Look at the way the Dowager had transformed her apartment, no doubt with her own funds. So what was Helen doing with hers? She wrote to Mr Seldon the story of her failure but told him she would continue digging.

Belle had developed an unaccustomed pallor; worried, Ursula persuaded her to come riding, a decision that was rewarded by the girl coming back with pink cheeks and high spirits.

Ever since the Colonel had left for London, simmering at the back of Ursula's mind had been the unanswered questions over Polly's death. Almost three weeks after the girl's funeral, Ursula sat with her knitting and forced herself to face certain conclusions that her examination of various facts had produced.

First, following the arguments produced by the Colonel, was the belief that the girl had definitely not committed suicide. Even if Polly had gone against her nature and decided the shame of carrying a bastard child was too much for her to bear, she would have chosen a more certain way to kill herself.

Second, although accident on the face of it was a possibility, it was surely unlikely. Her personal experience was that no one would tackle that slope without real reason and there was no evidence to suggest that there was anything that could have meant Polly would have voluntarily tackled that climb. All right, she herself had been crazy enough to try it but Polly would have been better acquainted with its dangers.

If she accepted these conclusions, the only viable possibility left was that someone had killed Polly. But why? The most obvious reason was that the girl insisted that her lover should take her away and either marry her or set her up with a home in which she could bring up their child. He had been unwilling to consider either arrangement and did not want her to name him as the father.

It was a most unpleasant conclusion and Ursula was sure the reason why it had taken her so long to face it was because the next question had to be: who was the father?

There were a number of possibilities but no actual evidence against any of them. If she waited, would something emerge that would point to one or another? For a moment she wished passionately that the Colonel was available to discuss the question. In his absence she was horribly aware that she might be living alongside a murderer.

The one bright spot that Ursula could see at present was that the Countess was at last involving Belle with the arrangements for her coming out ball. There were lunches and dinners, both at Mountstanton and with neighbours, establishing friendships with girls who were also making their debut that season, together with a number of eligible young men.

Helen had also arranged for a small dance one evening with some sixteen couples, mainly young, who Belle had been introduced to in the surrounding neighbourhood. The drawing room carpet was lifted and the floor polished. Ursula was happy to play for dancing while parents and guardians were offered cards in an adjacent reception room. A buffet supper was served and the evening was a great success, with Belle behaving delightfully. Ursula's one disappointment was that the charming Mr Russell was not among the guests. She supposed, perhaps, that being a contemporary of the Earl's, he was a little old for such entertainment.

The day after Ursula had faced the possibility Mountstanton was harbouring a murderer, news came of the death of Lady Frances. The Earl insisted he would attend the funeral and would cable his brother, asking him to come home so he could also attend. The Colonel, however, did not return.

Nor had Mr Warburton returned and Belle was prone to sulks and depressions. One evening some four weeks after the inquest, following dinner with just the family, Belle gave up trying to render a simple piece on the piano. 'It's no good, I'll never be able to play properly,' she said despairingly.

'Practise, that's what you need, my girl,' said the Dowager tartly. 'You'll never get anywhere in this world without effort. You're a scatterhead, that's your trouble.' She closed her book, rose and clicked her fingers at Honey. 'I shall say goodnight.'

The Dowager sailed magisterially out of the room and Belle stuck her tongue out at her departing back.

The Earl had removed himself to his study after dinner and Helen had already retired to her boudoir, so if anyone was to admonish Belle it would have to be Ursula.

'Belle, dear,' she said.

'Oh, don't you start.' The girl abandoned the piano, her face petulant. 'All anyone ever does these days is scold me. Papa said that everything would be done to entertain me: visits to the races, theatres, and Helen would take me to London, to Paris, to Monte Carlo.' She gazed disconsolately at Ursula. 'All I do is meet boring, boring people. There's far too much talking. Why can't we have another dance? I love dancing.'

Belle held up her arms to an invisible partner and swayed gracefully round the room for a moment, then burst out. 'Oh, Ursula, can't you talk to Helen? It's no good me saying anything, she just tells me I'm a spoilt brat, and she's introducing me to lots of girls and young men who will invite me to all sorts of events once we reach London and I make my debut. But it's *now* I want to have fun. And William hasn't sent me so much as a note. It's as though he's vanished down a hole like Alice in Wonderland. How could he desert me like that?' Belle plumped herself down in a chair beside the gently dying fire and gazed resentfully at Ursula. 'Why can't we just go to London and have some fun? No wonder that odd Colonel has gone.'

'I wish you wouldn't refer to him in that way.' Ursula immediately regretted her words.

'Why not? He is odd. Don't you see how he looks at Helen? Why you all want me to marry him, I can't imagine.'

'I've never said I wanted you and he to marry.' Ursula put down her knitting and tried to think of a way to send Belle off to bed in a better humour.

'That's probably because you want to marry him yourself.' Belle darted a sly look at her. 'You were always having little chats with him and since he's gone to London you have quite lost your sparkle.'

Ursula couldn't help laughing. 'Sparkle? Honestly, Belle, what on earth have you been reading?'

'Well, I shouldn't get any hopes up because I think he's the one who pushed that nursemaid into the river.'

'What a dreadful thing to suggest, Belle,' Ursula said coldly. Her knitting lay forgotten in her lap. 'Apart from the fact that you know of no motive for such a thing, the Colonel was not even at Mountstanton when Polly disappeared.'

'How do you know he didn't come here, push her into the river and then go off again? And how do you know he didn't have a motive? Sarah told me that Polly was in a delicate condition. And she told me that the Colonel spent a lot of time in Harry's nursery talking to Polly when he was last here.'

'You should not gossip with servants. Anyway, that was a long time ago, after he came home injured from the fighting in South Africa.'

'See, you know about it too!' Belle sounded triumphant. 'So it must be true. Maybe he met her in secret afterwards?'

'But he went back there.' Ursula felt hysteria rising; she had to convince Belle she was talking nonsense. The very thought that she might repeat any of this to anyone else was appalling.

'Oh, Ursula, you are so simple! I thought you were intelligent, yet you just accept whatever that man says. Helen is the same.' Belle leant forward and narrowed her eyes. 'The war ended last year and nobody knows why he has left the army. If he is such a wonderful soldier, why doesn't he stay on and become a General? I think he's done something shifty and he's been asked to leave. And that's why they all want me to marry him, because he needs money to make another life. Which is why he can't be interested in you, because you haven't got any.' She stood up and shook the skirt of her pink silk dress into place. 'Well, they can whistle but I won't dance to their tune. And Papa won't expect me to. I'm going to write to him and say what a boring time I'm having and can he please arrange for you to take me to Paris. He's bound to know someone who can give us a good time there. Loads of Americans spend months and months in Paris and Monte Carlo.'

Ursula was speechless for several moments.

'Belle, I can't imagine what sort of rubbishy romantic novels you read,' she managed finally. 'It's been a long time since I heard such a farrago, such a hotchpotch, such a load of nonsense. Please, please do not repeat any of that to anyone else, particularly any of your sister's staff. She would be mortified.'

'Ho hum, Ursula! No, I won't repeat any of it. Not until it becomes obvious to you all. But you think about it. And I shall certainly write to Papa about Paris. Goodnight.'

She flounced out of the room.

It took a long time that night for Ursula to get to sleep and when she did, her dreams were confused and unhappy.

★ ★ ★

With the improvement of her sprained ankle, Ursula had developed the habit of an early morning ride. Occasionally she persuaded Belle to join her, but the morning after Belle's extraordinary words on the Colonel, Ursula went riding on her own. For the moment she felt out of sympathy with the girl.

She explored a new area of countryside and came upon another river; very different from the one so close to Mountstanton. Narrow, it ran chuckling and busy beneath trees; sun shone through the leaves, dappling both the water and the low banks. So attractive was the prospect, Ursula stopped and enjoyed a few minutes taking in the view.

After a little, her eyes adjusted to the half-light and she saw that, a little lower down the river, there was a fisherman. There was something familiar about the figure sitting on a small stool, a woven basket at his feet, rod held steady over the water. Approaching, she saw it was Mr Russell.

She was almost upon him before he realised he was no longer alone and looked up. Immediately he rose to his feet.

'Miss Grandison, what a pleasure to see you. What brings you to these parts?'

'A desire to experience a little more of this beautiful countryside. What do you fish?'

'Trout.' He looked at the rod still held in his hand. 'I have not had much luck but it is a pleasant way to pass the time and sort through one's thoughts.'

'I was so sorry to hear the sad news concerning Lady Frances. Losing a parent is a bitter blow that takes some adjusting to; you have my deepest sympathy.'

He turned his gaze towards the river. His face was drawn and he looked as though sleep was a stranger to him. 'I knew she was slipping away and that soon I would be an orphan but, somehow, I still can't quite believe it. It is not helped, perhaps, by my imminent departure forcing me to sort out possessions. Luckily they are few and I have now almost completed the task.'

They remained for a few moments without speaking, Ursula on her mount, Mr Russell standing beside her. Then he gave her a lopsided smile. 'Can I persuade you to join me in contemplating the river for a while? I am afraid I do not have another rod but, if you care to fish, you are welcome to borrow mine.'

Ursula thought the idea sounded delightful and was interested to hear his plans for the future. Before she could respond though, Mr Russell's rod almost sprang out of his hand.

'Ah, a bite!'

'Please, do whatever it is fishermen do, Mr Russell. I shall enjoy watching you in action.'

With a smile he started to play the fish on the end of his line, walking to and fro, reeling in and letting out. Ursula noted the tautness of the line and how its pull bent the slender top of the rod, and realised the trout he had on the end of it must be a big one. It could, she thought, be some considerable time before the fish was exhausted enough to be landed and her horse was getting restive.

She gave a wave, wished Mr Russell luck with the fish, and moved away from the river. The chat would have to wait.

Ursula headed back towards Mountstanton. She had not gone far before she saw, across the fields, another rider going towards the river. The grey horse identified him as the Earl.

Once again the facts as far as she knew them concerning Polly's death nagged away at Ursula's mind. All at once she thought of a course of action she could follow.

Chapter Twenty

Five o'clock in the morning. The cockerel announced a new day and the dog stirred in his kennel.

Slumped in his chair beside the cold ashes of last night's fire, Adam Gray opened bleary eyes and cursed. He flung the empty brandy bottle against the wall; the noise of the shattering glass threatened to break open his aching brain. Wrenching off jacket and shirt, he stumbled out of the house and thrust his head beneath the pump in the backyard, then drank gratefully of the icy water.

Adam pushed back his wet hair and stood for a moment, taking in the morning. Summer was almost here. Mist softened every outline and promised heat later in the day. All was fresh and new. Beyond the stables, a gentle hill rose, white sheep embroidering the green of the meadows. Over by the river, cattle grazed; rich brown Jerseys, their udders bulging with creamy milk. In the distance, the green shoots of wheat were decorating earthy furrows.

The futility of last night's drinking session hit him hard. When did alcohol ever solve problems? He shook his gradually clearing head. What had his life become? Since the day of the inquest, it had slid into a dark hole.

The day after, the Earl had caught him as he rode back from a meeting with one of the tenant farmers, a matter of some worn-out pig sties on one of the tenant farms and where the money to replace them was to be found.

'What's this I hear about you and Polly?' he had demanded.

Richard Stanhope had never been known for ease of manner. He had inherited none of his father's famous charm. Instead, there was his mother's pride and cold authority.

Adam sat on Barney, his stolid chestnut horse, and gazed unblinking at his employer, resentful of his language, resentful of his authority, resentful of all the Mountstanton family had done to bring down his beloved Polly.

'Gray!'

'My lord?'

'I've been told Mrs Parsons caught you and the nursemaid in a compromising position.'

Adam felt a familiar fury build within him. He wanted so much to strike the man. He wanted to bring him down off his horse and trample him into the ground, use his whip to slash that proud face.

With enormous effort he controlled himself. 'It was not compromising, my lord. I merely put an arm around the girl. She was very upset.' He hesitated, then decided that he might as well say everything he was prepared to admit to rather than have it screwed out of him.

He took a deep breath. 'Polly had trusted a man who betrayed her. She suspected she was with child. She had no one to turn to but me, her friend. I told her to keep her counsel while I tried to work out what could be done.'

The Earl sat very still, holding his reins tightly. 'You mean she revealed the identity of the man responsible for her condition?'

If only she had! 'No, my lord. She refused to say.' Adam bared his teeth in an uncontrollable grimace. 'She feared that I would do the man some damage.'

A tic twitched in the Earl's right eyelid. 'Yes, we know your reputation, Gray.'

Adam didn't flinch. He was known as a man not to cross in an alehouse; easy to anger, quick to use his fists and with a strong right arm that could launch a punishing blow. He was, though, judged a fair fighter.

'So you have no idea who Polly was walking out with?'

'No, my lord.'

Was that an infinitesimal relaxation in the Earl's shoulders?

'The jury's verdict was just,' the Earl said. 'She could not live with the shame.'

Another little piece of Adam died at this.

The Earl lifted his whip in a semblance of farewell, dug his heels into his horse and was gone.

Since then, Adam had tried to forget the encounter. For once, he was relieved that his employer showed so little interest in his estate.

The evenings were the worst. When his disabled wife, Deirdre, had been helped to bed and his sister, Adele, had retired, there were too many hours before Adam could bring himself to take to his bed, knowing that sleep was unlikely to come. That was when Adam made alcohol his companion.

Now he stood in the yard and found a stone to discourage the cockerel's hoarse claiming of his territory.

It was too early for their housekeeper to be up, so Adam riddled the stove. When the blaze was going well, he made coffee and fried himself bacon and eggs.

'Lord bless us,' said Jenny, his housekeeper, as she entered, tying on her apron, 'but you're up before times. Nothing wrong with madam, is there?'

Adam shook his head. 'I hope she and my sister are still asleep.'

The process of getting a woman up who had no use of her legs was long and tedious, even when Adam was there to help. While he was away, Deirdre chose to remain in her bed rather than call on outside help to lift and carry her downstairs to the invalid carriage she used during the day.

When he was there, the first part of Adam's day was spent aiding Adele to bathe and dress his wife, then carrying her downstairs. Only after that could Adam turn his attention to his job as Mountstanton agent. There were mornings when her joints were in agony and the process was slow and desperate; Deirdre's courage never failed to cut through Adam as though a knife stabbed him.

Jenny took a broom and swept up the broken bottle without comment.

Later, with Deirdre settled downstairs, he prepared to go out. 'I'll be back around midday, so count me in for luncheon,' he said, running a soothing finger along her right eyebrow.

Just as he was leaving to go to the stables, a horse and rider cantered in and he recognised the woman who had found Polly's body.

'Miss Grandison,' he said, coming reluctantly towards her. 'To what do I owe this pleasure?'

She sat on her horse, a docile mare belonging to the Mountstanton stable, and looked down at him with clear grey eyes. She was not beautiful, not like the Countess, but her face was attractive: strong cheekbones, a generous but firm mouth and wide-set eyes that gave her a very honest look. Her dark green habit had style, and she sported a jaunty little tricorne hat. Her expression was serious.

'Mr Gray, I wonder if you would speak to me about Polly.'

He was taken aback. 'Why?'

'Because I am not happy with the verdict of suicide.'

'But what is it to do with you?'

She looked intently at him for a moment then said, 'I do not think we can converse like this. Will you help me dismount, please?'

He would have preferred to send her on her way, but had to do as she asked.

She almost fell as she reached the ground and he had to grasp her firmly round the waist. 'I remember, you were using crutches at the inquest, were you not?"

She nodded. 'My ankle is much better now, Mr Gray, but a stick would be helpful.'

There was nothing self-pitying about her and he found it no hardship to assist her to the bench outside the stables and fetch a trusty ash stick, chosen for its straightness and natural handle. She thanked him and sat with her gloved hands folded on it, watching as he tied her horse to a hitching post and loosened the girth of her saddle.

Then she turned so she could look at him as he leant against the stable, his hands in the pockets of his breeches.

'Mr Gray, you asked me what the verdict on Polly's death had to do with me. I was the one who found her body in the river. I am sure you understand that it was a distressing experience.'

Her eyes closed briefly as though she could still see Polly's partially decomposed body. Even as she spoke, Adam's own stomach muscles clenched and his mind revolted against the picture she conjured up.

She took a deep breath and continued. 'I am sure you also can imagine how overwhelming an experience staying at Mountstanton is, especially for an American who knows very little about the English aristocracy; what their rules of behaviour are, how they expect guests to conduct themselves, all that. However, when I understood that it was the body of Lord Henry's nursemaid I had discovered, I could not understand how her disappearance from the household had been so easily accepted.'

'Did you think one of them had been responsible for her death?' he said, astounded. His own thinking was far more confused.

She twisted the ash stick for a moment. 'I wanted to know what sort of person Polly was,' she said slowly, appearing to choose her words carefully. 'Why no one had been surprised that she suddenly decided to leave what must surely have been a very desirable post? You should not be fooled by my appearance. There have been times when I was desperate to find a job, any job. So I know the value of one that offers security and a relatively comfortable living and I am sure that Polly did too.'

He found it difficult to believe what she said. Everything about her suggested someone who belonged to a privileged class.

'So I spoke to Mrs Comfort, the Countess, Mrs Parsons, other members of the staff, oh, and the Colonel.'

Was it his imagination or did she colour slightly as she mentioned the last name? He dismissed the thought. In his opinion, there was nothing romantic about Colonel Stanhope.

'The more I was told about Polly, the less likely it seemed to me that she had committed suicide. The Colonel agreed. I understand he spent time at Mountstanton, recovering from a wound sustained in the Boer War, much of it in the nursery with Harry and, of course, Polly. He seems to have admired her.'

'Do you mean they could have become close?' He tried to control his horror at the thought. He remembered the Earl's unease when he asked if Adam knew who had seduced Polly. Surely neither he nor his brother could have abused their position in that way? Then he remembered the Earl's father.

She looked at him thoughtfully. 'The Colonel does not seem to have been at Mountstanton during the critical period.'

The way she phrased it unsettled Adam. She had not rejected the idea altogether, merely pointed out that the facts, as presented to her, did not support such a theory.

'Mrs Parsons,' continued Miss Grandison, 'seemed to be convinced that she glimpsed you and Polly *in flagrante delicto*.'

'She saw what she wanted to see,' Adam said sourly. 'Her imagination is too vivid.'

The grey eyes studied him. 'Then there is Mr Snell. Before he died he went around saying he knew something about Polly that he would tell at the inquest. Have you any idea what that could be?'

Adam kicked at a stone. 'Miss Grandison, there is no reason for me to tell you anything.'

'You think I'm a nosey-parker spinster with a gory interest in death, is that it?' She sat very straight on the bench and looked directly at him.

He shrugged belligerently.

'Mr Gray, at the inquest I gained the impression that you were very fond of Polly. Perhaps it would not be too strong to say that you loved her, however mistaken Mrs Parsons was about what she saw in the woods.' Her warm smile said she wanted to be on terms of equality with him. 'I have not always lived amongst rich folk who have others to serve them and a position in society that must be maintained. I have been at the bottom of the heap, scratching a living, never knowing where the next meal would come from. Somehow, though, I believed in the possibility that life could suddenly turn around and, like some fairytale, give me and those I loved everything we needed and more. I have always been ready to grab life and live it to the full. I think Polly was like that. I know it must be difficult for you to talk about her. You are the Earl's employee; I understand you would not want, in thought, word or deed, to feel you might be in some sense betraying the Stanhopes. But think of Polly!'

Adam closed his eyes. How much he longed to talk about Polly and what she meant to him. He had no one he could even mention her name to without them drawing the wrong conclusions. Could he be frank with this American woman who seemed to understand so much already, and who was so open and straightforward?

Across the yard he saw the back door of the house open and Adele push Deirdre through in her invalid carriage. He went forward to help, not knowing whether to feel resentment or relief at the interruption.

Deirdre looked up at him, mischief in her eyes. 'Consorting with strange women behind my back, Adam?'

'It is Miss Grandison, my dear. Miss Seldon's American companion, asking about my work. Come and meet her.'

Immediately her face was alive with interest. Adam checked that the light rug which hid the hateful twisting of her legs was in place, then took over pushing the carriage. He brought it to Miss Grandison, standing and supporting herself with the ash stick. As Adam performed introductions, she held out her hand to Deirdre, who took it.

'How lovely to meet you, Miss Grandison. The village has been agog with the arrival of Miss Seldon. I have heard how beautiful she is and how well she rides. Every glimpse of her is cherished and talked over.' Her face shone with excitement.

Adele smiled. 'My sister-in-law loves to hear any detail of life at Mountstanton, Miss Grandison. For the most part we live very quietly here. Maybe you would like to come and take tea with us one day and tell us about life in America?'

'I should like that very much, Miss Gray.'

'Then we shall expect you soon, Miss Grandison,' Deirdre said. She waved a hand, 'Onward, dearest Adele. We must not miss a minute of this lovely sunshine.'

Adele pushed Deirdre down the carefully smoothed path to the arbour at the end of the garden. This was supplied with chairs and a view over a sweep of fields and woods. Here the two women would sit, sewing or making lace, comfortably chatting until it was time for lunch.

Adam Gray watched them go, trying to clear his mind. Had he brought about Polly's death by not opening up before about what he knew? Did he have anything to lose by telling at least some of the story? As though he had mentally tossed a coin, he made his decision.

'Miss Grandison, let me tell you what I know about Polly.'

Ursula sat down, her back very straight. Adam picked up a twig, came and sat down beside her and twisted the forked piece of branch in his hand as he talked.

'I have to go back a little way,' he started. 'My father was land agent to the Mountstanton estate before me. I grew up here, in this very cottage.' He looked up at the top left-hand window, the one belonging to his bedroom. 'It was always understood that I would, in time, take over from my father. I came back from the end of my schooling for a short period before beginning my training with a friend of my father's in Derbyshire. I rode all over the Mountstanton land to get a proper feel for the place and to understand what was involved in its running. Occasionally, the fifth Earl, the present Earl's father, came with me. He made me aware of many aspects of the estate that I might not, at that stage, have noticed.'

He paused for a moment. In his mind's eye he could see the tall, handsome man with his quick laugh and easy manner; godlike to a nineteen-year-old girl.

Miss Grandison said nothing, but her alert expression assured him she was taking in everything he was telling her.

'One day in late August, I was riding along the river. It was early evening and I was nicely tired and looking forward to dinner with my parents. Then I heard someone shout for help and I saw that a girl was stranded halfway up that escarpment you fell down when you found Polly.'

'So you became the cavalry charging to the rescue,' said Miss Grandison.

Adam looked down at his fingers still playing with the twig. 'I certainly went to her aid. She had been out blackberrying; the fruit was early that year. She thought she saw a particularly lush bush just below the top of that dreadful slope. She slipped, though, and was lucky not to tumble the whole way down. Well, I climbed up, helped her to the top, then walked her back to Hinton Parva before retrieving my horse. She was a maid of all work for the local teacher.'

'Miss Ranner?'

Adam nodded, pausing again. The facts were simple enough to state. What he had no words for was the impression the girl had made on him. He thought her face was the sweetest he had ever seen; her hair was golden, tied back neatly, which seemed to make more of its colour's extravagance; her slight figure was dressed in the simplest of gowns and her eyes were the most mischievous he had ever seen.

'I was smitten by the girl,' he said stiffly. 'And after that I suppose I went out of my way to encounter her as often as I could.'

'And she was happy to spend time with you, I am sure,' said Miss Grandison, sounding as though she completely understood the situation.

Adam nodded. 'These days I think she would be known as a bit of a minx,' he said slowly. 'I was too naive then to notice. I just felt myself incredibly lucky that such a pretty girl seemed happy to spend time with me, be affectionate.'

Something subtle changed in Miss Grandison's expression. 'By "affectionate" what, exactly, do you mean, Mr Gray?' she asked quietly, almost apologetically.

'Nothing more than a hand in mine, a kiss on my cheek, a finger on my lips. That is, until the last night before I left for Derbyshire.'

There was a long silence. Miss Grandison looked at him, a question in her eyes.

'When I came back a year later for two weeks' leave, I went down to Miss Ranner's to see Mary – that was her name – but the teacher said she was no longer with her. I was totally unprepared for how shocked and disappointed I was. I realised then how much I had been thinking about her, you see. Remembering her gestures, her smiles, her blue eyes and golden hair.' His voice faded as he saw again Mary with all her captivating ways.

'Dare I imagine I know why Mary disappeared?' Miss Grandison asked very gently.

Adam gave her a haunted look. 'Miss Ranner said she didn't have an address for Mary and I was to forget about her. Two weeks later I was back in Derbyshire and was soon so busy that I did almost forget. Two years later, I met Deirdre and we were married.'

'Did she lose the use of her legs through an accident?' came the next gentle enquiry.

Adam rose and strode over to where his visitor's horse stood patiently and caressed the mare's neck for a moment. 'She fell down some stairs,' he said. 'She lost not only the use of her legs but also our baby.'

'Oh, how very, very sad.'

Adam pushed away the anger, frustration and guilt he always felt when he remembered that time.

'It must have made life very difficult for you both.'

His face carefully schooled, Adam came back and once again leant against the stable. 'We managed. Seven years ago my father died, and I was offered the position of Mountstanton agent. My mother went to live with her sister in Devon and we came here. My sister, Adele, said she would help to look after Deirdre, and I settled into learning all about the estate. A year or so later, the Earl died and his son, the present Earl, took over. And, just before that, Lord Harry was born.' He stopped.

Miss Grandison said nothing.

Adam took a deep breath. 'Riding around the estate as I do every day, I used to come across Polly out with the youngster, first pushing him in his perambulator, then they'd either be walking or Lord Harry was on his pony and Polly riding a bicycle. As soon as I laid eyes on her, I recognised Mary in her face and also in her ease of manner. As my experience of girls had grown, I had realised that Mary was the sort of girl who gave her affections easily. Now I recognised the same lightness of character in Polly. I thought I also recognised something else.'

'What did you do?'

He gave a bitter laugh. 'I went to see Miss Ranner. I insisted she told me the truth about Mary. After a little bleating about not breaking promises and the importance of confidences, she finally admitted that Mary had been in trouble. She was sympathetic, she said, but had to tell her she could not keep her on. She arranged for Mary to go to an old friend she knew. When she died in childbirth, Miss Ranner then organised for the baby girl to be taken into the local orphanage. She said that way she could keep an eye on her.'

'And that was Polly?'

He nodded.

'And you felt you knew who her father was?'

Another bitter laugh. 'Oh, I was certain. Without courting attention, I tried to run into her and Lord Harry as often as possible. Only a word here and there but gradually they added up and she began to think of me as a friend.'

'And so she told you when she discovered she was in trouble?'

He nodded. His voice trembled as he said, 'I begged her to tell me who had been responsible but she refused. She said I'd do him an injury and she could not bear that. She would not believe me when I said he'd be safe from me,' he paused for a moment. 'I . . . I think she was right not to trust me.' He felt again the rage that had filled him as she'd confessed. 'She . . . she said she just wanted my advice.'

'And what advice did you give her?'

'Why to say to the man, whoever he was, that she would tell me his name if he did not do the decent thing by her.' He thrust his hands deep into his pockets, his rage now blackened with a deep sense of guilt. 'I was responsible for her death, Miss Grandison. When she told him that, he killed her, he must have done. And I was not here. His lordship had sent me to try and sort out trouble in the Mountstanton Yorkshire mine. It took longer than either of us had expected. There is deep feeling running against the owner there.'

There was silence for a long time.

'What a shock it must have been to find that Polly was dead,' Miss Grandison said finally. 'But you surely cannot hold yourself responsible for your daughter's death.'

'I shall always hold that I brought about Polly's death, Miss Grandison. But you are wrong; *I* was wrong; Polly was not my daughter.'

Chapter Twenty-One

Richard Simon Arthur Philip Stanhope, sixth Earl of Mount-stanton, approached the portrait of his father, Simon Richard Arthur Philip Stanhope, the fifth Earl, with caution.

The walls of the picture gallery were hung with works browned with age; their heavily ornamented frames often offering more interest than the pictures themselves. More recent additions, though, leapt out with fresh colours to charm the visitor.

The art-laden walls seemed to hang about Richard like prison chains, dragging him down into a dungeon of history from which escape was impossible. He felt the eyes of his ancestors judging and dismissing him as the least of their number; three hundred years of Stanhope history pinning him to the spot.

There, towards the end of the gallery, was the portrait of the man who had dominated so much of his life. He almost turned back, as though it was a sleeping animal he feared would wake. Instead, he confronted the vibrant figure that seemed to glory in his youth and strength.

The eighteen-year-old Mountstanton heir stood on a hill beneath a spreading tree, looking slightly to his left, beyond the viewer, down at the house.

A visitor, one familiar with portraiture, once looked at the work and said of the artist, 'Ah, he always makes a statement with his paintings. Look at the simplicity of the landscape, the authority that is conveyed in the subject. He holds a gun, broken over his arm, ready for shooting. His breeches and waistcoat are almost nondescript, yet with them he sports a long and stylish coat that can hardly be held suitable wear for a country pursuit. However, the absurd combination is carried off in an entirely natural manner. It is the portrait of a man of position who cares not what others think. A complex character, I think, perfectly captured by the artist.'

Richard had listened sourly to this assessment. When he was eight, his father had once explained the reason for the coat. 'The painter was the old man's choice; I was to be captured for posterity, as he had been.' Over the other side of the gallery was a portrait of the fourth Earl, Richard's grandfather, arrayed in his Grenadier Guards' uniform, keen blue eyes looking out with humour and dash. 'I didn't want the bother of posing,' his father had continued. 'I agreed as long as I didn't have to dress up in some absurd fashion. But the artist feller said he didn't like my tweed jacket, he wanted something with "a bit more drama", was the way he put it. He took off his coat and told me to put it on, said it was just the job, and so that was that.' The fifth Earl had laughed. 'What shall we dress you up in when the time comes for your portrait, eh?'

Richard had looked up at his father. 'Can I be a pirate?'

Richard recognised with dread the expression of distaste that so often appeared on his father's face when in the company of his elder son, then he had given another laugh. 'Don't think so, old chap. Your mother wouldn't like it.'

Richard looked now at the arrogant tilt of the head in the portrait, the autocratic line of the slightly hooked nose. As Belle had observed, he himself had inherited the Mountstanton nose – and the finger – but not the arrogance; that had been painfully acquired and never enjoyed.

Was there anything he enjoyed in life now?

Helen came up with a piece of paper in her hand. 'I've been looking for you everywhere. What on earth are you doing here in the picture gallery?'

'Wanted a look at the old man.'

Helen turned her attention to her dead father-in-law. 'It's a good likeness,' she said after a moment, as if she had never seen it before. Richard remembered, though, how keen she had been on her first arrival for a grand tour of Mountstanton.

She had taken in everything, commenting as they went in her soft voice that contained only a hint of an American accent. She had been horrified at the decay she saw all around her; bubbling over with plans for rescuing what she called 'its heritage'. Funny, Richard had never noticed any decay. The place was ... well ... just Mountstanton. He was comfortable with it. Had been comfortable with it.

'He was a devil, all right,' Helen said with a reluctant chuckle, gazing at the picture with affection. Richard looked at her properly; saw how tired and stressed she seemed, and how, most unusually for Helen, a strand of hair had come adrift from her carefully arranged coiffure and hung beside her beautifully formed right ear.

'Did I ever tell you it was my father who insisted I went to America to look for a bride?' Richard remembered with frightful clarity that awful session with his father. The Earl had been in his most autocratic mode; Richard, filled with a terrible sick feeling, unable to meet his condemning eyes.

'No, you didn't.' Helen looked at him with a glint in her eye that she hadn't seen since the early days. 'You didn't seem reluctant to be there when I met you.'

He'd been thinking about those early days for some little time now; now that his options seemed to be narrowing dangerously. 'Not after I arrived in Manhattan.'

There was another glimmer of the old Helen as she smiled. 'I remember. You were full of how you wanted to see everything. You were going to tour the Rockies, Mexico, California ...'

For an instant he was back there, with that feeling of freedom he had sensed the moment the boat docked. In America he had been sure he could do anything, be anyone. 'But then I met you.'

'It was that party at Newport; someone introduced us, said you had just arrived and would I look after you.'

'And you did.' He had a sudden vision of her standing on that wide Newport lawn that led down to the water, dressed in a slim gown of white watered-silk with a blue silk belt that showed off her tiny waist and matched her eyes. Her only jewellery had been a single string of magnificent pearls. She had smiled at him with such friendliness that he had been enchanted.

As she looked at him now, he knew she also remembered that moment.

'Where did it go wrong?' he said quietly, more to himself than to her. Would matters have gone differently if they had remained in America?

'As you have to ask . . . ' she snapped and the moment of togetherness passed.

'Why were you looking for me, Helen?'

She seemed to gather herself together and dismiss memories of those weeks in New York. 'It's about the fireworks for your mother's fête.'

Over the years, increasingly lavish rituals had surrounded his mother's birthday celebrations. Every year now, a party was held in the grounds for all the Mountstanton staff and the villagers, complete with an entertainment. It would end with a firework display, for which an expert would be brought in. Despite the work it made, everyone seemed to enjoy this annual party.

'The designer wants to know if we would prefer her name spelt out in a fiery finale or, as he puts it . . . ,' Helen looked at the piece of paper she held, '"to have the sky alight with cascading diamond waterfalls". Hmm, I didn't know he had so much poetry in him. Well? What do you think?'

With an effort, he tried to focus on the matter. It all seemed so unimportant. He raised a hand in a helpless gesture.

Helen shrugged. 'If you have no particular feelings, I think Mama would consider finishing the display with an outline of her name in sputtering fireworks incredibly vulgar. I'll tell him we would prefer to end on "cascading diamond waterfalls". You have organised a gift for her, haven't you, Richard?'

A gift! 'Of course, Helen.' He had better go into Salisbury that afternoon and find something.

'I wrote off for a Kashmiri shawl she admired. And Belle will give her a Chinese lacquer box; Father organised it.' Helen paused for a moment. Richard said nothing. 'I hope Belle will enjoy the fête; the fireworks should please her. I'm a little worried about her. She has seemed quite peaky recently.'

Richard found he did not care whether Belle was pleased or not.

He had never quite understood why Helen had been so keen on inviting her younger sister to Mountstanton. Had she and his mother really plotted to make a match between her and Charles? More fool them if they had. He had raised no objection to the visit; thought a young girl could not interfere with his life. That, though, was before her companion had found Polly's body.

Helen took another look at her list. 'Have you heard if Charles is returning for tomorrow?'

'You mean, you haven't?' Richard could not resist the comment.

Another shrug. 'Your brother forgets he isn't still in the army. He needs to be more considerate of his family's feelings. He's been away now nearly four weeks without a word to say when we can expect him back.'

'Charles is a law unto himself,' he said at his most bored.

Helen tapped a foot in controlled irritation. 'He hasn't told you what his plans are now that he has resigned his commission?' Was that why she had tracked him down? To see if he knew what Charles had in mind for himself?

Richard looked again at the portrait of his father. All that vitality, all that youth, all that supreme self-confidence. His brother had inherited more of it than he had.

'And young Warburton? Will he be back for tomorrow?'

Ah, the very slightest of flushes on Helen's cheeks.

'His mother is much recovered; he returns today.'

'Then he can help me with some papers this afternoon,' Richard said pleasantly. 'Good morning, my dear.' He strode past Helen and along the corridor.

Charles was another matter he needed to give thought to. Who could have imagined his brother would give up his army career like that? Richard felt uneasy; he had been unable to extract even a hint of Charles's intentions and felt his brother had always been a darn sight too intelligent to be comfortable around. He'd left for London without any explanation. What was he doing there?

* * *

Walking purposefully, Richard passed the servants as though they had melted into the fabric of the mansion. He had learned early on the trick of always appearing to have business elsewhere and they, of course, were not allowed eye contact.

He both envied and despised Helen's ability to hold a conversation that appeared to suggest equality without losing an ounce of dignity.

Once outside, Richard skirted the haha where the pyrotechnic specialist was supervising the erection of the framework for his display. He paused for a moment to assess progress, then caught sight of Helen emerging from the house, obviously intent on delivering the firework finale verdict. Richard walked through the yew-framed parterre with its intricate box hedges, then the rose garden, reaching the herbaceous-bordered lawn, which led up to the little belvedere that stood in the far corner. With its pillars and stone seating, it almost matched the pavilion on the roof. He and Charles had played in both as young boys, their games almost always involving brave soldiers repelling invading forces. Charles had gone on to realise their imaginary dramas and Richard – Richard had tried to live up to his father's expectations – and failed.

He sat on the stone bench, his back to the house, and stared out over the green parkland. Its specimen trees that led down to the silver band of river flowed prettily round the wooded hill and made such an attractive feature. It was a view of pastoral delight. That was what a belvedere was all about, his mother had told him and Charles years ago, objecting to their use of it as a battleground.

Now Richard could not look down the parkland without thinking of Polly ending up in those swiftly flowing waters; of her body being found by that sharp-eyed Grandison woman.

After a moment, he rose and walked slowly round the house to the stables.

★ ★ ★

In the yard, four horses were being harnessed to the closed carriage, its glossy finish receiving a final polish. Helen had hardly looked dressed for going out; it must be for the use of his mother. Richard felt relief. There would be no summons for him to attend her this afternoon. The last trace being secured and the stable boy holding the harness of the lead animal, the coachman swung himself up onto the box. The grooms got onto the back platform and the stable boy let go. Slowly, in

stately style, the heavy equipage moved round the corner on its
way to the front of the house.

Richard helped himself to a carrot from the bowl that was
always ready just inside the stables, and went to check on his
much-loved horse, Snowy.

'What sort of a name is that?' his father had snorted as
Richard proudly led his new mount around the yard.

'It matches his colour,' Richard had said belligerently, putting
his foot into the stirrup and lightly gaining the saddle. The thor-
oughbred horse had, of course, a much more elevated name,
but Richard had insisted on keeping to the one he'd given him.
Confident in little else, he knew his ability to choose first-class
horseflesh could not be challenged by his father.

As he approached the stable, there came from round the side
of the house the most extraordinary honking sound followed
by screeches, panic-stricken shouts, horses frantically neighing,
and a grinding of gravel under wheels.

Dropping the carrot, and followed by several stable lads,
Richard ran to see what had happened.

On the side-drive the carriage stood at an angle, the horses
snorting, throwing their heads in the air and pulling in different
directions as the coachman and grooms tried to pacify them.

Facing the terrified horses was a polished, dark green motor
vehicle. As Richard ran up, a badly shaken driver stepped down
onto the gravelled drive. A youngish man; he wore a dark
jacket with embossed brass buttons, what looked like dark blue
jodhpurs, a peaked cap and goggles.

'What the hell are you doing?' Richard threw at him.

'Sorry, sir, it was a surprise, see; coming round the corner of
the house and meeting that carriage.'

'And sounding your horn seemed appropriate, did it?'

The driver took off his goggles, revealing unhappy eyes set in
circles of clean flesh in a dusty face. 'Like I said, sir, I'm sorry.'

The coachman handed over the now steadied lead horse to
one of the stable lads and approached.

'You'll address his lordship as "my lord",' he said, his face an
angry red. 'This is the Earl of Mountstanton and these are his
prime matched bays you've frightened out of their senses.'

'Thank you, Ford,' Richard said. 'Do you think the horses
are able to proceed now?'

The coachman looked back at his charges: eyes rolled, rumps quivered and the animals moved nervously, but they were no longer out of control. He nodded. 'They'll be all right, my lord, and all the better for being under way.' He looked at the driver. 'Think you can move that *thing* out of our way without putting the fear of God into them again?'

'Perhaps,' suggested Richard, 'if it was pushed back a bit? The lads could help.'

The driver looked relieved and nodded. Standing on the ground next to the driver's seat, he let off the brake and took hold of the wheel. With the help of two of the stable lads, the machine was pushed into the side of the drive.

A few minutes later the carriage moved slowly round to the front of the house.

'I await an explanation,' Richard said to the driver.

The young man flushed. 'As I said, I'm sorry, sir . . . my lord. I wasn't expecting . . . well, I was told to go round the house, like, to the stable yard.'

'Stable yard, yes. And nothing suggested to you that horses could be coming out of the yard, not to mention a carriage, and that your infernal machine could frighten the wits out of them? That without due care you could cause a hell of an accident?'

Richard caught himself. He should have learned by now there was no point in losing his temper. After a brief pause he added, 'Where are you from?'

'Salisbury, Sir . . . my lord.'

'Who sent you?'

'Colonel Stanhope, sir; I mean, my lord.'

'Colonel Stanhope?'

'Yes, sir. The machine is his . . . and I'm his mechanic. Roberts is the name.'

'Well, Roberts, you had better proceed to the stable yard.'

Richard watched as the driver switched on the engine, swung the starter handle at the front of the machine, climbed back into the vehicle, replaced his cap but not the goggles, and slowly drove off.

Richard followed him round to the stable yard. By the time he reached it, the glossy green machine was stopped in the middle of the yard, surrounded by all the grooms, and Roberts was looking around with lively interest.

Where the hell was Charles? What was he thinking of, acquiring such an infernal machine, not to mention a mechanic, without a word to anyone?

Richard singled out the Head Groom. 'Higgs, apparently this machine belongs to Colonel Stanhope and that is Roberts, the mechanic. Both man and machine will require accommodation.'

'Very good, my lord.' Higgs looked thoughtful. 'There'll be room in the stable lads' quarters for 'im, my lord,' nodding at Roberts, 'but I doesn't know about the machine. We got a couple of empty stalls but it'll never get through the doors.'

Richard sighed. 'Find something for it, Higgs.'

'Will the Colonel be back today, my lord?'

Richard was saved having to answer by the arrival of Miss Grandison mounted on the quietest of the Mountstanton mares. He went to its head. 'Morning, Miss Grandison. Back from your morning ride?'

She looked down at him with her easy charm. 'Good morning, my lord. I very much appreciate being supplied with Daisy,' she gave the horse a loving pat. 'The exercise is very beneficial and I am enjoying your beautiful countryside.'

Richard helped her dismount. He wondered just where she rode. He thought he might have caught a glimpse of her this morning on Viscount Broome's estate. No doubt she didn't realise she had travelled beyond Mountstanton land. She couldn't, though, have returned home immediately for he had been back some time.

'I hope you have had a pleasant outing?'

She nodded, removing her gloves, then caught sight of the motor vehicle. 'Good heavens, I did not expect to see such a modern convenience at Mountstanton! Have you advanced into the twentieth century, my lord?' She shot him a teasing glance.

'It appears to belong to my brother, Miss Grandison. He would seem to have obtained it from Salisbury.'

'Indeed!' She limped over to the vehicle and was soon in conversation with Roberts.

Richard sank his hands into his trouser pockets and watched as Belle's companion was given a tour of the machine. He almost expected her to climb into the driving seat and ask for it to be started up.

Higgs, who had disappeared after Miss Grandison rode into the yard, now reappeared. 'I've had a word with Gradgrass, my lord. There's that outbuilding where the wheelbarrows and gardening trailors are kept. He thinks it best if it's cleared out and the machine placed in there for the present.'

Richard wondered what pressure had been brought to bear on the head gardener.

Higgs rubbed at one of his ears. 'Seems to think it's time he was provided with somewhere more commodious, my lord,' he said, all expression carefully wiped from his face.

So that explained that. Richard watched Higgs go over to the driver. A moment later, they disappeared off towards the horticultural area.

Miss Grandison limped back to Richard. 'It seems an impressive machine, my lord. Roberts says it is a one-cylinder engine but that the power-to-weight ratio produces up to twenty-five miles an hour.'

'You seem to know a great deal about motor vehicles, Miss Grandison.'

She shrugged. 'They are the future, my lord. Mr Seldon has one and enjoys being driven in it.'

At that moment the station fly arrived. Stepping down from it was his brother, Colonel The Honourable Charles Stanhope.

Chapter Twenty-Two

The Colonel jumped down from the fly. He was wearing a formal dark suit with a wing collar and a bowler hat. The driver lifted out his case and handed it to a groom. The transport was dismissed. Charles Stanhope tipped his hat with the briefest of smiles to Ursula and turned to the motor vehicle.

Ursula had thought she would be delighted to see him after his protracted stay in London. Now her feelings were confused. Questions had arisen that suggested he might not be quite everything he seemed. Belle's verbal attack on him, despite Ursula's immediate rejection of everything she said, had left a mark, like stains on linen that only appear after time has passed. And today she had been presented with facts that made her uneasy. She needed time to think.

'Ah, my new toy has arrived. Sorry, Richard, I meant to be here before Roberts brought it round but business made me miss a train.' He went over and laid a hand on the motor's bonnet.

Ursula thought that he might just as well have been caressing a well-loved horse, even a woman. She repressed the shiver that went through her.

'A nasty accident was only just avoided,' said his brother coldly.

Charles Stanhope listened to the details of the incident. 'I am extremely sorry, Richard, and relieved that no harm appears to have been done. I shall have to talk with Roberts. Nothing like that must be allowed to happen again.'

Ursula had retrieved the stick left in the stable when she had mounted that morning, and hoped to escape into the house before he spoke to her. Her limp slowed her down too much.

'Miss Grandison, I am very pleased to see you in a habit. This must mean that you are able to ride again.'

She nodded. 'My ankle is much recovered, thank you, Colonel.' She knew her words were stiff and saw him frown. 'Forgive me, I must go and change.'

Ursula limped into the house, conscious that the Colonel's intent gaze followed her.

Upstairs in her bedroom, she went to the window and caught sight of the polished, dark-green motor vehicle disappearing with the Colonel driving. The details vouchsafed by Roberts echoed uneasily in her mind. She undid the buttons of her habit with irritated fingers. Emotion had to be banished, facts faced.

By the time she had carefully put away her habit and changed into a severe, ivory poplin shirt and matching linen skirt, Ursula had managed to achieve a certain calm. She brushed her hair into a knot at the back of her head, securing it with a host of pins.

Halfway down the last flight of stairs into the main hall, Ursula was in time to see Mr Warburton hand his hat and gloves to Benson. Then, in a flurry of rose-patterned muslin, Belle ran up to him.

'William – you're here! How wonderful!' She grabbed his hands and stood looking eagerly at him, her bosom rising and falling with excitement, her cheeks flushed, eyes sparkling with delight. No maidenly modesty for Belle, thought Ursula, transfixed on the staircase.

'Miss Seldon. Thank you for being so pleased to see me.'

At the formality of his tone, Belle's joy faded. 'William?' Her voice was hurt, her eyes searched his face.

Gently he removed his hands from her grip. 'Have you been enjoying yourself, Miss Seldon?'

'Belle!' Helen advanced down the corridor. 'I need to talk to you.' Her voice was cool.

'You only ever have one thing to say to me,' Belle shouted and fled past her sister.

'I am glad to see you back, William,' said Helen austerely. 'We will speak later.' She followed after Belle.

Ursula sighed. She felt infinitely sorry for Belle and would cheerfully do serious injury to the young man who was causing her such pain.

She was the first to enter the dining room for luncheon. Then Helen came in, followed by William Warburton.

'Belle will be taking her meal in her room; she is a little under the weather,' Helen said. 'Mr Warburton, I trust your mother has recovered from her indisposition?'

He coloured very faintly and made his way to his usual place. 'Thank you, my lady, she is feeling much improved and the doctor is confident she will make a complete recovery.'

The Earl and his brother entered. They seemed at ease with one another and yet Ursula thought she detected an undercurrent. Could it have been caused by the arrival of the motor vehicle?

'Charles,' said Helen as the Colonel sat down. 'We are delighted you have been able to return in time for Mama's birthday celebrations.'

'Would not have missed them for the world,' he said easily.

'And we want to know everything you have been up to in London; the exhibitions you have seen, the people you have met – all your activities.'

'Dear Helen, I am afraid you would find such a recital very boring. Tell me instead of all you have arranged for tomorrow.'

Helen was more than happy to talk of the singers, acrobats and tumblers who were to provide the entertainment for the Dowager's birthday fête. 'And the fireworks should be particularly spectacular this year. Charles, it's no use you raising an eyebrow at me. You know how Mama looks forward to her birthday fête.'

The servants, having served the first course, had disappeared. The Colonel said, 'My dear Helen, I am well aware of Mama's dependence on the outward sign of her standing in the local community. Indeed, I sometimes think she extends that standing to a good part of the country. She is lucky to have a daughter-in-law who is willing to pander to her foibles.'

Ursula waited for Helen to blush. Instead, she stared haughtily at the Colonel. 'I wish I could think you were being honest and that you do know I care for her.'

'Yes, Charles,' said the Earl caustically. 'You have been absent from Mountstanton too much. Had you been here you would have seen how much Mama depends on Helen.'

The Colonel held up his hands in surrender. 'I am put in my place. I will say no more on the matter. Miss Grandison, how have you been spending your time over the last few weeks?'

'I have enjoyed becoming better acquainted with Mountstanton, its history and traditions. Mr Benson has been kind enough to give me a tour of the picture gallery and I have learnt from Mrs Parsons something of what it takes to run a house of this magnitude. It has all been most educational.'

Helen looked at her with astonishment. 'Ursula, I had no idea that was what you were up to.'

'You make it sound as though I have been indulging in something underhand. I thought you would be pleased to hear I was so interested in this wonderful house and estate.'

'If I had known of your curiosity, I would have made time to satisfy it myself,' Helen said glacially.

'I hope, Miss Grandison, that you will allow me to extend your knowledge of Mountstanton,' said the Colonel smoothly.

Her poise perfectly in place, Ursula gave a little dip of her head and said, 'That would be most kind, Colonel.'

He gave her a slightly puzzled look, as though he recognised a change in her attitude towards him and was unable to account for it.

'Have we told you our plans for London, Charles?' said Helen brightly. Having regained control of the conversation, she regaled her brother-in-law with details of balls, race meetings, regattas and other excitements until the end of the meal.

As they left the dining room, Ursula said, 'I think I should visit Belle, see how she is.'

'I would rather she were left sleeping undisturbed,' said Helen cooly.

'Charles, I want you to take me in that motor carriage of yours to Salisbury,' said the Earl. 'I have an urgent errand there.'

'I shall be delighted. Would you care to accompany us, Miss Grandison?'

'Alas, I have letters to write,' said Ursula. She moved off down the corridor, conscious that the Colonel was unhappy with her attitude.

She had not written to Mr Seldon for several days. Recently, there had not been a great deal worth telling him. Today, however, she had gained new details. In the library she helped

herself to a supply of crested notepaper, borrowed the pen
from the desk-stand and sat down to write to Helen's father.
The letter took her some considerable time and her clear, inci-
sive hand covered several sheets of paper.

Having read what she had written, she picked up the
pen again:

From what I have told you, I think you will agree that
the question of Polly's parentage has been answered.
What is not clear is how many others are aware of the
identity of her father, or whether it played any part in
her death. Still a mystery is the identity of the man who
fathered her unborn child. It is possible that the coroner
was correct, that Polly did commit suicide. Her death
could have been an accident, but the more information that comes to light, the less probable it seems. I am
extremely reluctant to come to the conclusion that she
was killed, but as time passes I feel it more and more
likely. At Mountstanton, every effort is being made to put
everything connected with her in the past. She has been
buried and that should be that, is what the family seem
to be saying.

This household is not a happy one. As you have heard,
there are currents and cross-currents. Belle is unhappy
and, much as it distresses me, I have to confess that Helen
seems to be contributing to that unhappiness. Though I
have not been able to discover what she has done with
her dowry, I have seen enough of her marriage to the
Earl to be certain that there is something very wrong
between them. The Dowager Countess attempts to exercise her authority over her sons, particularly the Earl, not
always successfully. She also seems far too concerned with
what I term 'the honour of the family'.

Once again, she paused and reread what she had written. After
a little hesitation, she picked up the pen and continued:

There is the matter of the death of Mr Snell. How long
before Miss Ranner tells someone else what she says she
saw that night is impossible to say. I am certain she told

me because she believed I would ensure the information was acted upon. But in what way?

Mr Seldon, do you remember talking to me one day about your purchase of a motor vehicle? I recollect vividly the frustration you expressed over the time it took to arrive. This has alerted me to an upsetting possibility, which I will investigate before reporting on it to you.

I do feel, sir, that if your business could possibly allow, you should come over and see for yourself the situation with both your daughters. I do not feel competent to assess exactly what has been happening here and I am very afraid that some other tragedy could be in the making.

I am, sir, your devoted servant,

Ursula signed her name and, without further rereading, placed the pages within a large envelope and sealed but did not address it. She would not put it out for Benson to send; tomorrow morning she would ride down to Hinton Parva and post it herself.

★ ★ ★

The weather for the Dowager Countess's birthday fête was cloudless, sunny and warm.

There had been old friends of hers at dinner the previous evening and, to Ursula, it seemed the claustrophobic atmosphere at Mountstanton slightly lifted, until she realised that the Earl scarcely spoke and Helen's conversation was too bright. Belle looked pretty but pale and gazed hopelessly across the table at William Warburton. However, she quite properly confined her conversation to the two elderly gentlemen she was seated between. Each appeared enchanted by her and, as the meal progressed, Belle cheered a little.

When the gentlemen joined the ladies for coffee, the Earl was not among them. The Colonel, as Ursula had feared, made straight for her.

'I have this strange feeling that you are avoiding me,' he said. His eyes were clear and frank as they studied her face.

Ursula smiled in a polite way; she could think of nothing to say.

He frowned. 'What has happened, Miss Grandison? I know something has.'

'Nothing has happened, Colonel Stanhope. Tell me, how did you occupy yourself in London? Are there interesting exhibitions to be seen?'

He gave a slight exclamation of annoyance and said, 'Do you really want a polite conversation about nothing at all?'

Ursula felt a flush come to her face. 'Colonel, I . . . '

'Charles, such a delight to see you; it must be at least twelve years since we have met. Such a shame you were seated at the other end of the table.' A woman of some fifty years of age appeared by the Colonel's side.

He turned to her. 'My lady, what a pleasure to meet you again.'

Ursula moved away.

Helen stretched out an arm towards her and suggested she play to them. 'Something light and soft,' she said.

Ursula launched into some Debussy. Not as light as Helen would have liked, she was sure, but she needed to play a piece that would tax her. As she finished the piece, the Colonel came to stand beside the piano.

The evening was coming to an end. The Earl had reappeared with apologies for the business he had been forced to attend to and guests were leaving.

'I don't know what that was but I enjoyed it,' he said as she closed the piano lid. 'You have a way of playing that brings music to life.'

'Thank you, Colonel Stanhope. If you will forgive me, I am very tired.'

He placed a hand on her arm. 'Miss Grandison, I need to talk to you. Dare I ask that you spare me a little time tomorrow morning?'

She stood up and looked squarely at him. 'We should indeed talk, Colonel. Now, I must go.' She said goodnight to Helen then left the room. Slowly mounting the stairs, she cursed herself for handling the situation so badly. It was unfair not to allow the Colonel to explain himself. But not yet. She needed to be absolutely clear in her mind exactly what she suspected him of.

★ ★ ★

In the morning, Ursula sent a message to the stables to saddle Daisy, the mare she usually rode. By the time she presented herself, the horse was all ready and snickered in a welcoming way.

The fresh air and warm sunshine were a benison. As she rode, Ursula began to feel lighter in spirit. On reaching the village, she tied Daisy up outside the shop, which also did duty as a post office.

'America, did you say?' asked Mr Partridge, weighing her envelope. 'You will need an address before it can be sent.'

'Oh,' Ursula said, affecting surprise. 'How stupid of me. Perhaps you will be good enough to provide sufficient postage and I will add the recipient's address.'

She took back the stamped envelope and, using the pen and ink supplied on the counter, wrote Mr Seldon's address on the envelope. Then she hurried from the shop.

Outside, she was accosted by a man in a bowler hat, not particularly tall, and dressed like a clerk. 'I believe I have the fortune of addressing Miss Grandison?' he said.

His accent was slightly nasal and clipped, very different from the slow, broad way of speaking Ursula had become used to in this part of the country. Had the man been a local, she would not have queried the identification, but that this stranger should address her by name was odd. 'How did you know me?' she asked.

'You have been described to me, Miss Grandison, in a manner quite unmistakeable.' He had bright, enquiring eyes, and appeared to be some forty years of age. 'I'm Thomas Jackman.'

He said it in a way that suggested his name was one she should recognise.

'Mr Jackman, I am pleased to meet you. Now, you will oblige me by allowing me to reach my horse.'

For a moment he looked puzzled, then it was as though a shutter came down over his face. 'Of course, miss,' he said and stepped aside. 'Sorry to inconvenience you.'

Grateful for the mounting block outside the village store, Ursula hoisted herself into the saddle, lifted her whip in acknowledgement to Mr Jackman, and put the horse into a gentle trot, wondering about the little encounter.

Miss Ranner was outside her house, talking to a neighbour. As Ursula rode towards her, she waved and hurried across. 'Miss Grandison, good morning! I hope you are well. So nice to see you riding. Your ankle is much better?'

Ursula assured her it was and said she soon hoped to be mobile enough to visit with Miss Ranner.

'I hope you don't mind my mentioning it, Miss Grandison, but I saw you talking with that funny little man. Who is he?'

'I have no idea.'

'He has been hanging around the village all morning. He stayed last night at the Lion and Lamb and apparently the landlord says he has booked himself in for a week. This morning he was in the village shop making himself very pleasant to Mr Partridge and asking all sorts of questions.'

'Questions, Miss Ranner?' Ursula's sense of unease communicated itself to her horse, who gave a slight sidestep and tossed her head. Ursula tightened the reins.

'Nothing in particular, you understand, Miss Grandison. Merely what sort of village Hinton Parva is, the extent it covers, how very pleasant the villagers seem and is the weather going to continue so fine, that sort of thing. We all think, though, that there is something very odd about him. What is he doing here for a week?'

What was he doing here at all? Ursula wondered. 'He looks like some sort of clerk,' she said. 'Maybe he is taking a holiday.'

Miss Ranner's face cleared. 'Of course, that must be it. I must not keep you, Miss Grandison. I'm sure up at Mountstanton there must be a great to-do going on.'

Having ascertained that Miss Ranner was invited to the fête, Ursula took her leave and rode to the postbox she had noticed at the edge of the village.

The heavy letter slipped inside the bright red box and landed with a thud. Ursula wondered if she was being foolish taking such precautionary measures. What did it matter who knew she was writing to Mr Seldon?

★ ★ ★

Back at Mountstanton, there was indeed a great to-do. A marquee had been erected on the main lawn to one side of the house. Long tables were being laid with damask cloths and piles of plates and cutlery. Folding chairs had been placed on the lawn. A small band was practising.

'Ursula!' Belle called, running towards her. 'At last I have caught you on your own. I need to speak with you.' Belle caught hold of her arm and gave her a pleading look.

'Of course, dear. It is too long since we had a proper talk. Shall we go to your room?'

Belle made a face. 'That busy-miss French maid will interrupt us. Let's go to yours.'

Upstairs Ursula settled Belle on her bed and sat beside her. 'Now,' she said, 'tell me what it is that is worrying you. Is it Mr Warburton?'

The response was instant. Belle collapsed in a torrent of tears. 'I thought he loved me, Ursula,' she wailed. 'He acted as though he did. He made me think he did!'

'Men are notoriously unreliable,' said Ursula compassionately. 'I am afraid, Belle, you will have your heart broken a good many more times before you find the man of your dreams.' She stroked the girl's hair. After a moment she added, 'Have you spoken to your sister about your feelings?'

Belle choked back her tears and sat up. 'I cannot speak to Helen about this.' She spat the words out, her face turning from that of an upset kitten to a vengeful cat. 'She wants William for herself.'

'And do you think Mr Warburton responds?' Ursula realised she had skipped over the step of protesting that Helen was a respectable married woman.

'I expect he wants us both!' The crying started again.

Ursula tried to soothe her while she considered the situation. There had been the odd incident, which suggested that Helen had a *tendresse* for the handsome young secretary, but could she be serious about him? And was William Warburton really going to ignore all the benefits that a match with Belle could bring?

'Have you had any private conversation with Mr Warburton since his return to Mountstanton yesterday?'

Belle raised a tear-stained face. 'No, Ursula! I've tried so hard but he slips away whenever I approach him. If only he would speak to me.' She burst into loud sobs.

Ursula took the girl in her arms and rocked her until she quietened.

'Darling Belle, I know how painful this must be for you. We feel everything so sharply when we're young.' Not only then, she thought. 'I don't suppose it is any use my saying that Mr Warburton is not worth your tears?'

It took a long time for Ursula to calm Belle but finally the sobs abated.

'You know, darling,' she said when only the odd hiccup signalled the girl's distress. 'One of the reasons girls are not supposed to be too informal with young men, or spend time alone in their company, is that the men have to prove worthy of your trust in them. Far too many men take advantage of loving and open girls.'

Belle bowed her head and fiddled with the handkerchief Ursula had supplied her with, now soaked right through.

'But I fell in love the moment I met him, and . . . and he said it was the same for him!' Belle wailed afresh.

Ursula wished William Warburton at the bottom of some ocean.

'I thought when he returned from visiting his mother that we would become engaged. We could be married and I could make my debut, but it would be as a married woman and all the other girls would be so jealous of me. Oh, Ursula, what am I going to do?'

Ursula could not help feeling sorry for this foolish, head-strong girl.

★ ★ ★

The fête was a triumphant success. The weather could not have behaved better. The Dowager Countess looked superb in black ribbed silk and appeared to be thoroughly enjoying herself, passing amongst her guests, being gracious to villagers and staff. When Ursula appeared with Belle, she beckoned them over.

'Your presence was missed at luncheon. Where were you both?'

'Belle was helping me make myself look presentable for your birthday celebrations, and we had something on a tray,' said Ursula easily. 'May I wish you a very happy day, my lady.'

'How kind.' A penetrating gaze took in the plain, pearl-grey muslin gown Ursula was wearing and appeared to approve.

Then she assessed Belle's white, broderie anglaise dress and gave a nod. 'Belle, my dear, the japanned box you gave me is exquisite. I thank you most sincerely.'

'I am glad you like it, your ladyship.' Belle bobbed a little curtsey.

'And I have to thank you, Miss Grandison, for your gift. It was well chosen, I enjoy Mr James's works.'

With a twirl of her parasol, the Dowager moved on.

'Who is Mr James?' Belle asked.

'He is an author. When I accompanied yourself and Helen to Salisbury the other day, I was able to purchase his latest work in the bookshop there.'

Helen beckoned Belle over. Ursula watched as the Countess appeared to speak winningly to her sister. Then, with a shock, she thought she saw Mr Jackman standing by the haha, looking around himself like a visitor to a foreign land. A swirl of guests moved between her and the man, blocking him from Ursula's view. When she managed to work her way through to where she had seen him, there was no one there. However, she was able to spend a little time with Miss Ranner, who introduced her to other villagers. Then she spent a little time with Mrs Comfort and a very excited Lord Harry, followed by an encounter with Mrs Parsons, whom she congratulated on her organisation. 'It must have taken a great deal of time,' she said. The woman seemed grateful for the praise but her eyes never stopped checking every aspect of the occasion.

Ursula walked up to the terrace and stood for a moment studying the scene, appreciating the atmosphere of enjoyment.

'You seem amused by the natives, Miss Grandison,' the Colonel said.

Somehow it seemed natural that he should appear beside her. 'I was thinking how well behaved everyone is. Were this an American gathering, high spirits would have taken over by now. Youngsters would be playing in the fountain, others jumping over the edge of the haha; their mothers would be having hysterics and fathers making vain attempts to restore control.'

'Ah, but this is Mountstanton, Miss Grandison.'

'Indeed,' Ursula said gravely. Almost without her realising it, they had returned to the easy relationship that had existed before he disappeared to London.

'You are not eating. May I fetch you a plate of the delightful collation that has been prepared to do my mother honour?'

'Thank you, I am not hungry.'

'Nor I. Cold chicken in aspic does not tempt me.' He paused for a moment. 'Miss Grandison,' he started, only to be interrupted by his brother.

'Charles, I am about to make my birthday speech to Mama. I wish you to be with me.'

'Of course, Richard. Miss Grandison, please, do not disappear.'

The Earl's speech, with his wife and brother standing beside him, Helen holding Lord Harry by the shoulders, was exactly as might have been expected.

Afterwards, Ursula would attempt to remember exactly what he said, and try to look behind the actual words. All she could recall were the hackneyed phrases of tribute to his mother and the pleasure displayed by the Dowager. Helen had been calm and the Colonel, well, the Colonel, as usual, looked slightly apart from the scene.

After the speech came the entertainment. Music hall and folk songs were loudly applauded; tumblers and acrobats greeted with gasps of astonishment. A knock-about act between two comedians met with acclaim. The small band performed with aplomb.

Then it was time for the firework display.

Though it was dusk rather than dark, Ursula found the pyrotechnics the greatest success of the whole event. Set pieces of static fireworks fizzed and rotated, with sparks flying off in all directions, making wondrous patterns against the dark of the background woods. There were fireworks that banged, leaping over the ground, to the great delight of the youngsters, and making the loudest of noises at unexpected intervals. Rockets soared into the air and showered the sky with massive handfuls of iridescent gems to oohs and aahs. A finale of a battalion of rockets all fired at the same time, lit up the sky with the generosity of a caliph firing cannons loaded with diamonds.

Then it was all over and guests and entertainers gradually dispersed.

Ursula found Helen. 'Have you seen Belle?' she asked. 'I seem to have lost her.'

'I sent her to bed. She looked quite exhausted.'

Ursula thought that Helen herself looked tired.

The Dowager came up. 'I cannot find Richard anywhere. I particularly wished to thank him for his gracious speech. I cannot retire until I have done so.'

Helen sighed. 'He's vanished. You know how he cannot stand the entertainment. He says it is too banal for words.'

'The servants and villagers find it delightful,' said the Dowager chidingly. 'Charles,' she called over to her younger son. 'Find Richard for me, will you?'

'Certainly, Mama.' He disappeared.

Ursula gave her thanks for a splendid party and went inside. She started up the stairs to her bedroom, then paused. The house was full of the sound of servants coming in from outside, chattering amongst themselves, with Mrs Parsons shooing maids upstairs. It seemed as though part of the fun of the fête was to be allowed the run of the house.

Ursula changed her mind about going upstairs. She needed solitude and peace.

Outside all seemed quiet. Tables had been stripped of the remains of food and drink, and the damask cloths removed. In the silver moonlight, the abandoned chairs and naked tables reminded Ursula of the last lines of *The Tempest*, except that these revellers had left more than the odd wrack behind.

She wandered through to the rose garden and wondered how long before it would be redolent with heady scent. There was a stone bench where the paths that ran between the carefully laid-out beds crossed. Ursula sat down and tried to unpick the various threads in the tapestry she had created since her discovery of Polly's body. If only she could stitch them into a different pattern.

She was too tired for any of it to make sense and she gave herself up to the solitude and quiet of the garden, dew gathering on the grassy paths.

'Miss Grandison, is that you?'

Ursula turned and saw the Dowager coming towards her. In the moonlight her features were rigid as stone. Ursula rose and a hand grasped her wrist with the strength of steel.

'Come with me. I have seen something in the belvedere.'

She pulled Ursula along the way she had come.

The moon lit the scene with the charm of a romantic stage set. There was the stone pavilion, floating in an unearthly manner above the haha with the river far below, tonight a stream of molten silver.

The Dowager's tension transmitted itself through that steely grip.

The apprehension that had been building up in Ursula over the last two days rose with choking power. She wanted to pull her wrist free, refuse to go any further, but the Dowager's hold was too strong.

By now the woman was panting heavily. 'I must know,' she said. 'I must know.'

Together the two women climbed the stone steps up into the belvedere.

Lying on the stone bench was a body. The head had been shattered, an arm hung loosely down. On the ground, beneath the open fingers, was a shotgun. Richard, sixth Earl of Mountstanton, was no more.

Chapter Twenty-Three

Charles Stanhope finished searching the stables for his brother with mounting frustration.

This was typical of Richard – disappearing when he must have known people wanted to say goodbye after the fireworks. And typical of their mother to insist she had to speak to her elder son before going to bed.

Charles stood for a moment in the stable yard and wondered where to look next. He had drawn a blank with the billiard room, the library, and all the reception rooms. Richard was not in his bedroom or his dressing room; his valet had not seen the Earl after he had given the birthday tribute to the Dowager Countess.

Charles looked up at the roof of Mountstanton. The moon flooded the white stone with unearthly light. Could his brother have gone up there for a quiet smoke? It seemed unlikely; the roof had long been known both to Charles and the Earl as a retreat and assignation point for members of the Mountstanton staff. Even if Richard had wanted an assignation with a servant – Charles unconsciously pulled a face at the thought – he would have chosen another spot. But tonight was surely not the night for that.

None of the horses were missing from the stables, so he could not have gone riding. No hope for it; Charles would have to start exploring more of Mountstanton's vast collection of rooms.

As he approached the house, however, Barnes, his mother's maid, came towards him. Barnes had small feet and Richard and he used to say she walked like a pigeon with bowel problems. Charles smiled to himself as she came up.

'Colonel Charles, there you are! The Countess wishes you to attend on her immediately.'

Just for a moment, he thought Helen had asked for him, then realised his mistake. 'My mother, that would be, Barnes?'

'Of course, sir,' the maid said sharply. Then she modified her tone. 'Miss Grandison it was that actually said I should fetch you.'

He had already started walking in the direction of his mother's apartment when that almost brought him to a stop. 'Miss Grandison?'

'Yes, sir.' There was a slight pause before Barnes added, 'They came in from the garden together, sir.'

'I see,' said Charles, unable to make any sense of the situation.

'And Miss Grandison, she told me to tell you that you must come at once, sir.'

There was no point in Charles worrying about reasons; if sensible Ursula Grandison said he should come at once, then he would. He lengthened his stride and took the side door into his mother's wing at a fast pace, Barnes running behind in an effort to keep up.

As Charles entered the room, he heard his mother say, 'I disown him. No son of mine could . . . ' for a moment she faltered, 'could do that!'

The Dowager Countess was sitting bolt upright in a Sheraton armchair, holding a half-empty glass of what looked like brandy. Patches of red flared on her cheeks; her eyes stared ahead as though into some abyss.

Kneeling beside her was Ursula Grandison, her face pale as a wraith. 'My lady,' she said in an imploring voice and took the Countess's free hand in both of hers, as though it was cold and needed warming.

His mother saw him. 'Charles!' she said as she disengaged her hand and held it out towards him.

Charles glanced at the woman on the ground and was startled to see a look of such warmth and relief on her face, he might have been bringing a battalion to raise a siege.

'Mama,' he said, taking her hand. 'What has happened?'

The Countess closed her eyes. 'Show him!' she commanded.

Miss Grandison flinched. Then she rose, picked up a glass of brandy and drank it in one swift motion.

Charles sent her a questioning look.

'You must show him.' His mother's voice spelt out the words one by one as though Miss Grandison was a child.

Ursula put down the glass and without a backward look went out through the French windows.

Charles gave a quick glance at his mother, then followed.

Nothing was said as they crossed through the rose garden towards the belvedere.

Half way there, Miss Grandison stopped and faced him. Her large grey eyes looked into his with such pain, Charles knew that something terrible had happened.

He grasped her hands and held them tight. 'Tell me,' he said softly.

Her hands returned his grasp. 'Your brother has shot himself, in the belvedere.' She gulped and her eyes closed for an instant. 'He used a shotgun. The moon, it's so bright; it's . . . it's remorseless.'

He dropped her hands. 'Go back to my mother, look after her.'

She did not move. Somehow his mind refused to acknowledge what waited for him in that graceful stone outlook. The outlook, that was what he and Richard had always called the belvedere.

Ursula held out her hand to him. 'I will wait here,' she said.

All feeling closed down as he climbed the steps towards the figure lying on the stone bench.

For a long moment he stood looking down at what was left of his brother. The shotgun had shattered much of his head. Blood bespattered the columns and the floor. The weapon had fallen to the ground. It was one that had belonged to their father. Both he and Richard had shot with it. His brother's right arm and hand hung down, almost touching the gun. Not far from it was an empty champagne bottle.

Without thought, Charles carefully laid the dangling arm on the dead man's breast. His head might be mangled, but the hands were intact. Such beautiful hands with their long fingers but with the odd bend in the top joint of the little right finger. Mountstanton hands. They were his too.

Charles found his sight blurring. He blinked hard. About to turn away, he saw a piece of paper anchored beneath the dead man's right foot. He tugged it out.

Charles, forgive me. I have no other option.

That was all there was.

He slipped it into his pocket and gave a shuddering sigh. On the edge of his consciousness questions crowded; they marshalled themselves alongside a host of things that also started to line up, all needing to be done. And only he to do them. The burden of all that waited for him was almost too much. He had lost his brother; Richard, his childhood companion. Richard, who he had played with, argued with, competed with – but never envied. He ran his hand down his face, as though it could wipe away what he had seen.

He turned back towards the house – and found Miss Grandison at his side. She looked anxiously at his face.

'There's nothing I can say except that you have my deepest sympathy.'

Her eyes seemed full of compassion and for a moment he wanted to drown in them and forget what lay in the belvedere. He forced himself to ignore everything but what lay ahead. He tried to smile at her, placed a hand on her elbow and started moving them towards the house, his steps stiff and jerky.

'Was it my mother who found him?' The idea was horrific but seemed inescapable.

'She thought she had seen something in the belvedere and asked if I would go with her.'

'I would not have had that happen for the world.' Fury took Charles. How unutterably selfish of Richard not to make arrangements that would ensure it was his brother who found him. And what did that nonsense, 'I have no other option,' mean?

He realised Ursula Grandison was walking without a stick and limping badly. He held out his arm. 'Please, lean on me,' he said, suddenly aware that, once again, the Stanhopes had been responsible for her making a shocking discovery.

After a moment's hesitation, she slipped her hand into the crook of his arm and his strength seemed to ease her progress. Whatever had caused her withdrawal from him since his return from London appeared, for the moment, to have been forgotten.

'I am glad my mother had you with her,' he said. 'I can imagine no one who would be a greater support.'

'I wish it had not been she who had to discover him,' she said, her voice low.

'I, too.'

As they approached the French windows, she removed her hand from his arm. 'Thank you. I am so glad the family has you here to help with everything that will follow from this. It will be a terrible time.'

He held the French window open for her to pass inside.

The Dowager Countess had drunk her brandy but otherwise seemed not to have moved since they left. Her eyes, those pools of darkness, searched Charles's face. What she saw there seemed to satisfy her. She gave a slight nod.

'I have sent for Benson, Charles. There will be things to organise.'

He marvelled at her ability to rise above shock. He picked up her hand, held it in both of his, looking searchingly into her frozen face, then kissed her fingers. 'I will do all I can, Mama. Have you also sent for Helen?'

Some fleeting emotion passed over her features, gone before it could be identified. 'After Benson, I thought.'

No doubt she was right but Helen had to be informed as soon as possible. He glanced at Miss Grandison.

She picked up her cue. 'Would you like me to bring her here?'

A slow nod from the Dowager Countess.

'It would be best not to tell her what has happened.' Charles realised he had taken command, as he had to.

'Of course.' Ursula left the room.

A moment later a tap on the door signalled Benson's arrival.

For once, the butler's famous ability to absorb extraordinary events failed him.

'Lord Richard!' he said faintly. 'Dead? Shot?'

Charles was suddenly aware how long the man had been a pillar of the Mountstanton establishment. He laid a hand on his shoulder. 'I'm afraid so, Benson. We are all relying on you to manage what has to be done.'

With a visible effort, looking as if he had aged ten years in ten seconds, the butler pulled himself together. 'Of course, Colonel Charles. What would you have me do?'

Charles sat down at his mother's desk and dashed off two quick notes. He handed the envelopes to Benson. 'One for the doctor and the other to Mr Jackman at the Lion and Lamb. Send a groom with them immediately. Then bring some form of substantial covering to the belvedere.'

'At once, sir.' He took the envelopes, looked at them for a moment as if they might contain explosive material, then left the room.

'Jackman? Who, pray, is Jackman?' his mother asked.

Charles wondered how much he should tell her. 'Just someone who may be able to help,' he said. 'The police will have to be told but they can wait until the morning.'

It seemed enough. For a moment both of them were silent. Then: 'He was never the man your father was,' his mother said suddenly. 'It was always a sadness to Simon.'

Charles sighed. It was not the first time he had heard this. 'Richard never forgot his duty, he was a good man,' he said firmly.

The door was thrust open and the room filled with fragrance. Helen, her face pale and distraught – long, fair hair tumbling down the back of a Chinese dressing gown, over which sprawled a burning red dragon – marched up to her mother-in-law.

'How dare you send Ursula to summon me here? She refuses to tell me what has happened – only that it is nothing to do with Harry.'

'Helen, I am afraid it is Richard,' said Charles, coming forward.

'Richard?' she said sharply. 'What has he done?' She did not add 'now', but the word vibrated silently.

'He is dead,' said the Dowager Countess. 'He has shot himself. It is the act of a coward.'

'Mama!' protested Charles.

'Shot himself?' Helen whispered. She looked at Charles as though for reassurance it hadn't happened.

'I am afraid it is true.'

'Where is he? I must see him.'

'Please, no, Helen, not yet.'

'What do you mean, "not yet"? He is my husband, of course I must see him.' She sounded imperious.

'I've brought these.' Ursula stood just inside the door looking drawn and very tired. She held a collection of linen. 'Tablecloths. I found them in a pile gathered from the garden. I thought you could use them ... ', her voice trailed away as she held them out to Charles.

'Of course.' He took them, grateful for her typically practical approach. 'Will you give me a few minutes?' he said to his sister-in-law. He looked again at Miss Grandison, 'Perhaps you would be good enough to accompany Helen?'

'If she will allow me to do so.'

Making his mind a blank, Charles went back to the belvedere. He used one of the smaller cloths to cover the bloody remains of the dead man's head, then spread a larger one over the body. He carefully arranged the hands over the breast so they were in full view.

By then Helen was approaching with Ursula.

She slowly climbed the steps and stood by the shrouded body. Charles laid a comforting hand on her shoulder.

With an irritated gesture, she shook it off. 'Leave me,' she commanded.

He retreated down the steps.

'It's the shock,' Ursula murmured. She stood at the bottom of the steps.

Strange, Charles thought, it was almost as though he was on a battlefield; all feeling cut off, action somehow muffled.

He made a sudden movement forward as Helen stripped the cloth off Richard, but Ursula caught his arm. 'She is doing what she has to do.'

It was all he could do to stay where he was as Helen then raised the smaller cloth so that she could see the bloody mess beneath; beside him Miss Grandison drew in a sharp breath and raised a hand to her mouth.

Helen dropped the cloth with a smothered cry. She snatched up the large cloth and vomited into its folds.

Ursula ran up the steps and placed an arm around her, murmuring into her ear.

Carefully, Helen folded the linen into a bundle and gave it to her companion, who placed it on the ground. Then Helen started to undo the buttons of Richard's jacket and waistcoat. 'Help me,' she instructed Ursula. After a moment's hesitation, she obeyed. Charles watched, unbelieving, as the two women revealed Richard's naked breast. Then Helen flung herself on to it and let out an animal cry that cut to Charles's heart.

Ursula managed to raise the weeping woman off the body. 'There is nothing you can do,' she said, enfolding her in her arms. 'There, there; cry all you want; it will help, Helen, I promise you.'

For a moment the two women stood as though classical figures on a vase of grief. Then Helen allowed herself to be walked down the steps. As she passed Charles, he saw how ravaged her face was and felt pierced as he realised how much she had, indeed, loved his brother.

He picked up another of the cloths, covered the head again and refastened Richard's clothes so that his brother was once more respectably dressed.

Inside the Dowager Countess's drawing room, Helen sat huddled in a chair with Miss Grandison sitting on the arm and holding her around the shoulders. Charles looked at his mother. Her eyes were closed. It was impossible to tell whether she was conscious of anything that was happening or not.

Benson came in. 'Your messages have been sent, Colonel Charles.'

Weariness threatened to consume him. 'Thank you. Let me know when either the doctor or Mr Jackman arrives.' He sensed rather than saw Miss Grandison react to the name.

Helen suddenly sat upright. 'Organise a stretcher, Benson. Then have his lordship carried to his room. Have warm water and towels brought there. I will prepare him for burial.'

The butler looked at Charles.

He crouched down in front of his sister-in-law. 'Helen, dearest, Richard cannot be moved until he has been officially declared dead and someone in authority has viewed his body. I will arrange for that in the morning. There may have to be an autopsy.' He gave a nod to Benson, who melted from the room.

Helen looked mutinously at Charles. 'Why should there have to be an autopsy? It is perfectly obvious how he died. Nobody should be allowed to touch his body but me.' He said nothing and after a moment she touched his cheek with her hand. 'Dear Charles, you must understand; he was my husband. Maybe I was not the best wife he could have had but we did love each other. Surely it is I who should prepare him?'

The Dowager opened her eyes. 'I do not approve of some-one in Helen's position undertaking such a task but she has the right attitude. Charles, surely our rank still counts for some-thing? Surely we can order these things as we see fit?'

The weight of competing demands was heavy. He stood up and looked down at Helen. The hem of her dressing gown was wet with dew but the writhing red dragon, that covered so much of the silk, disguised the bloodstains it had absorbed.

'I will do what I can,' he said. 'And I will keep vigil by Richard until the doctor arrives.'

Helen rose, lifted a hand, then let it drop in a helpless gesture. 'If you will not allow me to do anything, then I shall retire.' She looked at her mother-in-law. 'You should, too, Mama. Tomorrow will be ... difficult.'

Ursula rose. 'Shall I come with you?'

'No. I ... I need to be alone.'

Even through her grief, Helen managed to leave the room as though she was exiting a stage.

Ursula turned to the Dowager Countess. 'Shall I find Barnes for you, your ladyship?'

She received a weary nod.

Charles was left alone with his mother. He helped her to rise.

'Thank you, Charles. At least I have you.'

He kissed her cold cheek. 'Always, Mama.'

She stood erect, indomitable. 'You will take charge. And make sure that Miss Grandison does not leave us until all this is over. One can rely on her to act in the right way. The Mountstanton way.'

He watched her greet her maid.

As Charles walked back to his brother's body, his mother's description of Miss Grandison echoed in his mind. Yes, the American woman was someone who could be relied upon. But to act in the Mountstanton way? That was a different matter.

Chapter Twenty-Four

Ursula's uneasy sleep was broken by a knocking at her door.

For a moment, she thought that she was in California and the banging came from the door of her wooden shack. Then, with a sickening lurch in her stomach, she remembered. She was at Mountstanton and the Earl had shot himself.

'Come in,' she called, levering herself into a sitting position.

'Oh, Miss,' Sarah said, putting a jug of hot water on the washstand, her round, usually happy face stunned. 'Have you heard?'

Ursula nodded.

'To think of that happening whilst we were having our fun!' Sarah's eyes were moist and swollen, her mobcap pulled to one side. 'Mr Benson told us all this morning. Inside and outside we were all there; like Sunday morning prayer meeting it was.'

Ursula had a sudden vision of the Mountstanton staff gathered to hear the news: maids in aprons, footmen in livery, Benson and Mrs Parker in their formal dress. In many ways they were like a family.

'It's terrible.'

Ursula had not seen any sign that the Earl had been greatly loved – not as his father was – if all she had heard could be relied upon.

'Oh, Miss, I doesn't know what I'm doing. I should 'ave brought you your tea before your water.'

'Don't worry, Sarah.' Ursula longed for a cup of tea but the girl's distress was obvious.

'I'll get it right now, miss.'

★ ★ ★

By the time Ursula reached the Morning Room, it was clear that, though the staff were struggling to act as normal, the usually smooth and unobtrusive service was today clumsy and ill-prepared. She saw the butler pass through the hall, his face stolid with repressed grief, then pause to admonish a footman whose trembling hands had scattered a pile of mail.

In the Morning Room, a flustered maid hastily cleared away plates, apologising for not having done so before. It seemed that at least two other members of the household had break-fasted already.

Ursula found she had no appetite. She toyed with a roll, drank a cup of coffee, then went along to Helen's boudoir and knocked on the door, hoping she was not still in bed. A low voice said, 'Come in'.

Helen sat in her pretty buttoned chair, last night's red dragon silk kimono replaced by a white lace negligée. Her long, fair hair looked as though it had not seen a brush since she woke up. Her eyes were red, though her mouth was full and relaxed. By the window stood William Warburton, a slight flush on his cheeks, his hands in the trouser pockets of his dark suit.

'I came to see how you were,' said Ursula, standing just inside the door.

Helen shrugged. The distraught girl from last night had van-ished; the controlled woman was back.

'I am as you see me, a widow in her grief.'

Behind the words Ursula heard animosity.

Helen stretched out a hand towards the man standing behind her. 'William has been very kind. He will help sort out Richard's papers.'

Ursula had to stop herself from saying that surely Richard's brother should do that. After all, if Mr Warburton really had been the Earl's secretary, he must be acquainted with his corre-spondence at the very least and the Colonel would have many calls upon his time.

Helen rose in an easy, languid movement. 'I must dress. Harry has to be told he no longer has a father and that he is now – poor child – the Earl of Mountstanton. William, I will see you later.'

He gave her a graceful nod of his head. 'Of course, your ladyship.'

She went into her bedroom.

Ursula looked across at the secretary. 'Have you seen Belle this morning, Mr Warburton?'

The slight flush on his cheeks deepened. He shook his head.

'Has she heard about the Earl's death, do you know?'

'I . . . that is, I am not sure. Surely someone will have told her?'

Not if she had been asleep when the Earl's body was discovered. But her maid would tell her as soon as she woke. Ursula wondered how the girl would react. Belle had not liked the Earl of Mountstanton. However, he had been her brother-in-law.

'I had better go to her,' she said, and realised that the shock of finding his body had been so great, she hadn't given thought to how much she would miss the Earl. More than she might have expected, given how little contact she had had with him, she concluded. There had been glimpses of a reserved, even shy, man beneath the unyielding front he seemed to have adopted for the outside world. If only he could have let go and shown the charm of his brother – somewhat eccentric though that charm might be. Perhaps the duties and responsibilities of the Earldom meant it hadn't been possible.

Ursula shivered as she thought of little Harry, now the seventh Earl.

As she approached Belle's room, a footman hurried towards her.

'Miss Grandison, Colonel Charles would be grateful if you could join him in the library.'

'Thank you, John.' He had lost his teasing air. Like all the Mountstanton staff, he looked shaken and bereft.

In the library, the Colonel sat in one of the deep leather armchairs. Ursula could not help remembering the last time she had seen him in this room, when it had seemed so clear to her that he doubted his brother's word and believed the Earl had indeed visited Mr Snell the night the man died.

The Colonel stood up as she entered. He looked desperately tired and Ursula thought it probable he had not been to bed that night, but instead had merely bathed and changed his clothes.

'Miss Grandison, thank you for coming. May I introduce Thomas Jackman?'

Ursula had not realised anyone else was in the room.

Standing by one of the book-lined shelves was a man she immediately recognised as the one who had accosted her in Hinton Parva the previous day; the one who had known her name and seemed to assume that she would recognise his. It was a shock to realise that hardly twenty-four hours had passed since they'd met.

He nodded at her, his bright eyes taking in every aspect of her hastily knotted hair, cream linen skirt and cambric shirt.

The Colonel waved towards another of the leather arm-chairs. 'Please, Miss Grandison, will you sit?'

She sank down and looked questioningly at him.

He sat also and lent towards Ursula, his manner confiding. 'I had hoped to tell you all about Mr Jackman before you met him in the village. Unfortunately, my return from London was delayed and I had no opportunity for a private conversation with you.'

No, Ursula had made certain of that. Looking at his exhausted expression now, she tried to remember exactly why she had been so determined not to let him slip under her defences. She knew there were questions he needed to answer – but they could wait until later. She tried to look alert and interested.

'Like you, I was not at all satisfied with the coroner's verdict on Polly's death. It seemed to me that, without my brother's backing, we were unlikely to make progress down here and so I went up to London.'

Well, there was one unasked question answered.

He gave her the slightest of smiles, as though he had worked out at least one reason for her sudden antagonism towards him.

Ursula felt a momentary regret at not having had more faith in him – but also a sudden spurt of anger that he couldn't have told her what he was doing. She was also very conscious of Mr Jackman's keen attention and strove to keep her expression non-committal.

'Through an old friend, I made contact with the Home Secretary and asked for an introduction to Scotland Yard.'

American she might be but Ursula knew exactly what Scotland Yard represented.

'And, finally, after a little time, I got an introduction. But apparently what I was able to produce by way of facts was not enough for them to send down a detective for an investigation. However, it was suggested that if I was set on pursuing the matter, I contact one Thomas Jackman.' He glanced over at the other man, who took a step forward.

'Until recently I was a detective officer in the Metropolitan Police,' Jackman said in a matter-of-fact way. 'And I now pursue a calling, as you might say, as a private investigator.'

'That is why Mr Jackman is in the village. He has booked himself into the Lion and Lamb and is pursuing enquiries.'

Ursula remembered Miss Russell's indignation at this stranger questioning villagers.

'What reason have you been giving for making these "enquiries" as you have it, Mr Jackman?'

'Why that there is a gentleman of fortune who has come to see the error of youthful indiscretions and is now anxious to trace the possible offspring of a relationship he enjoyed in this area some twenty odd years ago.'

How that skimmed the truth!

'When pursuing investigatory matters, miss, while being circumspect, I find it best to stick as near to the facts as is known.' He glanced at the Colonel as though handing the conversation back to him.

'As Jackman was in the neighbourhood, I sent him a note last night asking him to attend on me here,' said the Colonel. 'I wanted him to see my brother's body before the authorities took over.'

Ursula felt the hairs on the back of her neck rise.

'Local authorities seldom take notice of evidence in the way we do at the Yard,' Thomas Jackman said sententiously.

The Colonel leaned back in his chair. 'Tell Miss Grandison what you said to me after your inspection of the scene in the belvedere.'

The detective turned to Ursula.

'As soon as I saw the deceased, every instinct and all my experience as a detective said that it was not suicide.'

Ursula gasped. 'How do you know that?'

'Suicides do not shoot themselves lying down, miss.'

'Are you sure?'

'Never known one yet.'

'Why don't they?' The question seemed idiotic but she could not stop herself.

He shrugged. 'Who's to say? Perhaps because it's awkward if a shotgun is used, as in his lordship's case, though it seems if the deed is done with a pistol, the victim still prefers to be sitting or standing. Whatever the reason, I hold his lordship's death to have been by some other hand than his own.'

'Thank you, Jackman. Would you be good enough to wait in the hall while Miss Grandison and I discuss the situation?'

'Of course, sir.'

The detective quietly left the room.

Ursula swallowed hard and tried to take in the enormity of what had been said. She turned back to the Colonel, now studying her through half-closed eyes. 'Forgive me, but are you really taking that man's word that your brother did not commit suicide? I realise such a verdict would have terrible consequences. Polly's death has taught me that.'

His eyes were haunted. 'The shame threatens to devastate my mother.'

'But who could possibly have wanted to kill him?' Later she realised that the thought of an accident had not occurred to her.

'I knew I could trust you to go to the heart of the matter, Miss Grandison. You have raised the two crucial issues: First, can I rely on Jackman's experience in these matters? Second, if I can, who could have had reason to shoot Richard?'

She saw one reason why he had been a successful army officer; personal feelings could be put aside when they had to be. Ursula wished she could manage to do the same. 'Do you know what the view of the authorities is? Have they attended on you yet?'

'Dr Mason came last night, pronounced Richard dead and said he would inform the coroner. I expect him and the Chief Constable to arrive at any moment.'

'Should you not wait to hear what they say? And why are you telling me all this?'

The Colonel's singularly charming smile broke through the exhaustion. 'I asked Jackman to tell you his conclusions because I have the greatest respect for your common sense and superior intelligence. There is no one else in this household I can trust the way I do you.'

His words and the sincerity with which they were uttered were so unexpected, Ursula gazed at him in astonishment.

'I do not expect the coroner to agree with Jackman's verdict,' he continued, 'nor do I expect our Chief Constable to call on Scotland Yard to instigate a thorough investigation.'

Ursula tried to grapple with the situation. 'But surely, sir, you are now the head of the Mountstanton household? Oh, I know it's Harry who must be Earl but, until he is grown, you have to be in charge.' He said nothing and she considered for a moment. For the first time an alternative presented itself. 'What is being suggested here is surely impossible. If, and I cannot take it as more than *if*, Mr Jackman is correct in saying your brother could not have committed suicide, could there not have been some sort of accident?'

He regarded her steadily and his lip curled slightly. 'I am sure my mother and sister-in-law would prefer a verdict of death by misadventure.'

'Misadventure?' Having suggested an accident, Ursula now found she was sceptical.

Charles sighed heavily and said nothing.

'You think that your brother was shot by someone else? But that would make it a homicide!'

The word echoed round the quiet room.

Ursula looked at the Colonel in horror and saw that this was what he believed. 'Can you take the word of that former policeman? Can he really be certain that people never shoot themselves lying down?'

He walked to the door. 'Let us allow him to speak for himself.'

A moment later Thomas Jackman reappeared in the library and Ursula expressed her doubts.

'I can understand, miss, that it is a hard matter to accept,' he said. 'Perhaps if I could suggest that we visit the scene?'

Ursula flinched.

'You may stay here, Miss Grandison,' the Colonel said quickly. 'We will report back.'

She pulled herself together. If Colonel Stanhope had called her in because he felt her opinions could be valuable, she must not let him down. 'I shall accompany you, sir.'

'Are you sure?' His voice was concerned.

'Absolutely.'

Her reward was a warm smile.

'Then let us go.'

'A moment, sir,' Mr Jackman said. 'I think we shall need to conduct a small experiment. Is there a shotgun similar to the one used last night?'

The Colonel nodded. 'I will fetch it from the gun room.'

'And if we could take a couple of wooden chairs with us?'

'Of course.'

★ ★ ★

Outside, clear skies and a warm sun said it was going to be another glorious day.

It was a curious little procession. First came the Colonel, a shotgun broken over his arm; then followed Mr Jackman carrying two plain wooden chairs from the servants' dining hall, and lastly came Ursula.

She found her steps slowing as they approached the belvedere. But the Earl's body was covered with a tarpaulin; only the gun was visible. It lay neatly alongside the stone bench, beneath the hand, once again dangling down, its fingers just visible.

Mr Jackman halted short of that dreadful scene and put down the chairs, one alongside the other with a gap in between. He waved at the gun on the ground beneath the Earl's hand. 'Please, take note of its position.'

Ursula and the Colonel looked at it and then back at Mr Jackman.

'If I could have the shotgun you are holding, sir?'

The Colonel handed it over.

The detective checked it was unloaded. Then he snapped the stock back onto the barrel and released the safety catch. Finally he adjusted the position of the two chairs so they stood a little further apart.

'How is my height in relation to that of the deceased?' he asked the Colonel.

'You are several inches shorter, Jackman, my brother was taller than I am.'

'Should not be critical.'

He lay down across the two chairs and Ursula put a hand to her mouth and swallowed hard as she saw what he was about to do. She closed her eyes as the ex-policeman brought the barrel of the gun up to his mouth. She heard a click followed by a thud and then silence. She opened her eyes.

Thomas Jackman was inching himself off the chairs. On the ground lay the shotgun.

'You see, sir, miss?'

The gun lay at an angle to the line of the chairs.

'But perhaps it could sometimes fall as that one did,' the Colonel waved a hand towards last night's weapon.

'I could repeat this experiment as many times as you like, sir, but the result will never be as neat as that gun there.' He gestured towards it. 'Also, this one was not loaded; there was no recoil. You saw how when my finger loosened its grip off the trigger, the weapon slipped and then bounced on the ground. With the recoil, it would have landed further away.'

Ursula and the Colonel both looked again at the weapon that lay on the floor of the belvedere, so neatly positioned below the Earl's dead hand.

'And the champagne bottle?' the Colonel asked.

'Could have been placed there to suggest the dead man had drunk it to prepare himself for the final act.'

'What are you doing?' The voice was sharp. Coming towards them across the grass was the Dowager Countess.

Chapter Twenty-Five

The Colonel went to meet his mother. Mr Jackman picked up the gun he had used for his experiment and laid it carefully on one of the chairs. He looked at Ursula.

'Do you understand, miss?'

She nodded slowly. She might not trust the ex-policeman the way the Colonel obviously did but the demonstration had convinced her. It seemed incontrovertible that the Earl had not killed himself.

The Dowager made an angry gesture at her son and continued on towards Ursula and Mr Jackman.

'Young man, I am the Dowager Countess of Mountstanton. I understand my son has hired you to investigate the tragedy that happened here last night,' she said, looking the detective straight in the eye. 'You may go home now. We know what happened: there was an accident.'

She stood as if prepared for roots to grow from her feet. 'The coroner and the Chief Constable will soon be here and will pronounce officially that an accident occurred. I ask you to remove those macabre items from my lawn.' She waved a hand at the chairs then turned to Ursula. 'I am surprised to find you taking part in this extraordinary exercise, Miss Grandison. I thought better of you.'

With superb control, her head held high, her back ramrod straight, the Dowager Countess returned to her apartment.

Mr Jackman placed one chair upside down on the other.

The Colonel saw his mother into her apartment then hurried back to where the two of them were standing.

'Accident?' asked Ursula blankly. She had suggested this possibility herself; now it seemed unlikely if not impossible.

'Richard was often known to take his shotgun after pigeons. My mother believes he grew bored with last night's festivities and decided that shooting a few would offer better entertainment. She thinks a malfunction in the weapon caused the accident.'

'Pigeons, Colonel, at that time of night?' said Ursula.

He gave a hopeless shrug. 'That is what my mother appears to believe. Mr Jackman, you have convinced me that my brother might well have been shot by someone unknown. I would be grateful if you would attempt to discover from those villagers who were here at yesterday's celebrations, what time they left and if they saw anyone approach the belvedere. It cannot be seen from where the marquee was placed but someone might have noticed a person coming up from the river towards it, for instance. I think it unlikely anyone would have been bold enough to come round the house.'

'Certainly, sir. When would you like me to report to you?'

Charles thought for a moment then suggested around six o'clock that evening.

Mr Jackman handed over the shotgun he had used for his demonstration, picked up the two chairs and walked swiftly away, just as two men appeared.

The Colonel straightened his shoulders. 'Ah, the coroner and the Chief Constable. Miss Grandison, would you . . . ?'

'Of course.'

'I will come and find you after they have conducted their examination.'

'Will you . . . ?'

'Tell them the result of Mr Jackman's little experiment? I will indeed, Miss Grandison.' He seemed hurt that she would think anything else.

★ ★ ★

Ursula went back into the house feeling shattered. What was being suggested seemed impossible. And yet . . .

No sooner had she returned inside than Belle found her.

'Oh, Ursula, isn't it awful?' Her pretty face was crumpled with distress. 'And did you really find him? Come to my room and tell me what happened; no! That nosy maid of mine will interrupt us. Let's go to yours instead.'

So once again they sought privacy in Ursula's bedroom. Belle didn't seem to want to talk until they were safely there. Passing the door of the nursery, Ursula thought that she heard Harry crying.

Belle sat on the bed and pulled Ursula down beside her. Then she wiped away tears from eyes already red with crying. 'Now, tell me everything.'

'How much do you know?'

'Didier woke me with the news. She said that there had been a terrible accident and that the Earl had been shot.' She looked up at Ursula. 'I can't believe it! Richard dead! She couldn't tell me anything else, except that he had been found by the Dowager Countess and you.' She sounded incredulous. 'Helen is with Harry,' she continued, 'and I can't find William.' Suddenly she dissolved in a flood of tears.

Ursula put her arm around the girl and held her tightly. 'I'm afraid it is all true.' She swallowed hard. 'There's . . . there's a sort of investigation going on.'

'What do you mean?' Belle's eyes were huge, distraught.

Ursula took a deep breath and tried to put her thoughts into order. 'We, that is the Dowager Countess and I, found the Earl's body lying on the stone bench in the belvedere. A shotgun was on the ground beside him. The Dowager is certain there was an accident, that he was shooting pigeons and the gun misfired.' To her own ears it sounded a ridiculously improbable event. 'Have you spoken with Helen?'

Belle shook her head. She had lost all her colour and sat working her hands together in a distressed way.

'Helen will need your support now,' Ursula suggested. 'It's good that she will have you at her side.' Surely Belle would be able to summon sisterly compassion, allow Helen to pour out her sorrow? Ursula could not see her doing so to her mother-in-law or, most especially, to herself. But she must need someone to confide her feelings in.

Belle did not look at all sympathetic. 'She's a widow now, isn't she?'

Ursula nodded.

'She'll want to marry William,' Belle suddenly wailed. 'I know she will.' Huge sobs followed.

For a moment Ursula was stunned. Then she realised how distressed the girl was and gathered her tightly into her arms again. 'Shhh, shhh, you don't know that.'

Belle pulled back with a pout. 'She warned me off William when we first arrived. Told me straight he was not for me. I knew what she meant by that. She's always been selfish.' Despite the fact Helen had spent the last seven years in England, there was a history of sisterly resentment in Belle's voice. 'And now I won't get to make my debut!' she wailed. 'We will all have to go into mourning for months and months. I am getting measured for two black outfits this afternoon to be made by tomorrow. You are to have one as well. By the time the mourning is over, the Season will be too.'

'It's only a matter of dances,' Ursula tried to comfort her.

'Balls!' Belle protested. 'And being presented. Hardly anyone in New York is presented to royalty.'

'Maybe a private presentation to their Majesties can be arranged.' Ursula had no idea whether this was possible, yet, somehow, she had to get Belle thinking positively. 'Perhaps you and Helen can go to Paris or Italy and do some sightseeing instead.' What on earth, she wondered, was the form for English aristocrats dealing with recent widowhood? Whatever the rituals the Dowager would consider appropriate, Ursula was certain Helen would follow her own desires.

Would they really include marrying William Warburton? Did he have anything to offer beyond good looks and a neat figure? Surely Helen would need more?

'She won't want to do anything for me, Ursula. Helen only ever wants to do what she wants. And I'm sure that means marrying William!'

'Darling Belle, I am sure Helen hasn't any such thought in mind. She will have far, far too much to cope with over the coming months even to think of marriage. And can you see the Dowager Countess countenancing Harry's mama doing any such thing?'

Belle seemed struck by this. She took the handkerchief Ursula offered and wiped her eyes. 'You mean, I can get

together with William while Helen gets on with . . . well, whatever she has to get on with?'

Somehow Ursula managed not to sigh. 'He obviously finds
you very attractive,' she said encouragingly. 'You can make him
laugh and men love that.'

'Oh, you are right, Ursula! And I do make him laugh. And
he loves horseback riding with me. Helen won't have time for
that.'

It took a little more time but Belle was at last more cheerful
and Ursula sent her off to find William Warburton.

With her hand on the doorknob, Belle turned back for a
moment. 'You do not know, Ursula, how determined my sister
can be. I do not think there is anything she would not do to
gain her way. But she is not going to get William.'

★ ★ ★

Ursula walked slowly through the rose garden. Looking
towards the belvedere, she saw the coroner and the Chief
Constable talking with Colonel Stanhope. As she watched, the
three men started towards the Dowager's apartment. Ursula
retreated.

She went to the library and found a couple of sheets of paper
and a pencil. The sun slanted in through the windows, motes
dancing in its rays. The atmosphere was calm and peaceful and
Ursula longed to stay there but the Colonel would almost certainly bring the two officials in for further discussion.

She went to the hall and asked Albert, the footman on duty,
if there was a quiet room where she would not be disturbed.

She was shown into the smoking room. Square, permeated
with the aroma of cigars, the walls badly discoloured and hung
with hunting scenes, it was furnished with more leather chairs.
The harshly masculine atmosphere made Ursula feel uncomfortable.

Shivering and telling herself that it was lack of sleep that
made her feel so cold, she sat in a chair that caught the sun.
Her head throbbed with tension. So many unacceptable details
fought around her mind and she wanted to deny them all.

There were the various facts and suppositions that had been
thrown at her by Thomas Jackman. There was the suspicion

that the Colonel was so willing to accept the detective's vision of events because he could not bear to believe that his brother may have shot himself. There was the unpleasant feeling she had experienced in Helen's boudoir that morning. And there was Belle's distress.

Ursula put aside the problem of Belle and Mr Warburton for the moment and tried to consider the trustworthiness of Thomas Jackman. Why, she wondered, had he left the police force? Surely the Colonel must have been given a solid reference for him by whatever senior Scotland Yard official had produced the recommendation. Apart from that, she had to admit that there was a quiet confidence about the man that suggested he was not someone who would lay claim to a competence he did not have.

Ursula turned her reluctant mind to consider the possibility that the Earl really had committed suicide. Quite apart from the shock and the shame, it was no wonder the Colonel did not want to accept that his brother had been in such a desperate state that he found death a more attractive option than life. Why would the Earl not have turned to him for help? He would read suicide as a bitter rejection of himself. But why should the Earl kill himself? He seemed to have everything: a magnificent, if decrepit, home, a beautiful wife and a gorgeous son. How could he want to leave all that?

Ursula began to make brief notes, supporting her paper on some hunting magazines.

As she worked, the quiet of the room and warmth of the sun began to calm her. Her pencil moved increasingly slowly. Gradually it stopped. Almost without her realising it, Ursula's eyes closed.

She had no idea how long she dozed or what woke her but when she opened her eyes she saw that, sitting opposite, was the Colonel.

He smiled at her. She felt a curious lethargy and wished they could go on sitting quietly together like this, ignoring the world outside.

He raised the piece of paper he held. 'I hope I did not disturb you. Albert told me where you were hiding and I found you sleeping so peacefully. This paper was on the ground by your chair. Forgive me, I have been reading your notes.'

She would not have chosen to show him what she had written but perhaps it was for the best.

'"Possibilities",' he read. '"One: the Earl did commit suicide despite Mr Jackman's expertise. Questions: Why would he? Is there a farewell note? Two: He suffered an accident with his gun. How likely is this? Does the Dowager really believe it? Three," your pencil has dug into the paper here as though you had to force yourself to contemplate this possibility. "Three: Someone else shot him. Again, why? And who?"' He looked up at her. 'A stark but efficient summing up of the situation. You have saved me from making a similar list of points. But I do not understand what you have added at the end.' He frowned. 'Here is William Warburton's name with two arrows, one pointing towards Belle's name and the other to Helen's. Then below that you have written: "Polly".' He gave her a keen look. 'Would you be prepared to share your thoughts with me?'

Ursula pulled herself upright and forced her mind to concentrate.

'I'm not sure I can,' she said slowly.

His eyes narrowed. 'You do not trust me?'

She shook her head. 'It's nothing to do with trust.'

'Ah, a matter of keeping confidences?'

She felt a small jolt of pleasure at his quick understanding but said nothing.

'Let me see.' Another frown as he studied the paper again. 'Miss Seldon has formed an attachment to Mr Warburton. Is that it?'

Again Ursula said nothing.

'But surely you aren't suggesting that Helen has also formed an attachment?'

He sounded as though that was impossible. For the first time Ursula realised that Helen's widowhood might encourage the Colonel to think he could comfort her. Marriage was forbidden between such close relatives but Helen would not let that stop her forming a liaison, if that was what she wanted. She dismissed the thought.

'Belle, poor girl, is desperately in love with Mr Warburton and has formed the idea that now her sister is a widow, she will want to marry him.'

'Has she – or you – seen or heard anything to suggest that that would be the case?' His voice was perfectly even.

'No, nothing,' Ursula said firmly. After all, she told herself, she might have misread that morning's atmosphere. 'At least, not as far as I am concerned. And Belle couldn't tell me why she believes it.' She paused for a moment. 'She is a girl who seems to follow instinct rather than rational thought.'

The Colonel went back to studying Ursula's notes. 'And you have added Polly's name because?'

Glad to have moved on from the subject of Helen, Ursula said, 'Two violent deaths within such a short space of time must surely give rise to speculation that they could in some way be connected.'

'Hmmm.'

Ursula waited.

Then, 'Let us consider each of your points in turn. First, I have no reason not to trust Jackman but no proof that he is so experienced in these matters that he can be considered a true expert.'

'Why is he no longer serving at Scotland Yard?'

'A good question. I understand it was a matter of a personality clash between him and his superior officer. Jackman preferred to resign rather than be demoted. Which could mean he failed in some way. However, he was recommended to me by someone whose judgement I respect.' He returned his attention to the paper. 'You are quite right to ask if Richard left a note.' He felt in his pocket. 'I found this poking out from beneath one of his feet.'

Ursula took the piece of paper with a slight shiver. Even in the depths of his shock, the Colonel had been in control of himself enough to notice this scrap – it was no more than that: *Charles, forgive me. I have no other option.*

'Is it your brother's handwriting?'

'I have had few letters from him; he has never been a good correspondent, but, yes, it looks like his. However, he might well have started a note to me and been distracted. Maybe he changed his mind and threw it into a waste paper basket – from where it was rescued by someone else.'

'That would mean they had access to his study.' Ursula shivered again. The unlikely possibility that the Earl had been shot by another hand than his own was gradually beginning to look as though it should be seriously considered.

'And why should,' the Colonel continued, 'Richard put it underneath his foot? Surely if he wanted to leave a note apologising for his action, he would have said more and left it in his bedroom or study?'

Ursula suddenly thought of something. 'Did you not take your brother in your motor vehicle to Salisbury yesterday afternoon?'

He nodded.

'How did he seem? Depressed? Moody?'

'You mean, could he have been considering shooting himself? Far from it. He seemed almost light-hearted, like he was when we were growing up together.' He smiled reminiscently. 'He even said motoring was a damn, forgive me, a damn good way of getting about and he'd go out and get a vehicle like mine!'

'No wonder you are so sure Mr Jackman is right. What about the coroner and, what did you call him, the Chief Constable? To be called a constable doesn't suggest a very high rank but I suppose put "chief" in front and it becomes more respectable.'

'He is the titular head of this area's police force, a man of considerable standing. Neither he nor the coroner will allow Jackman's theories to hold much water. It was probably a mistake to mention his name. Then the coroner announced that my mother had insisted they relate their findings to her.'

'Did she tell them that she believed it was an accident?'

He nodded, his face blank. 'Nothing would shake her from that view.' He pocketed the piece of paper and leaned forward. 'Forgive me for what I am about to say. I do not think for one moment it is the truth but you have to understand it is what my mother believes. Last night she told me we must ensure a verdict of death by misadventure is returned because she is certain Richard shot himself because he could no longer live with the fact that his wife was being unfaithful to him with a series of men. When I challenged her to produce some proof, she told me I was a romantic fool.'

Ursula drew a sharp breath. 'That is the last thing I would call you.'

He smiled ruefully. 'I'm not at all sure that is a compliment.'

Ursula moved swiftly on. 'Surely, though, your mother is desperate to prove your brother's death wasn't suicide because of the slur on the Mountstanton reputation, rather than because she doesn't want your brother's motives for suicide questioned.'

'It appears she has succeeded. Both the coroner and Chief Constable left here stating that the inquest would find that Richard's death was due to accidental causes.'

Ursula was astonished. 'I find that hard to believe.'

He looked at her steadily. 'Any other verdict would mean the Mountstanton name spread all over the gutter press, and newspaper men haunting the area; every aspect of the family would be dug up and displayed for the common man to salivate over. When my mother invokes the full power of the Mountstanton name and status, it takes an extraordinarily strong and independent man to stand against her.' His tired eyes held hers in a compelling way. 'I was told that the inquest is to be held in private. It will be a rubber-stamping exercise.'

'Surely, if there is any possibility that someone killed your brother,' Ursula swallowed painfully, 'surely every effort must be made to discover whether that is, in fact, the truth and, if so, who it was that shot him?' Ursula was suddenly very angry. She rose and stalked to the other end of the room.

Charles rose as well.

She turned and faced him, hands on hips. He said nothing but his eyes continued their steady gaze. 'You are the senior Mountstanton male. You are the strong and independent man you said was needed to stand up to your mother. It seems to me this is now a battlefield. You are a soldier, you must know exactly what has to be done. You can make those officials do the right and proper thing. You did it for Polly, what is preventing you doing it for your brother?' Her breath coming fast, she finally stopped, too angry to be appalled at her behaviour.

'Thank you, Miss Grandison. It was what I had decided must be done but I needed someone else to believe it as well. Richard must have justice.'

Ursula sank back into her chair. 'I'm sorry,' she whispered. 'You have your mother and Helen – and Harry – to consider. I had no right to say what I did.'

'You were absolutely right to speak so!' He took her hand and kissed it. 'You are an Amazon and I am grateful to you.'

Ursula felt a rare blush staining her neck and face as he sat down again. She sought a return to solid ground. 'What of the possibility that your brother's death could be connected with Polly's? That was why you brought Mr Jackman down, to investigate how she had died. Maybe his questions in Hinton Parva alerted someone to the possibility of something regarding Polly coming to light. Though why that should mean the Earl had to be killed, I can't imagine.'

'Now surely you can understand why I need your help? You are not entangled with the bloody, forgive my language, the bloody Mountstanton way of doing things. Our family's autocratic way of viewing its position can be poisonous. I told you once that I had tried to escape its influence. Now it appears that it is up to me to see that Harry grows up unencumbered with false ideas of what and who he is.'

Ursula thought of the little boy whose shoulders now bore such a burden. Would an investigation of his father's death mean his life would forever be scarred with scandal?

Chapter Twenty-Six

The May afternoon was gliding smoothly towards evening. Its warmth and beauty were lost on Thomas Jackman as he plodded up the hill and along the wooded path that would take him to Mountstanton.

Frustration ran through his veins like a rat through a run. He'd had no sleep the previous night. Colonel Stanhope's message had reached the Lion and Lamb as he and Sam Fry, the landlord, were ending a quiet session discussing the locals over a pint of Sam's Special Ale.

Soon after Thomas had arrived at the Lion and Lamb, he had discovered that the landlord had a dearly loved nephew in the Metropolitan force. To learn all about police work from someone who knew it from the inside was joy to Sam. He had produced jugs of his ale that first night and on subsequent evenings. During their conversations, it was not difficult for the former detective to extract a wealth of information about the villagers of Mountstanton – and about the family up in the big house.

The family up in the big house . . .

For a moment, as he negotiated the woodland track, Thomas wondered exactly what he had got himself into. When Colonel Stanhope had first approached him, it seemed a heaven-sent opportunity. Now it looked more like a lifeline turning into a rope that could strangle him.

Losing his job in the detective section of the Metropolitan force had been devastating. His ability as a constable on the beat to search out evidence and assemble cases against various East End villains had quickly produced an offer to join the elite team of detectives. Thomas had soon realised he'd found a totally absorbing career. The cases mostly involved petty thieves, fraudsters and such like, but he had grown increasingly involved with the process of winkling out the truth. Once facts had been collected and witnesses found and interviewed, most cases proved simple enough. The villains he dealt with possessed a certain low cunning rather than high intelligence. Even the craftier type of rascals, making a good living from crime, were no match for Thomas. He learned to disguise his appearance with different outfits, sometimes using a wig or false moustache; nothing too blatant. He learned the value of subtlety. He gained a reputation for being able to crack the most difficult of cases and put what were sometimes called 'master minds' behind bars.

It was only later he realised how naive he'd been not to see how eaten-up with jealousy his superior officer was becoming.

The cases Thomas found most difficult were those that involved the upper classes. Humble policemen, even detectives, were not expected to point the finger of responsibility at those who were so far above them in the social scale.

It was a case not unlike the one he was involved with at the moment that had caused the final showdown with his boss. A maid in the home of a marquis had been strangled. Her body had been found in Green Park, no more than a stone's throw from the back garden of the house where she was employed.

Initially, such evidence as there was had pointed at one of the marquis's footmen as her killer. He had pleaded innocence, and swore that the girl had been seduced by a member of the household. One of the other maids said the girl had told her she was with child. She had been very cut up, she said, and had declared she would make the man who had brought about her ruin 'do right by her'.

What was mainly circumstantial evidence had convinced Thomas that the seducer was a nephew of the marquis and that he had most probably killed the girl to protect his reputation. Thomas wanted to take him in for questioning in the hope of extracting a confession. That was when the power of the aristocracy had been brought into play. Thomas was told that one of the down-and-outs, in the habit of sleeping in the park, must have killed the maid. When he asked what evidence there was to support this theory, his boss told him, 'The case stops here.'

Suddenly Thomas had recognised not only the inspector's jealousy of the attention his junior officer was receiving as he closed case after case, but also his ambition, the obsequious manner the man used to the upper classes. Thomas respected those in authority but his mission was to see justice done. The vision of the dead girl's face, the eyes bulging, tongue swollen and lolling out, haunted him. He had pressed for a warrant to bring the man in.

Perhaps if Rose, his wife, had still been alive, Thomas would not have reacted the way he had. Rose had always listened to his worries, shared in his problems, his triumphs. With a few soft words she had the knack of removing pressures and making any difficulty easier to deal with. But Rose had died of a fever.

So Thomas had challenged the detective inspector and accused him of pandering to the power of privilege. He had lost his job.

He should, of course, have accepted his superior's diktat without question. Instead he had tried to go over his head.

His career had ended in an interview with the Chief Constable. Later, he'd realised how unusual this had been and wondered if there hadn't been something he could have done to save himself. At the time he had been consumed with right-eous anger. He had stood rigidly to attention in front of the huge, highly polished desk.

The Chief Constable had stood looking out of the window, his hands held locked together behind his back, underneath the skirts of his frock coat. He hardly seemed to notice that Thomas was waiting.

'Well, Jackman,' he'd said finally. 'A fine mess you've made of things.'

'Sir!'

The Chief turned. His swarthy face with its strong bone structure combined power and intelligence. He sat down behind the desk and regarded his wayward officer, then said, 'Your conduct cannot be overlooked. You have to go.'

It had been a vain hope to expect anything else.

For a long moment the dark eyes regarded him without emotion. 'You're a good detective, Jackman, probably the best there is at the moment. Trouble is, you are not someone who can accept discipline or who understands what it is to be part of a team.'

Thomas felt resentment join his anger but knew there was nothing he could say.

'Set yourself up as someone who can investigate privately, man. You should be able to make a good living; perhaps even better than as a member of the force.'

The suggestion came as a complete surprise.

A few minutes later, Thomas was on his way out.

Back in his empty home in Holborn, he tried to ignore the loss of his career and think instead of what he should do now. Lacking any sort of plan, he went round to his local. There the landlord left him alone for a bit, as did the regulars. They had no wish to cross a policeman. The unusual sight, though, of Thomas Jackman sinking pint after pint, uninterested in the doings of the local villainy, finally led the landlord to enquire how things were.

A few days after that, there was a knock on Thomas's door and there was the pot boy from the pub. Thomas had been scanning his newspaper's employment columns. A sense of hopelessness rather than curiosity made him answer the land-lord's summons.

It had not taken him long to identify the villain responsible for a number of thefts connected with the pub; the police had given up on the case almost immediately and Thomas was almost certain it was because of a close connection between one of the constables and the villain. He had handed over the miscreant and enjoyed the gratitude of several locals.

Nothing else came along. Thomas took to doing odd jobs while he sought proper employment; anything to get him out of the empty house where everything reminded him of Rose.

Then one morning Colonel Stanhope had arrived on his doorstep.

'There's something I'd like to discuss with you, Mr Jackman,' he'd said, introducing himself. 'Can we go inside?'

Being addressed as 'Mr' by his visitor suggested a measure of equality between the two of them. But Thomas had known immediately that the Colonel was a member of the upper class. Everything about him breathed privilege, from the clearly bespoke clothes, classy shoes and military bearing to the well-ordered features and clipped accent.

Yet, despite an air of authority so natural the man had probably been born with it, his attitude as Thomas invited him to sit in the small living room, in the chair that had been Rose's, was that of a man without a trace of arrogance.

'The Chief Constable gave me your name and suggested you might be able to help me.'

As he'd listened to the Colonel outlining his problem, Thomas felt how ironic it was. One dead maid in an aristocratic household had finished his career, now it seemed another one might offer him a new chance. Something in this story, though, seemed odd. He took the Colonel through the facts, checking details, establishing the limits of what the Colonel knew about both the victim and her end.

'Well?' said the Colonel finally, his keen eyes fixed on Thomas's. 'Will you take this assignment on?'

For a moment Thomas sat surveying his visitor. How far could he trust this man? He was a member of the class that had caused his downfall. He might seem to be straightforward and honest, but Thomas could not run the risk of privilege, once again, burying truth. And what about the nursemaid who had died? If someone, as this man seemed to believe, had been responsible for her death, he should at least try to reveal her killer and make him pay for his crime, shouldn't he?

'One thing is not clear to me,' he said. 'The nursemaid was a member of your family's household but you want me to open my investigations in the village. Surely I need to start with the people she worked with?' For it was almost certainly someone in the household who had got the girl pregnant.

The Colonel took his gold fob watch out of his waistcoat pocket and consulted the time. 'As I think I told you, all the necessary enquiries have been conducted in the house. I may not have mentioned, though, that my brother, the Earl, is not in agreement with me that the matter of Polly's death should be taken further.'

Brilliant, thought Thomas sourly, a family feud! He almost refused the assignment there and then.

'In addition,' the Colonel continued, 'there is to be a fête at the house in a couple of days to celebrate my mother's birthday. Until that's over, nobody will have time to answer questions. It will, therefore, be best for you to begin your enquiries in Hinton Parva; I am sure there will be information to be unearthed. Polly came from the nearby orphanage and spent such time off as she had in the village. It will probably be best if you provide some other reason why you are there than that you have been asked to make enquiries on my behalf.'

That might well be, but Thomas was certain that the Mountstanton household would yield more important answers. He sat considering matters while the Colonel returned his watch to its pocket and sat patiently watching him.

'What if you do not like what I discover? There will be nothing official about my investigation; you could well decide to ignore my findings.'

The Colonel's gaze remained steady. 'I want justice for Polly. If you can establish how she died, I shall do everything I can to see that the law swings into action.'

This was the soldier speaking. Thomas, though, had a niggling feeling that there was something this man was not telling him; that if he said 'yes', he would be stepping into a situation beyond his control. But the temptation to accept this chance was too great.

'If you really mean what you say, sir, then I will take the case on.'

Colonel Stanhope stood up with an air of relief. 'Good man. Now, you will need directions on how to get down to Hinton Parva. You are on your own when you arrive but I will contact you after you have had an opportunity to conduct some enquiries.' He retrieved an envelope from an inside pocket and handed it to Thomas. 'Here are the details, some expenses and an advance on your fee.'

This man had been very confident he would be willing to do what he asked. He looked again at the decisive set of the Colonel's shoulders and did not know whether to be reassured or wary. He put the envelope on a table.

'Thank you, sir,' he said. 'I will go down to Hinton Parva this afternoon.' He opened the door to show his visitor out.

The Colonel, though, stayed where he was. 'Miss Grandison, the American woman who found Polly's body, is a person of sense. She also is dissatisfied with the coroner's verdict. Her current mobility is limited; she walks with a stick, owing to her ankle injury. So if you come across her in Hinton Parva, she should be instantly recognisable.' He paused for a moment. 'She is unusual, has a lively mind and is not afraid to speak it. On my return to Mountstanton, I shall tell her that you are to investigate the matter. If you do meet up, you may find it valuable to discuss any findings you have made with her.'

Thomas hid how startled he was. In his experience, gentlemen, especially military gentlemen, did not regard women as worthy partners in this sort of investigation. Miss Grandison must be a remarkable female.

That had all taken place three days ago. Since then much had happened. He had managed to extract several useful pieces of information from certain villagers and the landlord had been most helpful. Yesterday, while the fête had taken place, the village had been deserted, so Thomas had walked through the wood to Mountstanton. He had inspected the slope the nursemaid had fallen down, then slipped into the celebrations. Nobody had challenged him but the size and majesty of the house had made him realise the complexity of his assignment. He had returned to the pub and a productive few hours with Sam Fry.

Now he shifted the box he was carrying from one arm to the other and took another look at the escarpment where Polly had met her death. He tried to imagine what Miss Grandison had seen from here.

The Colonel had been right that he would have no trouble in recognising the woman from America. What he had not told Thomas was how attractive she was. Not a beauty, certainly, but with very fine grey eyes, a creamy complexion and a lively expression. As he'd confronted her outside the village shop, he'd admired the perky little tricorne hat that rested on the rich chestnut hair. Altogether, Miss Grandison presented a most pleasing picture. Yet the Colonel had chosen to describe her as a woman of sense!

Thomas's initial pleasure in meeting her rapidly vanished at her cold response to his greeting. The Colonel could not have alerted her to his presence in Hinton Parva. So he'd withdrawn and hoped that by the time they next met, she would know exactly who he was and why he was there. But her reception of him that morning at the big house had not been any warmer.

He looked down the precipitous slope. How would the haughty Miss Grandison have looked plunging down the hill, her long legs tumbling over and over before landing with a huge splash in the river? Thomas chided himself; he was here to give himself another chance to work out what had happened to the nursemaid, Polly, as requested, not to daydream about a woman who had made it plain she had no time for an ex-detective of police.

Thomas glanced again down the treacherous slope to the river. Unless you stood right at the edge of the little plateau, he reckoned there was no danger of falling. Miss Grandison, if he understood aright, had not fallen from here, she had decided to climb down. Studying what she had taken on, Thomas could not help feeling a certain respect for a woman who could set out so dauntlessly, or should that be recklessly?

He placed his burden, wrapped in a piece of chenille fabric, onto the soft turf, sat beside it and turned his attention back to the nursemaid. She could surely not have fallen from here by accident. He had already inspected the clear spot further back in the wood that he'd learned in Hinton Parva was known as 'lovers' lawn'. The trees and undergrowth that gave it shelter also provided perfect cover for eavesdroppers, enabling them to spy without danger of being spotted.

Is that what Mr Snell had been in the habit of doing? The man had been known as the village busybody, always sticking his nose into other people's business. He appeared to have resented his unpopularity, constantly trying to repay slights with malevolence.

Thomas reviewed what he knew about Snell's death the night before the inquest. The doctor had apparently claimed he recognised pinpoints of blood in the dead man's eyes, an unmistakeable indication that he had been smothered – in other words, unlawfully killed. But after that, nothing seemed to have happened. Sam Fry had told Thomas that the doctor had later said he'd made a mistake. The light in the bedroom had not been good. When the body had been transferred into the local morgue, he'd found no bloody pinpricks in the eyes.

'I reckon he was right sorry he'd come out with something like that. Should have kept any such opinion to hisself,' Sam had said yesterday afternoon, refilling their ale glasses.

Had this, wondered Thomas, been another case of privilege circumventing due processes of law? Or had the doctor got carried away with the drama of the situation? In his mind's eye he could see the lad running in with the news that Mr Snell was dead and the doctor bustling over, perhaps already half convinced he was going to find something strange. Had he, in fact, ever seen those 'pin pricks of blood' in the eyes of anyone who had been smothered? Had it been a case of a pillow lying on the floor beside the bed that suggested such a matter to him?

He'd questioned Sam.

'No one cares,' Sam had said. 'No one liked that long-nosed good-for-nothing, who never bought no round for no one. We was all heartily glad he died.'

Had anyone sorted out his possessions? Thomas asked nonchalantly. And what of his nearest kin?

'Nah,' Sam had spat onto the floor. 'No one's come forward yet. House is locked up. Constable has the key.'

Thomas had tidied away the information in the back of his mind.

Then had come his summons to Mountstanton House.

Now the Earl's death had thrown his embryonic theories as to what had happened to the nursemaid up into the air. It was, perhaps, natural that the Colonel was not thinking straight enough after his brother's death to connect it with the previous one, but Thomas was certain there had to be a connection. Just as he was certain that the Earl had not taken his own life; if ever a death scene had been staged, it was that one. Someone had killed him.

Had that person also killed Polly and Snell? If so, why?

Thomas stood up again, and tried to imagine exactly what had happened on this sunny spot.

The edge of the escarpment did not look a suitable spot for meeting anyone. He was certain that Polly had had an assignation with someone but that it would surely have been at lover's lawn. The post-mortem had detected a blow to the head and the coroner had decided it had been inflicted by one of the stones on the slope as she had crashed to her death. Thomas could think of other possibilities.

Until last night's summons, Thomas had been moving towards the theory that the Earl was responsible for both the girl's condition and her death, and probably for the death of Snell as well, if Miss Grandison's report of what Miss Ranner had seen on the night of his death could be believed. There was, though, a remarkable lack of evidence. And it was evidence that Thomas needed; without that, theories could never be transformed into arrests. Thomas had not been relishing the necessity of informing the Colonel how important it was that he talked to the household staff. Staff always knew exactly what was going on with their masters and mistresses, especially when it involved one of themselves. Now his theory was out of the window.

Which was why, late this afternoon, he had broken the law.

Armed with the note of authority given to him by the Colonel, Thomas's day had been spent questioning villagers. More than anything, this was the source of his frustration. These were not streetwise cockneys and it wasn't as if he was still trying to obtain information regarding the dead nursemaid. No, it had been merely a few enquiries into what people had seen during the Mountstanton fête. With them all concerned about the shocking news of the Earl's death, you would have thought questioning them would have been a piece of cake.

Instead, he'd met with blank stares and replies of such extreme stupidity, he knew some misplaced sense of loyalty to the big house had gripped everyone he spoke to. His usual ability to charm witnesses into talking had failed. Perhaps he had been foolish to imagine it would work here. He was used to urban localities where rivalries were rife and he could manipulate witnesses to spill the dirt on others; he was not used to societies that could bind together with such blind loyalty. It was as if the Stanhopes owned them.

He looked again at the item sitting on the grass beside him. His next step was clear. Thomas got to his feet and resumed walking towards the Mountstanton estate.

The butler was not exactly frosty but he made Thomas feel he should have applied to the back door. 'Colonel Stanhope is expecting me,' Thomas said.

'Colonel Charles is engaged,' the butler said. 'He has asked not to be disturbed.'

'Is Miss Grandison available?'

'Will you wait here whilst I enquire?' The butler eyed the chenille-wrapped burden Thomas was carrying, but disappeared without comment.

Well used to the Mountstanton hall by now, Thomas ignored its various uncomfortable chairs and waited by the long table at the back, which seemed to offer some sort of game. While he waited, he amused himself studying the markings along its length.

Before he could work out their import, there came the tap of a stick and Miss Grandison's voice. 'Mr Jackman?'

He turned.

Dressed in the cream skirt and shirt she had worn that morning, the American woman's expression was reserved. Once again Thomas was faced with the feeling that she did not trust him. Was it just that she was a foreigner and did not understand the English? Or had she some reason for not giving him the same confidence as the Colonel seemed to offer?

'You have something to report, I am sure.'

He saw her take note of what he carried. 'The Colonel is with lawyers; they were summoned from London this morning. He does not expect to be available for some time. Please, come with me.'

He followed her along a corridor and into a room with little of the faded glory that seemed to be the style of the house he had seen so far. Its aura of tobacco and lack of flimflams made him feel almost comfortable.

Thomas unwrapped and set down his burden, then looked straight at the woman. 'You don't trust me, do you, Miss Grandison?'

He expected her to be taken aback at the directness of his approach. Instead she answered, 'I have learned to wait before trusting people I know nothing about, Mr Jackman. Is that hatbox you are carrying Polly's? If so, are you about to tell me where you found it and what it contains?'

He had wanted it to be the Colonel he confronted with this evidence. Once again, he wondered what the relationship was between this suspicious woman and the Colonel. She seemed to have his confidence, but from the way he'd described her there seemed no chance of what Thomas thought of as a normal relationship a man would have with a woman.

The box sat on a table between them. 'I found it in Mr Snell's house. It stuck out; not something that belonged, if you know what I mean. So I opened it and found this . . .' He took off the lid, removed a note and held it out to her.

Miss Grandison made no move to take it from him. 'What were you doing in Mr Snell's house?'

'Ah, well, I heard it had just been left, see? Waiting for someone to claim the contents, so my landlord said. Didn't sound as though Constable Roberts had searched the place so I reckoned there was a good chance of unfinished business there. Maybe evidence of some sort.'

Her glance was keen. 'If Mr Snell's death had happened on your patch, Mr Jackman, would you have taken his house apart?'

He nodded. 'Indeed, Miss Grandison. So this afternoon I called on Constable Roberts and produced the letter of authority Colonel Stanhope had fixed me up with. He found the key to the place and we went in there together. When I found this box and said I needed to produce it to the Colonel, he had no objection.'

There was the faintest flicker of amusement in Miss Grandison's eyes. 'You, I assume, Mr Jackman, in his place would have objected?'

He nodded. 'Against the law my taking it is. It should have been listed, see?'

Then, at last, she took and looked at the piece of paper he offered.

For a long moment she said nothing.

Finally she waved him to a chair. 'Please, take a seat Mr Jackman. The Colonel needs to see this without delay.' She left the room.

Chapter Twenty-Seven

Helen felt as if she had spent hours standing for dress fittings. At last the local seamstress finished discussing styles and wielding her measuring tape. Such a nuisance having to depend on this rustic woman, skilful as she was, for her immediate needs. A cable had already been sent to her usual London couturier. Tomorrow or the next day should see the arrival of a *modiste* to arrange a fashionable mourning wardrobe.

When Helen's father-in-law, the fifth Earl, had died, the end had been foreshadowed and there had been time for discreet arrangements to be made so that when the melancholy event actually took place, a suitable wardrobe was all ready.

Helen had been taken aback by the calmly efficient way her mother-in-law had organised matters. 'It's as if she doesn't care that your father is dying,' she said to Richard.

'She cares very much.' He threw the morning's *Times* irritably onto the breakfast table.

'And isn't making arrangements for a passing on before it's happened taking on God? I think it's asking for bad luck, gives me the shivers.'

Richard poured himself more coffee and made no move to fill her cup.

'I asked if I could sit with him yesterday, perhaps read to him; he has always liked my voice, he says it is low and gentle and that my accent is attractive. Mama said he was beyond hearing but how does she know? I think she wants to keep everyone but herself out of his room. She even refused you permission to visit him; I heard her tell you that it was bad for him to have people in there. Your own father! Why do you let her dictate to you like that?'

'She's my mother,' he said softly, picking up the paper again.

There was no talking to Richard when he was in that sort of mood. Helen had learnt during their marriage that any discussion of his relationship with his parents was forbidden territory. Never one to accept boundaries, she had tried various ways of trespassing, but it was always the same. Her husband retreated inside himself.

At the time of the fifth Earl's last illness, Helen had been in a 'delicate condition'. She had been able to give the news to her father-in-law before the decline in his health had reached the point where the Countess banned visitors. Joy sprang into his eyes and he managed to lift himself up and grasp her hand tightly. Fighting for every breath he said, 'That's wonderful, darling girl.' Still holding her hand, he looked across at Richard, standing just behind Helen, smiled and in a halting whisper got out, 'Knew you could do it, my boy. Champagne, must drink to little feller's birth. Beatrice . . .' He collapsed back onto his pillows, his once handsome face gaunt and riven with pain.

The Countess summoned a footman. 'It is very good news,' she said quietly as she returned to the bedside. 'Congratulations to you both.' She smiled at Helen, who thought she saw genuine affection in her face for the first time.

Richard put his arm round her shoulders and pressed her against him. 'We need you to get well, Papa, so you can hold your first grandchild.'

'Grandson!' For Richard's father, there was no question over the embryonic child's gender.

Perhaps it was the news of a Mountstanton heir that gave him new life, for the Earl had rallied and lived to see his grandson, dying three weeks later.

Now the sixth Earl had followed his father into the family mausoleum.

The boudoir door closed behind the seamstress with her tape measure and collection of fashion plates, her expression worried, her lips silently moving as she no doubt counted up the various garments she was expected to produce without delay.

She would be working far into the night to produce the first of the mourning gowns by the next day.

Jenkins, Helen's maid, fussed around her, talking too much and pressing offers of refreshment on her mistress. Helen waved helpless hands and told her to go away and not come back until sent for, then she collapsed into her favourite buttoned chair. Exhaustion made it difficult to think, and the horror of the previous night had that day been briefly eclipsed by the realisation that she faced two years of mourning. Nothing but black to be worn and, for the first year, seclusion. No balls, no parties, no theatres, no concerts, no entertaining. Visitors were not supposed to be received, nor visits paid. After the fifth Earl's death, Helen's mother-in-law, now transformed into a Dowager, had had her own apartment created in the west wing and retired there, to pass her two years of mourning seemingly without chafing at the restrictions. She surrounded herself with images of her dead husband: photographs, of which there were many; a bust that had been sculpted in his early twenties, and a portrait painted soon after they were married. Helen wondered how Richard had dissuaded her from adding to her collection the much larger portrait that hung in the picture gallery.

Helen's own year of mourning for her father-in-law had been restrictive but because she had just given birth, her social activities would in any case have been severely curtailed. At least it had meant time to enjoy Harry's babyhood. From the moment her son was placed upon her breast and she had looked down into the wrinkled face – the pink rosebud mouth yawning, the blue eyes half closed – she had fallen in love. He was so tiny and so perfect.

'He has the Mountstanton nose,' had been Richard's comment on first setting eyes on his heir. 'And I am sure he has the finger as well.'

'How can you tell? They look just like a nose and a finger to me,' Helen had protested. It mattered not a jot to her. Harry was her son and a total delight. She instructed Mrs Comfort to bring him down to her bedroom every morning so they could spend a delicious hour together, laughing and playing. Even when the mourning period gradually lightened and social life began to resume, Helen kept on with the practice – until Harry was three, when Richard said that he needed to grow up.

She had failed to persuade him otherwise and the morning romps in her bed had ceased.

Helen lay back in the chair and closed her eyes, willing away the aches of exhaustion. Harry had been devastated at the news of his father's death. 'Why?' he'd shouted at her. 'Why has he gone to heaven? I want Papa here. I want Papa with me.'

Suddenly grief overtook her. The full extent of her loss was a flood that saturated every corner of her mind and body. A long moan emerged spontaneously, then whatever dam that had been holding back the tears broke and they started pouring down her face. She could hear his voice, feel the touch of his hands, even remember his special smell when naked. She also remembered his coldness when she overstepped whatever mark it was he had laid down, the way he would retreat from her before passion was renewed, and how cruel he could be. There had been little closeness between them over the last few years but the memory of what they had once shared would never leave her.

Gradually she choked back her sobs. There was so much that had to be done, so much that the Dowager would expect from her.

A light tap came on the door. Helen ran her hands over her face, trying to obliterate the signs of her breakdown. 'Yes?'

Charles entered. He was carrying a piece of paper. Behind him was Ursula.

Helen pulled her wrap a little closer around herself. 'Yes?' she said again coldly, glad to see that Ursula looked nervous.

'I am sorry to disturb you.'

Helen could see that Charles was in his soldierly mode. There was something he felt should be done and he was here to do it. Was this something connected with the funeral arrangements? Somehow she did not think so. A tiny trickle of unease ran down her spine.

'A letter has come to light.' Charles raised the piece of paper he was holding. 'We think you should see it.'

Helen noted the 'we'. Were he and Ursula in some kind of partnership? Surely after all they had been through together she could still count on Charles's support? But ever since Polly's body had been discovered, he had been behaving in a most peculiar way. She took the letter.

At first the words did not make any sense, yet they were plain enough. She read it again:

My dear Polly,
I am certain you are a Mountstanton. Armed with this knowledge, you should be able to demand due recognition for both you and your child. I hope to discuss this matter with you in the very near future. Meantime, in haste,
Yours
A.G.

'We think,' said Charles, 'we think that "A.G." stands for Adam Gray.'

'We?'

He dropped his gaze for the briefest of moments. 'Miss Grandison and I.'

Helen looked at Ursula and received back a direct look that she recognised.

Charles said, 'Did Richard mention any of this to you?'

Another shiver of unease, colder and stronger. 'I hardly think that he would mention some bastard child to me, would you?'

'Do you mean, would I mention a bastard child to you or do I think Richard would?'

'Please, Charles. We all know there is nothing you would not talk about if you felt it necessary.'

He gave a short, exasperated sigh. 'Helen, we are dealing with murder here. Richard's murder.'

'Richard was not murdered. Mama says he had an accident. She says he was shooting pigeons. The gardeners have been complaining what a nuisance they are.' She looked down at the letter she held. 'In any case, this could have nothing to do with his death.'

Ursula knelt beside her chair and placed a hand on her arm. 'Please, Helen. I know it's a terrible thing to have to face, but it does seem that Richard was killed by someone who came to him in the belvedere last night. It must have happened when the fireworks were set off. That's why no one heard the shot.'

'Why should anyone want to kill him? And with his own gun?' Helen asked obstinately.

Ursula glanced up at Charles.

'The house was open,' he said, 'anyone could have gone to the gun room and helped themselves to a shotgun. Gray has said to me in the past that the key to the case should not be hung behind the door. But maybe Mama is right, that Richard did decide to shoot some rabbits, then had the gun wrested from him by whoever he met in the belvedere.'

Helen looked directly at him. 'Either suggestion is ridiculous.'

His gaze did not flicker. 'Murder may sound ridiculous but the fact remains that the evidence shows Richard did not kill himself. You should be relieved that there will not be the ignominy and shame of suicide.'

Unable to hold that steady look any longer, Helen bowed her head. 'Murder is nonsense,' she managed weakly.

Ursula's hand increased its pressure. 'Helen, forget about Richard's death for a moment. What about Polly's condition? Have you really no idea who she could have been seeing; who might be the father?'

'She was a silly girl. Mrs Palmer had spoken to her about her flirtatious ways. It was only because Harry was so fond of her that she had not been turned off. The father could have been any available male.'

'Someone in this house?'

Helen knew they would not let the matter rest; she forced herself to speak calmly. 'Before that wretched inquest, Richard and I asked Mrs Palmer if she knew of any liaison between Polly and a Mountstanton servant.'

'And did she?'

Helen shook her head. 'We put the same question to Benson and got the same answer.' She raised the letter. 'This should be burned. It is nothing but tittle-tattle.'

Charles quickly took the piece of paper from her.

Helen snatched it back and reread its few lines. 'Anybody could have written this,' she said dismissively. 'Perhaps it was Gray, but does he say he's got proof for what he claims? No.' She gave Charles a look full of challenge. 'Where was this found? And by whom? What is their connection to all this?'

Gently Ursula extracted the letter from Helen's fingers, folded and handed it back to Charles. 'Your questions are all pertinent and they deserve an answer. Colonel, tell her how it was discovered.'

Helen watched as he carefully slipped the paper into his pocket. Always safeguarding something, that was her brother-in-law.

'Polly's hatbox was found in Snell's house. You remember he was found dead at the time of the inquest? And that his death was considered suspicious – for a time?'

Helen remembered acutely how a furious Richard had called the doctor up to the house. She had not needed to be present to know just how insistent her husband would have been. Certainly after their meeting, the doctor had announced he must have been misled by the lack of light in the room and that closer examination had shown the man had died in his sleep.

'Well,' said Charles, 'Snell must have found the box after Polly ended up in the river. The letter was inside and, no doubt, that was why he was going around making veiled accusations against the Stanhopes.'

'Perhaps he was responsible for pushing her down that hill,' Helen suggested slowly, watching for his reaction.

'It's a possibility,' he acknowledged. 'However, there does not seem to be a motive.'

'So who found the hatbox in his house?'

'An investigator I hired.'

'You hired an investigator?' She was deeply shocked. 'How dare you!'

'There are circumstances surrounding Polly's death that have to be looked at, Helen.' He hesitated briefly, then added, 'Just as Richard's death needs investigating.'

A mixture of rage and panic surged through Helen. She rose. 'You are despicable. You too, Ursula. But you at least are not a Mountstanton. If Mama were here, she would tell you, her sole surviving son, Charles, exactly what a disgrace you are to the family name.'

The Colonel looked incredibly weary, like a soldier surveying a lost battlefield.

His expression suddenly softened. 'My dear Helen, you must be overcome with grief and I am a fool to have burdened you with this. Forgive us for this intrusion.'

He dipped his head but did not try to take her hand, merely turned and left the room.

Ursula had stood up. 'You need rest, Helen. Have you had anything to eat today? Can I arrange for some refreshment to be brought to you?'

The Countess shook her head violently; her need to have this woman who knew so much about her leave the room was intense. 'I wish to be alone.'

'Of course.' Ursula followed Charles out.

Left at last on her own, Helen went to the window and stood, her hands pressed against her forehead, looking out and seeing nothing. She tried to think rationally and calmly.

It was impossible. She walked around the room, wild thoughts chasing themselves around her mind.

For once, Helen was on the side of her mother-in-law. The Mountstanton name must be protected. Harry must be spared a tainted heritage. Why couldn't Charles understand that? Why had he returned here? If he had to leave the army, why couldn't he have gone somewhere else? Everything that was happening was his fault. How could he behave so irresponsibly?

'Investigator', the word hammered in her head. What sort of investigation was taking place?

Helen stopped her pacing and took two deep breaths. There was no need to panic. This was not an official investigation. Whatever fly-by-night rogue Charles had managed to get hold of – probably someone who had served with him, no doubt drummed out of the army in disgrace – well, whoever he was, he could have no standing in the eyes of the law.

Helen went into the corridor and glided gracefully towards the hall. All the window blinds were down. Benson was there. He seemed to have shrunk since yesterday.

'I shall take dinner in my boudoir, Benson.'

'Very well, my lady, I will see to it myself. I . . . I have arranged the mourning ornaments on the front door, my lady.' He waved a hand in a way that suggested she might like to inspect them. Helen shuddered.

'Thank you, Benson. Please see that I am not disturbed by anyone.'

'Of course, my lady.'

She continued on to Richard's study, the flimsy skirts of her robe floating out as she went.

The study seemed to be holding its breath. Richard's desk and the tables that stood against the walls were stacked with the usual untidy piles of paper; some sheets had fallen to the floor, more looked in danger of following. William had not managed to reduce anything to order. Had he tried? Had Richard prevented him?

For a long moment Helen stood irresolute, then started leafing through the papers on the desk. She had hardly made any inroads before William entered.

'Helen!' he exclaimed, coming towards her.

'I thought you were supposed to be acting as Richard's secretary?' she said, waving at the disorder all around them.

He gave her a slow smile. 'That's what my father arranged.' He surveyed the papers without a hint of distress. 'I have written various letters for the Earl, even managed a little research into possible ways of improving the shooting. Somehow it didn't seem anything more was necessary. Now, though, I have to assist with organising his funeral. The Dowager insists it must match the grandeur of the last one.' He sighed. 'There is just so much to be done!' But he smiled warmly at her. Then his eyes darkened, he moved closer and swept her into his arms. 'Oh, Helen, Helen, Helen! What does any of this matter?'

For an instant, as his mouth came down on hers, Helen almost succumbed. To be able to forget everything that had happened in the last twenty-four hours, to lose herself in earthy lust with this splendid specimen of uninhibited English manhood would be so wonderful.

His breathing quickened. He looked into her eyes, his pupils huge and dark. 'My dearest, dearest desire. Oh, Helen, I adore you. I've loved you ever since I first saw you. Ever since then you have been a shining, unattainable star. But now, now you can be totally mine. Say you will marry me.'

Again his mouth claimed hers and his arms tightened around her. Again a sort of crazy belief that this could solve all her problems took hold of Helen. William had a good relationship with Harry, his background was impeccable, and he knew how to make a woman's body respond. Maybe this wasn't exactly how she had planned things but maybe it would work.

She dug her fingers into his shoulders and allowed herself a moment's joyous delight before she drew back. 'William, dearest . . . ' she started.

Then she saw her sister standing in the doorway.

Chapter Twenty-Eight

The tension in the shabby smoking room vibrated through Ursula like a plucked wire.

The Colonel stood looking out of the window. His shoulders were rigid. The unflappable soldier appeared to be deeply upset. Was it, Ursula wondered, because of the claim that Polly had been a close relation, even a half-sister? Or was it something to do with Helen?

Frustration filled Ursula. Were charming, facile and self-indulgent women always to have strong men at their feet?

Helen had invited Belle over to England but how much had she done to make the visit enjoyable for her little sister? There was her husband, had she shared any of his problems? Until the night of his death, Ursula had seen little warmth in Helen's relationship with the Earl. Apart from that collapse over his dead body, the only genuine emotion she had displayed since Ursula's arrival seemed to have been for her little son. But weren't dynastic marriages supposed to produce more than one possible heir? And surely Helen should be involved with charitable works, not enjoying languishing looks from her husband's secretary?

Clouds had come up and the sunny day had turned dark. Ursula found she was shivering.

'She's frightened,' said the Colonel without turning. 'Helen is frightened.'

'Why? Why should she be?' But Ursula knew he was right.

He shrugged and left the window. 'Perhaps, like my mother, she is afraid of a slur on the good name of Mountstanton.' A touch of irony removed any pomposity from his words.

'Do you believe that Polly was a Mountstanton?' Ursula asked curiously.

Another shrug and a gesture that asked her permission to sit. Once again they faced each other, but the ease that had been between them earlier that day had vanished.

The Colonel's attention was claimed by a rip in the leather upholstery of his chair. 'My father, I regret to say, left a number of by-blows.' He looked up. 'I'm sorry, I should not use such language to you.'

Ursula gave a grim chuckle. 'As I think you know by now, I am used to far worse, Colonel. Nor, I am afraid, does the existence of illegitimate offspring distress me.' She thought for a moment. Would it be a betrayal of Helen to explain why the letter could have so disturbed her? Yes, she quickly decided, it would. It was past history and should remain so.

'Respectability is important to Helen, as important to her as it is to the Dowager Countess.'

'I don't think that can be true. My mother yields to no one in her fierce protection of the family name.'

For the first time, the full implications of the letter struck Ursula. 'You are saying your father deceived your mother. Isn't it possible another Mountstanton, your uncle, say, or a cousin, could have been the philanderer?'

'Ah, Miss Grandison, can you really be that naive?'

Ursula flushed.

'I know that my mother soon realised what sort of man she had married. But what could she do? The morals of English high society, Miss Grandison, are worse than those of the most depraved mining camp. The only rule, it seems, is that scandal must be avoided. Not long after my parents were married, scandal did threaten to ruin my father's reputation and my mother's happiness.'

Ursula tried to envision the overpowering Dowager Countess as a young girl devastated by the imminent collapse of her world. It was not easy.

'What happened?'

He sighed. 'My grandfather arranged matters somehow. But the repercussions have followed my mother to this day. Not only her,' he added, looking down again at the ripped leather and retreating into himself. After a moment he gave Ursula a strained smile. 'Ever since then Mama has tried to ensure that scandal could never threaten the family again. She has guarded both the Mountstanton name and her own. Double-dyed in family pride, you might say.'

'Did the incident you mentioned have anything to do with Polly?'

'Good heavens, no!' He seemed almost relieved to be back with the question of the nursemaid's parentage. 'It would be convenient, I suppose, if a Mountstanton other than my father might have sired her, particularly as far as Mama is concerned. But I am afraid it is not possible. My father's younger brother died in infancy and the two cousins that exist decided New Zealand offered greater chances than England for impover-ished younger members of an aristocratic family. They have been there for some thirty years.'

Ursula suddenly saw a way of revealing something of Helen's background without betraying her.

'Respectability for Helen is, you might almost say, the reverse of that of the Dowager Countess.'

'Ah! I think I understand. Forgive me for putting it this way, I mean no disrespect, but as far as she is concerned, there is no family reputation to be maintained, is there?'

Ursula could not help laughing. 'I hope you will not put it that way to Helen, but Mr Seldon would be the first to admit that he came from nowhere.'

'Born on a mid-west farm, I understand, that went under in a drought, came to New York and clawed his way to fortune, isn't that it?'

Ursula nodded. 'Railways, mining, newspapers, import, export; he has had a genius for seeing profit in many different ventures.' And never flinching from tough decisions, always taking risks that hardly ever failed, never hesitating to do down any man who dared to cross him. 'Respectability was never high on his agenda; with Mr Seldon, riches meant more than reputation. He has only ever wanted to be regarded as a hard and successful man.'

'Poor Helen.'

Ursula fought a fresh feeling of frustration. After all, hadn't she achieved exactly the reaction she wanted? 'However, New York society is as rigid as any continental place, perhaps even more so. Despite their wealth, the Seldon family could never be accepted into the higher echelons. No invitations for Helen and Belle from those pillars of respectability, Mrs Astor and Mrs Vanderbilt. Mr Seldon understood that but he knew his rapidly expanding fortune could achieve respectability for his daughters without their help. That is why he sent Helen to school in Paris rather than New York.'

'And you accompanied her, I understand. How did you fit into the picture, if I may ask?'

Ursula looked down at her hands. 'My father was in partnership with Mr Seldon.'

The Colonel stared at her. 'But you have no fortune?'

If she had, she would not be acting as Belle's companion. 'No. There was a falling out and my father lost all his assets.' She was not prepared to go into the details. 'Mr Seldon was fond of me and felt I should not be deprived of a good education. He said it could be my salvation.' For the briefest moment, Ursula remembered how he had looked when he'd said it, dropping it into the middle of her devastation, and how she had clung to that statement as though her fingernails held onto a window ledge high above an unyielding pavement. 'Anyway, Helen never felt her father's millions were enough to guarantee happiness. She has always needed respectability, to be accepted in the top circles.'

The Colonel shifted his position uneasily. 'So that is why she married my brother.'

'She had proposals from a number of foreigners,' Ursula said quickly.

'Foreigners!'

'Non-Americans, I mean. Helen wanted to live in Europe. There were French aristocrats, an Italian Count, a Prince from Scandinavia.' She was embellishing now, but all in a good cause. At least, Ursula wondered suddenly, was it a good cause? She remembered Helen's reactions just now in her boudoir, and all the ways she had rubbed at Ursula's sense of what was right. But it was too late now. 'Your brother had competition, Colonel, but he won her fair and square.'

He said nothing for a long time. Ursula could gather no hint of his thoughts. The man would be a triumph at the poker table.

The Colonel rose and took out his hunter. 'Time I was back with the lawyers, Miss Grandison. Look, you will have to go with Jackman to Adam Gray and get the truth out of him.'

Ursula looked at him with something like horror.

'He would talk to you, Colonel. I'm sure he won't to me or Mr Jackman,' she said quickly. Ursula did not know why she distrusted the investigator but the idea that they were to form some sort of team filled her with dismay.

'Nonsense. Didn't you tell me you'd already met Gray? I'm sure you can make him tell you anything you want to know. Anyway, Jackman has my note of authority and he knows how to interview suspects.'

'You think Mr Gray a suspect? What do you suspect him of? Seducing Polly?'

'No. I think he was extremely fond of her; she was someone you could easily get drawn to – attractive and full of life and fun. If Gray did write that letter, and I think he did, he might well take revenge on someone he considered responsible for her death.'

'You mean you suspect Mr Gray of shooting your brother?'

'It's a possibility that has to be considered.'

'But why should the Earl have been responsible for Polly's death? Or do you think he was her seducer?'

The Colonel shook his head. 'I don't think so but Gray might.'

'He does have an uncertain temper,' admitted Ursula, remembering the agent's performance at the inquest.

'You will be able to get at the truth, you and Jackman.' It was said with an authority that would allow no dissent and Ursula knew that further protest would get her nowhere.

While the Colonel and Ursula had been with Helen, Thomas Jackman had been sent to talk to Mrs Parsons about the movements of the staff at the fête.

Now a servant was despatched to the stables to issue instructions for the trap to be harnessed. Another one was ordered to tell Mr Jackman to meet Miss Grandison there. 'You can drive a trap?' the Colonel queried as an afterthought.

Ursula grinned. 'Fine time to ask! But, yes, your confidence is not misplaced.'

He gave her a heart-warming smile. 'My confidence in you, Miss Grandison, is never misplaced.'

★ ★ ★

Clad in a jacket against the cooling air, and abandoning the stick she had become so used to depending on, Ursula went out to the stables.

Thomas Jackman was already there, standing very still, and looking at the harnessed trap and horse with an expression of misgiving. It was his eyes that made her distrust him, Ursula decided. They seemed to assess everything he looked at – to find everything wanting. Anyone that cynical did not deserve her consideration.

'Ready?' she said briskly.

He nodded, took a firm grip on the side of the vehicle and hauled himself up.

Ursula thought he might have helped her first. She accepted the aid of the groom.

'Beauty's thrown a shoe so it's Barnaby you've got there, Miss Grandison. He's steady as they come, long as you keep him straight.'

She looked at the sturdy chestnut horse, at the way he rolled his eyes, and then at the groom with a tinge of distrust. 'What are you saying, Jem?'

His gaze slipped from hers. 'Nothing, miss, just that if you don't keep him straight, he can do a bit of a dance, like.'

'Bit of a dance,' repeated Ursula thoughtfully. 'Well, I'd better keep him straight, then.' She picked up the reins, flicked them at Barnaby's back and said, 'Gee up, there.'

'Know what you're doing and where we're going, do you?' asked Thomas Jackman.

She looked ahead, avoiding the penetrating eyes, nodded serenely and kept Barnaby trotting happily down the drive. The sun was low in the sky. Ursula decided that the interview with Mr Gray should be a short one; she wanted to be back at Mountstanton well before dark.

'Did you have a productive meeting with Mrs Parsons, Mr Jackman?'

'What a woman for talking round a subject without ever

getting to the heart of it. I learned a great deal about the way
Mountstanton is run without getting to know anything of use
to my investigation. Tell me what we're supposed to be doing
when we meet this Gray fellow.'

Ursula fought with renewed irritation. Both the task she
was faced with and the man who was with her were equally
distasteful. Then she took a deep breath and decided it was no
good wishing the Colonel was accompanying her instead of
this so-called investigator. She had been given a job to do and
it had to be carried through as successfully as possible.

'We're going to see Adam Gray, the Mountstanton agent, the
man the Colonel believes wrote that note to Polly.'

'Right. And how much do you know about him?'

Keeping Barnaby going straight ahead on the stony and
rutted road required constant attention and Ursula related all
she had learned from her talk with the agent as succinctly as
possible. It seemed like weeks rather than a couple of days had
passed since she had ridden over to see him.

'Believed he was this nursemaid's father, did he? And you
thought their relationship somewhat different?'

'Well, as I said, at the inquest it looked possible he might
have been, how shall I put it, involved with Polly? Mrs Parsons
claimed she had seen the two of them in what she called "a
compromising position".'

'But the Colonel and his brother did not think it worth
questioning him?'

Ursula sighed. 'They probably would have done . . . eventually.'

'Only you took it on yourself to tackle him. Why?'

Looking back, Ursula was surprised at the determined way
she had approached the agent. 'It was because I was so unhappy
with the inquest verdict. From all I had learned about Polly,
suicide seemed the last thing she would do.'

'Not got much of a future ahead of her, though, had she?
With child; due to lose her position as soon as it was known;
unlikely to get any sort of a reference for a new one; abandoned by the man who had got her into trouble. Exactly what,
Miss Grandison, did she have to live for?'

Ursula flinched at this, then corrected Barnaby's tendency
to move off the centre of the road.

'Put like that,' she said slowly, 'I have to say she had very little, if anything. But the Colonel also believes the coroner arrived at the wrong verdict. And . . . '

'Yes?' said Mr Jackman impatiently as she paused, remembering what had occurred to her as soon as she'd taken in the contents of that piece of paper. 'And what?'

'Once she'd read the letter, she must have thought she had a weapon she could use in a fight for justice, and a livelihood of some sort for herself and the unborn child.'

Mr Jackman clutched the side of the trap as they bounced over a particularly stony section of roadway. 'Mercy, Miss Grandison; this conveyance is unsafe. I doubt you can get us there safely, let alone back.'

She laughed. 'The Colonel has confidence in me, so should you.'

Jackman did not look particularly reassured. After a moment's nervous twitching he said, 'So, what do we want from this agent fellow?'

Ursula recalled exactly what the Colonel's instructions had been. 'First, confirmation he wrote the letter; second, how he found out who Polly's father was; and third, whether he has any suspicions as to who seduced her.' She did not mention the possibility that the agent had killed the Earl. She would see how the interview went first.

'You say Gray believes it is the nursemaid's seducer who killed her?'

'He thinks it was because his advice to Polly was to tell the man that, unless he did the decent thing, she would let others know who the father of her child was.'

Jackman made another grab at the sides of the trap as, once again, they bumped alarmingly over some ruts. 'Have a heart, miss, that ditch looks very close and a mite messy.'

Ursula tried to find a less rutted part of the road and for a while they travelled without conversation. As the trap at last began to move more smoothly she said, 'Do you think Mr Gray could be right about Polly having been killed by her seducer?'

'Could be.'

Suddenly Ursula could visualise what might have happened: 'They meet in the wood; she accuses him of behaving wretchedly towards her. He laughs, maybe says she asked for it.

Polly tells him she's a member of the Mountstanton family. He laughs some more and says she only means she's one of their bastards. She gets angry and threatens that she will appeal to them if he abandons her. His reputation will be ruined, he will lose his job, be refused a reference. He panics; perhaps he grabs and shakes her, pushes her over.'

'She strikes her head on a stone,' suggested Thomas Jackman, surprising Ursula by entering into her enactment. 'Maybe she's knocked out; maybe she's killed. Whatever, he knows he has to make sure she cannot bear witness against him. He's a callous sort of a chap; he picks her up, and throws her down the slope, then reckons that's sorted his little problem.'

For the first time since meeting Mr Jackman, Ursula felt they could work together.

'Tell you one thing,' he continued. 'If that's anywhere near close to what actually happened, it's no horny handed son of toil who was involved with your nursemaid, no, nor a lowly servant at the big house.'

Ursula immediately lost her sense of partnership. 'Why not?'

'Because they would have seen more profit out of standing by her. Upper-class nobs, like the Stanhopes, wouldn't want their name dragged in the dust by the likes of her; they'd pay up, send her and the kiddie somewhere far away with just enough to live on. Her and the kiddie and the man. See my point?'

'The man who hired you is one of those nobs,' said Ursula coldly. 'Why do you despise him so?'

'Who said I despised him? Not his fault he belongs to the class what keeps their boot on the neck of the lower classes.'

'Ah, you are a follower of Mr Marx.'

'I'm no Communist. I believe every man for himself. The capitalist system has advantages. It's the class system I despise, where what a man is born into instead of his achievements dictates how society views him.'

'Does that mean you are all for a revolution?'

To her surprise, he laughed. 'I'm no revolutionary. I just want justice for the lower classes. Now, Miss Grandison, let's get back to the matter in hand. Do I understand this Gray fellow has a hot temper?'

She nodded, flicking her whip at a wayward Barnaby.

'Good. The way we'll work it is you will be all aristocratic, look down your nose, stress it's his duty to respond to your questions. I'll hover humbly at the back but produce the Colonel's letter of authority if necessary.'

Ursula was surprised. She had assumed that Thomas Jackman would lead the questioning. And that he would almost certainly rile Adam Gray, perhaps to the point where he would refuse to answer any of their questions. Instead, it was going to be she who initiated the interrogation – she could not think of it as an interview. Would the agent consider her to be wearing a cloak of Mountstanton superiority?

'Have you any ideas how I should start, Mr Jackman?'

He looked at her thoughtfully. 'You're a straightforward woman. Be straightforward.'

Then they had arrived at the agent's home and Adam Gray appeared at the front door.

He stalked towards the trap, his heavy-featured face frowning. When Ursula said there were some questions she had been instructed to ask him, he was surly and it was as though he had to force himself to help her down from the trap.

'Will you be stopping long, Miss Grandison? Should I unharness the horse?'

Her unease about the coming confrontation increased. Gone was the pleasant man she had met the other day; instead here was the aggressive man who had invaded the inquest.

'I hope we shall only need a few words with you, Mr Gray. Shall we go inside?'

The glower deepened. 'We have only recently finished eating. Clearing away won't be done until my wife is settled. My sister and housekeeper are upstairs with her now.'

He led the way into an untidy living room; the remains of a meal on the table. The agent indicated a wooden armchair to Ursula then, for the first time, he seemed to notice Thomas Jackman.

'And who might you be?'

'Mr Gray, may I introduce Mr Jackman? He comes with the authority of Colonel Charles Stanhope.' There should have been an Honourable inserted in there somewhere but Ursula, ignored the pesky little title. The one he had earned in the army in her eyes was far more important.

'Authority? What for?'

For an instant Ursula waited for the investigator to answer then realised that she was expected to field the question. She produced the letter the Colonel had handed over to her and said as haughtily as she could manage, 'When did you write this to Polly?'

His eyes blank, Adam Gray took the piece of paper, laid it on the table, smoothed its creases and looked at it with eyes that surely were not registering any of the words. 'Why are you so sure I penned this, Miss Grandison?'

'They are your initials.' A momentary inspiration came. 'The writing has also been recognised as yours.' After all, if they had gone to the Earl's office, surely there would have been notes there from the agent and they could have compared the hand-writing with the letter. 'And who else would be writing to Polly?' She flung the words at him with careless authority.

He flicked at the paper and seemed too paralysed to speak.

'Who told you Polly was a Mountstanton?' she asked in the most arrogant voice she could produce. 'The Colonel has to know,' she added when no response was forthcoming. Behind her she could sense Thomas Jackman waiting, assessing the situation.

Adam Gray seemed to be dealing with an inner struggle. Several times he appeared about to speak, his face getting redder and redder, veins bulging in his neck and forehead.

'The possibility of Polly being a Mountstanton has never arisen before, even though she was working in the house,' Ursula said, not softening her voice. 'Either it is something dreamed up for some nefarious reason or someone knows something. You know which it is. You have to tell us.'

That did it. Adam Gray bellowed with pent up rage: 'You're all the same; puffed up aristocrats who think you can lord it over us; that we have been sent here merely to do your bidding. Polly was worth more than the lot of you put together. She had Mountstanton blood in her but because her mother was what you call lower class, she was abandoned. No respectability for her, unlike . . . unlike . . . '

'Those in the big house?' Ursula finished for him.

He closed his eyes for a moment, his whole face contorted.

'Mr Gray,' Ursula tried to sound stern, authoritative. 'Please. You have to tell us.'

'I have to tell you nothing,' he shouted. 'Nothing, do you hear?'

Ursula felt the whole situation was hopeless. The Colonel should have come; he would have known how to handle this bull of a man.

'I've been looking at this photograph,' said Thomas Jackman pleasantly, his quiet voice breaking into the heated atmosphere. 'You seem to have been something of a footballer. Do I have it right?'

He was over by the far wall, studying a photograph hanging there. Ursula could only see an array of men in striped shirts and knee-length shorts. They were in two lines; those at the back standing and the front ones sitting, arms crossed; the central man had a foot on a ball.

Adam Gray seemed nonplussed. He stared at the investigator as though he had suddenly arrived from outer space. Then he gave himself a little shake and appeared to shrink. He ran a hand through his thick hair.

'Only I was a keen player at one time. Even had a try out for one of the London clubs. Then I injured a knee and that was that.' Thomas Jackman's tone was easy, friendly.

The agent moved towards him as though sleepwalking. 'It was when I was working up north,' Jackman continued, jabbing a finger at the photograph. 'Bunch of lads and I made up a team. We were good, though I say it myself. Course, we didn't have time to make a real go of it but we won the local cup one time. Bet you played defence, shoulders like that.'

Adam Gray nodded.

'I was a wing; fast you see, until my knee got clobbered.'

Ursula watched, amazed, as the two men talked football for a couple of minutes, then, realising at last what the investigator was up to, sat down in the chair she had been shown on entering.

Jackman put his hand on the agent's shoulder. 'Sorry about all this questioning. You know how it is; for the little lass's sake we have to get to the bottom of things. It's plain as a pikestaff you've got hold of some information from somewhere and if we're to sort out who was responsible for her death, we need to know what you do. The Colonel has put his trust in me and I don't intend to let either the girl or him down.' He looked around the room, then steered the agent in the direction of a chair. 'Why don't we sit down and have a chat, eh?'

To Ursula's surprise, the two men sat. Thomas Jackman leaned confidentially towards Adam Gray.

'All we really need is to know who told you Polly was a Mountstanton.' He spoke quietly, persuasively, and Ursula knew that her part in the interrogation was over.

Adam Gray leaned back in his chair and closed his eyes; all at once he looked very tired. 'It was Miss Ranner,' he said eventually. 'Made me swear I'd never tell anyone else.'

Of course, it had to be. Miss Ranner had employed Polly's mother, Mary. She had helped her when she found the girl was with child. Mary would have told her who had been responsible for her condition.

'So you said you would keep it confidential, yes? Yet you told Polly.'

The big man rubbed his eyes with the heels of his hands. All belligerence had now drained out of him. 'She deserved to know. I wanted to talk to her, tell her how I thought she should handle it, but I was sent off to Yorkshire. No time for more than those few words. Never thought she'd do anything before I came back and we could discuss it.'

Ursula conjured up the picture of Polly she had put together: bright, knowing, lively; put a girl like that in possession of information that could prove her salvation and she would not wait before using it. How foolish of Adam Gray to imagine she would. He had completely misread his influence with her.

'So, the Mountstanton who had his way with this Polly's mother was the father of the Earl who died yesterday, was he?'

The agent sighed heavily. 'Earl Simon, the fifth Earl.'

'So we've got that sorted. Now, how about the bounder who took advantage of Polly? Have you really no idea who he could be? One of the servants up at the big house, maybe? Chap with plans to rise in the world perhaps but not above enjoying himself with a lovely maid along the way?'

Adam Gray shook his head. 'Polly thought herself better than them. Even with not knowing who her parents were, she had silly ideas about where she came from – and where she was going. Full of dreams and stupid ambition she was.' A heavy sigh followed.

Listening to the two men, Ursula suddenly remembered the little incident in the Mountstanton laundry. The girl, Maggie, pounding her fists into the footman's chest and accusing him of playing fast and loose with Polly.

'What about John, the tallest of the footmen?' she said quietly. 'You don't think he could have seduced her? He's very attractive.'

Another shake of the head. 'Wouldn't have said so. She could have flirted with him; Polly flirted with everyone – if they were attractive – but, like I said, she held herself to be better than the other servants.'

'It would have happened about four months ago,' Ursula said gently. 'Think back, did Polly seem at all different then? And were there any men visiting Hinton Parva who could have caught her fancy?'

Life seemed to come back into his eyes. 'I haven't been thinking straight about matters. Four months ago, that would have been mid-February, right? We were lambing, it's a busy time, but I did meet Polly one afternoon when she was out with young Lord Harry.' There was a long pause as he seemed to retreat into himself. Both of his inquisitors waited patiently.

'You know, you're right,' he said, coming back to life. 'She was so bright that afternoon, joshing with me and the boy. I said it was as though she'd been drinking from some life-giving fountain. And she looked at me, not with the mischief that was usually in her eyes; it was more a pure sort of joy. Funny, I don't usually notice things like that but, to tell you the truth, I was a bit bowled over by it.'

Ursula wondered if he had thought her joy was because she was together with him. Had he imagined she had feelings for him?

'She went almost shy, if you could ever say Polly was shy. Then she made some comment about how great it was to see the sun and the boy asked if he could stroke one of the lambs. So we had fun catching hold of one.' Another pause. 'As to visitors to the village, no, I don't remember any.'

'What about the Earl, and his brother, Colonel Stanhope?' asked Jackman. 'Could either of them have been responsible for her condition?'

The agent looked pole-axed by the question. For several seconds he sat looking at the investigator before saying, 'Nay, his lordship weren't the womaniser his father were.'

That seemed to dispel any idea the man could have shot his employer.

'And Colonel Charles was in London with his regiment all that time,' said Gray.

To Ursula it was significant that the only reason it seemed the agent ruled out the possibility of the Colonel seducing Polly was because he was not at home. For a moment she sat stunned. She had good reason to believe that the Colonel had indeed been in the area at the relevant time. Could he have taken advantage of an innocent girl, one who, unbeknownst to him, was also his half-sister? Then she steadied her whirling thoughts. The Colonel was not the sort of man to seduce a servant girl and, even if he had been, surely he could not have disguised the revulsion the letter would have provoked when he found out she was so closely related? Whatever had distressed him after their interview with Helen, it was not that. No, she decided, they could count the Colonel out.

Thomas Jackman rose. 'Mr Gray, thank you for being so co-operative. We shall take our leave and report back to Colonel Stanhope.'

'I would hope you can leave out Miss Ranner's name,' the agent said. 'I did promise not to reveal what she told me.'

Jackman held out his hand. Gray rose and shook it.

'We'll do what we can,' Jackman said soothingly.

'Thank you, Mr Gray,' said Ursula, standing also. 'I am sure the Colonel will be very grateful to hear what you have told us.'

There was the sound of footsteps on the stairs and Adele, the agent's sister, entered.

Polite conversation had to be made and by the time Ursula and Mr Jackman were able to take their leave, the light was going, dark clouds loomed and rain threatened.

Outside, Barnaby stood quietly, one leg bent, resting. He looked up hopefully as Ursula untied the reins from the hitching post, twitched his ears and gave his body a little shake.

Adam Gray helped Ursula into the trap, then they were off.

'Weather doesn't look good,' said Jackman.

Ursula's lips tightened and she made no reply. Yet she found that her feelings towards the investigator had improved. She had to admire the way he set her up to receive the agent's immediate onslaught, then had slipped underneath his defences. The Colonel had known what he was doing when he hired Thomas Jackman.

Ursula clicked the reins, encouraging Barnaby into a faster pace through the rapidly failing light.

The first part of the journey went well. Barnaby, no doubt aware that home lay ahead, trotted happily without veering from the centre of the road.

Then, from the direction of Mountstanton, came the sound of a horse galloping down the narrow road towards them.

Ursula expected it to slow as the rider saw them. But if anything the horse's speed increased. She saw that the rider was a woman, urging on her mount, her head close to its neck. As far as she was concerned, the trap might not have existed.

Ursula pulled at the reins, shouting at Barnaby and attempting to move him out of the way. Whereas before the horse had seemed to have an inexplicable fascination for the wayside ditches, now he appeared determined to remain in the centre of the road. As she tried to force him away from the oncoming danger, he broke into a series of small, sideways steps that she recognised as the 'dance' the groom had warned her about. The galloping horse came on, the ditch beckoned, Barnaby danced and threw up his head, snorting terribly; the trap wobbled on the verge, then its near side wheel slipped over the edge. Both passengers were thrown out into the water-lined ditch.

As the rider galloped past them, apparently unconscious of their plight, Ursula saw that it was Belle.

Chapter Twenty-Nine

The brief vision of Belle riding like a girl possessed etched itself on Ursula's mind. Then she found herself in the ditch. Before she could struggle to her feet, the trap slid inexorably down the bank, catching the folds of her skirt and petticoat beneath a wheel. She was trapped in the waterlogged depths.

Terrified screams came from Barnaby, held by the harness and dragged off his feet by the falling vehicle, his front legs flailing as they failed to gain any purchase.

Ursula tried to pull herself free but the material was firmly captured. Panic filled her. Then Jackman was there. Standing in the debris-strewn ditch, he put his shoulder to the back of the trap. The weight lifted just enough for Ursula to release her garments.

'Thank you, Mr Jackman.' She pushed herself into a sitting position. 'Are you hurt at all?'

He grunted and allowed the trap to drop back, one wheel in the ditch, the other perched precariously on the verge edge. 'Seem to have come off all right, thanks miss. How about yourself?'

Ursula gingerly stood and lifted first one foot and then the other, testing that each could bear her weight. 'Like you, I appear to have escaped injury.' Even the ankle that had been sprained seemed only slightly worse. She tried to climb up from the ditch but was hampered by the heavy weight of her soaked skirts.

'Let's be having you out of there.' Thomas Jackman reached down towards her.

'The horse needs calming, Mr Jackman. I can manage.'

'Never been any good with livestock, miss. Take my hand.'

A powerful tug from his strong arm pulled her onto dry land. It was wonderful to be free but Ursula found she was shaking with the shock of the crash. She thanked the detective with a voice that trembled. Then she pulled herself together and went to soothe Barnaby and to assess the situation.

'If I keep the horse quiet, Mr Jackman, can you release the harness?'

He studied the buckles as Barnaby, thrashing his legs, threw his head from side to side and blew threateningly through his nose. 'Can you stop the animal from kicking me.'

Several minutes later, Ursula had managed to quieten the horse.

As she was about to instruct the investigator on how the harness was fastened, Ursula realised there was no need.

More quickly than she had dared to hope, Barnaby was freed and able to struggle to his feet.

Thomas Jackman looked at the trap. 'Can't say I have your acquaintance with this sort of conveyance, Miss Grandison,' he said. 'But I've had enough doings with carts and drays. I'm afraid even if we can manage to get this onto the road, it's in no state to get us back to Mountstanton.'

One of the shafts had shattered under Barnaby's weight and the wheel that had pinned Ursula's skirts stuck out at a crazy angle.

'The axle's gone, see?' Jackman pointed underneath the trap. 'And those spokes look dodgy.'

Ursula stroked Barnaby's neck, feeling his shudders gradually lessening. 'We'd better walk back to the house; they can send what's necessary to get it back on the road.'

'What about the horse, miss?' He looked nervously at the animal.

'I'll lead it.' Ursula spoke more confidently than she felt. Her relief at discovering that her damaged ankle was only slightly worse was tempered by realising that since her sprain, she had not undertaken a walk anywhere near the length it would take to get back to Mountstanton. And foolishly she had left her stick behind.

'Why not ride?' suggested Thomas Jackman.

'Barnaby's been thoroughly shaken up by the accident; he needs time to recover himself.'

'Him and us both! Well, we'd better get going while we've still got enough light to show us the way.'

Ursula looked through the gloom in the direction Belle had galloped. The glimpse of her desperate face came back to haunt her. What had happened to make the girl set off into the countryside at this time of day? Where could she have been going? And why had she been so lost to everything but herself that she had not seen the trap coming towards her?

There were no answers nor any possibility of following Belle; she would be far away by now.

'We'd better step lively, Mr Jackman. It's about to rain.'

The going was not easy. Ursula did not know which was worse, coping with the ruts and pot holes of the badly maintained road or walking on the grass verge; the way her feet sank into the soft ground made progress exhausting. She chose the road.

'This Miss Ranner,' said Jackman, walking beside her. 'She a softly spoken spinster of some sixty summers, untidy brown hair poking out of a russet bonnet, sharp blue eyes?'

'I couldn't describe her better myself.'

'Talked to her regarding attendance at the birthday fête. She was able to place the position of various villagers in a highly satisfactory manner. Could have been a policeman; almost told her so.'

Ursula was amused and said she thought Miss Ranner would have been too.

'So how does she fit into the picture as regards the nursery maid?'

Ursula explained how Mary, Polly's mother, had worked for Miss Ranner, and how the woman had helped the girl when she realised she was with child. 'Mary died giving birth. Polly was placed in an orphanage but Miss Ranner supervised her education and provided the reference that secured her the position in the Mountstanton nursery.'

'I think she should be visited tomorrow,' Ursula said finally.

'You believe she has more information than she told that agent?'

'I believe she knows everything that goes on in the village. Whether she will tell us is another matter.' She looked ruefully at the investigator. 'Maybe you can work your way under her guard, as you did with Mr Gray.'

'With Miss Ranner, I think you will have a better chance than I, miss. She answered my questions but as a matter of duty. She told me no more than was strictly required. On your own, woman to woman, I am sure you could find out more.'

Ursula was surprised to feel a surge of pride that this ex-member of the Metropolitan Police Force trusted her to conduct an interview. Perhaps, she thought, they could, after all, work together in the way the Colonel obviously intended.

'Miss Grandison,' Jackman said, rubbing a hand along the back of his neck as though his jacket chafed him, 'Do you know of any reason why someone would want to kill the late Earl?'

Her mind went back to the discussion she'd had with the Colonel. 'I wish I could answer that.'

He gave her a quizzical look. 'Does that mean you know of something but are not able to tell me?'

'Not at all. I know of no reason why anyone should want to shoot the Earl but I wish I did. That is all.'

'You see, Miss Grandison, when considering murder, I look at three things: means, opportunity, and motive. Now, as to the means, the Earl was killed with his own gun. So who had the opportunity to access it? As to that, it appears that a large number of people would have known where it was kept, and that afternoon they could have helped themselves to it without difficulty. There is also the possibility that the Earl had it with him for some reason.

'His mother, you call her the Dowager Countess, do you not? Well, she seemed convinced he could have got bored with her birthday fête and decided to shoot pigeons.

'That little stone summerhouse – called a "belvedere" 'aint it – well, it was out of sight of the general company; any one of those guests could have arranged to meet his lordship there, armed themselves with the gun and taken the opportunity to shoot him.'

'So,' said Ursula as he paused. 'Means and opportunity can be identified but what could have been the motive?'

'You have it exactly,' he said in satisfaction. 'Find the motive and we find the man.'

'Or woman,' said Ursula without thinking.

Barnaby took a couple of steps towards the verge on the other side of the road and she pulled him back beside her.

'My, Miss Grandison, you do have the makings of an investigator,' Jackman said. 'Now, what makes you think it could have been a woman who wanted to remove his lordship from this life?'

'Nothing,' said Ursula, cursing her quick tongue. 'It was just that so often people talk of a man in circumstances when it could equally well be a woman. Womanhood is constantly assumed to lack the brains, energy and general ability of men. I find it very irritating and take every opportunity to correct such facile judgements. But it was stupid of me to do so in this situation.'

'From my investigations in Hinton Parva,' Jackman said slowly, kicking at a loose stone in the road as though it was a football, 'I received the impression that the dead man was not a popular figure. Estate cottages have not been maintained; servants have been turned off for minor offences without references; the hunt, of which he is apparently Master, has been careless of tenant holdings when riding in pursuit of a fox.'

Ursula was shocked. Then she remembered the Colonel's comments when the Earl had been complaining about the chairman of magistrates. 'How much of that would be due to the Earl and how much to his agent?'

'A useful point, Miss Grandison. But is not the master responsible for the actions of his servants?'

'The servants in the household seem happy enough, Mr Jackman.' Then Ursula wondered how much she had seen. What went on behind the green baize door that closed off the servant quarters?

'Which brings us back, Miss Grandison, to the question of who was responsible for the death of the nursery maid?'

'Then, like me, you believe the two deaths are connected?' Ursula tightened her hold on Barnaby's rein. Her ankle was aching. She began to wonder about her ability to reach their destination.

Thomas Jackman nodded. 'In my experience, the coincidence is too great for any other conclusion.'

Ursula stumbled over a nasty rut and could not stifle a cry.

'Hey, miss, you've got to be careful. You're too important to the investigation to be crippled.' He put a steadying hand beneath her elbow and studied her face. 'You all right to go on?'

She looked into his dark eyes and could see nothing but concern for her there. The cold, professional assessment that had so disconcerted her on their first meeting seemed for the moment to have vanished.

'I'm . . . I'm OK.'

Determinedly, she stepped forward.

'I like your American speech,' Jackman said. 'And the way you manage to carry on, whatever happens.'

Once again he had disconcerted her. 'How come you are investigating for the Colonel?' She wanted to move the conversation away from her situation but was also genuinely curious.

He gave a shrug. 'I came to the end of my career in the police force.'

Ursula was not satisfied with this answer and she questioned him until he revealed how he had run up against what he referred to as 'the establishment'.

'What establishment is that?'

'Why, the toffs; those that have the money and the power. Them like your Colonel and his late brother.'

'The Colonel isn't "mine", as you put it, and the Earl did not seem to have much money.'

'But he had position; that's what I was up against.'

Ursula sighed. 'English society seems to work in a very different way from the US. Money talks big over there. It may not buy you an *entrée* into the highest circles but it gives you the power to do everything else. Here, unless you have the background as well, it seems that money on its own will not talk loud enough.'

'Miss Grandison, you have it right.' He fell silent for a little time.

It was almost dark now. Ursula hoped Barnaby knew the way home to his stable and supper. Once more, Ursula wondered why Belle had been riding in that madcap way and where she was going.

'I told the Colonel that if he was going to interfere, should it look as if a toff were the responsible one, then I wouldn't investigate as he wanted.'

Ursula shivered. 'What did Colonel Stanhope say to that?'

'Told me he had no intention of allowing anyone to escape his just desserts. Snakes and ladders, it's starting to rain!'

It was more mist than rain but they were going to get wet, that was for sure.

'Now you got to get on that horse. I can run, see. No skirts to trip me up.' He took her by the arm. 'Make a stirrup shall I?' He bent down and offered his linked hands.

Ursula only hesitated a minute. Then she put her foot in the cupped hands and allowed him to toss her onto Barnaby's back. The horse gave a small step sideways but otherwise seemed untroubled by her weight. She gathered up the long driving reins she'd tucked into the harness and looped them into a manageable length.

'Let's go,' cried Jackman, breaking into a trot.

Perched on Barnaby's broad back, needing to concentrate on maintaining her seat without a saddle, Ursula was unable to converse further.

They were thoroughly drenched by the time they reached Mountstanton.

Jackman helped Ursula down as a groom ran out of the stables, exclaiming at the appearance of Barnaby without the trap.

'I'll leave you to explain everything,' said Ursula in an undertone. 'And please find out all you can about Belle and why she rode off.'

* * *

In the hall, Ursula was surprised to see Benson. It was well past the hour for dinner; why wasn't he overseeing its service?

'Miss Grandison, I am delighted you are returned. Colonel Charles is anxious for you to join him and her ladyship in the library.' Benson's jaw worked and his fingers twitched beside his pinstriped trousers.

Earlier, Benson appeared to have recovered some of the calm that had been torn apart by the violent death of Mountstanton's master. Now he seemed freshly disturbed.

'Have they finished dinner already?' Ursula had hoped to be able to share a supper with Thomas Jackman before they reported to the Colonel on the results of their encounter with the agent.

The butler drew a long breath and looked at his shoes. 'Dinner has been put back an hour, Miss Grandison.' Then he seemed to take in her condition and his impassive face worked for a moment.

Unnamed anxiety filled Ursula.

'Has Miss Seldon returned, Benson?'

'No, Miss Grandison.'

Ursula sensed he would like to have said more. Frustration filled her. She wanted to talk to the butler as an equal, ask him what he knew, what he thought had happened. But her place in the hierarchy of the household was ambiguous. She might dine with the family but she was not on their level. Nor was she a servant. As far as Benson was concerned, her position was undefined.

'I cannot present myself in this condition.' Ursula looked down at her wet clothing, her skirt filthy from the ditch and its hem ripped. She'd lost her hat and her hair was all over the place.

'Colonel Charles did say immediately on your return, Miss.'

'He and her ladyship will have to wait; I will not be long. May some hot water be sent up to me, Benson, please? And when Mr Jackman comes in from the stables, he will need a change of clothes, could that possibly be organised for him?'

Hurriedly climbing the stairs, Ursula thought again about Belle. She had been hired as her companion. It was no use telling herself that, after their arrival, responsibility for her charge had passed to Helen. She had seen how tenuous their relationship was and she knew how wayward the girl could be. No, she had become far too involved with the matter of Polly's death and had neglected her duty. With a terrible sense of foreboding, she remembered the look on Belle's face as she galloped past the trap. Something disastrous must have happened.

As Ursula passed the nursery, she heard a child crying with awful desperation. She knocked and entered.

Mrs Comfort was trying to hold a struggling boy on her lap. 'There, there, now, Lord Harry. Don't take on so. It will be all right in the morning.'

'Belle, I want Belle,' the boy screamed, his voice rising to a pitch of passion that was heartbreaking. 'She promised . . . she promised.'

Ursula knelt beside the nurse and caught one of the boy's flying hands.

'What did Belle promise you, Harry?'

Perhaps it was her sudden arrival, or because he associated her with his aunt, but the boy's screaming stopped and he caught his breath in a convulsive sob. 'Belle said she would go out with me this afternoon. She promised!' His voice started to rise again.

'Then she must have had to go somewhere on a most urgent mission, Harry. She will be very upset tomorrow that she could not keep her promise to you.' She spoke soothingly, matter-of-factly.

'There, isn't that just what I've been saying?' Mrs Comfort pulled down the little jacket that had rumpled itself up the boy's back and settled him more comfortably into her lap. 'Why, miss, what's happened to you? You look like you've been through a hedge backwards.'

Ursula laughed. 'You have it to rights, Mrs Comfort. That is almost exactly what's happened. Harry, I have had such an adventure.'

She held the little boy's hand in hers and remained crouched down by the nanny's side while she gave him a dramatic account of the accident, without identifying the rider who had caused the crash.

'Barnaby don't keep to the straight all the time,' Harry said wisely. He'd listened with attention, the passionate crying dying away to a series of snatched breaths. 'Jem says you got to make him work at it.'

'Jem is quite right, Harry. Now, I had better go and change. I can't go round looking like this.'

He gave her a weak smile. 'Hedge backwards!'

'Well, what a thing for a nicely brought up lady such as yourself to have to deal with! We're not quite ourselves, what with what's happened and all,' she added in an undertone, tightening her hold on the boy.

Ursula gently stroked Harry's blond hair then laid a finger on the Mountstanton nose that Belle had identified. 'We'll do all sorts of things tomorrow, I'm sure.'

'Promise?' he said fiercely.

'We'll have to see what is happening.'

He looked pleadingly at her. 'Everyone is always busy. But you'll do something with me, won't you?' His mouth wobbled dangerously. 'Please?'

'Cross my heart and hope to die,' Ursula said, dramatically crossing her chest and hoping that this was a promise she could keep.

In her room, the hot water she'd asked for was waiting. Washed and in clean underclothes, she ignored the grey silk dress that was her normal evening wear in favour of a plain gabardine skirt and jacket. She had no intention of going into dinner. Once she had discovered what had happened with Belle, she would beg the kitchen for some food to eat with Jackman. She tried to towel her hair dry, then drew the still damp tresses into a knot at the nape of her neck.

She moved as quickly as she could down the stairs, deeply troubled about Belle. She had grown used to the girl in a variety of moods: happy and laughing Belle, flirtatious Belle, mischievous Belle, sulky Belle, mutinous Belle, angry Belle – but never desperate.

Why hadn't Ursula spent more time with her? Why hadn't she been able to persuade Helen that the girl needed more entertainment, that waiting around for her season to start was too boring for her sister?

Benson was no longer in the hall; the footman, John, was on duty. Ursula handed him the boots she'd been wearing, their soft leather ruined by the water and debris in the ditch, they were her only ones. 'Would it be possible for something to be done with these, please?'

'Certainly, Miss Grandison. I will see to it immediately.'

There was none of the twinkle she was used to seeing in this fellow's eyes. 'It's a terrible time,' she said impulsively. 'For all of us; family and staff.'

Something flickered in his expression. 'At Mountstanton, we all think of ourselves as family.'

'Of course you do.' With this footman, Ursula felt none of that distancing Benson had achieved. 'And in the time I have been here with Miss Seldon, I feel I have become part of the family as well.' For an instant, Ursula imagined Helen's frozen rejection of these words.

Ursula walked swiftly towards the library. She tapped on the door and, without waiting for an answer, entered.

A fire was burning and lamps had been lit but there was little warmth in the room.

Helen, dressed in a black silk evening gown that provided a flattering contrast to her intricately arranged blonde hair, was walking in a distressed manner up and down the room, her face frozen into a mask that betrayed nothing of what she was feeling.

The Colonel had also changed for dinner. He stood against the stone-mullioned windows that ran almost from the ceiling to the floor. The curtains had not been drawn and the unforgiving dark outside seemed to push against the glass and demand entry.

The Colonel's expression was also unreadable.

'Where has Belle gone?' Ursula demanded, ignoring preliminaries.

'How should I know?' said Helen angrily. 'I get a message from the stables that she's taken my horse and galloped off. The girl has no idea how to behave.'

'Which do you care more about, your horse or your sister?'

Helen stopped her pacing, fury in her eyes. 'How dare you speak to me like that!' She raised her hand and advanced on Ursula. The Colonel caught her arm.

'Please! This will get us nowhere. Miss Grandison, we are desperately worried about Belle. We have no idea where she has gone or where to start looking for her.'

Helen threw herself into a chair. 'Where have you been, anyway? Charles said you and that ... that investigator went to see Gray about his preposterous letter. But that was hours ago. So what have you two been up to?'

She made it sound as though their behaviour had been highly suspect. Ursula tried to control herself. After the violent death of the Earl, Helen must be in a highly emotional state. Little wonder if she was unable to deal with Belle's disappearance.

'There was an accident,' she said, forcing herself to speak slowly and quietly. 'We ended up in a ditch. The trap was damaged and we had to walk back here with Barnaby. Mr Jackman is explaining the situation to the groom.'

Helen looked incredulous. 'In a ditch? Hard to believe when you don't seem to have a hair out of place.'

'Come and sit down, Miss Grandison,' the Colonel said. 'It sounds as though you and Jackman have had quite a time.

I hope neither of you have suffered any injury? How is that ankle?'

'She was able to walk on it,' Helen said waspishly.

'Please, Helen,' said the Colonel wearily. 'We all have to work together.'

'We, we! That means you and Ursula, does it not? Don't think I don't know what you are both up to.' Suddenly she broke into floods of tears. 'I'm sorry. I don't know what I'm saying. I'm so worried about Belle.'

Ursula's anger melted away. 'Of course you are worried, we all are. We only want to help.' She walked over and gently stroked the back of Helen's hand. Helen closed her eyes.

The Colonel went to the drinks table and poured three glasses from a decanter. 'I think we all need a little brandy,' he said.

Helen took the glass he offered and drank down half immediately. Her cheeks were wet but the tears had stopped.

Ursula accepted the glass offered to her and sat. The Colonel stood in front of the fire. 'Now, please tell us, Miss Grandison, exactly what happened. You assured me you were able to drive the trap.'

He seemed genuinely concerned to hear the facts. Ursula drank a little of the brandy; its warmth was comforting. 'We saw Belle – she galloped headlong towards us. She did not seem to realise anyone was on the road but herself, or that we had crashed.'

'Had she lost control of the horse?' the Colonel asked.

'Pocahontas is not an easy ride; Belle can't be capable of controlling her,' Helen exclaimed.

'She seemed in perfect control,' said Ursula.

'Richard said he was impressed with her horsemanship when she rode Pocahontas before,' the Colonel said unexpectedly. 'So, we know the road she took. That is a start. Miss Grandison, can you identify where you were when Belle appeared?'

Ursula explained as best she could, then said, 'Why was she taking a horse out at that hour?'

'I . . . that is to say, we do not know.' The Colonel looked at Helen.

'She and I had a misunderstanding,' said Helen in a monotone. She fiddled with the stem of her glass.

'What about?'

Helen raised her head. 'It was after that very upsetting talk we had when you and Charles showed me that stupid letter,' she burst out.

Ursula waited and the Colonel said nothing.

Helen drank the rest of the brandy. 'She . . . she misunderstood something she saw,' she added in a low voice. 'I was very upset . . . that letter . . . the imputations it made . . . I went to Richard's study; I thought I might find something there . . .'

'What sort of thing?' asked the Colonel in a level voice. It seemed to Ursula that he was forcing himself to be dispassionate.

Helen held out her glass. 'Might I have more brandy?'

Without a word the Colonel refilled her glass. He looked towards Ursula, but she had hardly touched hers.

Helen raised her full glass and, with closed eyes, swallowed all the contents. 'Mr Warburton was there.'

'Ah!' The Colonel said as though that explained everything.

'He could see how upset I was,' Helen protested. 'He comforted me.'

'And then Belle entered the room,' Ursula said quietly. She had no doubt as to what had happened and how devastated Belle would have been.

Helen nodded. 'I tried to explain but she wouldn't listen. She ran at William . . . at Mr Warburton and shouted at him. She was incoherent; neither of us could make out a single thing she was saying. She seemed to think . . . '

'To think what?' asked Ursula, as Helen appeared to have come to a halt.

'That he had betrayed her,' Ursula whispered.

'What happened next?' she asked.

Helen sat up straighter in the chair, looked at the empty glass, then placed it on a small table beside her. 'She ran off. I asked Mr Warburton if he knew what she meant but he said he didn't; that they had a friendly relationship but nothing more.' She looked at the Colonel with wide, innocent eyes. 'I was concerned about my sister, of course. I went to her room but the door was locked and she would not answer me. I thought I should let her calm down before I asked for an explanation.'

The Colonel placed his hands in his pockets and turned to face the fire.

'And then?' Ursula asked as the silence stretched.

'I went back after an hour,' Helen said reluctantly. 'Only to find out from her maid that Belle had gone riding. So I sent to the stable and discovered that she had taken Pocahontas.' She looked across at Ursula. 'What do *you* know about Belle and Mr Warburton?'

The Colonel turned. 'Do you know anything, Miss Grandison?'

'Only that Belle had a definite *tendre* for him.' Why oh why had she not tried to find out exactly what had passed between her and Mr Warburton? Ursula was sure that the young man was a fickle fortune-hunter. It looked as though he had held hopes of enticing Belle into marriage then, when the Earl died, decided that a greater prize was now available. 'Have you talked to her maid?'

'Pouf! No point, Belle does not like her. She would not have told her anything.'

The library door opened and the Dowager Countess entered.

She stood majestically. Her gaze flickered over the brandy glasses, dismissed Ursula, now on her feet, as insignificant, and her son's greeting as irrelevant, until her eyes fastened on her still-seated daughter-in-law.

'Well, Helen, this is a sordid can of worms your family has landed us with.'

'Mama!'

She waved an imperious hand at the Colonel. 'Leave this to me, Charles. Well, Helen?'

'I am not sure what you are referring to, Mama.'

'Don't play games with me, girl. Barnes has told me everything.'

'What does your maid know about the matter?'

'Tush! You know as well as I how servants gossip. That French bit you saw fit to employ for your sister could not wait to share the news with the staff at tea time that her mistress had had a rush of blood to the head, taken the Countess's favourite horse and ridden off who knew where.'

'And Barnes could not wait to share the information with you,' Helen said bitterly.

The Dowager Countess sat and looked at Helen for a long moment. 'Barnes, my dear, knows that the interests of this family matter more to me than anything else. I cannot be surprised at the girl's behaviour but I am concerned that it should not bring scandal upon the rest of us.'

'Scandal, Mama?' exclaimed the Colonel. 'Surely that is going a little far? Belle has only gone for a ride. She was distressed and may have met with an accident. When you entered, I was on the point of sending to the stable to inform them of the road she took so that a search party could be organised.'

'Then do so, Charles. No, don't ring the bell, go yourself.'

For a moment it seemed as if the Colonel would protest, then, giving his mother a hard look, he left the room.

The Dowager turned back to her daughter-in-law. Ursula wondered if she should also leave the room but decided that she would have been dismissed if her presence was not wanted. She sat down again.

'I heard you say as I entered that you did not think it worth questioning Belle's maid.'

'There would be no point,' Helen said coldly.

'My dear, you have no idea how to handle servants. Barnes's news, together with what I have observed taking place in this house, disturbed me profoundly. The obvious course of action was to extract what had been happening from the girl's maid.'

'You did not think to question me?' Helen said bitterly. At the look her mother-in-law gave her, she picked up her glass and helped herself to more brandy.

'So, what information did you "extract", Mama?' she asked, returning to her seat.

For the first time the Dowager seemed to falter. She looked across at Ursula. 'I see you, too, have been supplied with some strong spirit. Perhaps you would be good enough to pour me a small glass.'

With a deepening sense of foreboding, Ursula gave the Dowager a brandy.

She drank a little then set the glass down. 'It took some time but eventually the wretched woman confessed that your sister not only believes herself in love, no doubt that's what infatuation seems to her, but appears to be with child.'

Cold fingers clutched at Ursula's heart.

Helen looked horror-struck. 'She can't be?' she exclaimed. 'Anyway, how would Didier know?'

'Does your maid not know the passage of your monthly courses?' The Dowager drank more of her brandy.

'She could merely be late,' Helen blustered.

'Why should the girl be so nervous and worried if that was all?'

'Nervous and worried? Is that what you were told?'

'As I said, nothing can be hid from one's maid.'

'Did she also vouchsafe you the name of Belle's *amour*?'

The Dowager sighed deeply. 'Helen, by now you should know better than to try and dissemble with me. Of course she knew; you knew, I knew, and I am sure Miss Grandison knows.' She turned and fixed her penetrating gaze on Ursula. 'You do, do you not?'

Ursula repeated what she had said earlier.

'A *tendre*? I repeat, the girl thinks herself in love.' The Dowager was scornful.

'Were you able to learn why Belle went riding so suddenly and recklessly?' Ursula asked.

'The maid found her, as I believe they say in romantic novels, "crying her heart out". Didier isn't a woman I warmed to and she does not show much respect for her mistress. She said the girl was incoherent. The fact that the woman's command of English is far from perfect may have had something to do with that. However, she said that Belle eventually got angry. Apparently she said she needed to "get away from here" and insisted on changing into her riding habit. The girl then left and the maid went down to Mrs Parson's sanctum for tea.'

'She didn't think it strange Belle should want to go out riding at that time?' Ursula said, astonished.

'The woman's a fool. Had it been an English maid,' the Dowager threw a contemptuous glance at Helen, 'she would have raised the alarm immediately. Now I only hope that the idiot girl can be found.'

Suddenly there were the sounds of a scuffle outside the library with shouts that grew louder and more acrimonious.

The door opened and in came the Colonel and Thomas Jackman. Between them they held a still-struggling William Warburton.

The Colonel forced the young man into a chair. 'Now, are you or are you not a murderer?'

Chapter Thirty

William Warburton tried to rise from the chair. 'How dare you!' he spluttered. He had changed for dinner; his black tie was now adrift and hung down his white pique front. The dark hair was mussed and the blue eyes narrow and ugly. The easy charm had vanished.

Thomas Jackman pushed him down again. 'To think I should catch up with you here,' he said joyously.

The Colonel stood back and regarded the young man with a cold gaze.

'A murderer!' exclaimed the Dowager.

Helen had risen and for a moment Ursula thought she was about to dash forward. Then she sank back into her chair, a fist to her mouth, gnawing at her knuckles.

Suddenly Warburton surged up, attacking Thomas Jackman with a cry of rage. His fury was so intense Ursula expected he would knock the investigator to the floor before the Colonel could intervene. But with remarkable coolness Jackman laid hold of one of the young man's arms and twisted it behind him, turning the aggressor into a helpless, pain-racked prisoner. A moment later, he was once again in the chair with Jackman standing over him, his breathing only slightly faster than normal.

'You have no right to lay hands on me,' the secretary spat out, massaging his arm. 'Tell him, Stanhope.'

The Colonel stood with his arms folded, his expression chilling. 'I would prefer to hear the charge against you, Warburton.

Right, Jackman, tell us what you know. Out there,' he nodded towards the door, 'you accused him of being a murderer. An innocent man, Warburton, would not have reacted with the violence you displayed. So, I repeat, I want details.'

The Dowager advanced, her back ramrod straight. 'Rise, you miserable excuse for a man.'

She waited, implacable, and after a moment William Warburton struggled to his feet.

To Ursula it seemed as though, beneath her iron exterior, the Dowager was controlling an anger of volcanic proportions.

'I knew you were trouble as soon as you arrived,' she said, her voice like steel. 'I told my son to tell you to go. No, he said. You were the Marquis's nephew and the Marquis was his friend. *Noblesse oblige*, were the words he used. He said he'd learned them from me.'

She was tall for a woman, dressed all in black, her hair in a severe knot, her gaze unyielding.

'You seduced that girl, Belle Seldon,' she sounded as though she could hardly bear to utter Belle's name. 'You seduced her under our roof! Now she is with child.'

'What!' Ursula saw this was something he had not known. He rapidly assimilated the information, then smirked. With an attempt to recapture some of his customary insouciance, he said, 'If that is indeed the case, our engagement should be announced immediately.'

The Dowager slapped him hard across the face.

Helen screamed.

'Mama!' protested the Colonel.

Mr Warburton's knees buckled and Jackman took a grip on one of his upper arms.

'You are worthless,' the Dowager said without emotion. Then she swung round to fix her daughter-in-law with her basilisk stare. 'You have brought heartache and little else to Mountstanton. You are uncontrollable. I told my son how it would be. He would not listen. Nor would his father. He congratulated Richard, said he had done a great thing. What great thing?'

Helen gazed at her, white-faced.

'Mama,' repeated the Colonel, 'Please! This is not achieving anything. Leave it to me.'

'And this *investigator* you have brought in. How could you think we had anything that needed investigating?' She gave Jackman a scorching glance then brought her attention back to Warburton. 'Belle Seldon is a stupid girl but she is under our protection. You are venal. At the very least you have abused our hospitality. She is like the rock that lies beneath coastal waters waiting for luckless ships, merciless when they are fouled on her granite. You, on the other hand, are scum,' she said. With a last glare at William Warburton, she left the room.

Helen sat shaking, her head in her hands.

Ursula placed a hand beneath her elbow. 'Come with me,' she said and led her, unprotesting, towards the door.

The footman had said they were all a family at Mountstanton; but what an unhappy one. Ursula thought that having to live with the Dowager could make anyone seek comfort elsewhere. When Richard became Earl, he should have pensioned her off to some far county, not allowed her to establish a redoubt in the west wing. No wonder the Colonel spent so little time at Mountstanton.

At the door, Helen turned. 'Charles?' she pleaded.

He offered no comfort. 'Go with Miss Grandison,' he said evenly. 'With Jackman's help, I'll sort this out.'

Helen stumbled into the corridor, Ursula supporting her.

Once in the pretty boudoir, Ursula settled her into an arm-chair. 'Shall I ring for your maid?'

Helen shook her head, a minimal gesture that said she was incapable of either action or speech.

Ursula drew up another chair. 'Did you really not know about Belle's condition?'

Helen closed her eyes. 'No. I had no idea. You have to believe me.'

'But you knew she was infatuated with Mr Warburton?'

'She's a child; I thought it a passing fancy. As soon as she was in London, making her debut, attending the balls and going racing and everything, she would forget him. I still think so.'

'And you, are *you* infatuated with him?' Ursula asked bluntly.

'I ... I ... he has ... he has given me support.' A flush coloured her pale cheeks.

'How long has Mr Warburton been at Mountstanton?' Ursula was aware that she should have ascertained this information before.

'He arrived just before Christmas.' Helen looked down at her hands, tightly interlaced in her lap. 'He . . . he was such fun.'

Ursula could imagine how the secretary would have brightened the place. He was the sort of young man who could not resist flirting with any halfway attractive woman – and Helen was far more than that. If he had received any encouragement from her, and no warning from his employer, well, no wonder their friendship had become so intimate.

'What was the "*noblesse oblige*" business?'

Helen looked sightlessly around the room. 'Richard said there was some . . . some misdemeanour William had been caught up in. Nothing much, he said, only he could do with some help with his correspondence and, well, William was to stay with us for a couple of months or so.'

'A couple of months? But surely he has now been here for much longer.'

'Richard said he was useful.'

'He does not seem to do very much.'

Helen shrugged again. 'Apparently he has given satisfaction.'

Ursula stopped herself from suggesting the satisfaction might lie with the Countess rather than the Earl. She went to the window, tweaked the curtains and looked out at the dark. Rain lashed at the windowpanes. The thought of Belle out there was horrific.

'And you really have no idea where Belle might have gone? Could she have made friends with one or another of your neighbours?'

'She was so bored with everywhere I took her. It was so embarrassing for me.' Helen seemed to sense Ursula's condemnation. 'I am, of course, worried about where she is. Charles said he would send that investigator of his to Hinton Parva as soon as he returned; he thought she might have gone there. But now there's this interrogation of William going on.' Helen covered her eyes with the back of a hand. 'It is so ridiculous. William cannot have killed anyone.'

'Belle was not on her way to the village when she galloped past us.'

Ursula imagined the girl, wet through, at last slowing her helter-skelter ride. Would she start to wonder what she was doing? Regret her impetuous decision? Would she know where

she was? Be able to find her way back to Mountstanton? She
had not returned. Was she lying helpless somewhere out there?
Surely a search had to be instigated now? But how successful
could it be in the dark?

A knock came on the door of the boudoir and the Colonel
entered.

Helen looked at him hopefully. 'Belle, has she returned?'

'I'm sorry, Helen, she hasn't. We have to go and look for her.'

'Will you be able to see anything?' Ursula asked. He looked
tired and dispirited.

'Very little,' he acknowledged. 'The walking party, though,
will take lamps and the territory is well known. The grooms
and I will ride; she's likely to have gone beyond walking distance. We will cover as many of the tenant farms as we can,
together with the village. If we can't find her, in the morning
we can start on the neighbours.' He looked out of the window.
'If the rain eases and the clouds lift, the moon will provide illu-
mination, it's almost full.' It seemed a lot to ask for.

For a moment Ursula remembered discovering the Earl's
dead body; the belvedere and all around had been flooded with
silver light. Then it had seemed cruel; now it would be helpful.
'In what way can I assist?'

The Colonel gave her an absent-minded smile. 'Thank you,
the best thing you can do is keep Helen company.'

'What about Mr Warburton?' Helen asked urgently. 'Have
you cleared him of this ridiculous charge of murder?'

'We have hardly started,' he said grimly. 'He will remain in
his room until tomorrow. Food will be taken to him.'

'You haven't locked him in?'

'He has given me his word that he will remain there.'

'He is of course innocent of whatever foul deed your investigator is accusing him of,' said Helen. 'Richard would never have
employed him unless he was certain of that. If William has given
his word not to leave, I cannot understand why he may not have
the run of the house.'

The Colonel looked at her incredulously. 'After admitting to
seducing Belle and getting her with child, and being accused
of murder, I should have thought, Helen, you would want him
thrown in a dungeon. I hope you will not think of going to
speak with him.'

'Of course not, Charles,' she said sharply.

His expression softened slightly. 'I have told Benson to have food brought to you and Miss Grandison here.'

'He may bring me a tray. I am sure Ursula would prefer to be elsewhere. My mother-in-law might welcome her company.'

Ursula tried to remind herself that Helen was under enormous strain and it was no wonder she wanted to be on her own.

With a sigh of exasperation the Colonel held the door open for Ursula. Once outside he said, almost if trying to believe it, 'She is not responsible for her words.'

'I know.' They started down the corridor towards the hall.

'You are limping badly, Miss Grandison. Did that accident damage your ankle again?'

'No, it's fine,' she lied, 'I'm just tired. A night's rest will be all that's needed.'

'Good. There's too much going on for the reliable Miss Grandison to be handicapped.' Without a pause he added, 'Jackman has reported the result of your visit to Gray. I gather that he has admitted authorship of the letter, and denied paternity of Polly's child or knowledge of who did seduce her. Is that about it?'

She nodded. 'Succinctly put, Colonel. One more detail, though. It was Miss Ranner who told him who Polly's father was. Tomorrow morning Mr Jackman and I will try and see if she can contribute any further information.'

'Excellent.' He sounded, though, as if his mind was elsewhere.

'What about Mr Warburton? Is he really the man who caused Mr Jackman's resignation from the police force?'

The Colonel stopped in surprise. 'So, he told you about that?'

'In the context of something else. It seems an extraordinary coincidence.'

They continued walking, Ursula trying not to limp.

'As to that, I do not think it is such a coincidence. It was an old friend of mine who put me in touch with the Chief Constable. He suggested I contact Thomas Jackman. I am sure that before we met, he researched my background and he could well have known that William Warburton had been given what might be called sanctuary by my brother. The Chief Constable may have looked on it as "unfinished business".'

Ursula looked at the Colonel, appalled. 'That suggests he thought Mr Warburton could be guilty. Were you told why Mr Jackman had resigned?'

'Only the briefest of details. I gained the impression it was not a free choice on his part.'

'And I understand Mr Warburton arrived at Mountstanton just before Christmas?'

'I was not here then. If you remember, I only returned the day you discovered Polly's body.' He gave her a slight smile.

'But, Colonel, if you'll forgive me, you must have been at least in the neighbourhood early in the year to order your motor vehicle.'

He stopped and looked at her incredulously. 'Was that why you were suddenly so cold with me? You suspected I could have been involved with Polly?'

Ursula flushed. 'It seemed so strange you going off to London so suddenly and not returning for such a long time. Then when your vehicle arrived, I talked to Roberts. He told me when you had ordered it and that you had personally specified the body work. Salisbury is not so far from here.'

The Colonel gave her a grim smile. 'You should have faced me with this before now. Yes, I did order my motor vehicle personally but I never came near Mountstanton. I had very little time or inclination to do so. My recent stay in London lengthened because I had to sort out some left-over regimental matter that was more complicated than it should have been.'

Ursula felt ashamed. 'I never really doubted you, Colonel, but you are right, I should have mentioned the business with the car.'

As they continued towards the hall, she felt she had let him down. 'Did Mr Warburton not want to help search for Belle?'

'He said he was sure I would not allow it. Since he showed so little concern for her, I thought it best he kept to his room.'

Ursula stopped him short of the hall, out of hearing distance of any footman. 'I agree with the Dowager's assessment of him. And I do wonder if he could be the father of Polly's child.'

The Colonel nodded. 'I have come to the same conclusion. I should have suspected earlier. I cannot understand why it did not occur to either Richard or Helen.'

They continued into the hall. There was Thomas Jackman, freshly dressed in dry clothes.

'Forgive me,' the Colonel said, 'I must change. I'll not be more than a few minutes, Jackman. Are you sure you will not ride with me?'

'I am no horseman, sir. I shall accompany the foot party that goes to the village.'

The Colonel took the staircase in a series of running leaps.

'Would you like a sandwich to take with you?' Ursula asked Jackman. 'I am sure one can be produced very quickly.'

He shook his head. 'Thank you, miss, but I am used to working on an empty stomach. We need to find the little lass.'

He made his apologies, saying he was meeting his group of searchers in the stables.

Ursula stood alone in the hall. There wasn't even a footman there waiting for orders. She felt useless and abandoned. With an inward jolt, she realised that investigating Polly's death had become part of her life at Mountstanton. And a vital feature of that investigation had been Colonel Charles Stanhope, Helen's brother-in-law.

Ursula gave a deep sigh and faced her demons. The man had been as involving as the investigation. That was the reason she had so neglected Belle. She should never have allowed herself to be caught up in either Polly's or the Earl's death. Never mind that it should have been Helen ensuring her sister's happiness; part of the mission Chauncey Seldon had given her was to be companion to his younger daughter – who could now be lying somewhere unconscious, her clothing soaked, bones broken. Her mount could have run off and be anywhere. What Helen would say if her prized mare had to be put down, Ursula could not bear to think.

Helen, though, was the other reason Ursula had been sent to Mountstanton. Her father had sensed something was very wrong with the household and wanted an insider's viewpoint. Surely the Earl's death would bring him over, and Ursula would be interrogated over her failure to find out what, if anything, Helen had been doing with her extremely generous marriage settlement. It certainly had not been put to work bringing Mountstanton back to its glorious heyday.

Ursula felt frustrated. She desperately wanted to do something to help find Belle; but what? The Colonel would ensure she did not join any of the search parties. With her ankle once again causing problems, she would only slow them down. She toyed with the idea of going out on her own and rejected it; her knowledge of the terrain was slight; she was more likely to fall and cause an additional problem than to find Belle.

She made her way through to back areas and the kitchen. Three trays suggested food was being prepared for the Dowager, Helen and herself.

One of the cooks looked at her questioningly. Ursula said, 'I know as many people as possible are going out to look for Miss Seldon, I thought I would save you some trouble. If you have something you could put on one of those trays, I'll take it someplace out of the way.'

'Tell me where you care to dine, Miss Grandison, and I'll get your tray sent there.'

Ursula opted for the Morning Room. 'Only something simple, cook, please.'

Entering the room where breakfast was normally served, she found the lamps had not been lit. Light from the corridor allowed her to discover matches and a candelabra. Placed on the centre of the round table, it threw unsettling shadows and the flames' reflection flickered in the dark windowpanes. Ursula hurriedly drew the curtains with a hand she found was shaking. Perhaps that was why the ancient brocade came apart. It seemed as if the very fabric of Mountstanton was disintegrating.

Ursula sat at the empty table, and thought about all that had happened since her arrival all those weeks ago.

It had been plain from the outset that this was an unhappy household. Helen, who had once been her friend, could not have been less welcoming and Ursula was certain that this was not solely because of their past history. The passionate girl she remembered had metamorphosed into a cool, controlled woman who had no conscience about seducing a young man under her husband's eyes. For Ursula was sure Helen had made the first move in her relationship with William Warburton. Without that, he would surely have behaved himself. Why, though, had her husband not acted?

Then, almost it seemed on arrival, Belle had become infatuated with the young man her sister had marked out for her own amusement. Why had Ursula not seen what was going on?

She had, after all, with the help of Mr Russell, her dinner partner, been instrumental in rescuing Belle from compromising herself in the shrubbery with the secretary. For a moment, Ursula allowed her mind to be sidelined by enjoying the memory of the amusing Mr Russell. She wished she had been able to stay longer keeping him company while he fished. How soon was he planning to leave his home? He'd made it sound as though it could be almost immediate, talking about sorting out possessions. She had wanted to give him Mr Seldon's address as a contact in New York. But no doubt Helen would have supplied him with an introduction.

A knock on the door announced the arrival of her meal, brought in by Sarah, the maid who attended to her needs.

'Oh, Miss Grandison, nobody has lit the lamps!' She laid the tray on the table and proceeded to amend the oversight.

'Since no one expected the room to be occupied, I am not surprised,' Ursula said. 'Thank you for bringing me my supper.'

Sarah placed one brightly burning lamp on the sideboard and another on the mantelpiece. 'We all hopes Miss Belle will be found very soon, Miss Grandison.'

'Thank you, Sarah.'

'She's, well, she never puts on airs, she's always spoken to us like we were friends, if you'll pardon me saying so.'

Ursula smiled at the worried-looking maid. 'She's a delightful girl and I know that everything is being done to find her. She is probably with a neighbour that we didn't realise she knew well enough to visit with at this hour.'

Sarah's face cleared. 'That would make sense, miss. I hope you enjoys your meal.'

The tray contained a delicious-looking breast of chicken confection together with a selection of vegetables. There was a roll and butter, and trifle in a cut-glass dish. A small carafe of wine stood beside a glass.

Without a fire, the room was chilly. Ursula ate quickly and drank some of the wine. She started to take the tray back to the kitchen but was met on the way by Sarah.

'Oh, miss, you should have rung the bell.'

'I thought you all had enough to do with so many of the servants searching for Belle. Tell me, Sarah, is the fire in the library still burning? I don't want to cause extra work but it is so chilly this evening.'

'I'll go and see, miss.' But Ursula said she would attend to it.

Logs were needed on the library fire. Ursula built it up then warmed herself in front of its flames. She could not dispel the image of Belle, soaked through, chilled to the bone, searching desperately for shelter. Ursula herself had suffered from exposure to cold, rain and snow. In winter, the mining camps of the Sierra Nevada could be inhospitable. Jack had had no compunction in warming himself each evening in one of the many bars, downing the raw spirits that were all he could afford, while Ursula herself shivered in their shack, longing for him to return and offer the warmth of his body. 'Why not come with me,' he said each time he set off. 'I'll protect you from trouble.'

Ursula had known all too well that as soon as he had downed the first drink, Jack would forget all about her. It would be up to her to beat off the advances of miners starved of female companionship. A chilly demeanour and a glass of some vile-tasting, non-alcoholic drink would succeed for a short while. Then drunken leers would turn to aggression and she would have to leave before fighting broke out, stumbling from the small mining centre with a lamp to guide her through the dark, back to their freezing hut. Firewood had to be carefully husbanded for cooking their one hot meal of the day. Ursula had learned over time to cope with the cold, with Jack's uncertain temper, with the lack of mining success – the small amounts of silver they found did little more than buy essential supplies. Belle, though, had always been sheltered from all of life's storms – she had no experience of such wretched conditions.

As time went on and no news came back from the search parties, Ursula grew more and more worried. She could not help wondering whether she should go and see if Helen would, after all, welcome her company.

Then Sarah appeared. The girl looked full of suppressed excitement. 'I have a message from John, miss.'

'John?'

'You know, John the footman. He's found Miss Belle and wants to take you to her.'

'Is she injured?'

Sarah looked worried. 'I don't know, miss. He's waiting in the stables, says you better be ready to ride. He's on the old Earl's hunter.'

'There's no sign of Colonel Stanhope?'

'No, miss.'

'And John was riding? Wasn't the horse party searching together?'

'I don't know, miss. Only that John wants you to come as soon as possible.'

'You'd better take a message to her ladyship while I change into my habit.'

'No, miss,' Sarah said urgently. 'John said no else is to know.'

'Not even her ladyship?'

Sarah shook her head. 'He said to hurry, miss.'

'He hasn't asked me to bring any bandages or anything special?'

'No, just you.' Sarah could hardly contain her impatience.

'Then I'll go and change and be at the stables as soon as I can. But there's something very strange about this, Sarah.'

The maid looked embarrassed. 'John's always an odd one, miss. We never knows what he'll do next. He's even cheeked Mr Benson. Several times we thought he'd lose his job but somehow he's always managed to stay. Oh, Miss Grandison, he's found Miss Belle and he needs to take you to her.'

Ursula hesitated no longer. She went and hurriedly changed. Then she stuffed a holdall with a number of items. John might say nothing was needed, but life had taught her that most men had no idea of what could be required. Downstairs in the kitchen she begged some supplies and added them to her holdall. Then she limped along to the stables.

A number of lamps were burning both inside and outside. Hitched to a bridle post was Hector, the ancient hunter that had belonged to Richard's father. John was just finishing saddling Daisy. He was dressed in working breeches and a rough jacket and looked very different from the liveried footman Ursula was used to seeing – rougher and yet more in command.

'Have you really found Miss Seldon, John?'

He gave a last tug to the girth, straightened up and nodded. 'Yes, Miss Grandison.'

'She's not injured?'

He checked the harness, his face averted from her. 'Not sure, Miss Grandison.'

'Not sure! What does that mean?'

'It's just that I haven't actually seen her, miss.' She gave him the holdall, told him to secure it to one of their saddles then used the mounting block.

Arranging her legs securely and the folds of her skirt properly, Ursula said, 'I think you'd better explain exactly what has happened, John.'

Light from one of the lamps fell directly on his handsome face. It looked creased with worry and Ursula decided she could trust him.

'You can fill me in as we go,' she said crisply.

He mounted and they set off.

'Does Colonel Stanhope know you are riding Hector?'

He nodded. 'Said if I could handle him it were a good choice.'

'Where did you learn to ride?'

'My father were a farrier, miss. I were brought up with horses.'

'But you didn't want a life with them?'

'I want more, miss. A life in London, theatres, excitement, like. Reckoned being a footman could bring me that.'

Despite all her anxiety, Ursula was amused. 'And has it?'

'We goes to London for the Season, miss, and at other times, every now and then.'

They rode in the same direction she had driven the trap earlier that day.

'How many of you were in the riding party, John?'

'Six, Miss. Colonel Charles, the four grooms and me.'

'And where did you search?'

'Colonel Charles said we were to go to the tenant farms. He sent us all to different ones. We were to ask if anyone had seen Miss Seldon, to say that she had gone for a ride without a groom and we thought she had got lost. Then we were to meet up with him at Mr Adams's, the agent.'

'And did you go to one of the farms?'

'Yes, Miss. But they hadn't seen a trace of her. Then I thought I knew where she might be.'

By now the rain had almost stopped but a keen wind blew. Clouds scudded across the sky, alternately obscuring and revealing the moon. It was like a cinematograph showing Ursula had once attended: black and white images flashing across a screen, making a curious kind of sense but remote from reality.

They left the road and started to canter across open ground. Soon John moved into a gallop. In the half dark, Ursula kept as close as she could to the footman, afraid of losing touch with him in an unknown landscape. On her own, she would have no idea which way to take back to Mountstanton.

Unease gripped Ursula. She could think of no good reason why the footman should not have gone to the Colonel and given him the information he thought he had.

And just what was that information?

Their speed increased. Ursula concentrated grimly on following him across first fields, then a gently rising meadow and then onto a wide path that led into a wood.

Here the trees dripped water and the moonlight, fitful at best, hardly penetrated the darkness. Ahead of her, Hector seemed to move forward without hesitation. Ursula felt as if she had entered some sort of sinister fairytale. Her sense of foreboding increased.

All at once the trees lessened and opened into a small clearing. A sudden shaft of moonlight showed a cottage, the type a woodsman might inhabit. Off to the side, a horse snickered in welcome and Ursula realised that Helen's mare, Pocahontas, was tethered in a rough stall at the side of the cottage.

John dismounted then helped Ursula.

'Belle is here?'

He nodded. 'She wouldn't let me in, just begged me to bring you to her. She sounded, well, strange. I tried to batter my way in but she screamed and screamed, said she wanted you and no one else. I didn't know what to do, miss.'

He sounded so worried and unsure that Ursula couldn't help sympathising with him.

He looked at the cottage. 'When I left there was a candle burning inside.'

The single window was dark. Ursula ran to the door and banged on it. 'Belle, it's Ursula. I'm here. Let me in, please.'

There was no answer.

'Belle, please, are you all right?'

Still no sound from inside the cottage.

'John, please give me that holdall.'

He unfastened it from his saddle and handed it to her. Ursula extracted some matches and a small lamp, which she lit and held up high, examining the door. It was fastened with a simple latch but seemed to be secured on the inside.

'John, you need to force it open,' she said urgently.

'Stand clear.' He took a run at it, his right shoulder aiming for the latch.

At the third attempt, the hinges gave way. John managed to squeeze his way in. A moment later he had opened the latch and Ursula was able to enter, holding up her lamp and trying to make out the interior.

Then she saw Belle lying motionless and pale as death, one hand trailing from a rough bed set against the wall. She wasn't breathing.

Chapter Thirty-One

Ursula ran to the girl's side, dropped to her knees and felt for a pulse in Belle's neck. Then came a violent snore that vibrated through the dank atmosphere.

Ursula almost dropped her lantern with relief. Placing it securely on a chair, she examined the girl. Belle was breathing and there was a strong smell of alcohol. A brief look around revealed an empty, unmarked bottle underneath the bed, the clasp of its stopper open. Ursula dribbled the last few drops onto a finger and tasted gin. Then she pulled back the surprisingly soft couple of blankets that covered Belle. Underneath, the girl was only dressed in a corset over a chemise. Quickly, Ursula drew the covering back over her, and went outside.

The footman had secured Daisy beside Pocahontas and was tying Hector up outside the stall.

'Is the lass all right, Miss Grandison?'

'As far as I can judge, yes. Do you know if a fire can be lit in the cottage?'

'Yes, miss.'

'Please come and light it, and bring that holdall with you.'

The footman brought the bag into the cottage. 'Is she really all right, miss?' he asked as another loud snore shook the air.

'I think she is under the influence of alcohol, John. Which is why we need a fire. I have to try and bring her back to consciousness, then dress her.' She shook out clothes drawn from her own wardrobe. 'Then we need to sober her up before it's safe to put her back on Pocahontas.'

There appeared to be a generous stack of wood by the empty fireplace. John found a box of firelighters in a cupboard and soon had a warming blaze going.

'Thank you, that's very comforting. I'm sorry, but I have to ask you to go outside and stay there until I call you.'

'No matter, miss,' he said cheerfully. 'I brought some oats with us for the horses. I'll go and feed them.' He left, carefully balancing the door back in place on its damaged hinges.

The business of trying to bring the drunken Belle back to consciousness was not easy and Ursula combined her efforts with managing to remove the corset, then pulling a petticoat over her lolling body. She half carried, half pulled the groaning girl onto a chair. She managed to button her into a shirt, bring a skirt down over her head, then force her to stand like a sagging, human-sized doll while she did up sufficient fastenings to keep the clothes in place.

'Belle,' she said forcefully several times during this process. 'Wake up!' The only result was groans and grunts.

Ursula sat her back on the chair and managed to slip a stocking on each bare foot, making a roll at the bottom of the legs, then she added a pair of too-large shoes, lacing them as tightly as possible.

Belle was lolling dangerously on the chair. Holding her in place, Ursula looked around the little room. On the wall opposite the door was what looked like a very basic kitchen. A shelf above a draining board held a collection of plates and mugs together with a utilitarian, metal coffee pot. Below the shelf was a small collection of comestibles, including a tin marked 'coffee'.

Ursula called the footman back into the cottage. He came in with an air of helpful efficiency. 'Could you, do you think, manage to make some coffee while I support Belle?'

'Of course, Miss Grandison.'

'I've found,' said Ursula, 'that if you heat water in the pot, then add grounds – four tablespoons should be sufficient for that pot – and stir it well, a tolerable result can be obtained.'

There was a trivet by the fire and soon the coffee pot was sitting on it over glowing wood. John also found several candlesticks and candles. 'That's better,' he said, placing them so they provided a goodly light.

Ursula thanked him and said, 'I think we must try and get Miss Seldon moving. You take one side and I'll support her on the other.'

As with the dressing of the girl, it was a difficult task. Only half conscious, she was unwilling to make any effort. Ursula slapped her face then splashed cold water on it. Alternately encouraging and badgering, Ursula forced her to take unsteady steps. Belle responded with more groans and protests. Gradually, though, she seemed to be returning to a semblance of consciousness.

When the coffee was ready, they returned Belle to the chair and John supported her while Ursula used spoonfuls of cold water to settle the grounds. Then she poured the coffee into a mug and persuaded Belle to drink.

With Ursula supporting the girl again, John went and found a large bowl. He was rewarded with a smile. 'I appreciate your forethought,' Ursula said. 'You have obviously had some practise in dealing with the sobering of those who have over-indulged.'

'As do you, if you don't mind my saying so, Miss Grandison.'

She acknowledged this with a slight smile but said nothing. She had no intention of telling the footman about the sordid and messy times she had coped with after her husband had come home from the mining saloons.

Soon the bowl had to be utilised. Shortly after that, John suggested that fresh air might assist the sobering process. Ignoring Belle's protests, they took her outside. It did not take long for the girl to come to.

'Oh, Ursula, has anything happened?' The words were almost wailed. 'Didier said gin always works.'

'Hush, Belle. You have not suffered any injury apart from being vilely drunk. Until you are sober, we cannot return to Mountstanton.'

The girl gave a great sob. 'I'm cold – I want to go inside.'

Ursula had given Belle her own jacket and her knitted wrap but the linen skirt she had dressed her in was not very warm and in the chill of night she herself was shivering badly. 'A little longer, Belle, then you will feel much better.'

The girl couldn't seem to summon up the energy to pro-test further.

The footman took off his jacket and draped it round Ursula's shoulders. It smelled earthy, of man, and a faint aromatic odour that she did not have the time or space to identify. She was just grateful for the warmth.

After a little while longer of walking up and down the grassy path, Belle started to gulp the fresh air and her expression grew more lively. 'I know where we are,' she said eventually. 'It's the Hansel and Gretel cottage.'

'It was the woodman's,' said John firmly and unexpectedly.

'What happened to the woodman?' asked Ursula.

The footman shrugged his shoulders. 'I think he died. The old Earl, he bought this wood. That were many years ago.'

Ursula decided not to ask more questions. 'I think we can go inside now, Belle.'

She sat the girl back on the chair and wrapped the soft blanket round her shoulders while John added more wood to the fire. She returned his jacket with thanks. 'I think you should ride back to Mountstanton and tell them that Miss Seldon is safe but is a little faint and I am staying with her until she is well enough to ride. It should not be long. I think you need not mention anything else.' She eyed the empty bottle she'd placed on the draining board without further comment.

'I understand, Miss Grandison.' He looked at Belle. 'Poor girl, not fair is it?'

Ursula looked keenly at the footman. He was extremely handsome and she had seen Belle, more than once, sending him a laughing glance when asking for something or other. But there seemed nothing inappropriate in his expression, only sympathy and concern.

'I'll be off then.'

Ursula was left alone with Belle. Huddled in the blanket, her eyes closed, head leaning against the chair back, she looked shrunken and bereft. Ursula collected the wet clothes scattered round the room and placed them next to the fire, together with the sodden riding boots. They would all take several hours to dry.

'I feel awful,' Belle groaned. 'I've never felt this awful in my life before.'

'It's the alcohol, I'm afraid, darling. This is what it does. I will make some fresh coffee and maybe that will make you feel a little better. And I brought some food from Mountstanton.

I begged it from the kitchen because I was sure that you would be hungry. You can't have had anything to eat since lunchtime.'

Ursula dug out a roll with chicken, some cheese and a piece of fruitcake from her holdall. She found a plate and placed the food next to Belle on the cottage's little round table. 'Do try and eat something, it will make you feel better, I promise.'

Belle opened her eyes. 'I never want to eat again. Have you ever felt like this?'

Ursula laughed. 'You mean, have I ever drunk too much alcohol? Yes, Belle, I have. In my wild young days, several times I felt as you do now.'

The big blue eyes widened. 'Really, Ursula? Really?'

'Yes, really.' She hesitated for a moment then said, 'My husband wanted a wife who could drink along with him. It took me a little time to realise how stupid that was.' She smiled a small, painful smile. 'I'm afraid men are often not very sensible.'

'What happened to your husband?'

'He died.'

'Oh, Ursula, how sad! I am so sorry.'

Ursula said briskly, 'Life can be difficult. And very rarely is alcohol an answer.' She thought how prim and governess-like she sounded.

'And it hasn't worked,' Belle wailed. 'Didier said riding hard and gin would do it. There would be a lot of blood but then I would be all right.'

Where on earth had Helen found that French maid? How could Didier risk her mistress's life in this way? And only confess the half of it to the Dowager? On their return to Mountstanton, Ursula would see that she was immediately dismissed.

'Darling, it was a dreadful thing you tried to do. And to be all on your own! What were you going to do if you started bleeding? Out here, no one knowing where you were, no one to care for you, no one to make sure you were all right.' Ursula could not bear the thought of what might have happened. 'Why did you not come and talk to me?'

'I tried,' Belle started to cry. 'I wanted to tell you about my condition but I was so scared.'

'Scared of me?'

'Papa told me you would be able to let him know all about my life at Mountstanton.'

'Oh, Belle, I was not sent to spy on you.'

'And I knew you would not respect me anymore and I could not bear that. Oh, my head!' Belle buried it in her hands.

Ursula put a gentle hand round her shoulders. 'Darling, I will always love and respect you. Don't ever again feel you cannot talk to me whenever you are in need. Now, please eat something and I will make some fresh coffee. I promise you that your situation is not hopeless.'

Belle ignored the plate of food. But the tears stopped and she leant her head against the chair back.

Ursula built up the fire and prepared another pot of coffee.

With the coffee infusing on the trivet, she pulled up the other chair and peered into the shadows around the room, trying to read the story of the little cottage. Apart from the soft blankets and linen sheets on the low, rustic bed, no effort had been made to spruce it up. A religious tract on a wall was the only decoration. The utensils were the simplest. Yet the coffee was fresh and wood had been carefully stacked by the fireplace in readiness – for what? For whom?

'How did you know about this place?' Ursula asked gently.

'I found it one day; the day I borrowed Pocahontas. I thought it just like the one Hansel and Gretel found in the forest.' The tiniest hint of a smile entered her eyes. 'I did wonder if it was used for assignations. I found a button of Helen's on the floor. Later, after I realised why she did not want me to become close with William, I was sure she met him here.' She closed her eyes for a moment as though the thought was unbearably painful. 'But shortly after I started home, Richard caught up with me and we rode back together. So then I thought perhaps he was the one who had assignations here. I did not mean to come this evening,' she whispered, 'but when I thought I'd galloped long enough, I recognised where I was and I was wet through so I thought if I came in here I could take off my wet clothes and while I drank the gin they would get dry.'

Ursula almost smiled at Belle's ignorance of how long it took a wet habit to dry even under the best conditions.

'So I undressed, but I couldn't manage to undo my stays. Then I got into the bed. After I'd drunk half the gin, I was so cold I tried to get up again to see if I could light the fire, but everything swam. I couldn't manage to stand.' She sounded as though that was a total surprise. 'Everything was going round and round.'

'Did you hear John knocking at the door?'

Belle looked shamefaced. 'I couldn't let him see me as I was. I needed you! Then he went away and I thought I should drink the rest of the gin. I hoped it would all happen and that you would come.' She burst into more tears.

'Hush, hush. I am here now and everything is going to be all right.'

Ursula waited until Belle wiped her eyes and seemed a little more rational.

'Is this where you have been meeting Mr Warburton, Belle?'

'William and me here?' She clutched her make-do shawl more closely round her shoulders. 'Of course not.'

There seemed no 'of course not' about it to Ursula. 'Where *did* you meet?'

Belle fiddled with the satin-bound edge of the blanket. After a long pause she whispered, 'He took me up onto the roof of the house. There's a sort of pavilion there, over the entrance. You can see it from the drive as you come up.'

'How many times did you go there?'

Her face flushed. 'It was only that one time.' After a moment's hesitation she said in a rush. 'I wanted us to go there again. I asked him . . . several times,' the flush deepened, 'but he . . . he made some excuse. But I knew he wanted to, Ursula,' she added eagerly. 'It was just that he had correspondences to handle for the Earl, or he had to do something for him. Like go to Salisbury on business.' She trailed to a stop and gazed into the fire. Then in a whisper she said, 'I suppose you are going to tell me I have been foolish, aren't you, Ursula?'

'We are all foolish at some time in life, darling.'

'Like Mama and your papa, you mean?'

The connection startled Ursula.

'How much do you know of what happened, Belle?'

'Why, that Mama ran off with your papa. You and Helen weren't there for me!' The cry of an abandoned child.

'We were in school, in Paris,' Ursula murmured. 'Did Helen ever tell you they visited us?'

Belle nodded, the tears starting again.

'They were on their way to Italy,' Ursula said. 'They hoped to live quietly and cheaply there.' It had been such a painful meeting; Helen distraught and aggressive, Ursula herself heart-broken, the runaway lovers trying to contain their happiness and ask for a forgiveness that was not forthcoming.

'Papa said we were never to speak of Mama again.'

'He was very hurt,' Ursula said quietly. It had been a double betrayal for Chauncey Seldon; both his wife and his business partner. He could not forgive either. He made sure that Ogden Grandison was financially ruined. He had not understood that it was his neglect of his wife that had made her turn to the kind and sympathetic man who was so often present in the Seldon household.

'And when I begged and pleaded with him to let me write to Mama so she would write to me, he told me she was dead!'

'They died together, of typhoid in Florence.'

'Helen said we must never, ever talk about it. As far as the world knew, she said, both Mama and your papa died in a railway crash on one of Papa's trains in Colorado. Papa had escaped and he buried them there.'

Such a flimsy tale, with the lovers still alive then. Helen was always terrified that the truth would out and mean the end of the fragile hold she had on New York society. Even after typhoid had made the death part of the story true, the threat of exposure was always there. What would the Stanhopes have said if they had known about the scandal that had been so thoroughly suppressed?

'I missed her so much,' Belle cried. 'And not even being able to talk about her . . . it was so awful. And I know Papa will never forgive me for bringing disgrace on him and Helen.'

'You will not bring disgrace upon them,' Ursula said firmly. 'Something will be arranged.'

Belle started nibbling at the roll with its chicken stuffing. Ursula poured them both a mug of coffee.

'Up in the Sierra Nevada, I lived in a shack not much larger than this.' Ursula made an encompassing gesture.

'Really?'

'I got tired of living in a tent. It was freezing in the winter and there was no room for anything. I told Jack, my husband, that unless he built us a cabin, I would leave.'

Belle's eyes widened. 'Did you mean it?'

Ursula shrugged. 'Who knows? Everything was such hard work; keeping clean was impossible and cooking meals tried all my ingenuity.'

'And your husband, Jack, did he really build you a log cabin?'

'No, darling,' Ursula said, laughing. 'If he had tried, it would never have been finished. He won it in a poker game.'

'Oh, my! What did you do for money?' The roll and the cheese had been eaten. Now Belle reached for the fruitcake.

'Cooked at the local eatery, mended clothes for the miners, sewed dresses and curtains for women who could afford to pay someone. I never thought the sewing lessons at our Parisian *école* would come in so useful!'

Belle brushed away cake crumbs and said, 'I like having things done for me. I'd never be able to cook a meal or sew curtains. I'd go out and buy them.'

Ursula smiled. 'You look much better now, Belle, and I think a little sleep will help you regain enough strength to ride back home.'

'Mountstanton isn't home,' Belle said miserably. But she allowed Ursula to remove her skirt and settle her in the simple bed. Almost immediately she fell into a natural sleep.

Ursula sat by the fire, nursing her coffee and trying to think of a way to solve Belle's situation. Marriage to William Warburton did not seem a good idea, not with an accusation of murder levelled at him.

The time-honoured way for families to deal with such a problem was to send the girl abroad with a suitable aunt or other chaperone, living under a false name until the baby was born. It would then be adopted and the girl return home, having absorbed, as far as the world was concerned, some continental polish.

Would Belle consent to such a plan? Would Ursula be asked to accompany her? But she doubted that Chauncey Seldon would trust her again.

She took another look around the shadowy room. Was Belle right about her brother-in-law meeting some inamorata here? Is that why relations between him and Helen were so cool? Or had the assignations arisen as a result of the coolness?

It seemed much more likely that it was William Warburton and Helen who were making use of the cottage. Who, though, supplied the pristine sheets, the fresh coffee? Ursula could not see Helen doing it herself. She would organise a member of staff, swearing them to silence. Is that why the footman John knew so much about the place?

Then there were the questions surrounding Mr Warburton. Was he a murderer as well as a serial seducer?

In many ways he was like Jack. The same easy charm, the same inbuilt confidence, the same belief everything would turn out for the best. And the same irresponsibility, the same self-centredness; the same lack of principles.

The Colonel was everything they were not. Was that why she had been so attracted to him?

It had been a difficult day and she gradually realised she was exhausted and near to falling asleep.

She got up, put more wood on the fire, opened the broken door and went outside for a reviving breath of fresh air.

The sky had cleared but the encroaching trees prevented moonlight penetrating to the cottage. Only the grassy access path was lit by a pale glow. She wondered if John would return to guide them back home or if Helen would decide to come herself. In her place, Ursula certainly would. Best of all, of course, would be the Colonel, but, given the situation at Mountstanton, she thought it unlikely he could spare the time.

The horses snickered, as if asking when they were to return home.

Ursula shivered in the clear, chilly air and turned to go inside, then was stopped by the sound of approaching horses. And not only horses. Along the path came an open cart. And driving it was the Colonel.

Chapter Thirty-Two

The cart rattled back towards Mountstanton. Belle lay on a mattress with her head in Ursula's lap. She was half asleep, drowsily asking every now and then if they were nearly there.

Ursula soothed her, stroking the girl's forehead, and murmuring words of comfort.

When she had seen the Colonel driving the cart, she had felt a profound sense of relief. It had taken all her control not to rush up and fling herself upon him in delight. Instead, she waited for him to draw up at the little cottage. The footman was riding behind.

The Colonel climbed down.

'Thank you for coming,' Ursula said with a fair attempt at composure.

'As soon as John appeared with the news, Miss Grandison, I made the arrangements. I need hardly say how relieved we all were that Miss Seldon had been located. It was a surprise, though, to hear that you had been involved.'

Clouds covered the moon and meant she could not see his expression. He sounded reserved, as if he considered that Ursula had somehow been presumptuous, riding off in that way. She told herself it was the result of her having confessed to her doubts about him.

'It seemed more important to go to Belle than try and find you first,' she said.

'You were right to do so, of course,' he said in a warmer voice. 'And I am so glad Miss Seldon had you to look after her. John told me everything.'

Ursula sighed. The Colonel would be as skilled at extracting the last drop of information from men as his mother was from maids. How could she have thought the footman would be able to keep the gruesome details of Belle's adventure secret?

The jerky motion of the cart over rough ground disturbed Belle and Ursula stroked the girl's forehead until she went back to sleep.

John was riding Pocahontas and leading his mount. The Colonel had said Helen's precious mare was likely to be too skittish if she was led. Ursula admired the footman's riding skills; he had Pocahontas completely under control. The moon, now bright in an almost clear sky, shone on his handsome face. Exactly what was his position in the Mountstanton household? The natural authority with which he had brought her to Belle's aid suggested it was something more than merely a footman.

Ursula's horse was tethered to the back of the cart and seemed happy to follow along. They at last left rough ground and began to move more smoothly along a well-used track. 'How is she?' the Colonel threw over his shoulder.

'Asleep,' Ursula said in a soft but clear voice. She longed to talk to the Colonel but the difficulty of conducting a conversation under the current conditions, plus the possibility of Belle overhearing, meant she remained silent, only speaking when Belle required reassuring.

Ursula studied the girl's face in the moonlight. She seemed so pale and her blonde hair looked silver. Perhaps the moon bleached out colour and in a better light Belle would look healthier. Ursula could not repress a shudder as she thought of all the girl had gone through, remembering Mr Jackman saying how little he thought Polly had to live for: single, with child, unsupported by its father.

It was more than likely that the condition of both girls had been brought about by the same man. Mr Warburton would never have considered marriage to Polly. In Belle's case, he might well be willing to accept her if she came accompanied by a fortune. In Ursula's estimation, though, marriage to him would be a disaster, even if it could be proved he had nothing to do with Polly's death. A disaster which she was sure Belle's father would do almost anything to prevent.

How supportive of Belle was Helen going to be? Could she conjure into being a more suitable husband for her little sister than Mr Warburton? One willing to accept her condition?

Whatever lay ahead for Belle seemed potentially disastrous. Her young life blighted all because she gave way to momentary passion in the belief it was true love. At least Ursula hoped that this was what the girl had believed. She could not help remembering her mother, Mrs Seldon, the woman who had run away with Ursula's father, and Helen's outburst after the lovers had visited their daughters in Paris.

'She's nothing but a high class whore!' Helen had said, flinging a school book across their bedroom with vicious force.

Ursula had been shocked and said so.

'You are such an innocent!' Helen had flashed back. 'But, then, perhaps you don't know how often Mama was unavailable in the afternoons because she was receiving a male friend behind closed doors. I wouldn't be allowed to enter, nor any servants.' Helen had sat on her bed, chewing at a worn-down thumb nail. Suddenly she looked up at Ursula, her eyes bright and full of tears she was determined not to shed.

'Do you think I am like Mama?'

'You are just as beautiful.'

'I have Papa's patrician nose. My looks are going to bring me a successful marriage. My husband will be handsome and very rich. I shan't throw everything away by indulging base desires for a lesser mortal.'

Ursula had laughed at the time. But how like Helen that had been; haughty and proud, thinking she understood lust and could control it.

Belle had also inherited her mother's looks, including her nose, which turned up deliciously, giving a soft look to her face that was immensely appealing.

Back in that Paris bedroom, Ursula had not known what else to say. Helen had continued to sit on her bed, moodily gnawing at her thumb.

'Do you know what I think?' Helen had suddenly demanded. 'I think Papa sent me away to school to remove me from Mama's influence. And he arranged for you to come too because he thinks you are sensible and a good influence.

'That's ridiculous.'

'Is it? Aren't you always the sensible one?' Helen made it sound an insult.

Now Ursula looked down at Belle's sweet little nose and thought of Helen's pride in having her father's; she had felt the facial characteristic proclaimed her paternity. How ironic that Belle had identified a similar one amongst the Stanhopes.

The Colonel guided the cart onto the drive leading up to the big house. 'Nearly home,' he said with a note of relief.

No wonder, thought Ursula. It must be the small hours of the morning and he would have had little if any sleep the night before.

He brought the cart to a halt in front of the stately porch, untied Ursula's mount and handed the reins to the footman. 'Take the horses round to the stables, John.'

The front door opened, lights from the hall spreading a soft glow over the top step. Benson came hurrying down, his face lined with tiredness. He was followed by three footmen.

Ursula wondered how many of Mountstanton's staff had remained on duty. Then she saw how informally they were dressed and realised they had been part of the search party, no doubt anxious to see that the girl was really safe. Their concern touched her.

'Are we here?' said Belle faintly.

'Yes, darling, we are.'

The Colonel climbed into the cart, gently lifted Belle up and handed her over to one of the footmen. 'Take her into the hall,' he said. 'Be careful.' Then he helped Ursula to her feet. 'You must be exhausted.'

'No more so than you, Colonel.'

'A soldier gets used to doing without sleep. But I think we both need rest now.' He jumped down to the ground and held out a hand. Once Ursula was down, he scanned her face. 'Can you manage the stairs?'

She smiled faintly, unable to summon the energy for a grin. 'Indeed, but first I need to see that Belle is being taken care of.'

'Shall I order some refreshment for you?'

'No!' she was almost scandalised. 'Do all the English expect their servants to behave like automatons? Able to do without rest? We all need to retire now.'

He managed a lopsided smile. 'What a commander of troops you would make.'

'Do you mean that as a compliment?'

'Of course.'

'Then I will take it as such.'

Someone had taken charge of the cart, and the Colonel and Ursula went inside the hall. She turned to him. 'I must thank you most sincerely, Colonel, for all your efforts on Belle's behalf but particularly in coming to collect her.'

His smile was warm but very weary. 'I could do no less. We shall meet tomorrow, Miss Grandison.'

She went to Belle's bedroom, where she found Helen, wrapped in her red dragon kimono, kneeling at her sister's bedside, holding her hand. Helen's lovely face was very pale, her blue eyes huge. If she herself felt guilty for neglecting Belle, she thought, how much more so must her sister feel? Then she wondered if Helen was going to blame her for what had happened. She braced herself for harsh words.

Helen looked up at her. 'Thank you,' she mouthed.

Ursula smiled, dipped her head in acknowledgement and left the room for her own bed.

★ ★ ★

Ursula surprised herself by waking early. Drawing back the thin curtains, she saw the newly-risen sun not far above the horizon and long shadows on the garden below. No trace of yesterday afternoon's clouds and rain. She sighed. Her body ached from all she had put it through the previous day. Aching far more, though, was her heart for Belle and what she was going through. Ursula went back to bed and tried – unsuccessfully – to sleep some more.

Ursula's hot water was brought late by a maid she didn't know.

'I'm Annie, Miss.' A cheerful, chubby girl with rounded cheeks like red apples put the jug on the washstand and gave a little bob. Wiry ginger hair stuck out from under her white mobcap. 'Sarah's waiting on Miss Seldon; the French one's gone. None of us is sorry about that. Always looking down her nose at us she was. Still, to be sent off in the middle of the night! Jem took her to the station in the dog-cart, gone they were afore we were up. Oh, sorry, miss. I always lets my tongue run away, I do. Mrs Parsons says I'll talk myself out of a job if

I'm not careful. Is there anything more you need, miss? Only I need to clear out the downstair grates. Oh, and I was to say as how your mourning isn't ready and for you to keep within the house.'

Ursula thanked Annie and sent her off to her duties. She had no intention of following the instruction not to venture outside Mountstanton without mourning dress. Her brown skirt was ruined yesterday but she had a dark grey linen one with a black braided matching jacket. That would have to do.

Downstairs she found Mr Jackman sitting in the hall. He looked as tired as she felt.

He rose as she came towards him. 'Morning, Miss Grandison. You up to visiting the village after everything that happened last night?'

'I am if you are, Mr Jackman. Did you sleep here last night?'

'I was watching outside that Warburton fellow's door. Had an idea he might try and scarper. Would have confirmed his guilt if he'd done that.'

Ursula realised that, with all the drama surrounding Belle, she had forgotten about Mr Warburton, confined to his room.

'Colonel Stanhope said that, whatever he had done, he was a gentleman and once he'd given his word, he'd abide by it.' He paused for a moment. 'The Colonel's an astute fellow but he don't know nothing 'bout chaps like that.'

'Did Mr Warburton try to escape?'

Jackman laid a finger against his nose. 'I goes into his room at three in the morning; wakes him from sleep. Three in the morning's time to catch a man at his lowest. So I wakes him and I grills him, like I had him in my station.' The investigator looked highly satisfied. 'Got him so he didn't know if he was coming or going.'

'And did he confess?' Ursula was fascinated as much by Jackman himself as by what admission he had wrung from the secretary. He showed all the tenacity of a terrier after a rat.

'To seducing the young girl, Miss Seldon, yes. Said it was only the once.'

'As though that counted for anything! Belle was an innocent young girl, not a mature woman of the world; he . . . he deflowered her.' Ursula was incensed.

'As to that, miss, said she weren't a virgin; he wasn't the first.'

That shook Ursula. If true, it could explain a lot about Belle and Mr Seldon's desire for her to leave New York and visit England. But was it true? She put the question to one side for the moment.

'And what about Polly, the nursemaid?'

'As to that, he wouldn't admit to 'er. I think that was 'cause he didn't want to be accused of her murder. He denies killing either her or the maid at the Marquis's.'

'Do you believe him?'

Jackman looked defeated. 'At three o'clock in the morning, miss, I reckon I had to. Anyways, after that, I got some sleep – and he's still there in his room.'

'Have you breakfasted?'

He nodded.

'While I take mine, perhaps you might visit the stables and see what sort of vehicle they can provide for us this morning. I am afraid my ankle will not support a walk to Hinton Parva.'

He gave a half salute and disappeared.

★ ★ ★

Ursula emerged into the stable yard to see a small dog-cart harnessed up with a shaggy looking pony. She wondered if this was what had transported Belle's French maid to the station.

It seemed the investigator knew the bones of what had happened with Belle last night and did not press Ursula for more detail. She found herself more and more comfortable with his company. The sun was bright, as though washed by the previous day's rain. There seemed a fresh shine to the spring greens of the trees and hedgerows. Ursula tried to let the exuberance of the air lift her spirits.

'So, Mr Jackman, will you visit Miss Ranner with me or do you hold to your view that I will do better on my own?' she asked as they approached Hinton Parva.

'On your own, miss, that's the way forward. I'll dig away with the other villagers; there has to be more information got from them than I've managed so far. And I'd better make sure my room at the inn hasn't been given away.'

The comic way he raised his eyebrow convinced Ursula that he did not consider this a serious danger. She found a convenient place to tether the pony and cart and remembered Mr Seldon once saying, 'A major convenience of a motor is that I can leave it without worrying it needs walking or feeding.' She wondered if he would he be coming over for the Earl's funeral?

Mr Jackman strode off in the direction of the village shop and Ursula found Miss Ranner's little cottage.

Ellie opened the door to her. 'Oh, miss!' she said, her eyes wide.

'Who is it?' came Miss Ranner's voice.

'It be that American lady from the big house,' Ellie called, still holding the door.

'Show her in,' said the gentle but firm voice.

Miss Ranner was sitting in her tiny living room with a visitor. The window was open, admitting a fragrant breeze.

'Miss Grandison, how nice of you to call,' said her hostess, advancing all of two steps to meet her. 'Ellie, another cup for our guest. You will take tea with us, will you not?'

'I shall be delighted,' said Ursula smoothly. She hardly needed more liquid after her breakfast coffee but a refusal was impossible.

'And have you met Mrs Sutton? Betty, dear, this is Miss Grandison, who has accompanied the Countess's sister from America. Miss Grandison, Mrs Sutton is housekeeper to Lady Frances Russell. Oh, dear, I should say, was housekeeper. Poor Lady Frances has passed away.'

Ursula looked at the other visitor with interest. 'I think I visited the village shop at the same time as you just after I arrived, Mrs Sutton. You were buying eggs for Lady Frances.'

The housekeeper was a spare woman with severely pulled back grey hair and sinewy hands, and Ursula remembered her clearly; remembered her concern to be served as quickly as possible so she could return to her mistress. 'But I did not see you at the Dowager Countess's birthday fête.'

The woman sniffed disparagingly. 'I should think not, with Lady Frances so recently passed on. Not that I would have attended in any event. It was not my place. Judith, I will depart and leave you with your visitor.'

'Oh, please, Mrs Sutton, do not let my unexpected arrival disturb your *tête-à-tête* with Miss Ranner.'

'Can we not all sit down?' the hostess pleaded, fluttering her hands towards the chairs.

Mrs Sutton hesitated for a long moment.

'You know, Miss Grandison is Miss Seldon's companion, she is not related to any of the Stanhopes,' Miss Ranner said unexpectedly.

Ursula smiled beguilingly. 'I would so like to talk to you, Mrs Sutton. I had such a pleasant conversation with Mr Russell at dinner shortly after I arrived, and I met with him only a few days ago; he was fishing.'

The woman sat down again, her fingers beating an uncomfortable tattoo on the chair arm. A seat was found for Ursula.

Ellie brought in a cup and saucer and Miss Ranner poured tea for Ursula.

'Now we are all cosy,' she said, handing it over.

Ursula smiled her thanks and returned her attention to Mrs Sutton. 'You must forgive my curiosity, but as an American I find all these quaint customs involving hierarchy and someone's place very interesting. I understood all the villagers were invited to the fête. Would that not include yourself, Mrs Sutton?'

Miss Ranner stirred as though about to intervene, but her friend held up her hand. 'I am not a villager, Miss Grandison. But even if I was, I would not attend at Mountstanton. Their treatment of my poor mistress was not to be borne.' She offered her cup for a refill with a righteous smile.

Ursula gazed at her expectantly. 'Really?' she said, sensing that the woman only needed an audience to say more. Miss Ranner made a small, deprecating noise.

'Lady Frances was that pleased to be back here,' Mrs Sutton said in a rush. 'She said it was like coming home. And that was what it was, poor lady. What with her brother, the Viscount, only ten miles away and the parish where the Very Reverend Mr Russell had been officiating when they met almost next door. Then to meet with such discourtesy from Mountstanton!'

'Discourtesy?' Ursula could not help the sharpness in her voice. She quickly modulated it. 'But, as I said, I met Mr Russell, Lady Frances's son, at dinner there.'

Mrs Sutton sniffed. 'Oh, he managed to inveigle himself in. The Earl, he would ask him over for a shoot. But no invitation for my mistress. She never said anything, mind,' she added quickly, 'but I could see how it preyed on her.'

'I believe the Countess said she visited with Lady Frances, Mrs Sutton.'

Another sniff. 'Oh, she came every now and then. But the old Countess, never. Then Mr Russell went to be a secretary, my lady said, to a most learned gentleman. She told me it was because it was in Oxford, where he went to college, so he could study books.' She sniffed again. 'I thought it better he should be with his mother, seeing as how she was poorly. And he did return.' She thought for a moment. 'He was different, even my lady said so. And,' she looked surprised, 'then he became bitter about the big house and its treatment of my lady.'

'Tell me, Mrs Sutton, has Mr Russell left yet for America? He told me he intended visiting there after . . . that is, when his mother no longer needed him.'

Mrs Sutton finished her tea and set down the cup. 'Oh, yes. He was off two days ago.'

Ursula drew a quick breath. 'The day the Earl . . . had his accident?'

'That would have been it. Not that he would have known about the accident, of course, having left already.'

'Has he sailed then?' Miss Ranner asked, as though eager to move the conversation away from the death of the Earl.

Mrs Sutton rose. 'I don't think so. He said he was calling in on a friend on the way to Liverpool, he meant to sell him his horse.' She gave a deep sigh. 'That horse! I think he loves it as much as he did his mama.'

'I wanted to give him Mr Seldon's details so he could contact him,' said Urusla. 'I am sure Mr Seldon would be interested in meeting him. Do you know his friend's address?'

Mrs Sutton shook her head. 'He mentioned Derbyshire but I don't know more than that.'

'How about the boat he was to sail on? If I wrote him a letter care of the shipping company in Liverpool, it might catch him. Mr Seldon could be of considerable help to him in New York,' she added persuasively.

Mrs Sutton drew herself up proudly. 'Showed me his ticket, he did. A passport he called it. "Here's my passport to a brand new life. It's all there waiting for me." He was that excited. Made me recall when he was a student and off to Oxford for the first time.'

'And do you remember the name of the boat on the ticket?' Ursula asked.

'Of course! Now, let me see. Something to do with royalty it was. *Majesty*? No, that wasn't it. *Majestic*, that was it; the SS *Majestic*,' Mrs Sutton said with huge satisfaction. 'I think he said it left in a week's time. Now, I must take my leave. I can't stay gossiping all morning, there's the house to be cleared up. His lordship is to repossess it next week.'

Mrs Sutton took her leave and departed with an air of determination and self-importance.

'Do sit down again, Miss Grandison,' said Miss Ranner. 'Let me pour you another cup of tea. I must explain that Mrs Sutton was uncommonly devoted to her mistress. Lady Frances was already indisposed when she and Mr Russell moved into their little house. I am sure that no insult was intended towards her by the Earl and Countess.'

Ursula was certain Miss Ranner was wrong there. The conversation with Mrs Sutton had been illuminating. She now had two different areas she needed to explore. Or were they, in fact, the same?

'The accident to the Earl,' her hostess continued, 'has upset us all. It's just that we show our concern in different ways.'

'That is so true, Miss Ranner. Up at Mountstanton House everyone is in, well, I think turmoil best describes it.'

'Oh, yes. They are all going to feel the Earl's loss so keenly. That poor little Lord Harry. First he loses his nursemaid – he was so fond of Polly, Miss Grandison – and now his papa.'

Ursula seized the opening she had been offered. 'Miss Ranner, it is about Polly that I have come.'

'Really, Miss Grandison?'

'I have to apologise for my presence. It is just as I have said; such turmoil up at the house. It seems to have fallen to me to follow up a piece of information that has emerged.'

Miss Ranner leaned forward, 'Miss Grandison, you intrigue me. A piece of information, you say. May I be a party to it?'

'You very kindly explained to me some little while ago how close you were to both Polly and her mother, Mary.'

Miss Ranner nodded.

'And I think you are aware that the Stanhopes, well, the Colonel in particular, have not been happy with the verdict of the inquest into Polly's death?'

Again Miss Ranner nodded, her pale blue eyes now gazing intently at Ursula.

'In fact, the Colonel has enlisted the help of an investigator to see if we – he – can establish the exact cause of Polly's demise.'

'An investigator? Is that the London man who has been asking all those questions? Most think he's been up to no good!'

'It's always difficult to have a stranger arrive in your midst, especially when they are seeking information,' Ursula said soothingly. 'Now, at the inquest, I think Mrs Parsons misinterpreted a glimpse she had had of Polly with Mr Gray in the wood.'

Miss Ranner fluttered her hands. 'If only she had spoken to me. I could have put her straight. There's been nothing like that between Polly and Mr Gray.'

'As we have discovered. Miss Ranner, now I have to approach a most delicate matter and I do hope that you will forgive me.' Ursula put down her cup and leaned towards her hostess.

'Miss Grandison, please, let me know what it is that concerns you,' Miss Ranner said earnestly.

'We have spoken at some length to Mr Gray because it seemed that he might well have information that could be of use in the investigation. Now I have come to you for the same reason.'

'Miss Grandison, if I can be of help in any way in this matter, you have only to ask.'

'Thank you.' But just as Ursula was about to put her question, Ellie came in and asked if her mistress would like more tea to be made.

Miss Ranner waved her away. 'Please, Ellie, not now. Leave us alone until I ring.' With a look of curiosity, the girl disappeared into the kitchen.

'Mr Gray informed us that he learned from you that Polly's father had been the previous Earl, that is, the fifth Earl. Is that so?'

'Oh, dear! I did tell Mr Gray that information was to go no further. I only told him because he had conceived the notion that he himself had fathered Polly. I had to tell him it was no such thing. Mary was quite definite and the dates would not have matched, him going away and all.' Miss Ranner seemed very agitated.

'Did Polly tell you she was with child?'

Miss Ranner looked down at her hands, tightly held in her lap. 'She fainted one day. She said it was only because she had run too hard through the wood. Miss Grandison, I may be a spinster but my dear mama had so many babies that I have an intimate acquaintanceship with the early signs of a delicate condition.'

'And I am sure you were very concerned for Polly's future.'

'Oh, my dear Miss Grandison, of course! It seemed to be a case of her mother all over again.'

Ursula grew very cold. 'You feared she was with child by the Earl?'

'Oh, no! The Earl was not like his father. There has never been the slightest breath of anything like that. That was not what I meant; it was the fact that Polly had succumbed to the, well, I suppose one could call it the urgings of her body.'

'Did she tell you who she had been involved with?' Ursula held her breath.

Miss Ranner shook her head. 'I assumed it to have been one of the servants, though Polly had always said she would never take up with anyone like that. But if it was someone with a higher standing, then I told Polly they should take responsibility for her and the child.'

'The Earl did not seem to have taken much responsibility for Mary,' Ursula said.

'He never knew, Miss Grandison. By the time Mary was aware of her delicate condition, he and the Countess had gone abroad. He wished to visit his cousins in New Zealand. They were away for nearly a year. By the time they returned, poor Mary had had Polly and passed away. Before she departed this life, she made me swear I would never tell her daughter her parentage. She thought it would be too difficult a burden.' Miss Ranner stopped and thought for a moment, 'I think she was right. A girl like Polly, well, you would never know what she would do.'

Ursula wondered if she should tell Miss Ranner that Polly had been told who her father was and that the information may well have led to her death. Mr Jackman might be certain Mr Warburton had not killed her but she was not convinced.

Miss Ranner continued, 'After all, you heard Mrs Sutton say how bitter young Mr Russell is.' She suddenly clapped a hand over her mouth for an instant. 'Oh dear, Miss Grandison, I didn't mean anything by that. It was just that from things Mrs Sutton said from time to time, it seemed Mr Russell thought he was owed more out of life.' She wrung her hands together. 'His mother, Lady Frances, was such a special person.'

'What happened, Miss Ranner?' Ursula remembered the Colonel and his tale of a father over-eager to exercise a *droit du seigneur* and a scandal only just averted. 'I ask not through a taste for gossip but because it could be very important.'

'Important? Why? I don't understand.'

'I am not at liberty to explain but please be assured that I speak the truth when I say that the details could mean a great deal.'

Miss Ranner passed a hand over her eyes. 'All my life I have been educated not to gossip and particularly not to gossip about one's betters.'

'Never think that just because someone has a title or a large house or some great reputation that they are better than you, Miss Ranner. From what I have seen here, you are of sterling quality and should bow to no one.'

Her hostess gave a shaky laugh. 'Dear Miss Grandison, what are you saying?' She thought for a moment. 'Well, both of them have passed on now, though, of course, the Dowager is still with us.' She looked hard at Ursula. 'If you are sure it is of such importance, then I will tell you.'

She looked down at her knitted fingers. When she raised her gaze, she was completely composed. 'The Earl and the Countess had been married some three or four years. No children as yet and perhaps he was worried by that. He and Lady Frances met on the hunting field. She was a bruising rider to hounds, reckless as anything. She came off at a high hedge and lost consciousness. She and the Earl were the only ones foolish enough to try jumping that obstacle. He gathered her up and, well, I suppose it was what the poets like to talk of as love at first sight. Some called her beautiful and some ugly. She had come out several years earlier but somehow failed to find a husband, perhaps she was too selective.'

Ursula had a sudden picture of a strong-willed girl with out-of-the-ordinary looks suddenly meeting the love of her life and throwing every rule book out of the window.

'I don't know how long it took before the gossip started. I think he was as reckless as she. Then, suddenly, she was marrying the clergyman of a local parish and he had been given an advancement that took them into the Midlands. We saw no more of Lady Frances until seven or eight years ago. The reverend had died, the rectory had to be passed to the next incumbent and the present Viscount Broome, brother to Lady Frances, supplied her with a house.'

'The fifth Earl must have still been alive, was he not?'

Miss Ranner nodded.

'And at last discretion was observed,' said Ursula, thinking that the Dowager may well have had something to say in that. She must surely have been aware of what had transpired.

'It was as Mrs Sutton described.'

'Did gossip not start up again regarding Mr Max Russell? Now that I know the facts, I can see that there is a strong likeness to the Earl.' Except that Mr Russell had a presence the Earl had never managed to achieve.

'He was invited to Mountstanton. Only occasionally, you understand, when there were other folk around, just what might be expected, given Lady Frances's standing. Had there been a complete ignoring of the Russells, then gossip may well have been active.'

'You spoke earlier as though Mr Russell was aware of his parentage.'

'Oh, yes. Betty – Mrs Sutton – is a close friend and she has told me Lady Frances informed him of the truth many years ago.'

Ursula shook her head. What a terrible story! And the fifth Earl was a man supposedly held in high esteem and great fondness by all who knew him. How extraordinary it was that neither of his sons seemed to have taken after him. She remembered Mr Russell's easy charm and wondered if the fifth Earl had wanted to acknowledge him as at least one son who had inherited his own charisma. And how had the Dowager borne it? No wonder she had lashed out so strongly against Mr Warburton the previous night.

Then she thought about Helen and Belle's mother, for whom faithlessness had seemed a way of life. She wondered how long she would have remained with her own Papa had typhoid not claimed them both.

'Thank you, Miss Ranner, for telling me this.'

'Is it important, Miss Grandison?'

Ursula looked down at the gloves she had lain in her lap and stroked their grey suede. 'At this moment I cannot tell. But, yes, it could be of great importance.'

Miss Ranner looked pleased and relieved. After a moment she said, 'And how is your knitting going, Miss Grandison?'

Ursula explained she was half way through the wrap she was making from Miss Ranner's pattern but all the time she wanted to say goodbye. She needed to find Mr Jackman, to tell him how she thought she could now put together all the pieces surrounding the Earl's death.

Chapter Thirty-Three

Charles Stanhope stood in his brother's study, looked at his two investigators, and tried to take in what they had told him.

He was deathly tired. He kept telling himself he had suffered far worse hardship on campaign than he had here at home over the past forty-eight hours, but the heartbreak of his brother's death kept sweeping over him. It made the shock of Polly's demise a fleabite in comparison.

He had meant coming home after resigning his commission to be no more than a dutiful interlude before moving on to the next stage of his life. He had had it all planned. Now, almost literally, the grand design had been blown into useless pieces.

'Please, sit down.' He waved at a couple of none-too-comfortable chairs and waited until both Miss Grandison and Thomas Jackman were seated. 'Now, let me see if I have this straight.' He leant against a side table weighted with piles of Richard's papers. 'You are saying that Max Russell is one of my father's illegitimate offspring, that he comes up here on Mama's birthday fête filled with animosity towards my brother, helps himself to a shotgun, meets him in the belvedere and kills him, making it look like a suicide. Is that it?' He couldn't help the incredulous note in his voice.

Until now, he had considered Miss Grandison as a woman of more than usual intelligence. And courage! What other woman would have climbed down that treacherous slope in the way she had for a dog! Or, for that matter, ridden out on a loathsome night through the dark and rain to help a foolish girl when there were others she could have called on? How quickly he had become used to her presence, her frankness, her wit, her ability to think the way he did about matters such as Polly's death. He caught her sometimes at the dinner table surveying the diners as though they belonged in some zoological park. Then she would catch his eye and smile almost as though they were conspirators.

Now, though, it seemed she had let her imagination run away with her. Could she really believe the theory she had outlined?

'Sir,' said Thomas Jackman, 'I have to point out that Mr Russell's horse, an unmistakeable animal, blond as I understand . . .'

'A palomino' interjected Miss Grandison.

'Was seen in the early evening tethered at the trees not far from the bottom of the slope leading up to the belvedere.'

This hadn't been mentioned before. It rocked Charles, made him realise this theory might not be as ridiculous as he'd first thought.

'When did you discover this, Jackman?'

'This morning, sir. While Miss Grandison was visiting Miss Ranner, I talked with Sam, the barman at the Lamb and Lion. He said if I wanted to know more about who was at the fête, I should talk to Mr Russell because his horse was seen below the slope leading up to the west wing. I asked who had produced this information; he said a customer had mentioned it, someone, I gathered, who wouldn't want to be identified. From what Sam didn't say as much as what he did, I reckon that poaching is amongst this fellow's activities.'

Charles had a good idea of who the fellow was. Luke Southover scratched a living lending a hand to any farmer needing unskilled help, and poached regularly, filling the pot for his ever-growing family. Luke was sharp and sly. He knew everything going on in the neighbourhood. If he said he'd seen Max's horse, then the report could be relied upon.

'So I asked who this Mr Russell was,' Jackman continued.

'And what were you told?'

'That he was a gent, lived a little way outside Hinton Parva and was known to visit up at the big house. Nothing about his being any sort of relation,' Jackman added hurriedly. 'I obtained his directions and walked back toward the house Miss

Grandison was visiting, to inform her that I was intending to call on the said Mr Russell, when . . . '

'When I emerged from Miss Ranner's and was able to tell him what I had learned from both her and Mrs Sutton,' finished Ursula.

Charles looked at her in bemusement.

She fixed him with a steady gaze. 'How do you view Mr Russell, Colonel?'

How indeed? With an effort Charles brought himself back to the matter in hand. It was a question he would have difficulty in answering but answer it he must. 'Max Russell and his mother moved into The Beeches, which is a mile or so the other side of the village, some seven years ago. Lady Frances, Max's mother, was the sister of Viscount Broome, whose estate borders Mountstanton to the east.'

'We are aware of that, Colonel,' Miss Grandison broke in with a note of impatience. 'Please, may I ask if you were aware that Mr Russell is your half-brother?'

'I was away with my regiment when the Russells arrived. I came home on leave about a couple of years later and met Max for the first time out shooting with my father and Richard. He seemed a pleasant enough fellow. Then my brother broke the news. He . . . he . . . apparently he considered that Max's birth was not his fault and that it should not be held against him.' He swallowed hard.

'But you could not see it that way?' Miss Grandison asked gently.

He looked down at his shoes. 'I could not help seeing the presence in the neighbourhood of his mother and himself as an insult to my mother. Richard said that my mother had left her card with Lady Frances and that was all she intended doing.' He paused then said, with a certain amount of difficulty, 'It was obvious, though, that my father derived great pleasure from Max's company.'

'Did he visit Lady Frances?'

'No. I believe he did not. By then his physical condition was deteriorating and he rode little. But I know Max came over and played chess with him.' When Charles had told Richard how inappropriate he considered this practice, his brother said that it gave pleasure to their father, and his life, at that stage, did not offer many pleasures. Richard had always had an uneasy relationship with both their parents. As had Charles. But Richard was always attempting to live up to his father's expectations. Charles dealt with their differences by removing himself from the family circle. But for Miss Grandison to suggest that Max could have shot Richard was truly shocking.

He took a deep breath. 'So Max's horse was seen below the belvedere shortly before my brother died.'

'I came across Mr Russell the morning before the fête,' said Miss Grandison. 'He was fishing. After I left him I saw the Earl riding in that direction. They might well have made some arrangement to meet the following evening.'

'Or they might not have met at all. None of that is evidence of intent to murder.'

'Revenge is a powerful motive,' said Jackman.

'Revenge for what?'

'For being done out of the style of living the Earl and yourself have enjoyed, sir. Indeed, I understand Mr Russell was older than your brother?'

Charles nodded. 'By no more than a few months.'

'So, if his mother had been married to your father, on his death, Mr Russell would have been the Earl. Jealousy can do terrible things to a person, sir.'

'You were very dismissive of him when we met on that picnic, Colonel.' Another quiet interjection from Miss Grandison.

'Was I? I don't remember.' But he did. The sight of Maximilian Russell had destroyed for him what had been, up to that point, a delightful outing; brought home to him how much of what went on at Mountstanton he found repugnant. He and Richard had been so close as boys; when had they started to grow apart?

'The revenge motive that Mr Jackman mentioned,' Miss Grandison continued, 'could have included revenge on behalf of his mother. The Stanhopes had ruined her life. Forced her to be married to a man she would, I suggest, not ordinarily have chosen as a husband, then damaged her social acceptability when she returned to this area.'

Charles said nothing but he was seeing a certain logic to the argument being put before him.

'Then,' said Miss Grandison, 'there is the matter of the horse and rider Miss Ranner saw outside Mr Snell's house the night

he died. She identified it as your brother's because it was a grey.
I believe it is the only grey in the immediate neighbourhood.
However, in the moonlight, would not a pale gold horse seem
to be white, the same colour as a grey? And Mr Russell's figure
is very like your brother's. It could have been Mr Russell that
Miss Ranner saw that night.'

'But what would he have been doing there?'

'Was it possible that Mr Russell was the father of Polly's
child? And that Mr Snell had seen them together some time?'

Charles felt a chill go through him. 'But that would have
been ... ' he could not bring himself to say the actual words.

'He would not have known the details of Polly's parentage,'
said Miss Grandison, 'that they were half-sister and brother.
You did not know who her father was before seeing Mr Gray's
letter to her, did you?'

No, that at least was true. He wished he had. He shook his
head, then looked across at the investigator. 'Do you go along
with this theory, Jackman?'

'It fits a number of the facts, sir. Mr Russell would seem
to have had the opportunity and the means – he would have
known where the gun was kept and been able to help himself
while the company was otherwise engaged with the fête. And
Miss Grandison has come up with a viable motive.'

'I find it difficult to believe that Max would have become
involved with Polly.' Yet was it difficult? He could easily have
met her in or around Mountstanton, or going through that
damn wood. Max had all their father's charm, probably had his
propensity for seducing women as well. 'I think it much more
likely Mr Warburton was responsible for her condition.'

'He strongly denies it,' said Jackman. 'As he denies killing
her.' He paused for a moment then said thoughtfully, 'His deni-
als carry a certain amount of weight but it is possible he is a
particularly good liar.'

Charles looked at the investigator he had chosen for the
mission of discovering what had brought about Polly's death,
and at the American woman who had shown such courage
and common sense. Both of them appeared to think that Max
Russell had been capable of killing his brother.

He walked over to the window, stood looking out on the
parterre garden and tried to bring the man into focus. It was

difficult because he had spent so much time trying to deny his very existence. Had he not, though, considered that Richard treated Max's unexpected presence with far too much ease? 'I don't trust him,' he'd told his brother. 'There's something in his eyes when he thinks you're not looking at him which is . . . '

'What?' Richard had asked impatiently, sounding as though any such suggestion was ridiculous.

Charles had shrugged and let the matter go. What he had seen, or imagined he had seen, in Max's eyes was hatred. Was it just possible that the malevolence towards his half-brothers had festered and grown to the point when, about to depart for America and reckoning he could get away with it, he had shot Richard? The man who, if Jackman and Miss Grandison were to be believed, he reckoned had stolen his rightful heritage?

Charles swung round to face the room. 'The fact that Mr Russell did not make his presence at the fête known to anyone, other than perhaps my brother, could have been because he wished to spare my mother the pain of his presence there.' Even as he said this, Charles decided Max was unlikely to show such consideration. 'You have, though, convinced me enough to believe Mr Russell should be questioned about his presence at Mountstanton on that day.' What would the man's reaction be? Charles wondered if he was opening his family up to more scandal, scandal that almost certainly could not be controlled. But what alternative was there? Allow Max to sail away to New York without the possibility he was a murderer being properly investigated? No, that was not an option.

'If the information given to Miss Grandison is correct, he is now on his way to Liverpool to board a boat for America. What was the name you were given, Miss Grandison?'

'The SS *Majestic*, Colonel.'

'Do we know when it sails?'

'Mrs Sutton said she thought it was to be in a week's time. He was going to visit a friend on the way to Liverpool with the intention of selling his horse.'

'I would suggest I go into Salisbury this afternoon and ascertain the line which operates that vessel and its schedule, sir.'

'Excellent, Jackman. I'll get my driver to take you in my motor vehicle. That will be faster than the dog-cart.'

A look almost of panic came over the investigator's face. 'A motor vehicle? I seen them in London, sir, and highly dangerous they seem to be. They never should have lifted the speed limit on them. Man with a red flag walking in front was just the ticket.'

Charles laughed, and realised it was the first time he had done so since his brother died. 'Jackman, I am sorry, but you sum up the reactionary view of so many to the advance of technology. Take the ride and see if you don't think the motorised vehicle will revolutionise travel.'

'Yes, sir.'

'Eat luncheon before you go. We would seem to have a few days in hand.'

Jackman raised a hand in acknowledgement and left the room.

'Miss Grandison,' Charles said as she moved to follow the investigator. 'I would appreciate a few words with you.'

She stopped. 'Certainly, Colonel.'

He realised he didn't know what the words were. When he had arrived at that woodman's cottage last night, she had been waiting outside and the look on her face had been more than relief – surely it had been delight that it was he who had arrived and not Jem or the coachman? If that footman had not been following right behind, he would have jumped down, taken her in his arms and told her everything was going to be all right. Just as well, perhaps, that John had been there. That would have been no way to try and release himself from the chains that bound him. Now he fought an inclination to smooth away the worried line between her dark, questioning eyebrows.

'How do you find Jackman to work with?'

She gave him her open, frank smile. 'We have arrived, I think, at a *modus operandi*, Colonel.'

'You did not seem very willing at first, I think?'

She nodded gravely. 'You are right, sir. But I think I underestimated both Mr Jackman's capabilities and my own ability to adapt.'

How he appreciated that straightforwardness. How much he wanted to hear about her experiences in California, and for this horrorific scenario to be over when they could take another picnic.

He remembered her confusion over suspecting him of being involved with Polly. It was bright of her to make the connection between his ordering of the motor vehicle and availability to dally with the nursemaid at the critical time. He'd been puzzled over the change in her attitude when he returned from London. Now he could understand. With all they had shared over Polly and the inquest, he should have let her know why he had gone to London and why he wasn't able to return as soon as he'd hoped.

'When Mr Russell came up at our picnic, he appeared to have met you before.'

'He was my partner at the dinner the Countess gave just after Belle and I arrived at Mountstanton.'

For a moment Charles could hardly believe he had heard aright. Max invited to dinner?

'He was very charming and a great help when Mr Warburton disappeared with Belle into the shrubbery.'

'Indeed!'

'Yes, very understanding.'

'And yet you're willing to believe he could be a murderer?'

She paused. Charles leaned back against the side table and enjoyed watching her think about his question.

'At the time I sensed that he resented the restrictions his position in society made on his activities. He was ironic about the paucity of opportunities in England for younger sons or gentlemen with little income. He didn't say so, but I assumed that his own income was not large. It seemed a reason why he would want to travel to America. Now I think his resentment was deeper seated.'

Charles smiled. 'I can see why Jackman is very happy to work with you.'

'I am glad to hear that is his opinion, Colonel. When did he say that?'

'It is not necessary for him to say anything; I know when men are happy working with the partners they have been assigned. I am not so conversant with women.'

There was a silence but a comfortable one.

'Has the inquest into your brother's death taken place?'

Charles's tension returned and he felt an involuntary tightening of his innards. He did not like to think of the number of irregularities that were taking place. 'Not yet but I understand it is a formality.'

'Have you scheduled a date for the funeral?'

'There are some details still to be settled.' Chief amongst them was Helen's insistence that no date could be decided until she had heard from her father. 'I am sure he will want to come,' she had said this morning. 'Oh, Charles, I don't know how I am going to tell him about Belle.' He had laid a hand on her shoulder, trying to reassure her, the feel of that fragile shoulder sending a familiar jolt through him. 'And there is the matter of Mr Warburton. Papa is certain to hear about him.' He wondered if she meant the matter of Warburton's pursuit of herself or of his seduction of her sister. How could Richard have employed the wastrel?

Then she had looked up at him, her huge blue eyes pleading. 'You will be my support, won't you, Charles?'

The strands of the web still held him. 'Of course, you can count on me.'

At that moment Helen entered the study. She held a telegram.

'Charles, my father has wired to say he arrives in a few days on the *Oceanic*.' She turned to Ursula. 'I am glad you are here for Papa says you are to meet him at Liverpool.'

Chapter Thirty-Four

The SS *Majestic* lay alongside the landing stage, awaiting its passengers for New York, its single funnel bearing the White Star Line's distinctive livery of beige topped with black.

Thomas Jackman and Miss Grandison were waiting in an empty office, supplied by the company. It did not look much used. A bare desk was set against a wall, with a poster of the latest White Star Line ship hanging above. There were a couple of chairs, one of which, tucked away in a corner, Miss Grandison was sitting on; and a plain piece of carpet in the centre of the floor. Standing against a wall was a member of the harbour police.

Thomas stood looking out of the window.

Already passengers had started to walk along the wide, bleak stretch of the stage, with boarding papers ready to be presented at the gangway that would sweep them into the liner's interior. He hoped it would not be too long before Mr Maximilian Russell appeared.

Jackman had had a busy few days. He'd obtained all the necessary details regarding the *Majestic's* sailing. Then, after a discussion with the Colonel on how to tackle the interview with Mr Russell, he had gone to London armed with letters of authority and two appointments. One was with his old boss, the Chief Constable, the other with the White Star Line. When he reached the shipping company, Mr Seldon's name had seemed to carry more weight than the Mountstanton connection.

Afterwards, he'd spent the evening in his own house, mulling over evidence and theories. The next day he had met Miss Grandison's train from Salisbury at Paddington station.

'It's very good of you, Mr Jackman,' she'd said as he lifted down her small case. 'I told the Colonel that I am well able to travel on my own to Liverpool should you have needed to make other arrangements. However,' she'd added quickly, 'it is very pleasant to have your company.'

Jackman had been surprised at how comfortable he had felt in her company as they took the train to Liverpool, discussing the case and exchanging travel experiences. He enjoyed her quick mind and ability to conduct a conversation without fluttering her eyelashes or producing coy comments intended to demonstrate female susceptibilities.

In Liverpool they had visited the offices of the White Star Line, followed by an appointment with the harbour police. On both occasions, Miss Grandison had comported herself with the utmost discretion. Introduced as the bereaved Countess's representative, in her severely tailored black travelling costume she had seemed to melt into the background. Afterwards they had checked into the Adelphi Hotel. Jackman appreciated its grandeur and the air of smart efficiency. Miss Grandison suggested they make use of the luxurious dining room for their evening meal.

'You are not afraid of losing your reputation?' Jackman had asked.

'I am long past the need for a chaperon,' she replied lightly.

The dining room was most pleasant, without being overwhelming. Jackman felt comfortable with its upholstered chairs, immaculate white tablecloths, sparkling cutlery and glassware. He liked the touch of a small vase of rose buds in the centre of their table. The other diners looked most respectable and Miss Grandison, wearing her black travelling suit with her chestnut hair tied into a tight knot at the back of her neck, seemed to have turned off the light of her personality. Jackman thought what a useful attribute that must be.

During the meal, Miss Grandison confessed that she was nervous about the coming interview with Maximilian Russell. The idea that this self-confident American woman could be nervous was somehow reassuring. Jackman leaned back in his chair.

'Bearing in mind all the arrangements that have been made, I do not anticipate that he will cause us much trouble.'

'I have only met Mr Russell a few times; he has always been very pleasant, charming in fact, but I found him a powerful character.'

He regarded her thoughtfully. 'Do you mean that he could be dangerous?'

'If he felt threatened, yes, I think so.'

'The circumstantial evidence against him is strong but not conclusive. I think we can rely on his demeanour when faced with us tomorrow to declare his guilt or innocence.'

'It is the situation that will transpire if he is guilty that I am worried about, Mr Jackman.'

'Will Mr Russell recognise you?'

'He will not be expecting an encounter, but I am sure he will have no trouble in placing me.'

'So his reaction will almost certainly tell us what we need to know.'

Miss Grandison sighed. 'Despite my strong belief that he could be the Earl's assassin, I hope he is not.'

Towards the end of the meal, Miss Grandison asked him about London. 'I had hoped to see the Tower of London, Westminster Abbey, Madame Tussaud's. And now I fear I may have to return to the States without visiting any of them.'

'That would be a shame,' Jackman said, dismissing an urge to offer himself as escort for a trip round London.

She nodded regretfully. 'Mr Seldon may well decide Belle, Miss Seldon, should return straight home.'

Jackman could understand why. 'Surely, though, if she is escorted by her father, there would be no need for you to return as well?'

'I was hired to be her companion. Without Belle, there is no reason for me to remain in England.'

'Perhaps the Countess might need you to support her?'

She gave a brief, ironic laugh. 'No, Mr Jackman, there is no chance of that.'

★ ★ ★

More and more passengers were advancing on the gangway. Jackman knew that at any minute Mr Russell could be shown into the office. He felt tense and wondered if Miss Grandison had infected him with her apprehension over how this man could react to their questioning.

After all, only a few feet away was the boat Russell intended should take him to a new life. If he was guilty, might he fight for his freedom? Perhaps try and take Miss Grandison hostage?

Jackman told himself not to be ridiculous. The harbour police could perform an arrest and, if Russell attempted to resist he, Jackman, should be well able to deal with him. And the man could be innocent.

A movement at the bottom of the gangway caught Jackman's eye. A tall passenger was being questioned by the two officers checking boarding papers.

'I think Mr Russell might have arrived,' Jackman murmured.

The harbour policeman straightened his shoulders and moved one leg slightly apart from the other. Miss Grandison's gloved hands tightened on the small purse she held on her lap.

Yes, after some argument, one of the officers had taken charge of the passenger's carpet bag and was now escorting him in their direction. As the two men disappeared into the main building, Jackman could feel tension building in the office. They were about to be faced either with a killer, or an innocent man who might have valuable information for them.

A few minutes later, the door opened and a light, authoritative voice was heard to say, 'I cannot imagine what problem there could be with my papers.'

'I'm sure it'll all be sorted out very quickly, sir,' came the stolid, official response.

Then the passenger entered.

Afterwards, Jackman tried to work out the exact sequence of events. But everything had happened so swiftly, even his trained policeman's eye had difficulty sorting it all out.

The open door initially masked Miss Grandison and the passenger approached Jackman.

'What's this all about?' he asked. 'I see no reason for further checks on my papers.'

Jackman saw no sign of the charm Miss Grandison had mentioned. The man was well dressed with a long coat over a fine tweed suit, and he held himself with an easy command, but he looked tired and stressed, with an air of nervous energy that put the detective on his guard.

'Mr Russell,' he started, 'we have been sent by Colonel Stanhope . . . ' Before he could continue, Miss Grandison gasped and rose, her face white, and her purse slipped to the ground.

Russell turned. When he saw her, his expression froze and Jackman, not a fanciful man, later swore he had the look of a man facing his nemesis.

Jackman started again. 'Mr Russell, we understand you met with the late Earl of Mountstanton shortly before his death six days ago . . . '

He trailed off as, with a speed that took them all by surprise, the man reached into the pocket of his overcoat and produced a small but lethal looking pistol.

Miss Grandison uttered a strangled cry. The harbour policeman took a step forward and said, 'Now, now, sir.'

Jackman produced his own revolver. 'There is nowhere you can escape to, sir; give me your gun.'

The pistol was raised; a shot rang out in the small room.

Mr Russell's knees gave way; he sank to the ground, the pistol falling from his fingers, blood issuing from his ear. As he collapsed, Miss Grandison threw herself down by his side, pulled off his cravat, opened his shirt and pumped her hands on his chest. Jackman scooped up the gun, slipped on the safety catch, and put it in his pocket.

Miss Grandison seemed to realise her efforts were useless. The dying man's mouth moved. She bent so that an ear was directly above his lips. A moment later, he had gone, his eyes staring sightlessly up at the ceiling. Jackman checked for a pulse while Miss Grandison reached forward and pulled down the eyelids, her mouth a thin line of distaste. Jackman helped her to her feet, then sat her down in a chair.

'Are you all right? Can I send for anything?'

For an instant her eyelids fluttered and closed for a moment as she gave a deep sigh. Then, 'Thank you, Mr Jackman. I am quite all right.'

Knocking came on the door. The harbour policeman went outside and they could hear his voice assuring those outside that everything was in order.

'What did he say?' Jackman asked.

For a moment he thought she was not going to answer, then, very quietly, 'He whispered, "Forgive me, Helen".'

'Helen? Isn't that the name of the Countess?'

'I didn't realise how close their relationship was.' She spoke almost in a trance. 'It was all there, at that dinner party; I should have seen.' She looked up at him and seemed to come back to the present. 'What happens now, Mr Jackman?'

He looked down at the corpse. 'If ever guilt was displayed, we saw it today. But he has cheated the hangman.'

Miss Grandison shivered.

'We need a death certificate, of course, then . . . '

'We must take his body back to Mountstanton,' she declared, her voice suddenly strong.

'To Mountstanton?'

'The Colonel will need proof of what has happened.'

'Will not a death certificate be enough?'

She looked down at the dead man and shook her head. 'I think he will expect to see his body.'

Jackman remembered the character of the man who had hired him and knew she was right. 'Well, then, I had better start making arrangements,' he said. 'But first I will take you back to the hotel.'

She shook her head. 'Thank you, Mr Jackman, I appreciate your concern but I am sure you will have to deal with a great many official procedures. I will find my own way.' She picked up her purse, then put a hand to her forehead and swayed slightly. 'Oh, dear . . . ' she said faintly.

He caught her before she fell.

Chapter Thirty-Five

Ursula regained consciousness and found herself lying on a narrow bed in a small, bare room. She lay for a moment wondering where she was and what had happened.

She gradually realised the room was in the same style as the office where they had waited for Max Russell. Then memory flooded back and she wished she could return to oblivion.

What was Helen going to say? How was the Colonel going to take this news?

The door opened and in came a nurse in a blue cotton uniform, white starched apron and winged cap. 'How are we feeling?' She took Ursula's wrist and felt for her pulse.

'I'm fine,' Ursula murmured, wondering how accurate that statement was. 'I don't know what came over me.'

'Shock,' the nurse said in a kindly manner. 'I'll bring you a nice cup of tea and then I think you will do all right.'

'Where am I?' Ursula asked before she disappeared.

'It's a first aid area. We sometimes have passengers who need a little attention.' The nurse whisked out of the room before Ursula could pose any more questions.

Ursula discovered that her footwear had been removed and set neatly on the floor. Gingerly, she sat up, swung her legs off the bed and put on her shoes. She felt as though she was in a dream world.

The nurse brought in a cup of tea and tutted to see her up. 'Don't want you swooning again, Miss Grandison.'

Ursula drank the hot, sweet liquid and felt life gradually returning. 'How is Mr Jackman managing with ... with everything, nurse?'

'Would you like me to find out, Miss Grandison?'

'No, thank you,' Ursula said quickly. 'Is there, though, someone who could find me a cab to take me to my hotel?'

Back in her hotel room, the scene in the office returned again and again to haunt her. To shoot himself like that! But then Ursula remembered the look in his eyes as he saw her. He must have realised the game was up and that there was only one way out. He had come prepared; no wonder he had seemed nervous when he entered the office.

What had he intended to do in America? Assume a new identity? Or rely on the probability that no one there would be interested in Maximilian Russell?'

'Forgive me, Helen,' he had said with his dying breath.

Max Russell and Helen, Countess of Mountstanton.

Ursula remembered more and more about that first dinner party. How the two of them had hardly spoken. How, when you were aware of what could be the situation, it was noticeable how each had managed to be in a different part of the room from the other. Then how brief Helen's thanks had been when Ursula and Mr Russell had extricated Belle and Mr Warburton from the shrubbery.

Ursula remembered her conversation with Belle in that little woodman's cottage. Belle had been convinced that Helen used it for assignations with Mr Warburton. What if it hadn't been Mr Warburton but Maximilian Russell she had met there?

Ursula also remembered the antagonism the Colonel had shown towards the man when he had appeared at their picnic. She had wondered about that at the time, then dismissed the incident. Now she thought that the obvious explanation was that the Colonel had been aware of a liaison between Max Russell and Helen. He had been jealous!

And was it in fact jealousy that had led to the firing of the shotgun the night of the Dowager's birthday fête?

Ursula gave a deep, deep sigh. She had thought Helen had conquered her waywardness; managed to learn how to keep her sudden passions under control; had left behind the times when she had been every bit as reckless as Belle.

A shudder ran through Ursula as she remembered the mangled remains lying in the Belvedere. Just how much did Helen have to answer for?

Ursula lay down on her bed and drifted into an uneasy sleep. At some stage, she was sure, Mr Jackman would want to know if she was all right and if she would dine with him that evening.

She remembered enjoying their meal the previous night. But that was before today's events. If they ate together this evening, would he want to know exactly what lay behind those dying words? And then there was the question still to be answered of exactly who was responsible for Polly's death. Ursula did not feel up to dealing with the investigator yet. He would not be surprised to hear that she was stricken with a headache and would keep to her room.

She wondered how long all the formalities regarding the shooting would take. She and Mr Seldon would travel by train tomorrow to Mountstanton. Would the investigator, together with the coffin, be on the same one? A shudder ran through her. She turned her mind instead to the task of everything that had to be told to the Colonel.

How she wished he could have been in Liverpool this morning. Mr Jackman was immensely efficient and courteous, but . . .

Ursula decided it was time she took herself in hand. How could she accuse Helen of wayward thoughts and not be in control of her own?

She stood up and went over to the desk that stood in a corner of the commodious room she had been assigned, opened the hotel's writing folder, and began to record her version of everything that had happened at Mountstanton, not only what she had seen but also what she had deduced.

* * *

Early next morning Ursula was back at the landing stage, hair neatly coiled at the nape of her neck and wearing the black straw hat Annie, the cheerful maid who was now looking after her, had dug out from somewhere. Ursula would not have been surprised to learn that the housekeeper had supplied it; somehow its no-nonsense shape belonged with Mrs Parsons.

In her purse was a note from Mr Jackman. He hoped that she had recovered from the previous day's distressing events and wrote that it looked as though he might be able to set off with Mr Russell's coffin that afternoon. If not, he would come down with it the next day. She could, no doubt, explain what had happened to the Colonel. He would give an official report on his arrival at Mountstanton.

Ursula was pleased to be one of a large number assembled to greet the arrival of the RMS *Oceanic*. The hustle and bustle was somehow comforting.

Passengers thronged the decks. The *Oceanic* was the newest of the White Star Line ships and it looked as though there could be many on board of interest to the newspapermen waiting for their disembarkation.

Ursula searched for Mr Seldon's face. She was dreading this meeting. She had no good news for him and she had failed in the task he had given her.

Then she saw him; an upright figure flanked by Paul Haddam, his ever-present secretary. Ursula waved frantically. Eventually Mr Haddam saw her and waved back.

A gangway was installed and customs officials walked up. So much bureaucracy had to be observed before passengers could be allowed to leave the ship.

Finally passengers were cleared to disembark. First down the gangway came Mr Seldon and his secretary. Mr Haddam fended off the reporters and beckoned her forward.

'Ursula, my dear, thank you for coming,' Mr Seldon said. His gaze took in every aspect of her appearance. 'I hope you have not been too taxed by the necessity to meet me.' Which meant that he thought she looked exhausted.

'Of course not, Uncle Chauncey.'

'The boat train, sir,' murmured the secretary. 'It is this way.'

'Quite, quite; you have ordered the private carriage?'

'All arranged, sir.'

'Then I do not need to see you again until we change trains in London. You have the details?'

'Of course, sir.' The secretary opened the door to the private carriage, took charge of Ursula's case, and removed himself.

Once they were settled, Mr Seldon removed his outer coat, revealing a well-tailored suit in sober black. His grey silk cravat was secured with a pearl pin. His razor cheekbones were smooth and polished; his eyes were cold. Ursula's morale sank even further as she realised Mr Seldon was in no mood to be indulgent.

He sat down by a window and stretched out his legs. 'Curious how firm ground seems to move like the sea when one first disembarks. I never cease to be surprised.'

Ursula knew she was not expected to respond to this. She sat opposite him, her back to the engine, and waited.

He leaned his head against the pristine white antimacassar arranged over the comfortable padding, his figure very still. He waited until, with a whistle, several jerks and clouds of steam, the train slowly started on its journey.

'Now,' he said as their speed increased and progress became a little smoother. 'Perhaps you will tell me exactly what has been happening at Mountstanton and what my daughters have been up to.'

Ursula knew there was no 'perhaps' about it. The account she had written the previous evening had cleared her mind and put the events in reasonable order. Grateful for this, she started speaking. Occasionally he interrupted, asking for further elucidation on some point or other. For the most part, however, he let her tell the story as she wished.

Helen had told her that Belle's condition was not to be mentioned. 'Myself or Belle herself will tell him,' she'd said. 'He will not wish to hear the facts from anyone else.'

So she slid swiftly over this part of her tale. Then she came to the events of the previous day and found she could not continue.

Mr Seldon's eyes narrowed for a moment. He brushed some indiscernible fluff from his tailored trousers. 'You said that this investigator, Mr Jackman, right? So, this investigator and yourself were to interview Mr Russell once he had presented himself for boarding, yes? Presumably you were involved because I had asked for you to meet me?'

Ursula nodded. 'Also I had met Mr Russell and knew him slightly.'

'Ah.' After a pause he said, 'So, what happened? Is the villain who shot my daughter's husband in custody?'

'He is dead, sir.'

'Dead!'

As briefly as possible, Ursula related what had happened the previous day. The full ghastliness flooded over her as she spoke and she was forced at one stage to stop. Mr Seldon said nothing but waited for her to resume her account, one finger tapping at the arm of his seat.

'And the body? What is happening with that?' he asked.

'Mr Jackman is to bring it down to Mountstanton.'

He raised an eyebrow. 'Why?'

'I felt that Colonel Stanhope would want to assure himself Mr Russell had indeed died.'

'I see.' Mr Seldon appeared to be lost in thought for some considerable time.

'Well, then,' he said finally. 'Your account, together with the excellent letters you have sent me, outlines a quite remarkable series of incidents. However,' his gaze came back to Ursula, his piercing eyes making her feel distinctly uncomfortable, 'I think we need to examine several points in more depth.'

Ursula braced herself.

'This Maximilian Russell, are you suggesting he and Helen have been involved in a relationship?'

Ursula gripped her hands together. 'I don't know, sir.'

'If they haven't been, I fail to understand what has happened.'

Ursula said nothing.

'Now, this fellow Warburton. Belle mentioned him in both the letters she has sent me – which were two more than I had expected.' He looked out of the window for several minutes.

'Belle is a highly impressionable girl,' he continued. 'She can become infatuated with a young man at sight and she certainly seems to have done so with this chap. Do you agree?'

Ursula could feel her hands sweating inside her gloves. 'He is very attractive,' she admitted.

'Is she going to fall into my arms and beg me to let her marry the fellow?'

She looked at him helplessly.

Mr Seldon's gaze sharpened. 'I take it she is. Is there any reason why I should consider Mr Warburton's suit?'

Again Ursula found words impossible. Chauncey Seldon in this mood could tie her into knots.

'And don't try to lie to me, Ursula. You have never been good at lying.'

'I . . . I cannot see Mr Warburton as a suitable husband for Belle, Uncle Chauncey.'

'Because?'

What could she say? There was no evidence to suggest he had been responsible for Polly's death.

'I think he has charm but he is also a fortune hunter.'

'I hope he hasn't managed to seduce her yet,' he said, almost as a throwaway comment. The gimlet eyes suddenly pierced into Ursula again and he took a quick breath of disgust. 'Ah, I see he has. With the inevitable result I suppose. What a stupid girl.' Again he sat looking out of the window while Ursula hoped that Helen would understand that she had tried not to let her father know about Belle.

'I am afraid both my daughters take after their mother,' he murmured. Then he turned to Ursula. 'What were you doing allowing Belle to spend time with him?' There was menace in his tone.

Ursula looked at him steadily. 'I have been blaming myself ever since I found out about Belle's condition, sir,' she said in a low voice.

'Have you nothing to say in your defence?'

She shook her head.

'Too busy chasing a will-o-the-wisp idea that a slut of a nursemaid had been murdered.' Ursula closed her eyes for a moment at the slur on poor Polly. 'Not to mention making eyes at Helen's brother-in-law.'

At that Ursula sat a little straighter. 'No, sir! I deny that.'

His cold gaze surveyed her. She felt her very soul was exposed.

'Huh,' he said at last. 'So there is something you are prepared to offer a defence against.'

She said no more.

'Not only did you fail to protect Belle but you have not been able to ascertain why Helen has not, as she swore she would, proceeded with Mountstanton's restoration?'

Ursula shook her head. She had known this interview would be difficult, but it was proving far worse than she had feared. She was being treated like an unsatisfactory servant. In the past, he had seemed to view her as a surrogate daughter.

His finger tapped the arm thoughtfully. 'Do you think that she has been conserving her settlement with the idea of running off with this Russell fellow?'

Ursula glanced down at her tightly entwined fingers. 'She gave no indication that such an idea might be in her mind,' she said quietly.

'Hmm.'

There was a long pause, then, 'To think I sent Belle to stay in such a cess pit.'

A railway official knocked on the door and asked if they would like luncheon tickets. 'First sitting in half an hour, sir.'

Later, when they were seated in the restaurant car, Mr Seldon assessed Ursula's black travelling costume. 'I am glad that you are observing the conventions with your dress. Now, tell me about my grandson, Ursula. Tell me about Harry.'

Relief filled her, 'Oh, you'll love Harry. He's bright, he's got guts and he's such fun.'

There was no more interrogation. She could almost feel their relationship had returned to its previous warmth. Ursula entertained Mr Seldon with tales of the Hinton Parva villagers, even getting him to laugh at her description of the village shop.

'They're the same everywhere, local stores; hotbeds of gossip, ripping off the little people to make up for the fact the toffs don't pay their bills.'

Ursula said nothing but inside she felt a sense of triumph. Despite the severity of the interrogation, there was one fact she *had* managed to keep from Mr Seldon.

Chapter Thirty-Six

On arrival at the station for Mountstanton, Ursula and Mr Seldon descended from the train. Waiting to greet them was the Colonel. Ursula thought how typical that he appeared to know exactly which carriage door was theirs and be standing opposite it as the train drew to a halt.

For a few moments there was a flurry of activity. The secretary went to organise the luggage. The Colonel introduced himself to Mr Seldon and apologised for military action preventing him attending the wedding, eight years earlier, of Helen and his brother. He courteously welcomed Ursula's return without referring to the intended meeting with Maximilian Russell.

Ursula knew he would not want the matter spoken of before Mr Seldon. Nevertheless, there was in his demeanour and voice that told her something had happened. Immediately her thoughts flew to Belle. She tried to catch his eye without success. Instead, while Mr Haddam attended to cases and porters, Charles escorted Mr Seldon and herself out of the station to where his highly polished, dark green motor vehicle awaited them.

'I thought, sir, that you would appreciate this more than a horse-drawn carriage.'

Mr Seldon looked around. 'But where is Helen?'

'She wanted to stay with her sister; Belle is unwell,' the Colonel said soothingly.

'I have been acquainted with Belle's condition,' her father said sharply. 'I am anxious to see her.' He directed one of his piercing gazes at the Colonel. 'What is it you are not telling me?'

Anxiety gripped Ursula. 'Is Belle all right?' she asked.

He looked from one to the other. 'She has suffered a miscarriage,' he said simply. 'It was immediately after you left for Liverpool,' he said to Ursula. 'For a time her life was in danger but Dr Mason is now confident that the worst is over and she will recover.'

Ursula felt her knees wobble and steadied herself on the side of the motor vehicle. 'You didn't think to send me a cable? Let me know what was happening?'

'There was nothing you could do and we hoped that by the time you and Mr Seldon arrived here, there would be good news. As, indeed, there is.'

'Let us get on our way.' Mr Seldon opened the passenger's door. 'I see no chauffeur so I take it you will be driving this vehicle yourself?'

'I have left my mechanic behind. There is enough room for you, Miss Grandison and your secretary. I have brought duster coats for you all,' he indicated where they were draped, all ready to be donned, 'together with goggles. There is a cart for your luggage.' He waved a hand to where Jem was helping the porter load the cases under the supervision of Mr Haddam.

Mr Seldon gave a cursory look, reached for a duster coat and said, 'Miss Grandison and Mr Haddam will travel in the cart.'

The Colonel looked at Ursula, his left eyebrow ever so slightly raised. 'That sounds very suitable,' she said, smoothly moving to the cart.

Mr Haddam received the news of how they were to travel with a sardonic smile. 'At least I shall not need to have my notebook out but can admire the scenery,' he said and helped Ursula to climb up onto the front bench. First, though, she stroked Barnaby.

'Just as well it's a straightish road to Mountstanton,' she said to Jem.

'Aye,' he said with a grin. 'And I knows all his little tricks. We'll wait a moment to let the Colonel get clear. Barnaby don't like the noise that motor makes.'

'Say, that's a fellow with dash,' said Mr Haddam admiringly as he watched the Colonel swing the handle at the front of the

elegant vehicle, then climb aboard and set off with Mr Seldon.
'Army is he? Cavalry for sure.'

'Infantry,' said Jem laconically. 'Served in the Sudan as well as
fighting the Boers.'

Ursula was surprised, then told herself that servants always
knew everything about their employers, and would boast
about their doings to the servants of other households.

'You don't say? Just shows you never know about people.'

How true that was, Ursula thought as Jem set Barnaby
in motion.

She did, though, know that Mr Seldon would have told
the Colonel everything that had happened in Liverpool long
before she and Mr Haddam arrived at Mountstanton.

★ ★ ★

Benson welcomed Ursula back and assured her that Miss
Seldon was now considered out of danger. 'She had a fall, Miss
Grandison, which caused some internal bleeding. We were all
very worried for a while but Dr Mason says that she should
now recover fully.'

Ursula wondered just how much the staff knew about the
'internal bleeding', and decided that, though it would never be
mentioned, nothing would have escaped them.

'Benson, has anything been heard from Mr Jackman?'

'Yes, Miss Grandison, he has cabled that we are to expect
him later this evening on the eight-forty-two train.' Then, as
though he could not stop himself, the butler added, 'He has
requested to be met by a cart with a cover.'

'Thank you, Benson.'

Ursula climbed the stairs to her room, not knowing whether
to feel relief or frustration that most of what had happened in
Liverpool would have been told to the Colonel by Mr Seldon.
It was, though, now essential that she spoke with him before
Mr Jackman arrived. Would he send for her, or would she have
to ask for a meeting?

Annie brought her up a jug of hot water. Ursula remembered the huge bathroom with its piping hot water in the
Adelphi Hotel and wondered what Mr Seldon thought about
the sanitary arrangements at Mountstanton House.

'Hope you had a pleasant time in Liverpool,' Annie said brightly.

For a moment Ursula couldn't think how to respond. 'Mr Seldon's ship arrived on time,' she finally managed.

'That's good, miss.' Annie arranged a towel conveniently close to the washstand. 'Her ladyship has given me a message for you.' Which meant that Helen's maid had relayed it. Annie screwed up her face in concentration. 'Her ladyship would be grateful if Miss Grandison could sit with Miss Seldon while she and Mr Seldon dine this evening.' Her face broke into a broad smile. 'There, I got it exactly, miss.'

'Thank you, Annie. Would you please say that I shall be delighted to sit with Miss Seldon? I will go to her room as soon as I have freshened up.'

'Of course, miss.'

Ursula stripped off and washed away the dirt of the train journey, wondering what she should do now. Of course she wanted to sit with Belle but it was essential she met with the Colonel.

Or was it?

Dressed in the simple black evening gown she had been supplied with for her mourning, Ursula brushed her hair into the same plain knot she had worn since setting off for Liverpool, then searched in her case for the account she had written of everything that had happened at Mountstanton. She scribbled a couple of lines at the top, folded the sheets, placed them in an envelope, sealed it and wrote the Colonel's name on the front.

Downstairs, John was in the hall. She gave him the envelope and asked if it could be delivered to the Colonel as soon as possible.

'Of course, miss,' he said with a smile.

Confident the Colonel would receive it immediately, Ursula made her way to Belle's bedroom.

Sarah, now Belle's maid, was sitting with her.

'Her ladyship is changing for dinner, miss. She said she'll see you before going in.'

Ursula looked towards the bed where Belle appeared to be sleeping, her face pale but peaceful. 'How is she?'

'Much better, miss.'

'She's very weak,' said Helen in a low voice from the doorway. She beckoned Ursula outside. 'We nearly lost her.'

'What happened? Was it a fall?'

Helen shook her head. She looked as though she had aged over the last few days. There were dark circles beneath her eyes, her skin looked patchy and wrinkles had appeared on her forehead and beside her mouth. 'She didn't feel well enough to rise the morning you left. Sometime later she miscarried.' Helen closed her eyes. 'I've never seen so much blood.' She looked at Ursula for a brief moment. 'When Dr Mason arrived, I told him everything and he said the ride or the alcohol or both must have killed the baby. Apparently it can stay in the womb for several days before ... before ... Oh, Ursula, if she'd died, I'd never have forgiven myself.'

'Nor would I,' Ursula said fervently.

She looked at Helen and wondered if she had heard about Liverpool. Was this the moment to tell her of those last words?

Helen placed her hand on Ursula's arm. 'Thank you for sitting with Belle. Now, I must go, I am already late and you know what a stickler for time Papa is.'

Back at the bedside, Ursula found Belle awake. 'I'm so glad you're here, Ursula,' she said.

Ursula felt tears pricking at the back of her eyes. She took the girl's hand. 'And I'm so glad to see you, darling. How are you feeling?'

'Tired,' she said.

'Have you seen your father?'

Belle nodded. 'He wants me to get well very soon, then he's going to take me back to America.'

'Is that what you want?'

Belle moved restlessly in the bed. 'I suppose so.'

'Would you like something to drink?'

Ursula helped her to some barley water.

'Shall I read to you?'

'That would be nice. Helen has been reading *Little Women*. It's my favourite; it makes me think of home.'

Ursula picked up the book and opened it where marked. Before she could start, Belle, sounding a little stronger, said, 'I think of Meg as Helen. You are Jo, and I hope I'm Amy. I don't want to be Beth and die before I've done anything in life.'

Ursula took her hand. 'Of course you're Amy; a pretty, talented and sweet girl. You're going to get better and go off to Italy, or Paris, or London, and find the love of your life.'

Belle's eyes filled with tears. 'Really, Ursula? Is that really what is going to happen?'

'I'm sure it is,' said Ursula firmly as she opened the book. 'Now, where did Helen leave off?'

Gradually Belle drifted off into sleep again.

Ursula closed the book and sat quietly. Until there was a knock at the door.

Opening it, she found Mr Warburton.

'How is Belle?' he whispered. 'No one will tell me anything.'

He looked haggard and was dressed in his ordinary day clothes – no mourning outfit – with his hair unkempt.

Ursula slipped outside and closed Belle's door. 'She is recovering.'

He closed his eyes. 'Thank heavens. These last few days have been torture. I'm supposed to keep to my room. I think I'm still suspected of killing the Earl.' He looked at her, his eyes haunted. 'You believe I didn't do it, don't you, Miss Grandison?'

'I believe you,' she said quietly. 'And if you admit to seducing Polly, I think you will be allowed to go back to your family tomorrow.'

He looked askance at her. 'Only to seducing her? Not to causing her death as well?'

'Not unless you did!' But she was certain he hadn't.

He sighed and leaned back against the wall. There was no trace of his previous debonair charm. Slowly he nodded. 'She was so very pretty and such fun. I couldn't resist.' He pushed his hands into his trouser pockets and studied his shoes for a moment. Then he looked up at Ursula and somehow his eyes looked very honest. 'But I didn't kill her. I didn't even know she was with child.' He rubbed at his face. 'What has happened to remove me as a suspect in the case of the Earl's death?'

'New evidence,' Ursula said firmly. 'Thank you for admitting your involvement with Polly and, for what it is worth, I believe you didn't kill her. Now, I have to get back to Belle.'

He caught her arm. 'I'm so sorry, Miss Grandison. I never meant any of this to happen. I didn't think . . . '

'No, you didn't, did you Mr Warburton. I hope this has taught you a lesson and you will not take advantage of any female again.'

'Miss Grandison, I hate myself,' he said simply. 'It's as though someone has shone a bright light into my soul and all I can see is rotten matter.' He dashed a hand across his eyes. 'If I really can leave tomorrow, would it be possible to see Belle before I go?'

Ursula was shocked. 'I do not think the Countess will allow any such thing. Belle is very weak.'

'But you will ask?'

How different he was now from the charmer who could produce a fetching smile to gain whatever he wanted. Ursula almost felt sorry for him – almost. 'Goodbye, Mr Warburton.' She went back into Belle's room.

Would the girl want to see him? Ursula did not think she was strong enough to be faced with such an emotional decision.

Later Sarah returned. 'Dinner awaits you in the Morning Room, Miss Grandison. I will sit by Miss Seldon now.'

'I have read a little to her and now she is sleeping again.'

'Doctor said sleep was the best thing for her.'

In the Morning Room, Ursula found Mr Haddam finishing his meal.

'Some place, this,' he said as she came in. 'I thought Mr Seldon's the grandest house I'd ever been in but this has, I don't know, gravitas?'

'A good word, Mr Haddam.'

'But it sure needs work done on it. Seems to be falling apart.'

That could not be denied.

He rose. 'A number of cables have arrived for Mr Seldon. They require my attention so I regret to say that I have to take my leave of you, Miss Grandison.'

She was happy to be on her own.

When she'd finished her meal, she looked at the clock on the mantleshelf. Five past nine. Mr Jackman would be arriving any minute. Had the Colonel read the pages she had asked to be delivered to him?

Suddenly, there he was, holding her account in his hand.

'Miss Grandison, we need to talk.' He started to pull out a chair.

She nodded. 'Can we go somewhere else? They will need to clear in here.'

He gave her a brief smile. 'Thinking of the troops again, Miss Grandison?' He led the way to the Smoking Room and lit a couple of lamps. He waved her to a chair then sat opposite, placed the sheets of Adelphi Hotel paper on a table beside him and looked at her, his expression bleak. 'We should have talked as soon as you returned but Mr Seldon gave me such a clear account of what you had told him, I foolishly thought I had the full story. I should have known it was essential to speak to you as well.'

Now that they were together, she found there was nothing she wanted to say.

'How much does Jackman know?'

'As much as Mr Seldon.'

He fingered the pages. 'You make some assumptions about Helen's actions. Do you have evidence?'

She shook her head. 'I only wrote it down that way because it seemed to make sense to me. I did not intend you to have that account; I wanted to tell you face-to-face, so you could question my conclusions, but there seemed no opportunity. I thought it was important you should know everything before Mr Jackman arrived, and giving you that,' she indicated the pages, 'seemed the easiest way.'

'God what a mess!' he said violently, rising and plunging his fists into his pockets. He walked jerkily down the room. 'I apologise,' he said as he turned.

'There is no need, I quite understand.'

'But you at least can distance yourself to some extent.' He walked some more, then stopped again. 'I must see for myself.'

'That is why I persuaded Mr Jackman we must bring back his body. I told him you would want to make sure Mr Russell was really dead.'

Another bleak smile. 'Miss Grandison, once again I have to thank you for your good sense and foresight.'

'Have you given orders as to what is to happen to the coffin?'

He nodded. 'It is to be placed in the carriage house.' He seemed to reach deep down inside himself. 'I have told the stable staff it belongs to a friend who has died in an accident.'

She nodded, wondering if it would do.

There was a knock on the door. A footman came in and said that Mr Jackman had returned and would like to report to Colonel Stanhope.

He nodded, asked that the investigator be given dinner and to say that he would be with him shortly.

The door shut behind the footman.

The Colonel looked at Ursula. 'Will you come with me?'

She was too astonished to respond.

'You have been present at almost every stage of this sorry saga and I would be most grateful if you could be there now.'

'Of course.'

He led the way out through the garden door. The evening was light enough to see the way across the parterre to the stable yard. There he found a lantern and lit it.

When, though, he carefully opened the wide doors to the carriage house, there was already a lantern balanced on the back of one of the carriages, shining its light on the simple, unadorned pine coffin that was supported on two trestles.

Bent over it, using a chisel to try and force open the lid, the skirt of her black silk evening dress ripped and dragging over the dirt and dust of the stone floor, was Helen.

Chapter Thirty-Seven

The Colonel walked over and took away the chisel.

'Give me that.' Helen struggled to wrench it back. Her hair was all adrift, her eyes wild. 'I have to see him. I have to. Charles, you must understand.'

'I do,' he said gently, placing his lantern where it would intensify the light. 'I, too, have to see him.'

He had with him a hammer and another chisel.

Ursula tried to put her arm around Helen's shoulders but was shaken off.

With quick, skilled movements, the Colonel forced open the lid all the way round the coffin. He put down the tools and looked across at Helen. 'Are you ready?'

She nodded, swallowing hard.

He carefully lifted off the lid.

Ursula moved unobtrusively so that she could see Helen's reaction as she saw for the first time the coffin's contents. The little trail of blood from his ear had been cleaned away. The exit wound at the back was hidden and his face appeared undamaged. Exposed in the light of the lanterns, looking as though he slept, was the body of Richard, sixth Earl of Mountstanton.

The Colonel gave a long sigh. It was as if, even knowing what he was about to see, he'd somehow hoped that it would be different.

Helen closed her eyes, shuddered and swayed. Ursula held her tightly.

The Colonel balanced the lid back on top of the coffin, not quite matching the nails and the holes. He gave it a few light taps until it looked closed. 'I'll come back later and secure it properly,' he said. 'It'll take too long now, some of the nails are bent. Helen, take my arm, let's go somewhere comfortable so we can talk.'

Tears were streaming down her face. 'There's no point, you'll never understand,' she screamed at him. 'He wasn't like you.'

'You must make me understand; please, Helen.'

Ursula kept her arm around the woman's shoulders.

The Colonel extinguished the lanterns and shut the carriage-house door. 'Where is Mr Seldon?'

'Gone to bed,' Helen sobbed.

'He always goes early,' Ursula said.

'And my mother, thank heavens, has also retired. We'll go to the library.'

The night was warm but by the time they reached the room, both Helen and Ursula were shivering.

There was a fire already laid and the Colonel lit it. 'I don't think we need call a servant for this,' he said, applying a match then watching the flames catch and climb until he was sure the wood was satisfactorily ablaze. He went to the drinks table and poured out three brandies.

'Shall I fetch you a wrap, Helen?' Ursula asked.

Helen advanced to the fire and shook her head. 'I'll soon be warm.' After a moment she flung herself into one of the huge leather chairs.

Nothing was said for a while. Ursula sat down, sipped at her brandy and watched Helen dispose of hers, almost in one gulp, then hold out the glass for more.

The Colonel replenished it then took up a stance with his back to the fire.

'Where to start?' he asked.

'You can start with your father,' Helen said viciously.

'My father?'

'It's all his fault that Richard was how he was.'

The Colonel took a deep breath. 'Please, explain.'

'Running around the countryside, seducing any girl he wanted who would let him. As far as I could see, they all did! He was over sixty by the time I met him but even then I could see his charm. Neither of his sons could match it.'

The Colonel looked at his shoes, 'Yet you married Richard.'

'Oh, he was a big prize on the marriage mart and, thanks to my mother's behaviour, at any time I could have been exposed as damaged goods. If Society had found out that instead of being killed in a railway accident she'd run off with Ursula's father, well, goodbye to a successful marriage.'

The Colonel looked at Ursula and she realised he'd known nothing of this. He took a deep breath.

'By successful, I take it you mean money and status?'

'Of course, Charles. What else is there? Oh, you mean love? Love comes afterwards.' She drank more of her brandy. 'I liked Richard. He seemed to think he loved me. I thought we could make a go of it.'

She held out her brandy glass and the Colonel gave her more, recharging his own at the same time. Ursula declined, her glass was still over half full and she wanted to make sure she kept her head clear.

'Maybe we would have managed, if it hadn't been for your father. Not content with insisting that Richard emulate him in every other field, he wanted him to be successful in bed. Well, I'm afraid that wasn't possible.'

The Colonel looked across at her. 'You mean?'

'He was impotent.' Helen rubbed one hand along the leather arm of her chair. 'I asked if it was just me or whether it happened with other girls. He said he'd thought I'd be different. Turned out I wasn't.' More of her brandy disappeared. 'It didn't help that your father kept making remarks suggesting Richard wasn't really a man, asking when the heir to Mountstanton was to arrive.' She looked across at the Colonel. 'You came back on leave when we'd been married just over a year. You must remember the nasty remarks dearest Papa would make.'

He turned away and looked down into the fire.

'Come on, Charles, look at me. Look at me the way you used to, when I thought you were more than a little in love with me. I pointed it out to Richard and he actually suggested you could be a way out of our difficulties.'

Ursula took a gulp at her brandy. How could Helen behave like this? The Colonel had closed his eyes.

'It would have kept it in the family, you see? Didn't Richard explain it to you?' The Colonel opened his eyes but his face was expressionless. Helen continued, 'Oh you were far too upright, loyal and true blue to even contemplate the idea before you disappeared again, off to another theatre of war. But now, there in the wings, so to speak, was Max. You only had to look at him to realise he was part of the family. Your father thought he was wonderful. Typical chip off the old block, as he might have said if he was into the business of acknowledging his by-blows.'

'Helen, please!'

'Upsets you, does it, hearing your father spoken of that way? Well, I reckon he had some pretty unpleasant characteristics to hand on. Richard was a coward and Max, oh, Max was something else.'

Helen rose and walked over to the wide bay window, through which could be seen a three-quarters full moon floating serenely over the garden. Ursula remembered it in all its glory on the night of the Dowager's birthday fête.

The Colonel watched her.

'We had our affair and I – I fell in love for the second time in my life. The result was Harry and, for his sake, I can never regret our affair. I watch, though, I watch very carefully to see if he has inherited any of his father's less pleasant characteristics.'

'Such as?' asked the Colonel.

'Such as turning blackmailer.'

'Blackmailer?'

'Oh, yes. Max forced me to pay him not to reveal who Harry's father was. I told Richard and said that if it was my word against Max's, who would believe him? But Richard said I had to pay him because there were things Max knew that he couldn't allow to be general knowledge.'

'What things?' the Colonel ground out.

'Apparently when Richard was about eighteen, your father caught him fooling around with a stable lad. Yes, Charles, I mean exactly what, judging by your face, you don't want to believe. Impotence didn't play any part there.'

It was hard from what she said to know what Helen actually thought. Primarily it appeared to be bitterness at her father-in-law. 'Richard told me there was hell to pay. The stable lad was paid off, but somewhere Max had come across him. Max could get people to tell him anything. He said if he told what he knew, the scandal would ruin us; we'd have to go abroad. It would destroy your mother and what chance would Harry have?'

'How long has this been going on?' the Colonel asked incredulously.

'Five years, ever since Harry was born. Finally, when he knew his mother didn't have long to live, Max asked for enough money to set him up for a new life in America. I wanted to refuse but Richard said he was fed up with life at Mountstanton; he wanted to "be himself", whatever that meant. He told me to give Max half of what he was asking for in bearer bonds and to give the same amount to himself. He would then disappear; I could live exactly as I wanted and he'd see that Max didn't trouble me any more. All I had to do was provide the money and ask Max to dinner at Mountstanton for one last time, so I could tell him I'd agree to pay him off. He didn't want anything in writing.'

'How did you think he was going to make sure Max didn't ask for more?' the Colonel asked harshly.

Helen swung round. 'I don't know! I only know that I was going crazy. My father kept asking how the restoration of this place was going,' she glanced around the gracious room. 'A restoration Max had made impossible. Then Papa wanted me to invite Belle over. He was worried about her behaviour in New York. And all the time Richard became more and more distant. I needed a life! I needed to be told I was beautiful, that someone loved me, wanted to cherish me.' Tears were once again falling down her cheeks. 'I thought if I asked Belle over, gave her a debut Season, I would at least have some fun.'

'You seemed to be having fun with William Warburton,' Ursula could not resist saying as she tried to distance herself from the appalling tale Helen related.

'William was nothing more than a diversion,' Helen said dismissively. 'You must see that I needed one.'

'Did Richard tell you what he was going to do?' The Colonel's voice was urgent.

'No, merely that I was not to distress myself over anything that happened. He would give the bonds to Max and make sure he was warned off ever coming back. Then he would arrange his freedom with his share.'

'Was it Richard who asked Max to come to the belvedere the night of Mama's birthday fête?'

'He said he'd run into Max out riding. Max had booked a passage to America. He was going to, "shake the dust of England from his shoes and go somewhere that would appreciate him," was what Richard said he'd told him. Max then said he'd come and collect the bonds on his way to the boat. "A last look at what should have been his," was apparently the way he put it. It just happened to be the evening of the fête.'

'So you knew it wasn't Richard's body in the belvedere?'

She nodded. 'Yes, Charles. Though at first I thought it was. The face, of course, was unrecognisable but there was the Mountstanton finger, and Richard had been so moody and volatile recently I did for a moment think that this was his way out. But then I undid his waistcoat and shirt and I knew it was Max's body. He was more muscular than Richard, and hairier.' Her face crumpled. 'I remembered everything Max had once been to me and I wanted it to be Richard there,' she wailed.

Ursula remembered Helen's wild grief, how she'd thrown herself on the body.

For a little while the only sound in the library was Helen's crying.

The Colonel pulled his hand down his face as though to wipe away the pictures Helen's words had conjured. He helped himself to more brandy. Finally he came back to the fire, his shoulders square and resolute. 'So,' he said finally, 'Richard must have knocked Max out, then dressed him in his clothes – and that must have been some task; I should think he would have needed help. By using a shotgun, it meant Max's body could pass for his. Max's bearer bonds and passport were in his saddlebags. No doubt he had the bonds his darling wife,' he said bitterly, nodding at Helen, 'had given him ready to add to them. Then he had everything he needed to start a new life.'

There was silence.

'What about Polly, Helen?' asked the Colonel roughly. 'Did Richard kill her, too?'

'I don't know! I never thought it was important until you started interfering.'

'You never thought it was important?' Ursula repeated, horrified.

Helen managed to look ashamed. 'Well, at the start we just thought she'd gone off. She was like that. Once I knew who her father was, though, I reckoned she had brought her death upon herself.'

'What do you mean?' Ursula asked, wondering how she could make Helen realise how callous she was being.

'Because it was she who had seduced whoever was the father of her child. No wonder he wouldn't take responsibility for her. She flung herself down that hill because she couldn't bear the shame.'

'I don't believe Polly would ever have taken her own life,' the Colonel said.

Helen shrugged. 'Well, I don't suppose we'll ever know the truth.'

'I can tell you what happened,' said John.

They all turned. The footman, in full livery, stood in the doorway.

'*You* can?' said the Colonel. 'What do you know about it?'

Ursula was certain she knew what John was about to say and that the last aspect of this tragic story was about to be revealed.

'Well, Colonel Charles, I'd never tell this normal, like, but this isn't normal, is it, sir?'

'Get on with it, man.'

John, standing stolidly before them seemed to exude a quiet confidence and she remembered how efficient he had been the night Belle had disappeared.

'His lordship loved me, sir. And, well, I loved him. At first I thought it was just one of those things. I've always known what sort I am but I thought he was just amusing himself.' There seemed no bitterness in his tone; he was just a man who recognised what he was up against. 'But his lordship kept saying that with me he could be himself. He didn't have to drink or pretend to be someone he wasn't. And I could see what his father, that is, his late lordship, was doing to him.' John's expression twisted at the thought. 'We was very careful – used the woodman's cottage over the other side of the estate.'

No wonder he'd known exactly where to go to find Belle!

'But that's where Max and I . . .' started Helen, who then stopped and gazed at the footman horror-struck. 'Richard told me about it once; his father set it up, said it made an excellent location for a liaison.'

John shifted from one foot to the other. 'I know, my lady. His lordship always seemed to know when you would be there.'

'But what happened to Polly,' said the Colonel impatiently.

'She was a right little thing, she was,' John said, bitter at last. 'After me for a time, until I told her to keep her hands to herself.' He took a deep breath. 'His lordship told me he'd had a letter from her saying she'd found out she was his half-sister, that she was in the family way and needed him to take care of her.'

'My brother told you that?'

'He told me everything, sir,' John said simply. 'Told me what happened when he met up with Polly. He couldn't stand the thought that yet another of his father's bastards – forgive the word, my lady – wanted to blackmail him. That was the word he used.'

'He killed her to keep her quiet?' The Colonel sounded appalled.

'No, sir! It was an accident. He told me. He just got so angry with her because she'd started to make insinuations. About him! She couldn't have known anything, otherwise she'd have come out with it, but, well, she was always clever with her tongue. He lost his temper and hit her. She fell onto a rock and died. Just like that!'

It was the scenario Mr Jackman and she had discussed, Ursula realised. Except they had never envisioned it had been the Earl who struck the fatal blow.

The Colonel sighed deeply. 'Then he rolled her body down the slope?'

John nodded.

'And was it you who helped my brother change clothes with Mr Russell?'

'Not really, sir. His lordship had asked me to bring a bottle of champagne to the belvedere. No glasses, just the champagne. When I got there, Mr Russell was with him. They were laughing. His lordship bet him that he couldn't fool one of the guests at the fête that he was the Earl. All he had to do was change clothes with him and go and have a chat. If Mr Russell won, then he'd double the money.'

'What money?'

'Don't know, sir. But Mr Russell seemed to understand. I left them there.'

'So, when the body was discovered, you believed it was the Earl's?'

The footman shifted his feet again. 'Sort of, like. But the day before, his lordship had given me money for a fare to America. Said we were going to start a new life over there; that when he wrote to me, I was to come. So I did wonder a bit. I both wanted to believe it wasn't him and also that it was, if you can understand?' he said painfully.

'I think so, John. But you do know now?'

'Yes, sir. When I heard Mr Russell's body was in the carriage house in a coffin, I knew I had to have a look.'

'And who told you it was Mr Russell's body?'

'It had to be. We all knew Mr Jackman and Miss Grandison had gone up to Liverpool to interview him. Who else's could it have been?'

What was it the Dowager had said, that the servants always knew everything?

'Can we trust you not to let anyone else know?' the Colonel said.

John looked injured. 'I've kept his lordship's secret for six years, I'm not going to let anything out now.'

'Good man.'

Helen looked incredulous. 'You will have to go, you know that, don't you, John?'

He turned to her and said, gently, 'I shall be handing in my notice and buying that ticket for America.'

John gave them a small bow, turned and left the room.

The Colonel sighed and flung himself into a chair.

'So that's what Richard meant by "be himself",' Helen said, sounding disgusted. 'No wonder he didn't want to tell me everything.'

'What would you have done if he had?' the Colonel asked quietly.

'Left him, of course. I wouldn't have divorced him; the scandal wouldn't have done Harry – or me – any good. But at least I wouldn't have had to look at him, knowing what we've just been told.' The contempt in her voice was devastating.

The Colonel looked sad. 'I wish he'd confided in me. I'd have helped him work something out.'

'Maybe if you had been here,' Helen said viciously, 'he would have done.'

Ursula looked from one to the other of them. The air seemed to vibrate with shock, horror, despair.

After a few moments the Colonel stirred and said, 'What the hell do we do now?'

'Oh, for God's sake, Charles. It's obvious, isn't it? We don't do anything. Unless,' Helen's eyes narrowed, 'unless you are after the title? Let me warn you that, if you are, I'll fight you every step of the way. You won't make much of a figure in the witness box trying to fling mud at your brother and sister-in-law and turning your nephew into a bastard. He was born in wedlock, let me remind you.'

The Colonel rose and looked at her, stunned. 'Helen, I will assume that everything you have been through over the last week has addled your brains. Of course I'm not after the title. The last thing I want is to be Earl of Mountstanton.'

There weren't many men, Ursula thought, who could make that statement sound sincere but the Colonel was one of them.

Helen stood up. 'Then what is there to discuss? You have a funeral already arranged for your brother. You have his dead body. No doubt you can think of some way to switch the coffins. Though why it should matter which one of them lies in the family mausoleum is beyond me. You are the only one who has been pursuing the truth of how Polly died; officialdom has signed off on her. I assume you can pay off your bloody investigator. I am sure Ursula, sensible and confidential Ursula, will keep her mouth shut.'

'I always have,' Ursula said, rising from her chair. 'But there is one thing I have to tell you. Your husband's last words were, "Helen, forgive me".'

Helen stood still, then said very quietly, 'Thank you, Ursula.' Tears started to well up in her eyes. 'I must go and see how Belle is,' she said and walked swiftly from the room.

Ursula felt drained. She looked at the Colonel.

'I must go and nail down that coffin properly,' he said, picking up the hammer he'd put on the mantleshelf. 'I hope Max's uncle, the Viscount Broome, will not cause us difficulties. Something he said last time we met suggested Max was an embarrassment to him, especially over the last few years.'

'But for his death to be put down as suicide?'

'Instead of him being branded blackmailer?' The Colonel sighed deeply. 'And there's Helen's reputation to be protected, if only for Harry's sake. I foresee a difficult meeting with the viscount. I need to have a word with Jackman. Heavens, I promised to take his report tonight.'

'I don't suppose he will mind if it is postponed until tomorrow. Would you like me to find him and tell him?'

He looked at her gratefully. 'Once again, Miss Grandison, you come to my rescue.' He turned at the door. 'I tell you, if it's the last thing I do, I'll see to it that it isn't Russell's remains that lie in the Mountstanton mausoleum.'

Ursula watched him leave the room. Then she sat down again and emptied her glass of brandy. There seemed nothing left for her at Mountstanton and, in truth, it was not a place she wanted to spend any more time in.

Chapter Thirty-Eight

Ursula found Thomas Jackman in the Smoking Room, his feet up on a low table, puffing a large cigar, a glass of whisky at his side. He looked thoroughly content.

'Mr Benson gave me the freedom of his lordship's humidor and provided me with the whisky decanter,' he said, rising to his feet. 'How have you been doing, Miss Grandison? Have you come with a summons from the Colonel or can you join me for a few moments?'

She sat down and wondered if it was the brandy that made her feel so disconnected from reality. What, after all, was real about Mountstanton? So much of what Helen had told them she had already surmised, yet to hear it spelt out in that way made living in the rough and ready world of a Californian mining community seem a haven of sanity.

'I'm afraid the Colonel has got tied up, Mr Jackman. He asks if he can meet with you tomorrow instead of tonight.'

'Suits me.' The investigator settled down into his chair again and raised the cigar. 'Fine smoke, this. Cuban.' He waved it in the direction of a side table. 'Only thing is, that needs to be taken proper care of. Thought it should be put into the Colonel's care.'

Sitting on the table was a commodious carpet bag.

'Ah,' said Ursula. 'Was that Mr Russell's?'

Thomas Jackman nodded. 'The White Star Line officials were not too happy for me to take either it or the body. But, as I said, what were they to do with them if I didn't? Russell hadn't been arrested; neither they nor the harbour police had authority in the matter. Whereas I had the Colonel's authorisation and the backing of the Met's Chief Constable. They soon realised I could remove a nasty piece of nuisance.'

'How sensible you were to approach the Chief Constable before going up to Liverpool, Mr Jackman.'

'That was Colonel Stanhope's suggestion and it was his letter that swung it for us.'

Ursula was not surprised. She looked towards the carpet bag. 'Have you checked the contents?'

'One of the officials insisted we did that. Said he didn't want any complaints from the deceased's next of kin.'

Ursula remembered what the Colonel had said about the viscount.

'Anybody else know what's in there?' Mr Jackman asked, sounding slightly inebriated. 'Or can we abscond with the takings?'

Ursula laughed. 'Remove the dust of Mountstanton from our feet and, what, see the world?'

'There's an awful lot of world to see.'

'Is it really a lot of money?'

'It's bearer bonds, not quite ready money but they're accepted by any bank, no questions asked. There's enough to make us both very, very wealthy.'

'If only we were that sort of people.'

'People like Maximilian Russell?'

'Yes, Mr Jackman, people like Maximilian Russell.'

'Well, the fact that you obviously know about their existence must mean there's others as do. So, goodbye the world.'

'Goodbye the world,' she repeated gravely.

'Can I offer you a whisky instead?'

She shook her head and rose. 'I've already had a brandy, thank you. I think I need to retire.'

He stood up, put down his cigar and held out his hand. 'Miss Grandison, may I thank you for your help over the last week or so? And may I say that you have a real talent for this work.'

'What work?'

'Why, the work of detection. I'd be proud to have you at my side any time.'

'Mr Jackman, you do me too much honour. I don't feel I have done very much at all.'

'You can let me be the judge of that. Thank you, Miss Grandison.'

Ursula shook his hand. 'Thank you, Mr Jackman. I can't say it's been an enjoyable experience; I've been too emotionally involved, but I have admired your approach and ability.'

He gave a little bow. 'Any time, Miss Grandison.'

★ ★ ★

Over the next few days, Ursula spent most of her time sitting with Belle. She didn't attend the elaborate funeral the Colonel had arranged for his brother. She no longer ate with the family. She and Mr Haddam were served their meals in the Morning Room, timed so that Ursula could be free to attend on Belle while the family luncheon and dinner took place. Ursula enjoyed the secretary's company; he had a lively sense of humour and appeared to respect Mr Seldon, but was not in awe of him.

Ursula hardly saw the Colonel. Then he stopped her one day in the hall.

'You are looking pale, Miss Grandison. You must take more exercise. Have you been riding today?'

'No, Colonel.'

'I'll have a word with Helen. We can't have you spending all your time looking after an invalid.'

'It is what I am here for, sir,' she said quietly. 'I would prefer it if you did not speak to the Countess.'

The little encounter seemed to Ursula to demonstrate how their relationship had changed. It was unlikely, she thought, to return to the same ease she had enjoyed with him before the Earl's death.

★ ★ ★

Two days after the funeral, Belle rose and dressed for the first time since she had collapsed, and attended tea. Harry was there.

'Will you soon come riding with me, Aunt Belle? I'm very good at jumping now. Uncle Charles says so.'

'I hope very soon,' Belle said to her nephew with a lovely smile. But Ursula could see tears pricking at her eyes and she quickly drew Harry's attention to the jigsaw puzzle of a map of North America that Mr Seldon had brought and was now gradually being put together.

'I shall question you on the various states when you have finished that, Harry,' said the Dowager Countess.

'Yes,' said Helen quietly, 'you must remember that you are half American.'

Later, after an exhausted Belle was sleeping, Ursula went to the drawing room to report on how she had survived her first foray outside her bedroom. The door was a little open and she could hear Helen saying, 'Papa, I do not want Ursula Grandison around here a day longer than necessary.'

'Helen, surely she is your old friend?'

As so often with Mr Seldon, he managed to instil layers of possible meaning into even the lightest of utterances.

'No, Papa, she is not my friend. She stole my first and greatest love – and you stood by and let her!'

Ursula could not remain eavesdropping. She entered the room just as Mr Seldon said, 'Helen, do not be ridiculous.'

Helen was standing by the window, facing her father. Mr Seldon was seated in a wing chair with the glass of water he always commanded by his side.

'Ah, Ursula, you have arrived at a good moment. I am just telling Papa how I can dispense with your presence at Mountstanton. I cannot forget how you stole Jack from me. I know, Papa, you never thought much of him but he was the man I wanted. And Ursula took and married him.'

'I paid him to leave you alone,' Mr Seldon said dispassionately. He ran a finger round the top of the water glass. 'That should tell you what sort of man he was. I gave him enough money to take Ursula out of your hair as well.'

Ursula was stunned. 'You did what?'

'I think there is nothing wrong with your hearing, my dear. Your father walked off with my wife. Now my daughter had fallen for a despicable cad who was trifling with you as well. What was I supposed to do?'

Ursula, stunned, dropped into a chair. 'But you rescued me from running that sleazy boarding house in San Francisco.'

He drank a sip of water. 'I decided you had suffered enough. After all, hadn't you discovered your marriage was no marriage? That your so-called husband already had a wife who was laying hold of his silver mine?' He sipped a little more water. 'And I needed your help with Belle.'

Helen looked as stunned as Ursula felt. 'You knew Jack was married?'

'You didn't realise I had all your young men investigated, my dear?'

'In that case,' Ursula said, her mind whirling with the implications, 'why didn't you just tell Helen that – and me?'

'She would have hated me,' he said simply. 'Better she should hate you.'

Ursula stood up. 'My father was right to rescue Helen's mother from you.'

She was careful not to slam the door behind her. Then for a moment she stood, not knowing where to go, knowing all she wanted was to get away from Mountstanton and the Seldons.

Helen and Mr Seldon deserved each other, she said to herself, and found that she was shaking.

'Miss Grandison,' said the Colonel, 'you are upset. What has happened?'

He seemed to have arrived from nowhere. His expression and his voice were concerned.

'There is nothing wrong,' Ursula said and did not recognise her own voice.

He took her arm in a gentle grasp. 'Allow me to disagree, Miss Grandison. Come with me.'

He took her into the library, the room that had seen so many dramatic scenes, sat her down and took a chair opposite.

'My dear Miss Grandison, tell me what has happened. I will personally deal with the person responsible.'

She tried to hang onto her anger, she did not want to start crying.

'Colonel,' she jerked out, 'there is nothing you can do.'

'Can you not allow me to be the judge of that. And can you not call me Charles? Do we not know each other well enough now for you to grant me the privilege of using your name, Ursula?'

His kindness undid her and she buried her face in her hands. Then, resolutely, she lifted her head and dashed away the tears.

'It is only that I have just been disillusioned over someone I thought I respected.'

He looked at her searchingly. 'I will not ask who that was, though I think I can guess. May I say that I know what that experience feels like?'

All at once the anger left her. Instead she was filled with hopelessness. 'Once, Colonel, Charles, I thought I was married to a wonderful man. I gradually found out that he was weak, a bully and a liar. Then, final degradation, his real wife turned up.'

What she hadn't told him was how Jack had died. The scene she had so determinedly driven from her mind returned as vividly as any in a picture book.

One day, Jack had returned from the mine in triumph. 'We've done it!' he cried. 'A massive lode. All the silver anyone could want. You will have dresses and jewellery and we'll build a magnificent house. Come on, we must celebrate.'

He'd dragged her off to the sordid drinking den he patronised. Raw whisky was produced and all too soon cards appeared and a poker game was in progress. Jack won bigger and bigger pots; it was as though he couldn't lose. Then someone produced a revolver and said he should try his luck with that. Russian roulette, it was called, said the gun's owner, a despicable fellow who constantly jeered at Jack. You put one bullet in the gun, give the barrel a twirl then point it at your head and pull the trigger. If your luck was in, you survived. Jack, drunk with more than whisky, had grinned and said that was his sort of game. Ursula had begged him not to play something so stupid and dangerous. He'd pushed her out of the way with a curse. She would never forget the look of astonishment on his face as the bullet entered his brain. The subsequent inquest struggled for a verdict but finally ruled it misadventure.

It was after his death that Jack's first wife had turned up and announced that Jack's estate was hers and Ursula had no claim on his share of the silver strike. No one knew where she had come from or how she had known about the mine, and it had never occurred to Ursula to ask. Now she thought she knew exactly who had informed the woman.

The Colonel leaned forward and took her hands. 'I am so sorry, Ursula.'

How easy it would be if he took her into his arms and promised to look after and protect her! She knew it wasn't going to happen.

She rose, walked over to the window and stood with her arms folded across her breast, her back to him. 'What are you going to do, Charles? Follow your plan to stand for election to your Parliament?'

He came and stood beside her, looking out, as she was, at the garden. She knew neither of them saw it.

'I feel rather as Napoleon must have done after Waterloo. All around is a defeated battleground.' He gave her a wintry smile. 'My aim was to distance myself as much from Mountstanton as possible.'

'You'd make a brilliant politician.'

'Would I?'

'Of course you would. You'd speak the truth, fight for the rights of the people.'

'I'm not sure that's how to be a successful politician. And already I'm mired in lies and deceit. There is no other way out of this tangle if Harry and Mountstanton are to have a chance.'

'You cannot deny Mountstanton, can you?'

He shrugged, 'I find that you are right. I can't. Helen says she is returning with Harry and Belle to New York for a while. Someone will have to look after things here.'

'Harry's inheritance,' she said softly.

He nodded. 'But what about you, Ursula? What are you going to do? Return to America?'

'No!' The answer was as much of a surprise to her as it was to him. She felt a slow excitement begin to build within her. 'No, Charles, I'm not. If I can find a job, I'd like to experience London.'

'I'm sure with all our connections, we can find you something.'

'No!' He looked stung and she smiled. 'Sorry, Charles, I don't mean to be ungrateful but I have learned to distrust favours. I need to make my own way.' It was as though a huge burden had dropped from her shoulders and she suddenly felt as light as a cloud. She spread out her arms. 'It will be an adventure. I need an adventure.'

He caught her hands, brought them to his mouth and kissed them. 'Perhaps when you know where you are to be, you will be good enough to let me have your direction. Ursula Grandison, I would like to remain your friend.'

'And so I would with you, Charles Stanhope.'

THE END

Acknowledgements

Many thanks to the Writers' Group: Shelley, Gay, Georgie, Helena, and Maggie, who we miss so much. Without their always-constructive criticism, advice, friendship and support, this book would never have seen publication. Thanks also to Sir Anthony Dewey, Bt, for instruction in the use of shotguns; Dr Michael Dingle for medical advice; Dr Dorothy Gennard, Visiting Senior Research Fellow, School of Life Sciences, University of Lincoln, for forensic advice regarding the immersion of bodies; and Michael Thomas for reading and advising on the ms. Lastly, many thanks to my agent, Jane Conway-Gordon, whose expertise found a publisher for *Deadly Inheritance*, and to my editor, Matilda Richards, for her excellent eye for detail. Any resemblance to actual people, living or dead, can only be coincidence and all mistakes or inaccuracies are mine.

About the Author

Janet Laurence is the author of numerous books, including the Darina Lisle culinary crime novels (Macmillan). She was a weekly cookery columnist for the *Daily Telegraph* between 1984 and 1986, and has contributed to recipe collections and written cookery books. Janet was Chairman of the Crime Writers' Association (1998-1999), was included in *The Times'* '100 Masters of Crime' in 1998, and invited to run the crime writing workshop at the Cheltenham Festival of Literature in 2000. She was the Writer in Residence and Visiting Fellow at Jane Franklin College at the University of Tasmania in 2002 and has also run the Crime Writing Course at each of the Bristol-based CrimeFest conventions to date. She lives in Somerset.

Visit our website and discover thousands of other
History Press books.

www.thehistorypress.co.uk